THE

PROSPECTOR

OTHER VERBA MUNDI BOOKS

THE

PROSPECTOR

J. M. G. LE CLÉZIO

❊

*Translated from the French
by Carol Marks*

Verba Mundi
DAVID R. GODINE, PUBLISHER
Boston

A Verba Mundi Original

First published in 1993 by
DAVID R. GODINE, PUBLISHER, INC.
Horticultural Hall
300 Massachusetts Avenue
Boston, Massachusetts 02115

Originally published in French in 1985
as *Le Chercheur d'or* by Editions Gallimard, Paris

LIBRARY OF CONGRESS CATALOGING-IN-PUBLICATION DATA
Le Clézio, J.-M. G. (Jean-Marie Gustave), 1940–
[Chercheur d'or. English]
The prospector / J.M.G. Le Clézio; translated from the French by
Carol Marks. — 1st American ed.
p.   cm.
"A Verba mundi original" — T.p. verso.
I. Title. II. Series: Verba Mundi
PQ2672.E25C4813   1993
843'.914—dc20   93-36322
CIP

ISBN 0-87923-976-X

First American edition
Printed and bound in the United States of America

For my grandfather, Léon

CONTENTS

THE
PROSPECTOR

BOUCAN, 1892

A s FAR BACK as I can remember I have listened to the sea: to the sound of it mingling with the wind in the filao needles, the wind that never stopped blowing, even when one left the shore behind and crossed the sugarcane fields. It is the sound that cradled my childhood. I can hear it now, deep inside me; it will come with me wherever I go: the tireless lingering sound of the waves breaking in the distance on the coral reef, then coming to die on the banks of the Rivière Noire. Not a day went by when I didn't go to the sea; not a night when I didn't wake up with my back sweaty and damp, sitting up in my cot, parting the mosquito net and trying to see the tide, anxious and full of a desire I didn't understand.

I thought of the sea as human, and in the dark all senses were alert, the better to hear her arrival, the better to receive her. The giant waves leapt over the reefs and then tumbled into the lagoon; the noise made the air and earth vibrate like a boiler. I heard her, she moved, she breathed.

When the moon was full, I slid out of bed without a sound, careful not to make the worm-eaten floor creak. But I knew Laure was not asleep; I knew her eyes were open in the dark and that she was holding her breath. I scaled the window ledge and pushed at the wooden shutters, and then I was outside, in the night. The garden was bathed in white moonlight; it shone on the tops of the trees, swaying noisily in the wind, and I could make out the dark masses of rhododendrons and hibiscus. With a beating heart I walked down the lane that went toward the hills, where the fallow land began. A big chalta tree, which Laure called the tree of good and evil, stood very close to the crumbling wall; I climbed onto its highest branches so that I could see the sea over the treetops and the expanse of cane. The moon rolled between the clouds, throwing out splinters of light. Then suddenly, over the foliage and to the left of the Tourelle de Tamarin, I saw it: a great black slab alight with shining, sparkling dots. Did I really see it, did I really hear it? The sea was inside my head, and when I closed my eyes I saw and heard it best, clearly perceiving each wave as it crashed onto the reef and then came together again to unfurl on the shore.

I clung to the branches of the chalta tree for a long time, until my arms grew numb. The wind from the sea blew over the trees and the cane fields, and the moon shone on the leaves. Sometimes I stayed there until dawn, listening and dreaming. At the other end of the garden the big house was dark, closed in on itself like an abandoned wreck. The wind made the loose shingles bang and the framework creak. That, too, was the sound of the sea, as was the groaning of the tree trunk and the moaning of the filao needles. I was afraid to be alone in the tree, but I still didn't want to go back to the room and I resisted the chill wind and the fatigue that made my head heavy.

It was not really fear. It was more like standing on the edge of an abyss or a deep gully and staring down, heart beating so hard that it echoed painfully in my neck. And yet I knew I had to stay, and that if I did I would at least learn something of great worth. It was impossible for me to go back to the room as long as the tide was rising. I had to stay, clinging to the chalta tree, waiting for the moon to glide across the sky. Just before dawn, when the sky became gray over Mananava, I would go back and slide under the mosquito net. Laure would sigh because she had not slept either during all the time I was outside. She never talked about it. She merely looked at me during the day with dark questioning eyes, and then I was sorry I'd gone out to hear the sea.

Every day I went to the beach. I had to cross the fields, and the cane was so high that I ran blindly down the paths cut in it, and sometimes got lost amid the sharp stalks. Then I could no longer hear the sea. The burning late-winter sun stifled its sound. I knew when the shore was very close because the air became heavy, still, full of flies. Above me the dazzling blue sky stretched, empty of birds. The dust from the red earth reached up to my ankles; so as not to spoil my shoes I took them off and wore them, tied by the laces, around my neck. This way my hands were free. You had to use both hands when crossing a cane field because the stalks were very high and their leaves cut like swords. In order to move forward, you had to push the leaves aside with the flat of your hand. Cook, the chef, said they would be cut next month. Denis, Cook's grandson, was right ahead of me but I couldn't see him. He always went barefoot, armed only with his pole, but walked more quickly than I. To call each other we plucked twice on a grass harp, or howled twice: *Aouha!* When they were in the high cane the Indian men bayed like that as they slashed it with their long knives.

I heard Denis far ahead of me. *Aouha! Aouha!* I answered with my harp. There was no other sound. The sea was at her lowest ebb and wouldn't come in before noon. We were moving as fast as we could to the tidal pools, where the shrimp and octopus hid.

In the cane in front of me there was a heap of black lava stones. I climbed to the top so that I could see the green sweep of the fields and, far behind me now, lost in the jumble of trees and thickets, our shipwrecked house with its odd sky-colored roof and Cap'n Cook's little shanty; and farther still, Yemen's chimney and the high red mountains going straight up toward the sky. I spun around at the summit of my stone pyramid and I could see the whole countryside: the smoke from the sugar refineries, the Tamarin river meandering through the trees, the hills, and at last, the dark, glittering sea that had receded from the other side of the reefs.

This was what I loved. I believed I could stay at the top of that heap for hours, even days, doing nothing but looking.

Aouha! Aouha! Denis was calling from the other end of the field. He, too, was standing on a pyramid of black stones, a castaway on an islet in the middle of the sea. He was so far away that I could barely make him out. I could only see his long, insectlike silhouette at the top of the pile. I cupped my hands and called in response: *Aouha! Aouha!* We both climbed down and once more started walking through the cane to the sea.

❦

In the morning the sea was black and unfathomable because of the lava dust from Tamarin and Grande Rivière Noire. When you went North, or down to Morne in the south, the sea became clear again. From the shelter of the reefs Denis fished for octopus in the lagoon. I watched him as, pole in hand, he waded farther into the water on his long, stiltlike legs. He was not afraid of the sea urchins or scorpion fish. He walked through the dark pools of water, his shadow always behind him. As he waded farther away from the bank he disturbed the

flights of laffes, cormorants, and corbijous. I watched him
with my bare feet in the cold water. I often asked if I could go
with him, but he never let me. He said I was too small, and
that my soul was in his care. He said my father had entrusted
me to him. This wasn't true, my father had never spoken to
him. But I liked the way he said, "Your soul is in my care." I
was the only one he let accompany him to the riverbank. My
cousin Ferdinand was not allowed to, even though he was a bit
older than I, and Laure wasn't either because she was a girl. I
liked Denis a lot; he was my friend. My cousin Ferdinand said
he couldn't be a friend because he was black and Cook's
grandson. But I couldn't care less about that. Ferdinand only
said it because he was jealous, he wished *he* could walk
through the cane with Denis to the sea.

When the tide was very low, as it was early in the morning,
the black rocks became visible. There were great dark pools,
too, and others so clear you could almost believe that light
came from them. At the bottom the sea urchins were violet
spheres, anemones opened their blood-red corollas, and jellyfish slowly waved their long, hairy arms. I stared into the
depths of the pools while in the distance Denis prodded for octopus with the point of his stick.

Here, the sound of the sea was like beautiful music. Waves
blown up by the wind broke on the coral reefs far away; I could
feel their vibration in the rocks and the current that flows up to
the sky. It was as if there were a wall on the horizon that the sea
was trying to break down. Sometimes a burst of spray rose up,
only to fall back onto the reefs in the next instant. The tide had
started to come in. This was the moment when Denis could
spear the octopuses, for they felt the renewal of water from the
open sea in their tentacles and came out of their hiding places.
The pools were flooded one by one. The jellyfish waved their
arms in the current, clouds of small fish rose to the surface in

the swells, and I saw a coffre fish swim by, looking hurried and stupid. I had been going there for a long time, since I was very little. I knew every pool, every rock, and every nook; I knew where the octopuses were, where the fat sea cucumbers crawled, and where the eels and octopuses hid. I would stand very still and silent, so they'd forget I was there. How calm and beautiful the sea was at that moment. When the sun was high above the Tourelle de Tamarin, the water became light, pale blue, the color of the sky. The waves thundered onto the reefs with all their might. Dazzled by the light, I squinted to look for Denis. The sea had come through the inlet and was driving slow waves across the rocks.

When I got to the shore, to the estuary of the two rivers, I saw Denis sitting high up on the beach, in the shade of the veloutier trees. Ten or so octopuses hung like rags at the end of his pole. He waited for me without moving. The sun burned my shoulders and hair. I quickly stripped off my clothes and dived naked into the water, at the point where the two rivers met the sea. I swam against the current of the soft water until I could feel the sharp little pebbles on my stomach and knees. When I was totally immersed in the river I grabbed hold of a large stone and let the fresh water run over me to wash away the burn from the sun and the salty sea.

That was all there was. Only what I felt and saw: the very blue sky, the noise of the sea breaking on the reefs, the cold water running over my skin.

I got out of the water, shivering despite the heat, and dressed without drying. Sand gritted in my shirt and pants and scratched my feet in my shoes. My hair was still sticky with salt. Denis had been watching me without moving, his smooth, dark face indecipherable. Seated in the shade of the veloutier he remained immobile, his two hands resting on the pole from which the octopuses hung like tatters. He never swam in the sea; I didn't even know if he could. When he bathed it was at dusk, high up the Tamarin river or in the Bassin Salé stream. Sometimes he went a long way away, toward the mountains of Mananava, where he washed with plants from the streams in the gorge. He said his grandfather had taught him to do that so he would grow strong and have a man's penis.

I liked Denis, he knew so many things about trees and water and the sea. He learned everything he knew from his grandfather, and also from his grandmother, an old black woman who lived in Cases Noyales. He knew the names of all the fish and insects, he knew all the edible plants in the forest, all the wild fruit, and he could tell the trees apart by nothing more than their smell, or just by chewing a bit of their bark. He knew so many things that you couldn't ever be bored with him. Laure also liked him because he always brought her little presents, a fruit from the forest, or maybe a flower, a shell, a piece of white flint or an obsidian. Ferdinand called him Friday to make fun of us; he nicknamed me Robin Hood because Uncle Ludovic called me that one day when he saw me coming back from the mountain.

One day, a long time ago, at the beginning of our friendship, Denis brought Laure a strange little gray animal with a long sharp snout which he said was a musquash, but my father said it was only a shrew. Laure had it for a day and it slept on her bed in a little cardboard box, but in the evening, just when it was time to go to sleep, it woke up and started to run all over the place and it made so much noise that my father came in his nightshirt with a candle in his hand; he was angry and chased the little animal outside. After that we never saw it again. I think that hurt Laure deeply.

When the sun was really high Denis stood up, emerged from the shade of the veloutiers, and shouted, "Alek-sees!"

9

That's how he pronounced my name. Then we walked quickly across the cane fields up to Boucan. Denis stopped to eat at his grandfather's hut and I ran toward the big house with the sky-blue roof.

❧

At daybreak, when the sky was growing light behind the Trois Mamelles, my cousin Ferdinand and I walked along the dirt track that led to the Yemen cane fields. By climbing over high walls we got into the chase, where the deer of the big estates of Wolmar, Tamarin, Magenta, Barefoot, and Walhalla lived. Ferdinand knew where he was going. His father was very rich and had taken him to all the properties. He had even gone as far as the houses of Tamarin Estate; and right up to Wolmar and Médine far in the North. It was forbidden to go into the chase; my father would be very angry if he knew we were going into the estates. He said it was dangerous, that there could be hunters and that we could fall into a ditch, but I think it was mainly because he did not like the people who owned the big estates. He said everybody should stay on their own property, that there was no use wandering over other people's land.

We walked carefully, as if we were in enemy territory. In the distance, in the gray scrub, we glimpsed some shapes disappearing quickly into the undergrowth: deer.

Then Ferdinand said he wanted to go as far as Tamarin Estate. We came out of the chase and walked once more on the long dirt path. I'd never gone so far. Once I went with Denis to the top of the Tourelle, where you could see the countryside up to the Trois Mamelles and right to Morne, and from there I saw the roofs on the houses and the thick smoke coming from the sugar refinery's tall chimney.

It got hot very quickly because it was almost summer. The cane was very high; they started cutting it several days ago. All along the road we passed carts being pulled by oxen, wobbling beneath the weight of the cane. The bullocks were driven by young Indians with an air of indifference, almost as if they were dozing. The air was full of flies and horseflies. Ferdinand walked quickly and I had a hard time keeping up with him. Every time a car came by we jumped into the ditch because there was just enough room on the path for the big iron-ringed wheels.

The fields were full of working men and women. The men had their cutlasses and sickles and the women their hoes. They were wearing gunnies, coverings made from jute sacks, and their heads wrapped in old rags. The men's chests were bare and streaming with sweat. We heard the cries and calls of *Aouha!* The red dust rose in the pathways between the blocks of cane. There was a sour odor in the air, an odor of cane sap, dust, and men's sweat. Slightly drunk from it, we walked and ran toward the houses of Tamarin where the loads of cane were going. Nobody took any notice of us. There was so much dust on the roads that we were red from head to foot and our clothes looked like gunnies. Indian and African children ran with us, holding stalks of cane that had fallen to the ground. Everyone was going to the refinery to see the first presses.

At last we arrived at the buildings. I was a little afraid because it was the first time I'd been there. The carts had stopped in front of the high, whitewashed wall, and the men were unloading the cane that would be thrown into the drums. The chimney spat out a heavy rust-colored smoke that darkened the sky and choked us when the wind drove it down. Everywhere was noise and great jets of steam. Directly in front of us I saw a group of men tossing bundles of crushed cane into the furnace. They looked like giants, almost naked, the sweat running down their black backs, their faces twisted in pain from the heat of the fire. They did not talk, just took a bundle in their arms and threw it into the furnace, shouting *Huh!* each time.

I didn't know where Ferdinand was. I stood, unable to move, looking at the cast-iron chimney, the great steel vat that stood out like a giant's pot, and the wheels that drove the cylinders. Inside the refinery the men were busy, throwing fresh cane between the jaws of the vats and taking back the crushed cane to extract even more sap. There was so much noise and heat and steam that my head was swimming. The clear juice streamed over the cylinders and ran toward the boiling vats. The children were standing at the base of the separator. I saw Ferdinand waiting in front of the slowly turning vat where the syrup cooled. There were big waves in the vat and the sugar dripped over, hung in black clots and then fell onto the leaf- and straw-covered ground. The children rushed forward screaming, picked up the pieces of sugar, and took them away to suck in the sun. I did, too. I watched for an opportunity and when the sugar plopped out and fell on the ground I rushed forward and picked up a burning wedge covered with grass and shreds of cane. I took it outside and licked it as I squatted in the dust and watched the thick russet-colored smoke coming out of the chimney. The din, the cries of the children, and the men's movements made me feverish and I started to shake. Was it from the noise of the machines and the hissing steam, the rusty, acrid smoke around me, the sun's heat, or the harsh taste of the burned sugar? I couldn't see straight and I felt as if I was going to vomit. I called for my cousin to help me, but my voice was hoarse and it hurt my throat. I called for Denis and Laure, too. But nobody paid any attention. The children constantly rushed around the big turning vat, trying to see the exact moment when the valves opened and the hissing air penetrated the huge pot to send the wave of boiling syrup running along the troughs like a blond river. I suddenly felt so weak and lost that I rested my head on my knees and closed my eyes.

Then I felt a hand stroking my hair and heard a voice speaking softly to me in creole: "Why are you crying?" Through my tears I saw a large, beautiful Indian woman, wrapped in her red-stained gunny. She was standing in front of me, erect, calm and unsmiling; the upper part of her body was quite still because of the hoe balancing on the folded rags on top of her head. She spoke to me softly, asked where I came from, and then I was walking with her on the crowded road, squeezed against her dress, feeling the slow sway of her hips. When we got to the entrance to Boucan on the other side of the river she took me right to Cap'n Cook's hut. Then she left immediately, without waiting to be rewarded or thanked. I watched as she walked stiffly down the wide avenue between the jamroses, her hoe balanced on her head.

I looked at the big wooden house lit by the afternoon sun with its blue or green roof, a color so beautiful that I remember it today as the color of the sky at dawn. Once more I felt the heat from the red ground and the furnace on my face, and I shook off the dust and the wisps of straw covering my clothes. As I approached the house I heard Mam's voice reciting prayers to Laure on the shady veranda. Her voice was so sweet and clear that tears ran down my cheeks again and my heart began to beat very fast. I walked toward the house on my bare feet, across the drought-cracked ground. I continued on until I reached the water tank behind the pantry, then I drew the dark water from the basin with the enamel pitcher and washed my hands, face, neck, legs, and feet. The cool water made the scratches and cuts from the sharp cane leaves sting. Mosquitoes and water spiders ran across the surface of the basin, and grubs writhed on the stone walls. I heard the sweet evening voices of the birds and I smelled the smoke descending on the garden, as if announcing the night that started in Mananava's ravines. Then I went to Laure's tree at the end of the garden, the big chalta tree of good and evil. Everything I felt and everything I saw seemed eternal. I did not know that soon all of it would be gone.

THERE WAS ALSO Mam's voice. It's all that I remember of
her now, all I have left of her. In order to keep the memory of her voice undisturbed I have thrown away all the yel-
lowing photographs, the portraits, the letters and books that
she read. I always want to be able to hear her, like those whom
we love but whose faces we can no longer see. Her voice, the
sweetness of her voice, contained all of her: the warmth of her
hands, the smell of her hair, the dress she was wearing and the
afternoon light that was already waning when Laure and I
came onto the veranda to begin our lessons, our hearts beating
hard from having run. Mam spoke very softly, very slowly,
and we listened carefully, believing that if we did we would
understand. Mam repeated every day that Laure was more intelligent than I, that she knew how to ask the right questions.
We each took turns reading standing in front of Mam, who
rocked back and forth in her ebony chair. After we read, Mam
would ask us questions: first on grammar (the conjugation of
verbs and the agreement of participles and adjectives), then on
the meaning of what we had just read, of certain words and
expressions. She phrased the questions carefully and I listened
to her voice with pleasure and anxiety, for I was afraid of

disappointing her. I was embarrassed not to understand as quickly as Laure; I felt I did not deserve the moments of happiness that came from her look and her words, the sweetness of her voice and her perfume, the light at the end of the day that gilded the house and the trees.

Mam had been teaching us for more than a year, because we didn't have anyone else. Once, so long ago that I could hardly remember it, we'd had a teacher who came from Floreal three times a week. But my father's progressive financial ruin no longer allowed this kind of luxury. My father wanted to send us to boarding school but Mam was against it: Laure and I were still too young, she'd said. So it was she who taught us every day in the evenings, and sometimes in the morning. She taught us what we needed to know: writing, grammar, a bit of arithmetic, and Bible history. In the beginning my father was skeptical about the value of what she was teaching us, but one day when Joseph Lestang, the head teacher at the Royal College, visited, he was astonished by the extent of our knowledge. He even told my father that we were very advanced for our age, and after that my father completely accepted the way we were being taught.

Still, I could not say today what kind of teaching it really was. My father, Mam, Laure, and I lived back then in our own little world in the Boucan valley, bounded to the east by the jagged peaks of the Trois Mamelles, to the north by the immense plantations, to the south by the fallow lands of the Rivière Noire district, and to the west by the sea. In the evening, when the mynah birds chattered in the big trees in the garden, there was also the soft, young voice of Mam dictating a poem or reciting a prayer. What did she say? I no longer know. The meaning of her words has disappeared, like the birds' cries and the sound of the wind off the sea. Only the music remains, sweet and delicate, almost impossible to grasp, at one with the light on the leaves, the shaded porch, and the perfumed evening.

I listened to her voice without ever tiring of it. I heard its vibrations as it mingled with the birds' song. Sometimes I followed the flight of a flock of starlings with my eyes, as if their passage through the trees to their hideouts in the mountains could explain Mam's lesson. From time to time she brought me back to earth by slowly saying my name, as only she could, so slowly that I stopped breathing, "Alexis . . . Alexis?"

She and Denis were the only ones who called me by my name. The others called me Ali, perhaps following Laure's lead. My father never called anyone by their first name, except perhaps Mam. Once or twice I heard him. He said softly, "Anne, Anne." At the time I thought he said, "*âme*": soul. Perhaps he really did say *âme,* in the soft and serious voice he used only when he spoke to her. He truly loved her.

Mam was beautiful then, but I could not say how beautiful. I hear the sound of her voice and it immediately brings to mind the evening light at Boucan, us sitting on the porch surrounded by the glinting light of the bamboo and the clear sky across which flocks of mynahs fly. I think that all the beauty of that instant came from her: from her curly, thick, tawny brown hair that caught the slightest spark of light; from her blue eyes, her face still so full and young, and her long, strong pianist's hands. She was so calm and natural, so full of light. I stole a look at my sister, who was sitting very straight in her chair, her wrists resting on the edge of the table, holding in front of her the arithmetic book and the white exercise book that she kept open with the fingertips of her left hand. She wrote industriously, head cocked slightly toward her left shoulder and her thick black hair hanging over one side of her Indian face. She did not look like Mam, there was no resemblance at all;

but Laure's black eyes were shiny as stone as she looked at her, and I knew that she felt the same admiration for Mam as I did, the same fervor. The evening's shadow was long now, the golden twilight decreasing imperceptibly over the garden, taking with it the flight of the birds, carrying off the shouts of the workers in the fields and the sound of the carts on the road among the cane stalks.

Every evening the lesson was different—a poem, a story, a new problem—but today it seems to me that it was always the same lesson, interrupted by either the burning adventures of the day and the wanderings of the edge of the sea, or by the dreams of the night. When did all that exist? Mam, leaning over the table, explained arithmetic by showing us a pile of beans. "There are three beans here and I take away two, that makes two-thirds. Eight here and I take away five, that makes five-eighths. Ten here and I take away nine: What fraction have I taken away?" I sat watching her long hands with the tapering fingers I knew so well. I looked at them one by one. The very strong index finger of her left hand, the middle finger, and then the ring finger with its thin strip of gold, worn down by water and time. The fingers of her right hand were bigger and stronger, less fine; her little finger, which she lifted very high when the other fingers ran over the ivory piano keys, suddenly hit a sharp note: "Alexis, you aren't listening . . . You never listen to the arithmetic lessons. You will not be able to get into the Royal College." Did she really say that? No, I don't think so. Laure invented it. She was always so studious, so conscientious in working out the piles of beans. It was her way of showing her love for Mam.

I caught up when we came to dictation. It was the moment of the afternoon that I liked best, when, bending over the white page of my exercise book, pen in hand, I waited for

Mam's voice to pronounce the words one by one, very slowly, as if she were giving them to us, as if she were drawing them with her inflections. There were difficult words that she had chosen carefully, for she was the one who wrote the texts for our dictations. "Titillate," "insufferable," "matter-of-fact," "cavalcade," "harness," "trough," "perceive," and naturally, from time to time, to make us laugh, "brew," "hew," "cue," "true," and "few." I wrote as best I could, without hurrying, in order to prolong the duration of Mam's voice echoing in the silent twilight, waiting for the moment when she would say to me with a little shake of the head, as if it were the first time she had noticed it, "You have nice handwriting."

Then she would go on reading, but at her own pace, with a slight pause for the commas and a longer silence for the periods. I can never forget that, either; it was a long story that she read us evening after evening, with the same words and rhythms jumbled up and redistributed every time. At night, stretched out on my cot under the mosquito netting, just before falling asleep, listening to the familiar noises: my father's serious voice while reading a newspaper article or talking to Mam and Aunt Adelaide, Mam's soft laugh, the distant voices of the blacks sitting under the trees, waiting for the sound of the sea breeze in the filao needles—this same interminable story comes back to me, full of words and sounds slowly dictated by Mam, the acute accent she put on a syllable or the very long silence from which a word grew, and the light of her look shining on these incomprehensible and beautiful phrases. I think that I only went to sleep when I saw this shining light, when I made out that sparkle. One word, I needed nothing more than one word which I could take with me to sleep.

I also liked Mam's morality lessons, most often given early on Sunday mornings, before the recitation of the Mass. I liked the lessons because Mam always told a story, a new one every time, always in a family setting. Afterward she questioned Laure and me about the story. They weren't difficult questions and she looked at us and asked them simply, and I felt the very soft blue of her glance sink into the deepest part of me.

"This happened in a convent where there were a dozen boarders, twelve little orphan girls, as I was when I was your age. It is evening, at dinnertime. Do you know what is on the table? There are sardines on a big plate, which they like very much. They're poor, you understand, and for them sardines are a real treat! And it so happens that there are as many sardines on the plate as there are orphans, twelve sardines. No, no, there is one more, there are thirteen sardines altogether. When everyone has eaten, the nun points to the last sardine in the middle of the plate and asks, 'Who is going to eat it? Would someone like it?' Not one hand is raised, not one of the little girls replies. 'Very well,' says the nun gaily, 'this is what we'll do: we're going to blow out the candle and when it's dark the one who would like the sardine can eat it without being ashamed.' The nun blows out the candle and what do you think happens? Every little girl stretches out her hand in the darkness to take the sardine and meets the hand of another little girl. There are twelve little hands resting on the big plate!"

These were the kinds of stories Mam told us. I have never heard funnier or more beautiful ones.

But what I really liked were the Bible stories. The Bible was a big book covered with dark-red leather, an old book with a golden sun on its cover, from which twelve rays flowed. Sometimes Mam let Laure and me look at it. We turned the pages very slowly, looking at the pictures and reading the words written at the top, the captions. There were some etchings I liked better than others, like the Tower of Babel, or the one that said, "The prophet Jonah who lived for three days in a whale, coming out alive." In the distance, near the horizon line, there was a great sailing ship mixing with the clouds, and when I asked Mam who was in this vessel she couldn't tell me. It seemed to me that one day I would know who was traveling in that great ship so that they could see Jonah at the instant he came out of the whale's stomach. I also liked it when God made the "armies of the air" appear in the clouds over Jerusalem. And the battle of Eleazar against Antiochus, when a furious elephant suddenly appeared among the warriors. Laure's favorites were the beginnings, the creation of man and woman, and the picture where we saw the devil with the body of a snake and the head of a man coiled around the tree of good and evil. She recognized the chalta tree at the bottom of our garden from that picture, for they had the same leaves and bore the same fruit. In the evenings Laure loved to go to the tree, climb to its uppermost branches, and pick the thick-skinned fruit we were forbidden to eat. I was the only one she told about this.

Mam read us stories from the Holy Scriptures, like the one in which the Tower of Babel stretches up into the sky. And Abraham's sacrifice, and the story of Joseph, who was sold by his brothers. This happened in 2876 B.C., twelve years before Isaac's death. I remember that date well. I also liked the story of Moses being saved from the water, and Laure and I often asked Mam to read it to us. To keep the Pharaoh's soldiers from killing her child his mother put him in "a little cradle of intertwined rushes," says the Bible, "and then she put him in the Nile at its edge." Then Pharaoh's daughter, accompanied by all her servants, came to the riverside "to bathe herself. As soon as she saw the basket of rushes her curiosity was aroused and she sent one of her maidservants to fetch it. When she saw the crying baby in the cradle she was filled with compassion and the beauty of the child made her feel even more tender, and she resolved to save him." We could recite this story by heart, and we always ended where Pharaoh's daughter adopted the baby and gave him the name of Moses because she had saved him from the water.

But the story I liked best of all was the one about the Queen of Sheba. I don't know why I liked it so much, but because I talked about it so often I succeeded in making Laure like it, too. Mam knew how much I liked it and sometimes, with a smile, she opened the big red book to that chapter and started to read. To this day I know every sentence by heart: "After Solomon had built a magnificent temple to honor God he built a palace for himself which took fourteen years to build and gold shone from all its parts and the magnificence of the columns and sculptures drew everyone's eyes." Then the Queen of Sheba "came from the far south to see if everything that was said about this young prince was true. She wore beautiful clothes and she brought costly presents for Solomon: six times twenty talents of gold which equal more or less eight million pounds; very precious pearls and such wonderful perfumes the likes of which had never been seen before." It is not the words I followed but Mam's voice, which took me into Solomon's palace, where he rose from his throne while the beautiful Queen of Sheba directed the slaves who were laying out the treasures on the floor. Laure and I especially liked King Solomon, even though we didn't understand why at the end of his life he renounced God to worship idols. Mam said that is how it is, that even the most just and powerful men can sin. We did not understand how this was possible, but we still liked the way he rendered justice, and the magnificent palace that he built, and the parts involving the Queen of Sheba. But maybe what we really liked was the book with its gold sun on the red leather cover and the sound of Mam's soft, slow voice, her blue eyes that looked at us between each sentence, and the golden evening light on the trees in the garden, for never has another book made such a deep impression on me.

The afternoons when Mam's lessons finished early, Laure and I would go and explore beneath the roof of the house. There was a little wooden staircase that went up to the ceiling, and all one had to do was push up a trap door. The light under the shingled roof was gray and the heat was stifling, but we loved it here. At either end of the attic was a narrow, paneless window with uneven shutters on the inside. When we opened the shutters we could see far over the countryside, from the Yemen and Magenta cane fields and the mountain chain including the Trois Mamelles and the Rempart.

I liked to stay in our hideaway until dinner, and even later, when night had fallen. The place I liked best was the part right at the end of the roof on the mountain side. There was a lot of dusty furniture there, which had been gnawed by the termites and which was all that remained of what my great-grandfather had bought from the Compagnie des Indes. I would sit on a very low sewing chair and look through the window, toward the circle of mountains emerging from the shadows. In the center of the attic were big trunks full of old papers, magazines from France tied into bundles with string. My father kept all his old newspapers there. Every six months he made a parcel of them and put them on the floor near the trunks. Laure and I often went there to read and look at the pictures. We would lie on our stomachs in the dust in front of the piles of old magazines, slowly turning the pages. There was the *Travel Journal,* which always had a drawing of an extraordinary scene on the front page, a tiger hunt in India, or the Zulus attacking the English, or the Comanches rushing toward an American train. Inside the magazine, Laure read passages in a high voice from the *Marseillais Robinsons,* a serial she particularly liked. The magazine we were most fond of was the *Illustrated London News,* and since my English was bad I studied the pictures carefully so that I could guess what the text said. My father had started to teach Laure English, and she showed me the meaning of the words and how to pronounce them. Sometimes we didn't stay very long, because the dust stung our eyes and made us sneeze. Sometimes, however, we remained there for hours, like on days when it was too hot outside, or when we had a temperature and had to stay indoors.

In the magazines that didn't have pictures I looked at the advertisements, those for the Parisian Dry Cleaners, the A. Fleury & A. Toulorge Pharmacy, Coringhy's Tobacconist, for sumac blue-black ink, American pocket watches, and beautiful bicycles that we longed to own. We played at buying things and chose what we wanted from the advertisements. Laure wanted a bicycle, a real bicycle painted in black enamel, with a chrome handlebar and big wheels, fitted with a pump, like the ones we'd seen when we went to the Champ-de-Mars, in Port Louis. As for myself, I wanted several things, like the big drawing books, the paints, and the compass from Wimphen's, or the pen-knives with a dozen blades from the gunsmith. But there was nothing I wanted more than the Favre-Leuba fob watch imported from Geneva. It was always in the same place in the magazines, on the next-to-last page, with the hands showing the same hour and the second hand on noon. I always read the words of the advertisement aloud, describing it with the same relish, "in stainless steel with an enamel face, unbreakable, water and air resistant, a marvel of precision and strength ready to serve you for life."

And so we dreamed in our stifling hideaway beneath the burning roof. There was also the countryside that I could see through the window, the only landscape that I knew and loved,

that I would soon no longer see. Beyond the dark trees of the
garden was the green expanse of the cane fields, the gray and
blue stains of the Walhalla aloes, the smoking chimneys of
the refineries in Yemen, and even further, like a semicircular,
flaming red wall, the mountain chain from which the peaks of
the Trois Mamelles rose. Against the sky the points of the volcanoes were sharp and delicate, like the towers of a fairy castle.
I never tired of looking at them through the narrow window,
as if I were the lookout on a still ship, waiting for a signal,
listening to the noise of the sea beneath and behind me, rocked
by the tidal winds. And in truth, as the joists and struts of the
house frame creaked, I was in a ship, floating eternally in front
of the row of mountains. It was there that I heard the sea for
the first time, there that I felt it best when its big waves came
and forced their way into the pass, throwing spray high onto
the coral reefs.

❖

We never saw anyone during the time at Boucan, and Laure
and I became utter savages. As soon as we could we escaped
from the garden and walked through the cane field toward the
sea. The heat had come, the dry heat that Cap'n Cook said
"pricks." Did we realize how free we were? We didn't even
know the meaning of the word. We never left the Boucan valley, that imaginary domain bordered by two rivers, the mountains, and the sea.

Now that the long holiday period had begun my cousin Ferdinand came more often, while Uncle Ludovic visited his
Barefoot and Yemen estates. Ferdinand did not like me. He
called me "Robin Hood," like his father, and Denis "Friday,"
and one day he said, "Souls in black skins are dipped in pitch,"
and I got angry. Even though he was two years older than I, I

jumped on him and tried to get him in a neck lock, but he
quickly got the upper hand and squeezed my neck in the hollow of his arms until I could feel my bones crack and my eyes
water. He never came back to Boucan after that day. I hated
him and I also hated his father, Uncle Ludovic, because he was
big and strong and spoke loudly and always looked at us with
his black, ironic eyes and his strained smile. The last time he
came to the house, my father wasn't there and Mam didn't
want to see him. She sent word that she had a fever and that
she was tired. All the same, Uncle Ludovic sat himself down
in the dining room on one of our old chairs, which squealed
under his weight, and tried to talk to Laure and me. I remember him leaning toward Laure and saying to her, "What's your
name?" His black eyes shone as he looked at me as well. Laure
was pale, sitting stiffly in her chair, and she stared in front of
her without answering. She stayed like that for a long while,
not moving, looking straight in front of her, while Uncle Ludovic, to tease her, said, "What's the matter? Cat got your
tongue?" My heart pounded with anger, and I snapped at him,
"My sister doesn't want to talk to you." Then he got up without saying anything else, took his cane and his hat, and left. I
heard the sound of his footsteps on the porch, then on the dirt
path; and then we heard the noise of his car, the rattle of the
gears and the rumbling of the wheels, and we were very relieved. After that he stopped coming to the house.

At the time, we thought of it as a kind of victory. But Laure
and I never spoke about it, and nobody else ever knew what
had happened that afternoon. We hardly saw Ferdinand in the
years that followed. Besides, it was certainly that year, the year
of the cyclone, that his father made him a boarder at the Royal
College. As for us, we did not know that everything was
about to change, and that those were our final days of living in
the Boucan valley.

❖

It was around this time that Laure and I realized there was something wrong with my father's business. He never spoke of it to anyone, I don't think even to Mam, because he didn't want to worry her. But we could feel what was happening; we guessed it. One day, when we were stretched out in the attic in front of the bundles of old magazines, Laura said to me, "'Bankrupt.' What does that mean, 'bankrupt'?" She asked because she knew very well that I didn't know the answer. It was a word that simply existed, that she had heard and that echoed in her head. Later, she repeated other frightening words: "mortgage," "foreclosure," "draft." On a big sheet full of fine figures like flyspecks that I hastily read on my father's desk, there were some mysterious English words: "assets and liabilities." What did they mean? Laure didn't know the meaning of those words either, and she didn't dare ask Father. They were threatening words, bringing with them a danger that we didn't understand, as did the series of scratched-out, under-lined figures, certain of which were written in red.

Several times late at night I was awakened by the sound of voices. My sweat-soaked nightshirt clung to my skin as I slipped along the hallway to the lit dining room. Through the half-open door I could hear my father's serious voice, and other voices that I didn't recognize answering him. What were they talking about? Even if I listened to every word, I wouldn't be able to understand them. But I didn't listen to the words. I heard only the hum of voices, glasses clinking on the table, feet scraping the floor, and chairs creaking. Was Mam also there, sitting beside my father as at mealtimes? But the strong smell of tobacco told me she was not. Mam didn't like cigar smoke. She must have been in her room, in her brass bed, she too star-ing—like me, crouched in the dark passage—at the line of yellow light that came through the half-open door and listening to the sound of strangers' voices, to my father speaking, speaking for such a long time. Eventually I went back to the room and slid under the mosquito net. Laure didn't move, but I knew that she, too, was listening to the voices at the other end of the house. Lying on my cot I waited, holding my breath, until I heard the sounds of footsteps in the garden and the hum of the departing cars. Then I waited some more, until the noise of the sea came to me, the invisible night tide that made the wind blow in the filao needles and beat against the shutters. The frame of the house groaned like the hull of an old ship. Then I could go to sleep.

❀

Denis's lessons were the most enjoyable. He taught me about the sky, the sea, the caves at the foot of the mountains, and the fallow fields where we ran together that summer between the black pyramids or the walls built by the creoles. Sometimes we left at dawn when the mountaintops were still covered with mist, and in the distance the rocks protruded from the low tide. We went through the aloe plantations along narrow, quiet roads. Denis walked in front; I saw his tall, fine, lithe silhouette moving as if dancing. From time to time he would stop. He was like a dog who had found a wild animal's scent, some rabbit or hedgehog. When he stopped he would lift his right hand as a signal, and then I too would stop and listen. I heard the sound of the wind in the aloes, and the sound of my heart as well. The first ray of sunlight was shining on the red earth, lightening the dark leaves. The mist was getting thinner on the mountaintops and the sky was now a deep blue. I imagined the sea, which would be the color of azure near the coral reef but still black at the river's mouth. "Look!" Denis said.

He had come to a halt on the path and he pointed to the mountain on the side of the Rivière Noire gorges. Very high in the sky I saw a bird gliding in the air currents, its head turned a little to the side and its long white tail trailing behind it. "A bo'sun bird," Denis said. It was the first time I saw one. It drifted slowly above the ravines then disappeared toward Mananava.

Denis had started walking again. We were following the narrow valley of the Boucan stream toward the mountains. We crossed old cane fields that now lay fallow, where only low walls of lava buried under thorn bushes were left. I was no longer in a familiar place. I was in a strange land, the land of Denis and the blacks from the other side, those from Chamarel, Rivière Noire, and Cases Noyales. The farther Denis got from Boucan and the nearer he got to the forest and the mountains, the less suspicious he became; he spoke more and seemed freer. He was walking slowly now, his gestures were easier; even his face had brightened, and he smiled as he waited for me on the road. With his right hand he showed me the nearby mountains: "Grand Louis and Mont Terre Rouge." We were surrounded by silence. There was no wind, and I could no longer smell the sea. The undergrowth was so thick that we had to walk along a mountain stream in order to climb. I took off my shoes, which hung around my neck by the laces as they always did when I was with Denis. We were walking on sharp stones in the cold shallow stream. Denis stopped at the bends to search the water for shrimp and crayfish.

The sun was high when we arrived at the source of the Boucan, very near the high mountains. The January heat was intense and I found it difficult to breathe beneath the trees. Tiger mosquitoes came out from their shelters and danced before my eyes and I could also see them dancing around Denis's woolly hair. Denis stopped on the banks of the stream, took off his shirt and began to gather leaves. I came closer to look at the dark-green leaves covered with light gray down, which he was putting into his shirt now transformed into a sack. "Sonz leaves," Denis said. He put a little water in the hollow of a leaf and held it out to me. On the fine down the drop was held like a liquid diamond. Farther on he gathered other leaves: "Emballaze." He pointed to a creeper on a tree trunk: "A seven-year liana." Some palmate leaves were open in the form of a heart: "Fa'am." I knew that old Sara, Cap'n Cook's sister, was "yangue," that she made potions and cast spells, but it was the first time Denis had taken me when he went to gather plants for her. Sara was from Madagascar; she had come from Grand Terre with Cook, Denis's grandfather, when there were still slaves. One day Cook told Laure and me that he was so scared when he arrived at Port Louis with the other slaves that he perched on a tree at the commissariat and refused to come down, believing they were going to eat him right there on the dock. Sara lived at Rivière Noire; she used to come to visit her brother and she liked Laure and me a lot. Now she was too old to come anymore.

Denis continued to walk along the stream toward its source. The running water was thin and black and it flowed smoothly over the basalt rocks. The sun was so hot that Denis sprinkled water from the stream over his face and chest, and he told me to do the same in order to refresh myself. I drank the cool water straight from the stream. Denis went on along the narrow ravine, staying in front of me. He carried the bundle of leaves on his head. From time to time he stopped and indicated a tree deep in the forest, or a plant, or a creeper: "Binzoin," "cow's tongue," "zozo tree," "big balsam," "mamzel tree," "prune," "cabri tree," "tambour tree."

He picked a creeper with narrow leaves that he crushed between his thumb and index finger to smell them: "verbena."

Still farther on he went into the deep woods until he found a big tree with a brown trunk. He peeled off a bit of bark and cut into it with his flint, making the golden sap run: "Tatamaka." I walked behind him across the forest, bending low in order to avoid the scratchy branches. Denis moved easily in the middle of the forest, silently, all his senses alert. The ground was damp and warm under my bare feet. I was frightened but I still wanted to go farther, to penetrate into the heart of the forest. Denis stopped at a very straight trunk. He tore off a piece of bark and gave it to me to smell. Its scent made my head swim. Denis laughed and simply said, "Colophony wood."

We went on. Denis was walking more quickly, as if he had found an invisible path. The heat and humidity of the forest oppressed me and I had difficulty breathing. I saw Denis stop in front of a bush: "Maroon pistachio." Black seeds that looked like insects spilled from a long, half-open pod in his hand. I tasted a seed; it was tart and oily but it gave me strength. Denis said, "It was the food of the slaves who ran away with the great Sacalavou." It was the first time that he had spoken to me of Sacalavou. My father told us one time that he died here at the bottom of the mountains when the whites caught up with him. He threw himself from the cliff rather than be taken again. It made me feel strange to eat what he had eaten, here, in this forest with Denis. We were far from the stream now, already at the foot of Mount Terre Rouge. The ground was dry and the sun beat down through the light leaves of the acacias.

"Chicken claw," Denis said. "Kasi."

Suddenly he stopped. He had found what he was looking for. He went directly to a tree that stood alone in the middle of the undergrowth. It was a handsome, dark tree with low, extended branches bearing thick green leaves with coppery tints. Denis was squatting at the foot of the tree hidden in its shadow. When I came nearer he didn't look at me. He put his bundle on the ground.

"What is it?"

"Affouche." He was holding something in his left hand. Still squatting, he sang softly like the Indians when they pray. His body, hidden by the tree's shadow, swayed back and forth as he sang and I could see only his back, which was shining with sweat. When he finished his prayer he made a little hollow in the ground at the foot of the tree with his right hand. His left fist opened and in his palm I saw a coin. It slid off his hand to the bottom of the hole and he carefully covered it with earth and a piece of moss with roots. Then he got up and without taking any notice of me picked some leaves from the lowest branches and put them on the ground at the side of the bundle. With his sharp flint he sliced off some pieces of the smooth trunk and a clear milk flowed from the cut. Denis put the pieces of bark and the leaves from the affouche tree into his shirt and said, "Let's go." He didn't wait for me and quickly moved away as he crossed the undergrowth and went down the slopes of the hills toward the Boucan valley. The sun was already in the west. Above the trees, between the dark hills, I could see the fiery spot of the sea and the horizon where the waves were born. Behind me the wall of the mountains was red, reflecting the heat like an oven. I walked quickly, following in Denis's footsteps until we reached the stream that was the Boucan's source. It seemed to me that I had been gone for a long time, for days perhaps, and this made me giddy.

It was during that summer, in the year of the cyclone, that my father pushed ahead with his old plan for a power station on the Rivière Noire. When did it really start? I don't remember exactly, because at that time my father had dozens of different projects that he mulled over in silence, of which only faint echoes reached Laure and me. I believe he had a plan for a shipyard at the Rivière Noire estuary, and also one for an airplane to transport people between the Mascarenes and South Africa. But they all remained simply visions, and we only knew of these ideas from what Mam, or the people who sometimes came to visit, said. The power station project was certainly the oldest, and they only began to build it that summer, when my father's state of debt was already irremediable. It was Mam who told us about it one day after our lessons. She talked for a long time in an emotional voice, her eyes shining. A new era was going to begin, and we were at last going to be prosperous and not have to fear what the next day might bring. Our father had already cleared a place at the lake at Aigrettes, where the two branches of the Rivière Noire met.

This was the site he had chosen for the power station, which would provide electricity to the whole eastern region, from Médine to Bel Ombre. The generator he had mail-ordered from London had just been offloaded at Port Louis, and had traveled in an ox cart along the coast up to Rivière Noire. The time of oil lighting and steam engines would soon be over, and little by little, electricity, thanks to my father, would bring progress to the whole island. Mam also explained to us what electricity was, its properties and its uses, but we were too young to understand anything about it, except to verify, as we did every day back then, the mystery of the pieces of paper that could be magnetized by Mam's amber necklace.

One day we all went in the horse-drawn carriage to the Aigrettes basin, Mam, my father, Laure, and I. Because of the heat we left very early, as Mam wanted to be back before noon. In the second bend of the road that leads to Rivière Noire, we found the path that my father had cleared for the ox wagon carrying the generator. Our carriage went along in a big cloud of dust.

It was the first time that Laure and I had gone up the Rivière Noire and we looked curiously around us. The dust rose up from the road and enveloped us in an ochre cloud. Mam pulled a shawl around her face and she looked like an Indian woman. Father was full of joy and he talked as he guided the horse. I will never forget how he looked that day: very tall and thin and elegant in his gray-and-black suit, with his black hair combed back from his face. I can see his profile, his fine aquiline nose, his trimmed beard and his elegant hands that always held a cigarette like a pen between his thumb and index finger. Mam was also looking at him and I can see the brightness of her look that morning on the dusty road alongside the Rivière Noire.

When we were near the lake at Aigrettes basin my father tied the horse to the branch of a tamarind tree. The water in the pool was clear, the color of the sky, and the wind made ripples that moved the reeds. Laure and I said that we'd like to swim, but my father was already walking toward the construction that sheltered the generator. In a wooden hut he showed us the dynamo, which was tied to the turbine by ropes and belts. In the dark the machine shone with a strange light that frightened us a little. Father also showed us the pool of water that flowed out through a canal to rejoin the Rivière Noire. There were large reels of cable on the ground in front of the generator, and my father explained that the cables would extend all along the river to the sugar refinery, then from there across the hills to Tamarin and the Boucan valley. Later, after the plant had proven itself, the electricity would go farther north, to Médine, Wolmar, and perhaps even as far as Phoenix. My father spoke to us, but his face was turned away, toward another time, another world.

After that day we thought all the time about electricity. Laure and I believed every evening that it was going to come, and like a miracle suddenly illuminate the inside of our house and shine outside on the plants and trees like Saint Elmo's fire. "When will it come?" Mam smiled when we asked her. We wanted the mystery to be revealed. "Soon. . ." She explained that the turbine had to be connected, the damming consolidated, wooden posts put up and the cables hooked onto them. All that would take months, perhaps years. No, it was impossible to wait for so long.

My father was even more impatient. For him, electricity meant the end of his worries and the beginning of a new fortune. Uncle Ludovic would see, he'd understand, even though he refused to believe in it. When electric turbines replaced all the steam engines in the sugar refineries, then he would believe. My father went almost every day to Port Louis, to Rempart Street where he met with important men, bankers and businessmen. Uncle Ludovic did not come to Boucan anymore. It seemed that he did not believe in electricity, or at least in this electricity. Laure heard our father say that one evening. But if Uncle Ludovic didn't believe in it, how would it get here? For he owned all the land around here and the watercourse belonged to him. Even the Boucan land belonged to him. Laure and I spent the long month of January during that last summer stretched out on the floor in the attic, reading. We'd stop every time something came up about an electric machine, a dynamo, or even a simple electric lamp.

The nights were heavy, and now the moist sheets under the mosquito net were full of anticipation. It was as if we were waiting for something. Something had to happen. In the dark, I waited for the sound of the sea, and through the shutters I watched the moon rise. How could we know what was happening? Perhaps by Mam's face at lessons every evening. She forced herself not to let anything show, but her voice was not the same and her words were different. We sensed her anxiety and impatience. Sometimes she would stop in the middle of a dictation and look to the side of the big trees as if something was going to appear.

One day, at the end of the afternoon, as I was coming back from a long ramble with Denis in the woods by the gorges, I saw my father and Mam on the veranda. Laure was at their side, a little farther back. My heart tightened, for I immediately guessed that something bad had happened while I was in the forest. I was also afraid of being scolded by my father. He was standing near the stairs with a dark air, very thin in the black suit that floated around him. As usual, he held a cigarette between the thumb and index finger of his right hand.

"Where have you been?"

He asked me the question as I was coming up the stairs. I stopped but he didn't wait for my reply. He only said in a voice I didn't recognize, a strange and slightly muffled voice.

"Grave events shall come to pass. . ."

He couldn't continue.

It was Mam's turn to speak. She was pale and seemed distraught. That is what hurt me most of all. I wanted so much not to hear what she had to say.

"Alexis, we have to leave this house. We shall have to leave here forever."

Laure didn't say anything. She was standing very stiff on the veranda, staring straight in front of her. She had the same hard and impassive face that she'd had when Uncle Ludovic asked her her name.

It was already twilight. Night was falling softly on the lawn. In front of us, suddenly, above the trees, the first star burst forth with magical radiance. Laure and I looked at it, and

Mam too raised her head to look at the star, as if it were the first time she was seeing it above Rivière Noire.

For a long time we stood beneath the star, unmoving. The trees were in shadow and the night crackled with the sharp music of the mosquitoes.

Mam was the first to break the silence. She said with a sigh: "How beautiful it is!" Then playfully, as she descended from the porch:

"Come, we're going to name the stars."

My father came down, too. He walked slowly, slightly bent, hands behind his back. I was near him and Laure was arm-in-arm with Mam. Together we walked around the big house that was so like a beached shipwreck. In Cap'n Cook's hut there was a wavering light and we could hear the muffled sound of voices. He and his wife were the last ones to have stayed on the property. Where would they go? When he came for the first time to Boucan, in my grandfather's time, he must have been twenty years old. He had just been freed. I heard his voice echoing in the hut; he was speaking to himself or singing. In the distance, near the cane fields, other voices were also echoing; they came from the gunnies, who were gleaning and walking toward Tamarin on the La Coupe road. There was also the squeaking of the insects and the song of the toads in the ravine at the other end of the garden.

The sky lit up for us. We should forget everything and only think of the stars. Mam showed us the stars, and then she called my father to ask us questions. I heard his clear, young voice in the dark and I felt good, reassured.

"Look there . . . isn't that Betelgeuse above Orion? And Orion's Belt! Look to the north and you'll see the Big Dipper. What is the name of the little star right on the end of the Big Dipper, at the tip of the handle?

I looked as hard as I could. I wasn't sure I would see it.

"A very little star at the top of the Big Dipper, above the second star?" My father asked the question seriously, as if it were of utmost importance this evening.

"Yes, that's it. It's very small, I see it and then it disappears."

"It's called Alcor," my father said. "Also known as the Great Charioteer. The Arabs named it Alcor, which means 'test,' because it's so small that only very sharp eyes can find it." He was silent for a moment, and then he said to Mam in a lighter voice, "You have good eyes. I can't see it anymore."

I saw Alcor as well, or, rather, I dreamed that I saw it, fine as cinders above the end of the Big Dipper's handle. And seeing it erased all the bad memories, all the anxiety.

It was my father who taught us to love the night. Sometimes in the evening when he wasn't working in his study he would take us by the hand, Laure on his right and me on the left, and lead us down the path that crossed the garden to the south. He called it "the path of stars," because it went toward the fullest part of the sky. He smoked a cigarette while walking, and we smelled the sweet odor of the tobacco that hung in the night and saw the glimmer of red near his lips that lit his face. I liked the lingering smell of tobacco in the night.

The most beautiful evenings were in July, when we could see all the brilliant lights in the cold sky above the Rivière Noire mountains: Vega, Aquila the Eagle—Laure said it looked more like a stag beetle—and the third, whose name I could never remember, like a jewel at the top of the great cross. My father called these three stars shining like a triangle in the clear sky "the beauties of the night." Jupiter and Saturn were also there, hanging above the mountains far to the south. Laure and I looked especially at Saturn because our Aunt Adelaide had told us that it was our planet, the one that was ruling the sky when we were born in December. It looked beautiful as it shone with its slightly blue tinge above the trees, but there was something frightening in it, too: a sharp, piercing light like the one Laure's eyes sometimes had. Mars was not far from Saturn; it was red and vivid and its light attracted us too. My father didn't like the things people said about the stars. He said to us, "Come, we are going to look at the Southern Cross." He walked in front of us to the end of the path, near the chalta tree. In order to see the Southern Cross clearly one had to move far away from the house lights. As we looked up at the sky we hardly dared breathe. Suddenly I picked up the "followers," high in the sky behind the centaur. To the right the cross was pale and dim, bending slightly as it drifted like the sail of a canoe. Laure and I saw it at the same time and there was no need to say anything. Silently, we both looked at the cross. Mam came to join us and she did not talk to our father. We all stood where we were and it was as if we could hear the noise of the stars in the night. It was so beautiful that we didn't have to speak, but my heart hurt and my throat was tight because something had changed, and somehow I knew that all this had to come to an end. I thought that perhaps what we had to do, for nothing to change and for us to be saved, was written in the stars.

There were so many signs in the sky. I remember all those summer nights when we lay on the grass of the lawn keeping a lookout for shooting stars. One evening we saw a shower of stars and Mam immediately said, "It is a sign of war," but then she kept quiet because father didn't like us to say things like that. We watched the incandescent trails that crossed the sky from all directions for ages; some of them were so long we could follow them with our eyes, while others were very brief and exploded immediately. I am still sure today that Laure, like me, was trying to see the traces of fire in the summer skies that would show us our destiny and make secret wishes come true.

We looked at the sky with such concentration that our heads started to swim and we reeled giddily. I could hear Mam speaking softly to my father, but I couldn't understand what they were saying. The big pale river of our galaxy went right across the sky from east to north, forming islands near the Swan's Cross and then flowing on toward Orion.

A little farther up, in the area of our house I perceived, like a swarm of fireflies, the confused glimmer of the Pleiades. I knew every corner of the sky, every constellation. It was my father who taught us about the night sky, and every evening, or almost every evening, he showed us the position of the stars on a big map that was pinned to a wall in his office. "Those who know the sky have nothing to fear from the sea," my father said. He was usually so secretive, so silent, but when his subject was the stars he became animated and his eyes shone. Then he would tell us wonderful things about the world, about the sea, about God. He spoke of the great sailors who discovered the routes to the Indies, Oceania, and America. Engulfed in the smell of tobacco that hung in his study, I looked carefully at the maps. He spoke of Cook, Drake, and Magellan, who discovered the southern waters on the *Victoria* and who later died in the Sunda islands. He spoke of Tasman, Biscoe, and Wilkes, who traveled as far as the eternally icebound South Pole; and also of fabulous explorers like Marco Polo in China and de Soto in America; Orellana, who went up the Amazon; Gmelin, who went across Siberia; Mungo Park, Stanley, Livingstone, and Przevalski. I listened carefully to these stories and the names of the countries: Africa, Tibet, the South Sea islands. They were magic names, like the names of the stars and the drawings of the constellations. At night, lying on my cot, I listened to the noise of the incoming tide and the wind in the filao needles. Then I would think of all these names, and it felt as if the night sky had opened and I was on the infinite sea, on a ship with swollen sails, sailing all the way to the Moluccas, to Astrolabe Bay, to Fiji, to Moorea. Before falling asleep I saw the sky from the bridge of this ship as I had never seen it before, hanging so big and dark blue over the phosphorescent sea. I glided slowly over to the other side of the horizon and sailed toward Orion's Belt and the Southern Cross.

❀

I remember my first sea voyage. I think it was in January, because well before sunrise the heat was already torrid and there was not a breath of air over the Boucan valley. At the first glimmer of light I slipped quietly out of the room. There were no sounds outside yet, and in the house everybody was asleep. A lone light shone in Cap'n Cook's hut, but at this hour he didn't concern himself with anyone. He looked at the gray sky and waited for the day to begin. Perhaps the rice was already boiling in the big black pot above the fire. So as not to make any noise I walked barefoot to the end of the garden on the dry earth of the path. Denis was waiting for me under the big chalta tree, and when I arrived he got up without a word and began to walk toward the sea. He went quickly across the plantations without bothering about me and I lost my breath as I tried to keep up. Turtledoves ran fearfully among the cane but did not dare to fly. By daylight we had reached the road to Rivière Noire. The ground was hot under my feet and the air smelled of dust. The first ox carts were already going toward the plantation roads, and in the distance I could see the white smoke from the chimneys of the sugar refineries. I was waiting for the sound of the wind. Suddenly Denis stopped. We stood still in the middle of the cane and I could hear the sound of the waves on the reefs. "The surf is high," Denis said. The sea wind reached us.

We got to Rivière Noire at the moment when the sun came out from behind the mountains. I had never been so far from Boucan and my heart beat loudly as I ran behind Denis's black silhouette. We waded through the river near the estuary and the cold water reached up to our waists; then we walked in the black sand that came off the dunes. The fisherman's canoes were lined up on the beach and some of their bows were already in the water. The men held the cords from the sails, which cracked as they filled with the tidal wind, and pushed the pirogues into the waves. Denis's pirogue was at the end of the beach. Two men were pushing it into the sea: an old man with a wrinkled face the color of copper and a big, vigorous black man. A very beautiful young woman with her hair tied in a red scarf was standing on the beach with them. "That's my sister," Denis said proudly. "And he is her fiancé. The canoe is his." The young woman saw Denis and called to him. Together we pushed the canoe into the water. When the back of the canoe was taken by a wave Denis shouted to me, "Get in!" and he jumped in too. He ran forward and took hold of the pole to guide the canoe toward the ocean. The wind swelled the sail like a big white sheet and the canoe streaked across the waves. We were already far from the beach. Soaked by the waves that broke over the boat, I shivered as I watched the black earth recede. I had waited so long for this day! Once Denis had spoken to me about the sea and this canoe and I had asked him, "When will you take me with you?" He had looked at me without saying anything, as if he were thinking it over. I didn't say anything about it to anybody, not even to Laure, because I was afraid she'd tell father. Laure did not like the sea, and she might have been afraid I would drown. When

I had left that morning with bare feet so as not to make any noise, she had turned to the wall so as not to see me. What was going to happen when I got back? But I didn't want to think of it then; I felt as if I were never going back. The canoe plunged into the trough of the waves and the spray burst into the light. The old man and the fiancé had set the triangular sail on to the bowsprit and the strong winds that blew in from the channel rocked the canoe. Denis and I were soaked by the spray as we crouched in the front of the canoe, leaning against the vibrating sailcloth. Denis's eyes shone when he looked at me. Without speaking he indicated the high, dark-blue sea; or, far behind us, the black line of the beach and the outline of the mountains against the clear sky.

The pirogue spun out onto the high seas. I could hear the loud noise of the waves and the wind rushed by my ears. I was no longer cold or frightened. The sun beat down, making the crests of the waves sparkle. I didn't see anything else and I didn't think of anything else: there was only a deep-blue sea and the shimmering horizon, the wind and the taste of the sea. It was the first time I had been in a boat, and never before had I experienced anything so wonderful. The canoe crossed the channel and ran alongside the thundering waves as they broke on the reefs and sent spray flying into the air.

Denis was bent over the bow, looking into the dark water as if he were trying to find something. Then he lifted his hand and showed me a big eroded rock right in front of us.

"Morne."

I had never seen it from so close. Morne did not have any trees or plants on it; it rose straight up out of the sea like a lava stone. Lagoons and pale, sandy beaches stretched around it. It was as if we were going toward the end of the world. Screeching sea birds flew around us; gulls, terns, white petrels, and huge frigates. My heart was beating very hard and I was shaking with worry because it felt as if we had gone very far, to the other side of the sea. Slow-moving waves slapped across the beam and flooded the bottom of the canoe. Denis threaded his way under the sail; he picked two calabashes up off the floor of the pirogue and called to me. Together we bailed the water out. At the back of the canoe the big black man had one arm around Denis's sister while he held the sail with the other. The old man with the Indian face leaned on the tiller. They were streaming with seawater, but they laughed as we scooped up the water that always came back. Crouching at the bottom of the canoe, I threw the water overboard to leeward, and every now and then from under the sail I could see the high black wall of Morne and the marks of the spray on the reefs.

Then we changed course and the wind swept the big sail above our heads. Denis showed me the coast.

"There, at the channel. Bénitiers Island."

We stopped bailing and slipped to the front of the canoe for a better view. The white line of the reef opened before us. Pushed by the waves, we rushed straight toward Morne. The roar of the waves breaking on the coral reef was very near. Denis and I kept our eyes on the deep water, which was so blue it made our heads swim. The color of the water in front of the bow slowly lightened; we saw glimmers of green, clouds of gold. The seabed appeared, and blocks of coral, purplish blue balls of sea urchins, and banks of silvery fish rushed quickly by. We were in calm waters now and the wind had dropped. The collapsed sail flapped around the mast. We were in the Morne lagoon, where the men had come to fish.

The sun was high. The canoe, pushed by Denis's pole, glided silently over the calm waters. In the back, the fiancé, still not letting go of Denis's sister, rowed single-handedly with a little paddle. The old man, standing with his back to the sun, kept his eyes on the water; he was looking for fish hiding in the holes in the coral. He had a long line in his hand that whistled in the air as he tossed it out. After the violent, high, dark sea and the wind squalls and the spindrifts, this felt like a warm dream full of light. I could feel the sun beating down on my face and back. Denis had taken off his clothes to let them dry, and I did the same. When he was naked he dived, suddenly and almost soundlessly, into the clear water. I could see him swimming under the surface, but then he disappeared. When he resurfaced he was holding a big red fish that he had harpooned and he threw it into the bottom of the boat. He immediately dived again. His black body slipped under the water, resurfaced and then went under again. He brought up another fish with bluish scales and threw it, too, into the boat. We were very near the coral reef now. The big black man and the old man with the Indian face sank their lines. Several times they brought in fish, seawives, *dameberi* and *kardonye*.

They fished for a long time as the canoe drifted along the reefs. The sun burned in the center of a dark sky, but it was the sea that threw up the light, a light so blinding that it intoxicated me. I was bent over the stem, lying absolutely still, looking at the glistening water, but Denis touched my shoulder and brought me out of my torpor. His eyes were shining like black stones, and he said in Creole in a funny singsong voice, "*Lizé manimani*"—faraway eyes.

Dizziness, like a magic spell reflected from the sun onto the sea, took hold of me and sapped my strength. Despite the torrid heat I was cold. Denis's sister and her fiancé laid me down on the bottom of the boat in the shade of the sail, which flapped in the breeze. Denis put some seawater in his hands and moistened my face and body. Then pushing on the pole he steered the pirogue to the bank. Soon we landed on the white sand near the Morne headland. There were some shrubs and veloutier trees. Helped by Denis, I walked until we reached the shade of a veloutier. Denis's sister gave me something to drink in a gourd; it was sour and burned my tongue and throat, but it broke the spell. I wanted to get up and walk to the canoe, but Denis's sister said that I must stay in the shade until the sun started to set. The old man was still in the boat, leaning on the pole, and now they glided away over the shimmering water to continue fishing.

Denis stayed with me. He did not speak. He sat with me in the shade of the veloutier; his legs had traces of white sand on them. He was not like the other children, the ones who lived in beautiful houses. He did not need to speak. He was my friend and there at my side his silence was a way of saying it.

Everything was beautiful and peaceful in that spot. I looked at the green stretch of the lagoon, the fringe of spray along the coral reef, and the white sand of the beach, the dunes, the sand mixed with spiky bushes, the dark filao woods, the shadows from the veloutiers and the Indian almond trees, and in front of us the eroded rock of Morne, like a castle filled with sea birds. It was as if we had been shipwrecked there for months, far away from any dwelling, waiting for a ship to appear on the horizon and rescue us. I thought of Laure, who would be watching from the chalta tree; I thought of Mam and my father. I wished that moment would never end.

But the sun was sinking toward the sea, turning it into metal and opaque glass. The fishermen came back. Denis saw them first. As he walked on the white sand his lanky silhouette looked like the shadow of his shadow. He swam ahead to the canoe in the sparkling water. I jumped into the sea behind him. The cool water washed away my fatigue and I swam in Denis's wake to the canoe. The fiancé stretched out his hand to us and effortlessly hauled us in. The bottom of the canoe was full of all kinds of fish. There was even a little blue shark that the fiancé had killed with one thrust of the harpoon when it swam close to eat one of the catch. Pierced through the middle of the body, the shark was transfixed; its open mouth showed triangular teeth. Denis said that the Chinese eat shark and make necklaces with the teeth.

I shivered in spite of the sun's heat. I had taken off my clothes to let them dry on the bow. Now the canoe was gliding toward the channel, and already we could feel the big waves from the high seas that broke on the coral reef. Suddenly the sea became rough and violet. The wind came up when we crossed the channel alongside Bénitiers Island. The big sail strained and snapped next to me and the spray exploded on the prow. Denis and I quickly folded our clothes and hid them near the mast. The sea birds followed the canoe, smelling the fish. Sometimes they even tried to steal one, and Denis shouted and waved his arms to scare them off. Screeching black frigates with their piercing eyes hovered in the wind next to the canoe. Behind us, Morne receded farther away, looking in the misty twilight like a castle covered in shadow. The sun, very near the horizon, was broken up by long gray clouds.

I will never forget that day when I went to sea for the first time, a day that seemed to last months, or years. I wanted it never to end, I wanted it to go on forever. I would have liked the canoe to go on racing over the waves in the bursting spray until it got to India, even to Oceania, going from island to island, lit by a sun that never set.

It was dark when we landed at Rivière Noire. I walked quickly on my bare feet with Denis to Boucan. My clothes and hair were full of salt, and my face and back were burned from the sun's rays. When we got to the front of the house Denis left me without speaking. My heart beat fast as I walked up the path and saw my father on the porch. Standing in his black suit in the light of the storm lamp, he seemed taller and thinner than usual. His face was pale and drawn from worry and anger.

When I was standing in front of him he looked at me without saying anything, but his look was hard and cold and my throat tightened—not because of the punishment awaiting me, but because I knew that I would not be able to return to the sea, that it was over. In bed that night, despite the fatigue, hunger, and thirst, and indifferent to the mosquitoes and my burning back, I lay absolutely still, listening to the movement of the air, to every breath of wind and every lull that came to me from the sea.

L AURE AND I spent the last days of that summer, the summer of the cyclone, even more dependent on ourselves, more alone than usual, in the Boucan valley, where no one came to see us anymore. Perhaps because of this we felt strangely threatened, as if danger were approaching. Or maybe the isolation had made us sensitive to the premonitory signs that our days at Boucan were coming to an end. Perhaps it was also due to the oppressive heat that day and night pressed down on the slopes of the Tamarin valley. Even the sea winds couldn't lighten the weight of the heat on the plantations and the red earth. Near the Walhalla aloe fields of Tamarin the ground burned like the inside of an oven and the streams dried up. At night I watched the smoke from the Kah Hin distillery as it mixed with clouds of red dust. Laure spoke to me about the fire that God rained down on the damned towns of Sodom and Gomorrah, and also of the eruption of Vesuvius in the year A.D. 79, when the town of Pompeii was buried under a torrent of hot ashes. We searched the sky, but in vain: the sky above Rempart and the Trois Mamelles remained clear, barely marked by a few innocuous clouds. Yet sometimes, deep inside us, we sensed the danger.

For several weeks already Mam had been sick and had stopped teaching us. Our father was a somber, weary figure who stayed closeted in his study, reading, writing, or smoking while looking absently out the window. I think it was during this period that he started to speak to me about the Unknown Corsair and the documents he owned concerning him. I had first heard about him a long time ago, perhaps from Mam, who didn't believe in his existence. Father told me about him at length, as if he were telling me an important secret. What did he say? I can't remember with certainty because it is confused in my memory with everything that I later heard and read, but I remember how odd he looked that afternoon when he took me into his study.

It was a room that Laure and I entered only in secret, not because it had been forbidden us, but because something there intimidated us, even frightened us a bit. At the time my father's study was a long, narrow room at the end of the house, between my parents' bedroom and the living room; a silent north-facing room with a varnished wooden floor and walls, furnished only with a big writing table without drawers, an armchair, and several tin trunks containing papers. The table was pushed right against the window so that when the shutters were open Laure and I could see, from our hiding place behind some bushes in the garden, the outline of our father as he read or wrote, enveloped in clouds of cigarette smoke. From his study he could see the Trois Mamelles and the gorges of the Rivière Noire, and could watch the passing clouds.

I remember going into his study and almost holding my breath, looking at the books and magazines piled up on the floor and the maps pinned to the walls. The map I liked most was the one of the constellations, which he had already shown me to teach me astronomy. When we went into the study we excitedly read the names of the stars and their constellations:

Sagittarius, guided by the star Nunki. Lupus, Aquila, and
Orion. Bootes, which carried Alphecca in the east and Arcturus in the west. The menacing drawing of Scorpio with red
Antares in its head and the star Shaula, like a luminous dart, in
its tail. Ursa Major with all the stars in its curve: Alkaid, Alcor, Alioth, Megrez, Phecda, Dubhe, Merak, Auriga, and the
biggest star, whose name, Menikalinan, echoes strangely in
my memory.

I remember Canis Major, which carries beautiful Sirius in
its mouth like a fang, and at the bottom of the triangle the pulsating Adhara. I can still see the perfect drawing, the one that
I liked the most and looked for night after night in the summer
sky, to the south of Morne: the ship Argo that I sometimes
drew on the dusty paths like this:

My father remained standing as he talked, and I didn't understand much of what he said. He was not really speaking to
me, I a child with overlong hair, sunburned face, and clothes
torn from running through the brush and the cane fields. He
was talking to himself; his eyes shone and his voice was
slightly muffled by the depth of his emotion. He spoke of this
immense treasure that he was going to discover, for at least he

knew where it was hidden; he had discovered the island where the Unknown Corsair hid his treasure. He never said the Corsair's name, but always called him, as I read later in his papers, the Unknown Corsair, and today this name still seems more real and more filled with mystery than any other name.

He told me for the first time about Rodrigues Island, a dependency of Mauritius several days' boat ride away. On his study wall he had pinned a map of the island, which he had drawn in India ink and watercolors, covered with signs and landmarks. I remember reading these words at the bottom of the map: Rodrigues Island, and under them: Admiralty Chart, Wharton, 1876.

I listened to my father without hearing him, as if his voice were coming to me from a deep dream. The legend of the treasure, the attempts made to find it over the past century on Amber Island, at Flic en Flac, and in the Seychelles. Perhaps I became so agitated and overcome with emotion that I couldn't understand because I had guessed that what he was telling me was the most important thing in the world, a secret that could save us, if only we could solve it. It was no longer a question of electricity now, or of any other project. The light from the Rodrigues treasure dazzled me and made everything else pale by comparison. My father talked for a long time that afternoon as he walked up and down the narrow room, picking up papers to look at them, and then putting them down without showing them to me, while I stood next to his table without moving, looking furtively at the map of Rodrigues Island pinned to the wall next to the map of the firmament. Perhaps because of that, I would later retain the impression that everything that happened afterward—this adventure and this quest—was determined by the sky and not by the real world; that I had begun my voyage aboard the ship *Argo*.

❋

These were the last days of summer and they seemed very long, even though they were filled day and night with so many events: they were like months or years, profoundly changing the universe around us and leaving us old. There was a heat wave, and the air in the valley of the Tamarin was thick and heavy and humid, and we felt imprisoned in the circle of mountains. The clear sky changed momentarily when the wind blew clouds across it, their small shadows running over the burned hills. The last of the harvesting would soon be over, and the field hands grumbled angrily because then they would have nothing to eat. Sometimes at night I saw red smoke from fires in the cane fields and the sky turned a strange color, a threatening red that seared the eyes and squeezed the throat. In spite of the danger I crossed the fields nearly every day to see the fires. I went as far as Yemen and sometimes even as far as Tamarin Estate, or farther up toward Magenta and Belle Rive. From the top of the Tourelle I could see more smoke coming from the north, from around Clarence and Marcenay and as far as Wolmar. I was alone now. Since the trip on the canoe my father had forbidden me to see Denis, and he no longer came to Boucan. Laure said that she heard Cap'n Cook, his grandfather, shouting at him because he came to see him despite the interdiction. After that he disappeared. This had given me a feeling of emptiness, of great solitude, as if my parents, Laure, and I were the last inhabitants of Boucan.

I roamed far from the house, farther and farther away. I climbed to the top of the creole-built lava-rock walls and watched the smoke from the uprisings and ran across fields devastated by the revolts. In places there were still some workers, very poor old women dressed in gunnies, gleaning or cutting the whistling grass with their billhooks. When they saw me with my tanned face, barefoot, my shoes strung around my neck and my clothes streaked with red dust, they were frightened and they shouted and chased me away. A white had never been there before.

Sometimes the sirdars also insulted me and threw stones at me, and I ran as fast as I could through the cane until I lost my breath. I hated the sirdars. I despised them more than anything in the world because they were callous and wicked and because they beat the poor with a stick when they didn't load the bundles of cane quickly enough onto the cart. But at the end of the day they got double pay and became drunk on arak. They were cowardly and obsequious with the field managers, lifting their caps when they spoke to them and pretending to care for those they had just been maltreating. The men in the fields who pulled out the *chicots,* the stumps of old cane, with heavy iron pincers called *macchabées,* were almost naked, their bodies covered only with tattered bits of cloth. They carried the blocks of basalt on their shoulders to the ox carts and then they piled them up at the end of the field to make new pyramids. Mam called them "cane martyrs." They sang while they worked and as I sat on top of a black pyramid in the vast deserted plantations, I liked hearing their monotonous voices. I also liked to sing to myself the old creole song that Cap'n Cook sang for Laure and me when we were small:

> *Mo passé la rivière Tanier*
> *rencontré en' grand maman,*
> *Mo dire li qui li faire là*
> *Li dire mo mo la pes cabot*

> *Waï, waï, mo zenfant*
> *Faut travaï pou gagn' son pain*

Boucan, 1892

waï waï mo zenfant
Faut travaï pou gagn' son pain . . .

(When I was passing by the Tanier river
I met an old granny
I asked her what she was doing there
She said I am fishing for cabots.

Yes, yes, my dear child
You must work for your daily bread
Go, go, my dear child
You must work for your daily bread)

It was there, from the top of a mound of stones, that I saw the smoke from the fires in the area of Yemen and Walhalla. That morning they were very close, near the shacks on the Tamarin stream, and I realized that something very serious was happening. My heart beat very fast as I hurried down the pyramid and ran until I got to the dirt road. The light-blue roof of our house was too far away for me to warn Laure of what was happening. When I got to the bridge over the Boucan I could already hear the sound of the riot. It echoed in the mountain gorges, sounding like a storm that seemed to be coming from every side at the same time. There were shouts and grumbles and gunshots. Despite my fear I ignored the paths and ran through the cane. Suddenly I was in the middle of the noise, standing in front of the refinery, and I could see the disturbance. A crowd of gunnies were massed before the door, all shouting at the same time. In front of them were three men on horseback and I could hear the noise of the horses' hooves on the paving stones when the riders made them rear up. In the background I could see swirling sparks in the gaping jaws of the oven for the cane-trash.

The people advanced and retreated in a strange kind of dance that was modulated by their shrill cries. The men brandished cutlasses and scythes, the women hoes and billhooks. I was transfixed by fear as I stood still in the jostling crowd. Blinded by the dust, I was suffocating. With great difficulty I pushed my way to the refinery wall. As soon as I reached it, I saw, without understanding what was happening, the three horsemen rush at the crowd that hemmed them in. The horses' breastplates pushed against the men and women, and the riders struck at the people with clubs. Two horses escaped toward the plantations and were followed by the angry screams of the crowd. They passed so close to me that, fearful of being trampled, I threw myself down into the dust. When I got up I saw the third horseman. He had fallen from his horse and the men and women were holding him by the arms and pulling him about. In spite of the fear distorting his face, I recognized him. His name was Dumont, a relative of Ferdinand, the husband of a cousin, and he was a field manager on one of Uncle Ludovic's plantations. My father had said he was worse than a sirdar, that he beat the workers with cane stalks and stole the pay of those who complained about him. But now the plantation workers were abusing him, hitting him, insulting him, pulling him to the ground. The crowd continued to knock him about, and for a second he was so close to me that I could see his wild eyes and hear the raucous sound of his breathing. I was terrified because I knew he was going to die. Nausea gripped me by the throat, suffocating me. With eyes full of tears I beat my fists against the angry crowd, who didn't even see me. The men and women in gunnies continued shouting and doing their strange dance. When I managed to get out of the crowd I turned around and saw the white man. His clothes were torn and he was being dragged by half-naked black men to the mouth of the cane-trash furnace. He didn't shout or move. His face, as the blacks lifted him up by the arms and legs and began to swing him in front of the red curtain of fire, was a white stain of fear. I was alone in the middle of the road, petrified, listening to the voices that shouted louder and louder, sounding now like a slow, sad song setting the rhythm for the swinging of the body above the flames. Then the crowd moved as one and there was a great savage cry as the man disappeared into the furnace. Suddenly the clamor subsided and I could hear the deafening roar of the flames again and the gurgling of the juice in the huge shiny vats. I could not take my eyes from the flaming mouth of the cane-trash oven where blacks were now shoveling in dried cane as if nothing had happened. Then slowly the crowd dispersed. The women in gunnies walked in the dust with their faces hidden in their veils. The men went toward the cane fields with their sabres in their hands. There was no more clamor, no more noise, and as I walked toward the river there was only the silence of the wind on the cane leaves. The silence was in me, too; it filled me up and made me giddy, and I knew that I would not be able to tell anyone what I had seen.

❀

Sometimes when I went to the fields Laure came with me. We walked along the paths through the cut cane, and when the ground was too soft or there were piles of stacked cane in our way I carried her on my back so that she would not soil her dress and boots. She was just over a year older than I, but she was so slight and frail that it felt as if I were carrying a child. She liked it a lot when we walked like that and the sharp cane leaves parted before her face and then came together again be hind her. One day in the attic she showed me a back issue of the *Illustrated London News,* which had a drawing showing Naomi being carried on Ali's shoulders in the middle of the barley fields. Naomi was laughing loudly as she pulled out the ears of grain that brushed against her face. Laure said that this drawing was the reason she called me Ali. She also told me the story of Paul and Virginie, but I didn't like it because Virginie was so scared of taking her clothes off to go into the sea. I found it absurd and I told Laure that it couldn't be a true story, but that only made her cross. She said I didn't understand anything.

We went toward the hills where the Magenta estate and the chases belonging to the rich began. Laure did not want to go into the forest, so we went down together toward the source of the Boucan. The air in the hills was humid, as if the morning dew had remained for a long time on the foliage. We liked sitting in a glade where the night's shadow had hardly left the trees and watching the flight of the sea birds. Sometimes we saw a couple of bo'sun birds go by. The beautiful white birds came out of the Rivière Noire gorges near Mananava, where the mountain was black and the sky overcast. We believed the rain was born there.

"Some day I'll go to Mananava."

Laure said, "Cook says that there are still maroons on Mananava. If you go there they'll kill you."

"That's not true. There's nobody there. Denis went very near and he told me that when you get there everything goes black as if it had become night and then you have to go backward when you leave."

Laure shrugged. She didn't like to hear those things. She got up and looked at the sky from which the birds had disappeared. She said impatiently, "Let's go!"

We returned across the fields to Boucan. In the middle of the foliage the roof of our house shone like a pool.

❀

Since she had been sick with fever, Mam did not give us lessons anymore, only some recitations and religious instruction. She was thin and very pale and she only came out of her room to sit on the chaise lounge on the veranda. The doctor, who was called Koenig, came from Floreal in his horse and carriage. As he was leaving he said to my father that the fever had broken, but that if she had another crisis there would be no "remission." I could not forget that word; it was in my head every moment of the day and night. Because of it I couldn't stay still. I had to be moving all the time, up hill and down dale as my father said. From early morning I was either in the cane fields, burned by the sun, listening to the gunnies busy singing their monotonous songs, or at the seashore hoping to meet Denis when he came home from fishing.

There was something threatening us; I could feel it pressing down on Boucan. Laure felt it too. We didn't speak about it, but I could see it on her face and in her worried eyes. At night she didn't sleep and we both lay quietly listening to the sound of the sea. I could hear Laure's too regular breathing, and I knew that her eyes were open in the dark. I, too, lay still and awake in bed, the mosquito net pulled back because of the heat, listening to the mosquitoes dance. Since Mam had been sick I was not going out at night so as not to worry her, but just before dawn, while it was still dark, I began racing across the fields or went down to the sea, up to the edge of the Rivière Noire. I think that I still hoped to see Denis appearing through the brush or sitting under an almond tree. Sometimes I even called him with our signal. But he never came. Laure thought that he had gone to the other side of the island, to Ville Noire. I was alone now, like Robinson on his island. These days even Laure was quieter than usual.

In the *Illustrated London News* we read the weekly episodes about Nada the Lily, a story by Rider Haggard, which was illustrated with engravings that frightened us a little and made us dream. The magazine arrived every Monday, three or four weeks late, sometimes in parcels of three, on ships belonging to the British India Steam Navigation Company. Our father leafed absentmindedly through them and then left them on the hall table, which we had been watching for their arrival. We took them to our hiding place under the roof to read them at our ease, stretched out on the floor in the warm shadowy light. We read aloud without understanding most of the time, but with such conviction that the words have remained etched in my memory. Zweeke the sorcerer said, "You ask me, my father, to tell you the youth of Umslopogaas, who was named Bulalio the Slaughterer, and of his love for Nada, the most beautiful of Zulu women." Each one of those names was buried deep in me, like the names of the living people that we met that summer in the shadow of the house we were soon going to leave. "I am Mopo, who slew Chaka the king," said the old man. Dingaan the king, who died for Nada. Baleka, the young girl whose parents were killed by Chaka, and who was forced to become his wife. Koos, Mopo's dog, who the night he saw Chaka's army went to lie close to his master. The dead haunted the land conquered by Chaka: "We could not sleep, for we heard Itongo, the ghosts of the dead people, moving about and calling each other." I shivered when I heard Laure read and translate these words, and when Chaka appeared before his warriors:

"O Chaka, O Elephant! His justice is as brilliant and terrible as the sun!" I looked at the engravings where the vultures flew at twilight in front of the sun's disk, which had already half sunk into the horizon.

There was also Nada, Nada the Lily, with her big eyes, her curly hair, and her copper-colored skin, the descendant of a black princess and a white man, the only survivor of the kraal massacred by Chaka. In her animal skin she was beautiful and exotic. Umslopogaas, Chaka's son, whom she thought was her brother, was madly in love with her. I remember the day when Nada asked the young man to bring her back a lion cub and Umslopogaas slipped into the lion's den. Then the lions came back from hunting and the male roared "so loudly that the earth trembled." The Zulus killed the lion but the lioness carried off Umslopogaas in her maw and Nada cried over the death of her brother. How we loved to read this tale! Our father had begun to teach us English, and for us it was the language of legends. When we wanted to say something extraordinary, or secret, we said it in this language as if no one else could understand.

I also remember the warrior who hit Chaka in the face. "I smell out the Heavens above me," he said. And also the apparition of the Sky Queen Inkosazana-y-Zulu, who announced Chaka's next punishment: "And her beauty was terrible to see. . . ." When Nada the Lily walked to the assembly, "Nada's splendor was upon each of them. . . ." These are sentences that we never tired of repeating as we lay in the dim light of the waning day. Today I think they carried a particular meaning, the muted agitation that precedes metamorphosis.

❁

We still daydreamed over the pictures in the magazines, but now our dreams seemed out of reach: the Junon bicycles, or those from Coventry Machinists' & Co.; Lilliput opera glasses that I imagined would let me see into the depths of Mananava;

Benson's "keyless" watches, and the famous nickel Waterburys with their enamel faces. Laure and I solemnly read the inscription beneath the drawing of the watches as if it were a line of Shakespeare's poetry: "Compensation balance, duplex escapement, keyless, rustproof, shock-proof, non-magnetic." We also liked the advertisement for Brooke soap, which showed a monkey playing a mandolin on a crescent moon, and together we recited:

> *"We're a capital couple the Moon and I,*
> *I polish the earth, she brightens the sky. . . ."*

And then we'd burst out laughing. Christmas was already far behind us—very sad that year because of Mam's illness, Father's financial worries, and Boucan's isolation—but we played at choosing our presents from the pages of the magazines. Since it was only a game, we didn't hesitate to chose the most expensive objects. Laure chose a Chapell practice piano in ebony, a pearl necklace from the East, and an enamel and diamond brooch from Goldsmith & Silversmith shaped like a chick emerging from its egg! It cost nine pounds! I chose a decanter for her in silver and cut glass, and for Mam I had the ideal present: a leather toilet case from Mappin featuring an assortment of bottles, boxes, brushes, nail implements, etc. Laure liked these cases too and said that she would also have one, later when she was a young woman. For myself, I chose a Negretti & Zambra magic lantern, a gramophone with needles and records, and, of course, a Junon bicycle, which was the best make. Laure, who knew what I liked, chose a box of Tom Smith firecrackers for me, which made us both laugh.

We also read the news, which was already several months old, sometimes even several years, but what did it matter? We read accounts of shipwrecks and the earthquake in Osaka and we stared for a long time at the illustrations. There was also the tea with Mongolian lamas, the Eno's Fruit Salts lighthouse, the Haunted Dragoon, a fairy alone in the middle of a pride of lions in an "enchanted forest," and a drawing of one episode of Nada the Lily that made us shiver: "Ghost Mountain," a stone giant whose open mouth was the cavern in which the beautiful Nada was going to die.

Mixing with the sound of the wind in the filaos, these are the images I have of this time, when we lay in the heavy air of the overheated attic and when, little by little, night began to take over the garden around the house and the mynahs started chattering.

We waited without knowing what we were waiting for. At night under the mosquito net, before going to sleep, I dreamed I was in a ship with swollen sails advancing to the middle of the sea, from which I could see the sparks of the sun. I listened to Laure's slow and regular breathing and I knew that her eyes were also open. What was she thinking? I imagined we were all on a boat going north, to the island of the Unknown Corsair; the next instant I was transported to the bottom of the Rivière Noire gorges at Mananava, where the forest was dark and impenetrable, and where the sighs of the great Sacalavou, who had killed himself to escape the whites, could sometimes be heard. The forest was full of hiding places and poisons; it echoed with the screams of monkeys, and above me the white shadow of the bo'sun birds passed in front of the sun. Mananava, the land of dreams.

❀

The days that took us up to Thursday, April 29, seemed endless. They ran together one with the next, as if they were one long day interrupted by the nights and our dreams, bearing no resemblance to reality. The moment I became aware of one, it had already become a memory. I did not understand that these days carried with them the weight of our destiny. Without a point of reference, how could I know? The Tourelle, my look-out to the sea, which I could see in the distance between the trees, and the pointed rocky peaks of the Trois Mamelles and the Rempart Mountain on the other side, were the only frontiers guarding this world.

Starting at dawn the sun beat down, drying the red earth in the troughs hollowed out by rain streaming off the blue corrugated iron roof. There were storms in February; the northeasterly winds blew over the mountains and the rain furrowed the hills and the aloe plantations, and the torrents made huge stains in the blue lagoons.

My father stood on the veranda for whole days at a time then, looking at the curtain of rain rushing over the fields and covering the peaks near Machabé mountain and Brise-Fer, where the electric generator was. The drying ground glistened in the sun and I sat on the veranda steps, sculpting little mud statues for Mam: a dog, a horse, soldiers, and even a ship with masts made of twigs and leaves for sails.

My father often went to Port Louis, and from there took the Floréal train to visit my Aunt Adelaide. I was going to stay at her house the next year when I started at the Royal College. I had no interest in that. There was a threat weighing us down, something that hung over Boucan like an inexplicable storm.

I lived here, only here. I had looked at this landscape for so long without ever getting tired of it, and I knew every crevice, every bit of shade, and every hiding place in it—and always, behind me, the dark chasm of the Rivière Noire gorges and the mysterious Mananava ravine.

There were evening hiding places as well, like the tree of good and evil where I went with Laure. We perched on the highest branches, swinging our legs without speaking to each other, looking at the light as it darkened under the thick foliage. Near evening it began to rain and we listened to the drops falling on the big leaves as if it were music.

We had another hiding place. It was a ravine, at the bottom of which was a pool of running water that farther on joined the Boucan stream. The women sometimes came to bathe a little lower down, and here we saw a herd of goats chased by a little boy. Laure and I would go right to the bottom of the ravine, where there was a plateau with an old tamarind tree on it leaning out into nothingness. We'd crawl along the trunk on all fours toward the branches, and there we stayed with our heads pressed against the wood, daydreaming while we watched the water running over the lava stones on the ravine bed. Laure believed that there was gold in the stream and that the women came here to do their washing so that they could catch grains of gold dust in their clothes. We watched the running water endlessly and looked for the sun's reflection in the black sand of the beaches. When we were there we didn't think of anything else; we no longer felt threatened. We didn't think of Mam's illness, or of the money we needed, or of Uncle Ludovic who was busy buying up all our land for his plantations. That is why we went to these hiding places.

❧

One dawn my father went to Port Louis in the carriage. I immediately went into the fields: first to see the mountains I loved in the north, then I turned my back on Mananava, and walked toward the sea. I was alone. Laure couldn't come with me because she was unwell. It was the first time she had said this to me, the first time she'd told me of the blood women lose during a certain phase of the moon. After that she never spoke to me of it again, as if it had been accompanied by shame. I remember her that day, a pale little girl with long black hair and a stubborn expression, a beautiful, very stiff face that took stock of the world, and something else, something that had changed in her, that distanced her and made her seem like a stranger. Laure standing on the veranda, dressed in her light-blue cotton dress with the sleeves rolled up showing her thin arms; her smile when I left, as if to say: I am Robin Hood's sister.

I ran without stopping to the foot of the Tourelle de Tamarin; I was very near the sea. Because of the fishermen, I didn't go to the Riviere Noire beach anymore, nor the Tamarin sandbar. Since the adventure in the canoe, after which they had punished Denis and me by separating us, I didn't want to go to the places we used to visit together. I'd go to the top of the Tourelle or climb the mountain called l'Étoile and hide in the undergrowth, from where I watched the sea and the birds. Not even Laure knew where to find me.

I was alone and I talked aloud to myself. I made up questions and answers like these:

"Come, let's sit here."

"Where?"

"Here, on the flat rock."

"Are you looking for someone?"

"No, no, my friend, I'm looking at the sea."

"Do you want to see the corbijous?"

"Look, a boat is passing. Can you see its name?"

"I know it, it's the *Argo*. It's my boat, it's coming to fetch me."

"You're leaving?"

"Yes, I'll be leaving soon. Tomorrow, or the day after, I'm going to leave. . ."

Boucan, 1892

❈

I was on the mountain called Étoile when it started to rain.

It was a beautiful day. The sun burned my skin through my clothes, and in the distance I could see the chimneys smoking in the cane fields. I was watching the turbulent, dark-blue stretch of sea beyond the reefs.

The rain swept across the sea from Port Louis, a huge, semi-circular gray curtain coming toward me at top speed. It was so violent that I didn't even think of looking for shelter. My heart was pounding, but I stayed where I was on the rocky promontory. I liked to see the rain come.

At first there wasn't any wind and all sound died out, as if the mountains were holding their breath. This silence, which emptied the sky and froze everything, made my heart beat faster.

Suddenly the foliage was rippling and the wind was on me. I could see it making waves across the cane fields. It swirled around me, enveloping me in such strong gusts that I had to squat down on the rock so as not to be blown over. Around Rivière Noire the same thing was happening: a big, dark curtain was rushing toward me, covering the sea and land in its wake. I understood then that I had to get away from there very quickly. It was not a simple downpour, it was a tempest, a hurricane like the one in February that had lasted two days and two nights. But today there was this silence such as I had never experienced before. And yet I didn't move. I couldn't tear my eyes away from the huge gray curtain moving so quickly across the valley and over the sea, swallowing up hills, fields, and trees. It had already covered the reefs. Then Rempart and the Trois Mamelles disappeared. The dark cloud passed over them and wiped them out. Now it was rushing down the mountain slopes toward Tamarin and the Boucan valley. I suddenly thought of Laure and Mam alone in the house, and my fears for them pulled me away at last from the spectacle of the traveling rain. I jumped off the rock and climbed down the slopes of the Etoile as fast as I could, running across the brush without heeding the scratches on my face and legs. I ran as if I had a pack of mad dogs at my heels, as if I were an escaped deer. Without knowing how, I found all the shortcuts; I raced down a dry gully due east, and in a moment I was at Panon.

Then the wind and rain were on me. I have never felt anything like it. I was engulfed by water; it streamed down my face and went into my mouth and nostrils. I reeled in the wind, suffocated and blinded. Most frightening of all was the noise. It was a deep, heavy sound that echoed in the earth and made me think the mountains were starting to collapse. I turned my back to the storm and went on all fours through the thicket. Branches of uprooted trees whipped through the air like arrows. I crouched at the bottom of a big tree with my head in my arms and waited. An instant later the squall had passed. The rain was pouring down, but I could stand up straight, breathe, and see where I was. The brush on the edge of the ravine had been flattened. Nearby, a big tree like the one that had sheltered me was lying on its side, its roots still in the red ground. I began to walk again at random, then suddenly, in a lull, I saw the Saint Martin hill, the ruins of the ancient sugar refinery. There was no time to lose: I could take shelter there.

I knew these ruins. I had often seen them when I was running across the fallow lands with Denis. He never wanted to go near them, he'd called them Mouna Mouna's house and said that the "devil's drum" was played there. I squeezed myself into a nook in the old walls under a vaulted section. My sodden clothes stuck to my skin and I was shaking from cold and fear. I could hear the blasts coming across the valley. They sounded as if a huge animal were lying down on the trees, crushing the leaves and branches and breaking the trunks like little twigs. Columns of water advanced over the ground, surrounding the ruins and then rushing down toward the ravines. Rivers appeared as if the earth had just given birth to their springs. The water rushed by, parted, knotted, and turned into whirlpools. Sky and earth had disappeared; only this liquid mass was left, and the wind carrying off the trees, and the red mud. I looked straight ahead of me, hoping to see the sky through the wall of water. Where was I? The Panon ruins were perhaps the only thing left standing on the earth; maybe everyone was drowned in the flood. I wanted to pray but my teeth were chattering too much and I couldn't even remember the words. All I could remember was the story of the flood that Mam had read to us from the big red book, when the water rained down on the earth and covered it to the tops of the mountains, and Noah built a big boat to escape the flood and put two of each kind of animal on board. As for me, how would I make a boat? If Denis were here, perhaps he would know how to make a canoe or a raft out of tree trunks. And why was God punishing the earth again? Was it because people had become hardened, as my father said, and because what was on their tables was provided by the poverty of the plantation workers? Then I thought of Laure and Mam alone in the house and I was gripped by such anxiety that I could hardly breathe. What had happened to them? The violent winds and the liquid wall might have swallowed them up and carried them away. I imagined Laure flailing in the river of mud, trying to catch on to tree branches, slipping toward the ravine. Despite the squalls and the distance, I got up and shouted "Laure! Laure!"

But as my cries were drowned by the noise of the wind and water I realized that it wouldn't do any good. Then I squatted down again next to the wall and hid my face in my arms and the water streaming over my head mingled with my tears. I was overcome by despair, a black emptiness that swallowed me; I was powerless, and, still sitting on my heels, I fell across the liquid earth.

I lay there for a long time without moving. The sky changed above me and the walls of water advanced like waves. At last the rain diminished and the wind died down. I got up and started walking, my ears still deafened by the din that was now over. The sky had cleared in the north and I could see the outline of Rempart Mountain and the Trois Mamelles. Never before had they looked so beautiful to me. My heart beat loudly, as if they were human friends that I had lost and found again. They were dark-blue visions against the gray clouds. Every detail of their line, every rock, stood out as if etched. The sky around them was still now and it had cleared as far as the Tamarin valley, from where other rocks and hills were slowly emerging: the Tourelle, Terre Rouge, Brise-Fer, Morne Sec. And in the distance, lit by an incredible sun, Morne.

It was all so beautiful that I stood transfixed. I lingered, contemplating the wounded countryside and the tattered clouds above. From the Trois Mamelles to maybe as far as Cascades there was a magnificent rainbow. I wished that Laure could be there with me to see it. She said that rainbows were rain paths. It was a mighty rainbow that started at the base of the mountains in the east and stretched to the other side of the mountain peaks in Floréal or Phoenix. Big clouds were still rolling across the sky, but suddenly they were rent and above me I saw the pure blue, radiant sky. Then it was as if time had leapt backward and changed its course. Moments ago the light had been blotted out and it was night, an infinite night that led only to extinction. And now I saw that it was only noon; the sun was at its zenith and I could feel its heat and light on my face and hands.

I ran across the wet grass and down the hill to Boucan. Everywhere the ground was saturated. The streams were over-flowing with red and ochre water and broken trees were in my path, but I didn't pay any attention to them. It was over, it was over because the rainbow had appeared to confirm God's peace.

When I arrived in front of our house my worry sapped my strength. The garden and house were intact. There were only leaves and broken branches strewn over the path, and puddles of mud everywhere. But sunlight glistened on the pale roof, trees, and foliage, and everything seemed renewed.

Laure was on the veranda, and as soon as she saw me she shouted, "Alexis!" She ran up and hugged me. Mam was there, too, standing in front of the door, pale and worried. I said to her, "It's over, Mam, all over, there won't be any more downpours!" But it didn't do any good. She didn't smile, and only then did I remember that my father had gone to town. I felt sick inside. "But won't he come now? Won't he come?" Mam squeezed my arm and said in her husky voice, "Yes, of course he is going to come. . ." But she could not hide her worry, and it was I who pressed her hand with all my strength and repeated, "It's over now, there's nothing more to be afraid of."

We stood on the veranda with our arms around each other, peering at the bottom of the garden and studying the sky, which had again filled with big black clouds. Once more this strange and threatening silence pressed down on the valley around us, as if we were the only people left in the world. Cook's hut was empty. He and his wife had left that morning for Rivière Noire. There weren't any shouts or noises from the carts in the fields.

This threatening, deathly silence, a silence I will never be able to forget, entered into the deepest recesses of our bodies. No birds sang in the trees, there were no insect sounds, and not even the sound of the wind in the filao needles. The silence was more powerful than the noise: it swallowed it up and everything around us was emptied and reduced to nothing. We stayed where we were on the veranda. I shivered in my wet clothes. When we spoke our voices echoed strangely as if they came from far away, and our words disappeared as soon as they were uttered.

Then, like a herd stampeding across the plantations and the brush, the noise of the cyclone filled the valley, and I could also hear, frighteningly nearby, the sound of the sea. We stood petrified on the veranda. I knew the hurricane was not over and the nausea rose into my throat. When it was calm and silent, all it meant was that we were in the eye of the cyclone. Now I could hear the wind coming off the sea from the south and, louder and louder, the body of the huge, furious animal that would destroy everything in its path.

This time there wasn't a wall of rain, the wind came by itself. In the distance I could see the trees moving; the advancing clouds were like smoke, long sooty trails marked with violet stains. The sky was the most frightening of all. It was moving at full speed, opening and closing, and I felt as if I were sliding forward, falling.

"Quickly! Quickly, children!"

At last Mam spoke. Her voice was hoarse, but she had succeeded in breaking the spell of our horrified fascination with the sight of the sky destroying itself. She dragged and pushed us inside the house and into the dining room with its closed shutters. She bolted the door. The house was full of shadows. It was as if we were on a ship waiting for the wind to arrive. Despite the heavy heat I was trembling from cold and fear.

Mam noticed and went into her room to look for a blanket. While she was gone the wind fell on the house like an avalanche. Laure pressed herself against me and we listened to the creaking of the boards. Broken branches hit the walls and stones knocked against the shutters and the door.

Through the chinks in the shutters we saw the daylight suddenly disappear and I knew that the earth was again covered by clouds. Then the water gushed from the sky and beat against the veranda. It slid under the door, came through the windows and covered the floor around us with dark streams the color of blood. Laure watched it rushing toward us around the big table and chairs. Mam came back and I was so frightened by her eyes that I took the blanket to try to plug the space under the door, but the water instantly soaked through it. The wind screaming outside made us dizzy, and we could hear the sinister cracking of the woodwork and the reports of the shingles as they were ripped off. The rain was falling into the attic now, and I thought of our old magazines and books, everything we loved, being destroyed. The wind broke the skylights and screamed across the attic, smashing the furniture in its path. With a thunderous noise it uprooted a tree, shattering the southern wall of the house, ripping it open. We heard the sound of the veranda collapsing. Mam pulled us out of the dining room just as an enormous branch smashed through one of the windows.

The wind came in through the gap like a furious invisible animal, and for a moment it seemed as if the sky had fallen onto the house and was going to crush it. I heard the din as the furniture was wrecked and the windows fractured. Mam dragged us, I don't know how, to the other end of the house. We took refuge in my father's study and stayed there, all three of us huddled against the wall with the map of Rodrigues and the big drawing of the constellations. The shutters were closed, but despite this the hurricane had broken the window-panes and water ran over the floor and over the books and papers on my father's desk. Laure tried awkwardly to stack some papers but then sat down again, defeated. Outside, through the chinks in the shutters, the sky was so black you'd have thought it was night. The wind swirled around the house and whipped against the mountain barrier. And all around us was the ceaseless clamor of snapping trees.

"Let's pray," Mam said. She buried her face in her hands. Laure's face was pale as she looked unblinkingly at the window. I tried to think of the archangel Gabriel. I always thought of him when I was frightened. He was big, bathed in light and armed with a sword. Could he have condemned us and abandoned us to the fury of the sky and sea? It kept getting darker. The noise of the wind was raucous and sharp and I could feel the walls of the house trembling. Pieces of wood flew off the veranda, branches whirled against the windows like grass. Mam held us tight. She stared with gaping eyes as the roar of the wind made our hearts miss a beat. I didn't think of anything and I couldn't say a word. Even if I had wanted to talk there was so much noise that Mam and Laure couldn't have heard me. It was an endless rip tearing into the center of the earth, a wave of destruction unfurling slowly and inexorably over us.

It lasted for a long time and we fell through the torn sky, through the split earth. I heard the sea as I had never heard it before. It had crossed the coral reefs and was going up the estuaries, pushing torrents of water in front of it that spilled over the riverbanks. I heard the sea in the wind, I couldn't move: it was all over for us. Laure had covered her ears with her hands and she leaned against Mam without speaking. Mam stared with huge eyes at the dark place where the window was, as if she could keep the fury of the elements at bay with her look.

Our poor house had been shaken from top to bottom. The southern facade had lost part of its roof and torrents of water and wind had turned the eviscerated room upside down. The wooden partition of the study was cracking as well. Earlier, through the hole made by the falling tree, I had seen Cap'n Cook's hut being thrown up into the air like a toy. I also saw the big bamboo hedge bend and touch the ground as if an invisible hand were pushing it down. Farther away I could hear the wind rumbling thunderously against the mountains' ramparts and then joining with the sound of the unleashed sea going up the rivers.

When did I realize that the wind was dying down? I do not know, but I'm sure something was freed in me before the noise of the sea and the creaking of the trees stopped. I was able to breathe again; the vice squeezing my temples was loosened.

Then, suddenly, the wind fell and it was very quiet again. We could hear the water streaming everywhere in millions of little rivulets, on the roof, in the trees, and even in the house. Little by little daylight returned, the soft warm light of twilight. Mam opened the shutters. We stayed where we were without daring to move, huddled against each other, looking through the window at the outlines of the reassuringly familiar mountains emerging from the clouds.

At that moment Mam came to the end of her strength and began to cry; in the calm she suddenly lost her courage. I remember that Laure and I began to cry too; I think I have never cried like that. Then we lay down on the floor and slept with our arms around each other because of the cold.

At dawn our father's voice woke us up. Had he come back during the night? I remember his defeated face and his mud-stained clothes. He told us how during the strongest part of the hurricane he had jumped out of his coach and lain in a ditch at the edge of the road. The hurricane passed over him there, taking the carriage and horse with it, who knows where. He saw extraordinary things, boats hurled onto the land and even into trees as far as the Commissariat. The swollen sea overflowing the river banks and drowning people in their huts. And above all the wind, which overturned everything in its path, tearing off roofs, smashing the chimneys of the refineries, demolishing the depots, and destroying half of Port Louis. When he was able to get out of the ditch the roads were flooded and he took shelter for the night in the hut of some black people near Médine. At daylight an Indian took him in his cart up to Tamarin Estate; to get to Boucan my father had to cross the river through water that came up to his chest. He also spoke of the barometer. Father was in an office on Rempart Street when the barometer fell. He said it was unbelievable, terrifying. He had never before seen the barometer go so low so quickly. How could a fall of mercury be so terrifying? I didn't understand, but my father's voice when he spoke of it stayed in my ears and I could not forget it.

❦

Sometime later there was a sort of fever that marked the end of our happiness. We lived now in the north wing of the house, in the only rooms spared by the cyclone. Half the south side of the house was in ruins, ravaged by water and wind. The roof had collapsed and the veranda was gone. What I will never be able to forget either is the tree that broke the wall and the long black branch that came through the window shutter in the dining room. It was left there, looking like the claw of a legendary animal that had struck the house with the might of thunder.

Laure and I ventured up the broken staircase to the attic. The water had gushed through the holes in the roof and devastated everything. Only several sodden pages remained of the piles of books and magazines. We couldn't even walk under the roof because the floor had collapsed in several places and the framing had come apart. The faint breeze that came from the sea every evening made the weakened house's structure creak. Now our house really did look like a shipwreck.

We ran about the surrounding land to measure the extent of the disaster. We looked for what had been there before: beautiful trees, plantations of palm trees, guava trees, mango trees, masses of rhododendron bushes, bougainvillea, and hibiscus. We wandered around on unsteady legs, as if after a long illness. Everywhere we looked the earth had been battered and ruined: flattened grass, broken branches, and trees with their roots exposed to the sun. I went with Laure to the plantations around Yemen and Tamarin, and in all the fields the virgin cane had been broken as if by a gigantic scythe.

Even the sea had changed. From the top of the Étoile I could see big sheets of mud spreading across the lagoon. There was no longer a village at the mouth of the Rivière Noire. I thought of Denis. Had he been able to escape?

Laure and I stayed perched almost all day on top of a pyramid in the middle of the devastated fields. There was a strange odor in the air, a stale smell brought in by whiffs by the wind. Yet the sky was clear and the sun burned our faces and hands as it did during the hottest part of the summer. The mountains around Boucan were dark green and distinct and they seemed closer than before. No one was in the fields or walking on the paths. We looked at it, at the sea beyond the reefs and the brilliant sky and the battered earth; we simply looked through eyes burning with fatigue, and our minds were empty.

Our house was silent too. No one had come to see us since the cyclone. We ate just a little rice accompanied by warm tea.

Mam lay on a folding bed in our father's office and we slept in the hallways, for these were the only places that had been spared.

One morning I accompanied my father to the lake at Aigrettes. We crossed the ruined earth in silence, our throats squeezed tight by what we already knew we would find. Somewhere on the road an old black gunny was sitting in front of what remained of her house. When we passed she only moaned louder and my father stopped to give her a coin. Then we arrived at the basin and immediately saw what was left of the generator. The beautiful new machine had fallen over and was half immersed in the muddy water. The shed had disappeared and all that remained of the turbine was unrecognizable pieces of twisted metal. My father stopped, but only to say in a clear voice, "It's over." He was tall and pale and the sunlight shone on his hair and black beard. He went up to the generator without paying any attention to the mud that came halfway up his legs. With an almost childlike movement he tried to right the machine. Then he turned around and came back onto the path. When he was near me he put his hand on my neck and said, "Come on, let's go back." It was a truly tragic moment; it seemed to me that everything was over, forever, and my eyes and throat filled with tears. I quickly followed in my father's footsteps, watching his tall, thin, bent figure.

Everything was coming to an end now, but we didn't really know that yet. For Laure and me, the menace had now been more clearly defined. This happened when the first news from outside was spread by the plantation workers and the gunnies of Yemen and Walhalla. News of the ravaged island was repeated and amplified. Port Louis, said my father, had been reduced to nothing, as if it had been bombed. Most of the wooden houses had been destroyed and entire roads had disappeared: Madame Street and Emmikillen and Poivre as well.

From Montagne des Signaux to Champ-de-Mars there was nothing but ruins. All the public buildings and churches had collapsed and people had been burned alive when they exploded. My father told us that at four in the afternoon the barometer had reached its lowest point and the wind had blown at more than one hundred miles an hour, reaching, it was said, one hundred and twenty miles an hour. The names of the destroyed villages made a long list: Beau Bassin, Rose Hill, Quatre Bornes, Bacoas, Phoenix, Palma, Médine, and Beaux Songes. At Bassin, on the other side of the Trois Mamelles, a refinery roof had collapsed, burying a hundred and thirty men who had taken refuge there. Sixty men had been killed in Phoenix and others in Bambous, Belle Eau, and on the northern part of the island at Mapou, Mont Gout, and Forbach. The number of dead grew each day: people carried away by the river of mud or crushed by houses and trees. My father said there were several hundred dead, but in the following days the figure rose to a thousand, and then to fifteen hundred.

Laure and I stayed outside all day, hiding in the battered groves around the house, but not daring to go farther away. We went to the ravine where the still raging mountain stream brought down mud and broken branches. Or we climbed the chalta tree from where we could see the devastated fields lit by the sun. The women in gunnies were picking the virgin cane, pulling it out of the muddy soil. Hungry children came to steal the fallen fruit and palm tree hearts near our house.

Mam waited silently inside. She lay on the study floor wrapped in blankets despite the heat. Her face burned with fever and her eyes were red, glittering with pain. My father stood on the ruined porch smoking cigarettes and looking past the trees. He didn't say a word to anyone.

Afterward Cook came back with his daughter. He spoke a bit about Rivière Noire and the wrecked boats and destroyed houses. Cook, who was very old, said he had never known a hurricane like this one since he first came to the island as a slave. There was the cyclone that broke the chimney on Governor Barkly's residence and nearly killed him, but it was not as fierce as this one, he said. We imagined that because old Cook was not dead and because he had come back everything would be the same as before. But he shook his head as he looked at what remained of his hut, kicked at some pieces of wood with his toe, and then before we had realized it was gone. "Where's Cook?" Laure asked.

His daughter shrugged her shoulders. "Gone, mamzelle Laure."

"And where has he gone to?"

"To his house, mamzelle Laure."

"But is he coming back?" asked Laure in an anxious voice. "When is he coming back?"

Cook's daughter's reply made our hearts ache. "Only God knows, mamzelle Laure. Perhaps never." She had come to ask for food and a little money. Cap'n Cook would not live here anymore; we knew that he would never come back again.

❊

After the cyclone, Boucan was an isolated place, abandoned by the world. A black man from the plantations came with his oxen to pull out the tree trunk that had smashed into the dining room. Father and I collected the debris that was strewn over the house: papers, glass, and shards of crockery mixed with branches, leaves, and mud. With its punctured walls, ruined veranda, and roof through which one could see the sky, our house resembled a shipwreck even more. We were like shipwreck survivors, hanging on to our debris in the hope that everything would revert to what it had once been.

In order to fight our anxiety, which increased every day, Laure and I roamed farther and farther away, crossing the plantations and venturing to the edge of the forests. We went every day, drawn by the dark Mananava valley where the bo'sun birds lived, circling very high in the sky. But they, too, had disappeared. I thought the hurricane had taken them, either smashing them against the walls of the gorge or tossing them so far across the ocean that they would never be able to come back. We looked for them every day in the empty sky. The silence in the forest was frightening, as if the wind were going to return.

Where else could we go? There weren't any people left; we no longer heard dogs barking on the farms or children playing near the streams. There was no more smoke in the sky. We climbed a creole pyramid and studied the horizon from over by Clarence to Wolmar. There wasn't any smoke. The sky in the south toward Rivière Noire was clear, too. We didn't talk. We stayed there in the noonday sun, watching the sea in the distance until our eyes hurt.

In the evening we returned with sad hearts to Boucan. The partially collapsed wreck stood in the ruins of the devastated garden on the still moist ground. We slipped furtively into the house on our bare feet. The dirt was already making a layer of crunchy dust on the floor, but father hadn't even noticed our absence. Ravenous from our long wanderings we ate what we could find: fruit taken from the estates, eggs, and the dregs of the rice in the big pot that my father boiled every morning.

❧

One day while we were in the forest Dr. Koenig came from Floréal to see Mam. On our way back, Laure spotted the marks of his car wheels in the muddy road. I couldn't go on and waited, trembling, while Laure ran to the porch and leapt into the house. When I finally came in, Laure was holding Mam tight against her and pressing her head onto her chest. Despite her fatigue Mam smiled. She went to the alcove where the spirit lamp had been set. She wanted to warm the rice and make us tea.

"Eat, children, eat. It's so late. Where have you been?" She spoke quickly, in a tight kind of way, but her joy was real. "We're going to leave here. We are leaving Boucan."

"Where are we going, Mam?"

"Ah, I shouldn't have told you. It's not certain yet. That is, it hasn't been definitely decided yet. We're going to Forest Side. Your father has found a house for us not far from your Aunt Adelaide." She hugged us both. We could feel her happiness and that was enough.

My father had gone back to town, in Koenig's car, no doubt. He had to prepare for our departure and get the new house at Forest Side ready. Much later I learned of all he had done to hold back the inevitable. I heard about the papers he signed at the moneylender's, the promissory notes, the mortgages, and the pledge loans. Everything, all of the Boucan land, the uncultivated lands, the garden, the woods, and even the house itself were either mortgaged or sold. There was no way out for him. He'd put his last hope for survival into the extravagant plan for an electric generator on the reservoir at Aigretes, which was to bring progress to all the east of the island, and which ended up as a heap of scrap iron submerged in mud. How could we have understood that, we who were only children? But we didn't have to understand these things just then. We guessed, little by little, everything that wasn't told us. When the hurricane came we knew very well that everything was lost. It was like the flood in the Bible.

"Is Uncle Ludovic going to live here after we've gone?" Laure asked. There was so much anger and distress in her voice that Mam couldn't answer. She turned her head away. "It's his fault! It's all his fault," Laure said. I wished she would keep quiet. She was pale and trembling and her voice shook, too. "I hate him!"

"Keep quiet," said Mam. "You don't know what you're saying."

But Laure couldn't let go of it. For the first time she defied Mam, as if she were defending everything we loved, this ruin of a house, the garden, the big trees, our ravine, and even farther away the dark mountains, the sky, and the wind that carried the sound of the sea. "Why didn't he help us? Why didn't he do anything? Why does he want us to leave? Is it so he can take our house?" Mam was sitting on the chaise-lounge on the shady, ruined veranda, just as when she taught us to read the scriptures or began a dictation. But a lot of time ran out in a single day, and today we knew that nothing that had happened before would happen again.

That was why Laure shouted and her voice trembled and her eyes filled with tears: to express how hurt she was. "Why did he turn everyone against us when he only had to say one word, with all his money! Why does he want us to go? Is it because he wants to take our house and our garden and put cane everywhere?"

"Keep quiet, you keep quiet!" Mam shouted. Her face was twisted with anger and pain. Laure stopped shouting. She stood in front of us full of shame, her eyes shining with tears, and suddenly she turned around and jumped into the shadowy garden and ran away. I heard twigs snapping as she ran over them, and then there was only the silence of the night.

I ran after her. "Laure! Laure! Come back!" I looked for her but couldn't find her. Then I stopped and thought and I knew where she was, as if I had actually seen her cross the thicket. I went there for the last time. I knew she was in our hiding place at the other end of the ravaged field, on the highest branch of the tamarind tree above the ravine, listening to the sound of the running water. The light in the ravine was ashen; night had already begun. Several birds had come back already and I could hear the crackling noises of the insects.

Laure had not climbed the tree. She was sitting near the base on a big stone. Her pale-blue dress was mud-stained and she was barefoot.

When I got there she didn't move. She was not crying. She had the stubborn expression on her face that I liked so much. I thought she was pleased that I had come. I sat down beside her and put my arms around her. We talked. We didn't talk about Uncle Ludovic or our departure the next day; we didn't talk about any of that. We talked about other things. Of Denis, as if he were going to come back bringing strange objects with him like before, a tortoise egg, a feather from a condé's head, a tambalacoque seed or things from the sea, shells, pebbles, and amber. We also talked about Nada the Lily; we had a lot to say about her because the cyclone destroyed our collection of magazines, perhaps blew them to the top of the mountains. When it was really night we climbed the slanting trunk the way we used to and stayed suspended for a moment, without being able to see anything, swinging our arms and legs in the void.

❧

That night was long, like the night before a big journey. And the truth was that in leaving the Boucan valley we would be making our first journey. We didn't sleep, but lay on the floor wrapped in our blankets, looking at the wavering gleam from the nightlight at the end of the hall. If we sank into sleep it was only momentarily. In the quiet night we heard the rustling of Mam's long white dress as she walked in the empty study. We heard her sigh, and only when she came back to sit in the armchair near the window could we go to sleep.

My father came back at dawn. He brought with him a horse cart and an Indian from Port Louis whom we didn't know, a tall thin man who looked like a sailor. My father and the Indian packed the furniture that had been spared by the hurricane into the cart: some chairs, armchairs, tables, a cupboard that had been in Mam's room, her brass bed and her chaise-lounge. Then the trunks containing clothes and the papers about the treasure. For us it was not really a departure, since we had nothing to take with us. All our books and toys had disappeared in the storm and the bundles of magazines no longer existed. The only clothes we had were the ones we were wearing, and they were dirty and torn from our long wanderings in the brush. It was better this way. What would we have been able to take? What we wanted was the garden with its beautiful trees, the walls of our house and its sky-blue roof, Cap'n Cook's little hut, the Tamarin and Étoile hills, the mountains and the somber Mananava valley where the two bo'sun birds lived. We stood in the sun while my father put the last objects onto the cart.

A little before one o'clock, without having eaten, we left. My father sat in front beside the driver. Mam, Laure, and I sat under the canvas cover, amid chairs that slowly wobbled to and fro and crates in which loose bits of crockery rattled. We didn't even try to look through the holes in the canvas at the countryside we were leaving. This is how we left on Wednesday, August 31, how we left the only world that we knew. We were losing all of it, the big Boucan house where we were born; the veranda where Mam had read to us from the Holy

Scriptures, the story of Jacob and the Angel, Moses rescued from the water and the lush Garden of Eden with guava and mango trees like those at the Commissariat; the ravine with the leaning tamarind tree, the big chalta tree of good and evil, the path of the stars that led to the most populated part of the sky. We were leaving, we were leaving all of it, and we knew that none of it would ever exist again. It was like death, a journey from which we would never return.

FOREST SIDE

THE UNKNOWN CORSAIR, the "Privateer," as my father called him, became a part of me. He shared my life and my solitude as well. It was he with whom I really lived, first in the rainy, cold, shadowy Forest Side, and then at the Royal College in Curepipe. He was the Privateer, a man without a face or name, who had travelled the seas capturing Portuguese, English, and Dutch ships with his pirate crew, and who had disappeared one day without a trace, leaving behind nothing except these old papers, this map of a nameless island, and a cryptogram written in cuneiform characters.

At Forest Side, so far away from the sea, there was no real life. Since we had been driven from Boucan we no longer went to the coast. On holidays, most of my college friends and their families took the train to spend a few days at the campsites near Flic en Flac, or they went to the other side of the island, toward Mahébourg, and sometimes even as far as Poudre d'Or. Sometimes they went to Cerf Island, and afterward they would talk for a long time about their trip, about lunches and parties under the palm trees, and teas with young girls in pale dresses and parasols. We were poor and we never went anywhere. Besides, Mam wouldn't have wanted to. Since the day of the hurricane she hated the sea, heat, and fevers. She had been cured of them at Forest Side, even though she was still weak and listless. Laure stayed by her side all the time and saw no one. In the beginning she went to school like me, because she said she wanted to learn to work so that she would never have to get married. But because of Mam she had to stop going. Mam said that she needed her at home. We were so poor, who else would help her with the housework? Somebody had to go with Mam to the market, help her cook the meals and clean the house. Laure didn't say anything. She had resigned herself to not going to school, but she became somber, taciturn, and moody. She only cheered up when I came back from the College to spend Saturday night and Sunday at home. Sometimes she would come to meet me on Saturdays on the Royal Road. I would recognize her from afar, a tall, thin figure in a pale-blue belted dress. She didn't wear a hat and her black hair hung down her back in a thick plait. If it was drizzling she wore a big shawl around her head and shoulders like an Indian woman.

As soon as she saw me she would run toward me shouting, "Ali! Ali!" She would hug me and begin to talk, telling me about a lot of unimportant things that she had been bottling up all week. Her only friends were Indian women who were poorer than she and lived in the Forest Side hills; she took food and old clothes to them and chatted with them for a long time. Perhaps this is why she started to look a bit like them with her slim figure, her long black hair, and her big shawls.

I hardly listened to her because at that time I only thought of the sea and of the Corsair—his travels with his pirates to Antongil, Diego Suarez, and Monomotapa, and his expeditions, as swift as the wind, as far as Carnatic in India, to intercept the proud, heavily laden vessels of the Dutch, English, and French companies. I read books about pirates, and their names and exploits echoed in my imagination: Avery, nicknamed the "little king," who had ravished and captured the Great Mogul's daughter; Martel; Teach; and Major Stede Bonnet, who became a pirate because of the "chaos in his soul"; Captain England, Jean Rackham, Roberts Kennedy, Captain Anstis, Taylor, Davis, and the famous Olivier Le Vasseur, nicknamed the Buzzard, who with Taylor's help seized the viceroy of Goa and a ship carrying the fabulous diamonds from the Golconda treasury. But the one I liked the best was Misson, the philosopher-pirate who, helped by the defrocked monk Caraccioli, had founded at Diego Suarez the Republic of Libertalia, where all men were to live free and equal, regardless of their origins or race.

I never spoke of these things to Laure because she said they were daydreams like the ones that had ruined our family. But I sometimes shared my dreams of the sea and the Unknown Corsair with my father, and he let me look for long periods at the documents relating to the treasure that he kept in a lead-covered chest under the table that served as his desk. Every time I was at Forest Side, in the evening I would close myself in the long, damp, cold room, and by candlelight would study the letters, maps, and documents that my father had annotated, the calculations he had made according to information left by the Privateer. I carefully copied the documents and maps and took these copies back with me to the College to dream about.

The years went by like this, in even greater isolation than at Boucan, for my life in the cold College and its dormitories was sad and humiliating. There was the proximity of the other pupils, their smell, their touch, their jokes, which were often obscene, their taste for crude words, and their obsession with sex—all of which was unknown to me before, and which started when we were chased out of Boucan.

❈

There was a rainy season, not the violent rains of the storms of the coast but rather a fine, monotonous rain that fell incessantly over the houses and hills for days and weeks. In my free time, chilled to the bone, I would go to the Carnegie Library, where I read all the books I could find in French and English: *Voyages and Adventures on Two Desert Islands,* by François Leguat; *The Oriental Neptune,* by Après de Mannevillette; *Voyages to Madagascar, Morocco and India,* by Abbé Rochon; and also books by Charles Alleaume, Grenier, and Ohier de Grandpré. I also leafed through the magazines looking for pictures and names to nourish my dream of the sea.

At night, in the freezing dormitory, I would recite by heart the names of the navigators who had sailed the oceans, eluding the fleets and chasing dreams, mirages, and gold's elusive reflection. Avery, Captain Martel, and Teach, the one they called Blackbeard, who replied, when asked where he had hidden his gold, that "only he and the devil knew, and that the one who outlived the other would have it all"—that is what Charles Johnson said in his *History of the English Pirates.* Captain Winter and his adopted son, England. Howell Davis, who met the Buzzard's ship on his route one day and became the Buzzard's ally when both hoisted black flags and decided to sail the seas together. Cochlyn, the pirate, who helped them capture the fort of Sierra Leone. Mary Read, disguised as a man, and Anne Bonny, Jean Rackham's wife. Tew, who went to Mission and kept Libertalia going, Cornelius, Camden, John Plantain, who was the king of Rantabe, John Falember, Edward Johner, Daniel Darwin, Julien, Hardouin, François Le Frère, Guillaume Ottroff, John Allen, William Martin, Benjamin Melly, James Butter, Guillaume Plantier, and Adam Johnson.

And all the adventurers who sailed the boundless sea and discovered new lands. Dufougeray, Jonchée de la Goleterie, Charles Nicolas Mariette, and Captain Le Meyer, who perhaps saw passing not far from him Taylor's pirate ship *Cassandra,* "coming from China with booty worth five or six million that he had plundered there," according to Charles Alleaume. Jacob de Bucquoy, who helped Taylor in his agony and was perhaps given his ultimate secret. Grenier, who discovered the first Chagos archipelago; Sir Robert Farquhar; De Langle, who accompanied La Pérouse to Alaska; or again this man L'Étang, whose name I bear and who countersigned the deed of possession of the island of Mauritius, which was signed by Guillaume Dufresne, commander of the *Chasseur,* on September 20, 1715. These were the names that I heard at night in the dormitory where I lay with eyes wide open. I also saw the names of the ships, the most beautiful names in the world, written on the stern, tracing a white wake on the deep sea, written forever in the memory of sea, sky, and wind. The *Zodiaque;* the *Fortune;* the *Vengeur;* the *Victorieux,* commanded by the Buzzard, and the *Galderland,* which he captured; Taylor's *Defense;* Surcouf's *Revenant,* Camden's *Flying Dragon;* the *Volant,* which took Pingre to Rodrigues; the *Amphitrite* and the *Grande Hirondelle,* which the corsair Le Même commanded before he perished on the *Fortune.* The *Néréide,* the *Otter,* and the *Saphire,* which carried Rowley's English to Pointe aux Galets to conquer the Ile de France in September 1809. There were the names of islands as well, fabulous names that I also knew by heart, simple islets where the explorers and pirates stopped to look for water or bird's eggs hidden in caves in the hallowed bays, places where they built villages, palaces and kingdoms: the Bay of Diego Suarez, the Bay of Saint-Augustin, the Bay of Antongil in Madagascar, the island of Sainte-Marie, and Foulpointe Tintingue. The Comoros islands, Anjouan,

Maheli, Mayotte, the Seychelles and Amirantes archipelago, Alphonse Island, Coetivi, George, Roquepiz, Aldabra, Assumption Island, Cosmoledo, Astove, Saint Pierre, Providence, Juan de Nova, and the Chagos group: Diego Garcia, Egmont, Danger, Aigle, Trois Frères, Peros Banhos, Salomon, and Legour. The Cargados Carajos, and the marvelous Saint Brandon Island, where women were not allowed to go; Raphaël, Tromelin, Sable Island, Bank Saya de Malha, Bank Nazareth and Agalega . . . These were the names that I heard in the silent night, names that were distant yet so familiar. And now while I write my heart beats fast again, and I no longer know whether I actually went to see them or not.

❖

The times I came alive were when Laure and I met after a week's separation. As we walked, ignoring the people under their umbrellas, along the muddy path that bordered the railway as far as Eau Bleue and then went on to Forest Side, we relived our days at Boucan, talking about our adventures in the cane fields, the beauty of the garden, the ravine and the sound of the wind in the filaos. The words tumbled out and it seemed as if it was all a dream. "And Mananava?" Laure asked. I couldn't answer because the pain went straight to my heart, and I thought of the sleepless nights when, eyes open in the dark, listening to Laure's too regular breathing, I waited for the sea to come. Mananava, the dark valley where the rain was born and where we had never dared go. I also thought about the wind from the sea slowly carrying the two white bo'sun birds along like legendary spirits, and again I heard the echoes of their raucous cry like the noise of a rattle reverberating in the valley. Mananava, where old Cook's wife said that the descendants of the black runaway slaves who had killed their masters and burned the cane fields lived. Sengor fled there, and it was also there that the great Sacalavou threw himself from the top of a cliff to escape his white pursuers. She said that when the storms came you could hear groans coming from Mananava, an eternal wail.

Laure and I walked as we reminisced and held hands like lovers. I repeated the promise I had made to her so long ago: we will go to Mananava. How could the others have been our friends or equals? At Forest Side nobody knew of Mananava.

❧

We lived during those years in a poverty to which we'd learned indifference. Too poor for new clothes, we didn't receive any visitors and we didn't go to any teas or parties. Laure and I even took a kind of pleasure in our isolation. My father, to earn enough money for our keep, had taken work as an accountant in one of Uncle Ludovic's offices in Port Louis; Laure was furious that the man who had contributed the most to our ruin and our departure from Boucan was now feeding us, as if out of charity.

But we suffered less from our poverty than from our exile. I remember those dark afternoons in the wooden house at Forest Side, the damp, cold nights, and the noise of the water beating on the corrugated iron roof. The sea didn't exist for us anymore. We hardly noticed it on those occasions when we took the train to accompany our father to Port Louis, or went with Mam to the Champ-de-Mars side. In the distance the great expanse of water glittered in the sunlight between the roofs of the docks and the tops of the trees. But we didn't go any closer to it. Laure and I turned our eyes away, preferring to make them smart by staring at Montagne des Signaux's bare flanks.

At this time Mam spoke a lot about Europe and France. Even though she didn't have any family in Paris, she spoke about it as a refuge for us. We would take a British India Steam Navigation Company ship coming from Calcutta and would go to Marseilles. First we would cross the ocean to Suez, seeing on the way the cities of Mombassa, Aden, Alexandria, Athens, and Genoa. Then we would take the train to Paris, where one of our uncles lived—one of my father's brothers, who never wrote and whom we knew only as Uncle Pierre. He was an unmarried musician, who according to Father had a terrible temperament but was very generous. It was he who sent the money for our education and who later came to Mam's aid after Father's death. So Mam had decided we would go to live with him, at least when we first arrived, before we could find our own place. Even my father got caught up in the fever of this voyage and started imagining new projects. But I could not forget the Unknown Corsair or his secret. Would there be room for a Corsair in Paris?

And so we would live in this mysterious city where there were so many beautiful things and so many dangers. Laure had read an interminable serial novel called *The Mysteries of Paris,* which told of bandits, kidnappers, and criminals. But these dangers were minimized for her by the etchings that showed the Champ-de-Mars (the real one), the column, the big boulevards, and the fashions. During the long Saturday evenings we would talk about this journey while the rain drummed on the corrugated iron roof and the gunnies' carts rolled through the muddy road. Laure spoke of the places we would visit, particularly the circus, for she had seen drawings in my father's newspapers that showed a big tent under which tigers, lions, and elephants performed, ridden by young girls dressed like Indian dancers. Mam brought us back to more serious things: I would study law and Laure music and we would go to the museums and perhaps visit the great castles. A long silence followed this pronouncement, while we pursued our dreams.

But for Laure and me the best was when we spoke of the day—far away, of course—when we would return home, to Mauritius, like old adventurers trying to recapture their childhood. One day we would arrive, perhaps on the same steamboat that had taken us away, and we would walk the town streets without recognizing anything. We would go to a hotel somewhere in Port Louis, on the Wharf, perhaps, to the New Oriental, or maybe the Garden Hotel in Comedy Street. Or perhaps we would buy first-class tickets and go by train to the Family Hotel at Curepipe, where no one would guess who we were. I would write our names on the register:

Monsieur and Mademoiselle L'Etang, tourists

Then we would ride on horseback across the cane fields, west toward Quinze Cantons and beyond, and we would take the road that went between the peaks of the Trois Mamelles. Then we would go along the Magenta road, and it would be evening when we reached Boucan, and there, nothing would be changed. Our house with its painted sky-blue roof and the vines that overran the veranda would still be there, leaning a bit because of the hurricane. The garden would be wilder, and near the ravine, the big chalta tree of good and evil where the birds gathered at nightfall would also still be standing. We would even go as far as the forest, to the entrance to Mananava, where night began, and there would be two bo'sun birds in the sky as white as sea spray, circling slowly above us, making their strange rattling cries before they disappeared into the night.

The sea would be there, the smell of the sea brought by the wind, the sound of the sea, and we would shiver while we listened to its forgotten voice that said to us: *Don't go away again, don't go away again . . .*

But the trip to Europe never took place, because one evening in November, just before the birth of the new century, our father had a stroke and died. The news came in the night, brought by an Indian messenger. I was awakened in the College dormitory and taken to the principal's office, which was lit unusually brightly for this time of night. They told me tactfully what had happened, but all I felt was a great void. As soon as possible they took me by car to Forest Side, and when I got there, instead of the crowd that I had been dreading, there were only Laure and our Aunt Adelaide, and Mam, pale and exhausted, sitting in a chair next to the bed where my father lay fully dressed. This sudden death, coming after the loss of the house we were born in, was incomprehensible to Laure and me; it was a mortal blow, like a punishment from God. Mam never entirely got over it.

The first consequence of our father's death was an even greater poverty, especially for Mam. For the time being, Europe was out of the question. We were prisoners on our island, without any hope of escape. I began to detest this cold, rainy city, its roads full of wretched people, the carts endlessly transporting loads of cane to the sugar trains, and even the huge expanses of the plantations I had once loved so much. Would I have to work one day as a gunny, loading bundles of cane onto the ox wagons and then feeding them into the mill's mouth, every day of my life, without hope, without freedom?

It didn't come to that, but perhaps what happened was worse. When my scholarship at the College expired I had to find work, and I found it by taking the position my father had occupied in the gray offices of W. W. West, the insurance and export company owned by powerful Uncle Ludovic.

❄

I felt as if the ties that bound me to Mam and Laure had been broken, and I was overwhelmed as well by a feeling that I would never see Boucan or Mananava again.

Rempart Street was another world. I arrived every morning by train with the mass of errand boys and Chinese and Indian merchants coming to ply their wares. Important people, businessmen and lawyers in dark suits and carrying hats and canes, spilled from the first-class compartments. I was swept along by the stream of people to the W. W. West offices, where, in the hot, dim cubicle, account books and piles of bills waited for me. I stayed there until five in the evening, with half an hour at noon for lunch. My colleagues ate together at a Chinese restaurant in the rue Royale, but I, because of my poverty and also because I preferred to be alone, was content to nibble at some spicy cakes in front of the Chinaman's shop, and sometimes to have as a treat a large orange, which I would cut into quarters and eat sitting on a low wall in the shade of a tree, while watching the Indian peasant women returning from market.

It was a life devoid of shocks or surprises, and it often seemed to me that it wasn't real, that it was in fact a waking dream, all of it: the train, the figures on the ledgers, the smell of dust in the offices, the voices of the employees speaking English, and the Indian women walking slowly back from market, carrying their empty baskets on their heads, along streets that the sunlight made vast.

But there were the boats. Because of them I went to the port whenever I could, whenever I had a free hour before the W. W. West offices opened, or after five o'clock, when Rempart Street was empty. On holidays, when the young men walked arm-in-arm with their fiancées down the paths of the Champ-de-Mars, I preferred to dawdle on the quays among the fishing lines and nets, to hear the fishermen talk and look at the boats bobbing on the oily water, following with my eyes the inter-laced design of the rigging. I was already dreaming of leaving, but I had to content myself with reading the names of the boats on their sterns. Sometimes they were simple fishing boats that bore only a primitive drawing of a peacock, cockerel, or dol-phin. I stole looks at the sailors' faces, old Indians, blacks, and turbaned, almost motionless Comorians sitting under big, shady trees, smoking their cigars.

I remember to this day the names on the boats' sterns. They come back to me like the words of a song: *Gladys, Essalaam, Star of the Indian Sea, Friendship, Rose Belle, Kumuda, Rupanika, Tan Rouge, Rosalie, Gold Dust, Belle of the South*. To me they were the most beautiful names in the world, for they spoke of the sea, telling of big waves in the open seas, reefs, faraway archipelagos, and even storms. When I read them I was trans-ported far away from land, far from city streets, and far, most of all, from the dim, dusty offices and account books covered in figures.

One day Laure came with me to the quays and we walked for a long time near the boats, before the indifferent eyes of the sailors sitting under the trees. It was she who mentioned my secret dream first by asking me, "Will you be leaving on a boat soon?" Astonished by her question, I laughed a bit as if she had made a joke. But she didn't laugh back, and her dark, beautiful eyes were full of sadness as she looked at me. "Yes. Yes, I do think you could leave on any one of these boats and go anywhere, the way you did with Denis on the canoe." As I didn't reply, she suddenly said, almost gaily, "You know, I'd like to get on a boat and go wherever it was going—India, China, Australia, anywhere. But it's out of the question!"

"Do you remember when we were going to go to France?"

"I wouldn't like to go there anymore," Laure said. "To India, or China, or anywhere else, but not to France." She stopped talking then and we continued to look at the boats lying at the quay. I was happy, and I knew why I was happy every time a boat hoisted its sails and sailed off toward the open seas.

❈

That was the year I met Captain Bradmer and the *Zeta*. I'd like to recall every detail of that day, to relive it, for it was one of the most important days of my life.

At dawn one Sunday morning I had left the old Forest Side house and taken the train to Port Louis. I wandered as usual along the quays, among the fishermen who were already coming back from the sea with their hampers full of fish. The boats were still wet, their tired sails hanging out along the masts to dry in the sun. I loved being there when the fishermen returned, hearing the groaning of the hulls and smelling the odor of the sea that still clung to them. Then, among the fishing boats, the trawlers, and the crowd of canoes with sails, I saw it: already an old boat, with the fine, streamlined shape of a schooner, it had two masts that were raked slightly aft and two beautiful lateen sails that flapped in the wind. On the broad, raised black hull its strange name was written in white letters: *Zeta*.

In the midst of the other fishing boats, with its big, very white sails and its rigging that soared from topsail to bowsprit, it looked like a thoroughbred ready for the race. I stood admiring it for a long time. Where did it come from? Would it soon be leaving on a journey, which in my imagination had no end? A black Comorian sailor was sitting on the bridge and I asked him where he had come from. "Agalega," he replied.

When I asked him who owned the ship, I thought he said, "Captain Bras-de-Mer." Perhaps it was this name, reminiscent of the time of the corsairs, that ignited my imagination and drew me to the ship. Who was this "Arms-of-the Sea?" How could I meet him? I wanted to ask the sailor these questions, but the Comorian had turned his back on me and was sitting in an armchair aft, in the shade of the sails.

Worried at the thought that it could leave with the evening tide, I came back several times that day to look at the schooner lying in the quay. Each time the Comorian sailor was still sitting in the armchair, in the shade of the sails that flapped in the breeze. At about three that afternoon the tide began to come in and the sailor clewed the sail onto the yard. Then, after he had carefully padlocked the hatchway, he came down onto the quay. When he saw me again in front of the boat, he stopped and said, "Captain Bras-de-Mer will be here soon."

As I waited for him, the afternoon seemed very long. In order to get away from the fiery sun I sat for a long time under the trees of the Commissariat. The harbor people's business died down as the day progressed, and soon there was no one left except for a few beggars who were either sleeping under the trees or picking up the leavings from the market. The tide brought in the wind blowing off the sea and I could see the shining horizon in the distance, between the masts.

At twilight I went back to the *Zeta*. Secured by its lines, it hardly moved on the swell, and by way of a gangway, a simple plank grated as it followed the movement of the ship. In the golden evening light in the deserted port, where only a few gulls were flying and the light noise of the wind whistled in the rigging—and perhaps, too, because of my long wait in the sun, like the times when I ran in the fields—the ship had become something magical, with its tall, raked masts, its yards imprisoned in the entangled gear, and the pointed shaft of the bowsprit. On the shining bridge, the empty armchair placed in front of the wheel made it seem even stranger. It wasn't even a ship's chair: it was a wooden office chair, like the kind I saw every day at W. W. West! And it was there, on the poop of the ship, dulled by spray and carrying the marks of its trips across the ocean!

The pull was very strong. With one bound I had crossed the plank that served as a gangway and was on the bridge of the *Zeta*. I went to the armchair in front of the big wooden wheel and sat in it to wait. Sitting on the ship in the empty port, bathed in the golden light of the setting sun, I was so captivated by its magic that I didn't even hear the captain arrive. He came up to me and looked at me curiously, without anger; then he said in an odd tone that was at once mocking and serious: "Well, sir, when are we leaving?"

I remember the way he asked me this question, and the blush that covered my face because I didn't know what to reply. What did I say to excuse myself? Above all, I remember the impression the captain made on me: his huge body; his clothes which were as worn as his ship, studded with indelible stains like scars; his English face with its very red skin, heavy and serious except for his black, shining eyes and the childish, mocking light in them. He spoke with me for a moment, and I learned that "Bras-de-Mer" was in reality Captain Bradmer, an officer of the Royal Marines who had just finished one of his solitary voyages.

I think I knew it immediately: I would leave on the *Zeta*; it would be my *Argo*, the ship that would take me across the sea to the place of my dreams, to Rodrigues and my quest for the boundless treasure.

TOWARD RODRIGUES, 1910

I OPEN MY EYES and see the ocean. It is not the emerald
green color I used to see in the lagoons, nor is it black like
the water going into the Tamarin estuary. I have never seen a
sea like it before: free, wild, and so blue it makes my head
swim; a sea that slowly lifts the hull over wave after spume-
topped wave as we plow through its sparkling waters.

It must be late, as the sun is already high in the sky. I have
slept so deeply that I didn't even hear the ship getting under
way when the tide came in, nor the crossing of the channel.

Last night I walked on the quays until very late, breathing in
the smells of oil, saffron, and rotting fruit floating near the
market. I listened to the voices of the men from the boats,
heard the exclamations of the dice players, and could smell the
arak and tobacco. Then I boarded the ship and went to sleep on
deck to escape the stifling hold and the dust from the sacks of
rice. I leaned my head against my sea chest and looked at the
sky through the mast's rigging. I fought sleep until after midnight, gazing at the starless sky and listening to the voices, the
squeaking of the gangway against the dock, and guitar music
in the distance. I did not want to think of anyone. Only Laure
knew I was leaving, and she hadn't told Mam. She didn't shed

a tear—on the contrary, her eyes shone with a strange light. *We'll see each other soon*, I said. *We'll start a new life on Rodrigues. We'll have a big house with horses and trees.* Did she believe me? She didn't want me to reassure her. *You're leaving, you're going away, maybe forever. You have to see your quest to its conclusion, go to the end of the world if necessary.* That's what she was saying as she looked at me, but I couldn't understand. Now she's the one I am writing for, to tell her what it was like that first night sleeping on the *Zeta's* deck in the middle of the rigging, listening to the sailors' voices and the guitar playing the same creole song over and over. At one point the voice became louder: perhaps the wind had risen, or maybe the singer on the dark quay had turned to me.

> *Vale, vale, prête mo to fizi*
> *Avla l'oiseau prêt envolé*
> *Si no gagne bonher touyé l'oiseau*
> *Mo gagne l'arzent pou mo voyaze,*
> *En allant, en arrivant!*

> *(Go on, go on, lend me your gun*
> *The bird is ready to fly away*
> *If I'm lucky enough to kill the bird*
> *I'll have enough money for my trip,*
> *To go and come back!)*

I fell asleep listening to the words of this song. And when the tide came in, and the *Zeta* silently hoisted its sails and slid over the black water toward the powerful waves of the channel, I was not aware of any of it. With my head resting on my sea chest I slept on the deck beside Captain Bradmer.

I woke up in dazzling sunlight and when I looked around, I couldn't see any land. I immediately went to the stern and leaned over the rail. I watched the sea for as long as I could, the huge waves slipping under the hull and the wake like a sparkling road. I have waited so long for this moment! My heart pounds and my eyes are full of tears.

The *Zeta* slowly rolls as it glides through the waves, then straightens. As far as I can see there is nothing but this: sea, the deep troughs between the waves and the spray on their crests. I listen to the noise of the water as it slaps the hull and I hear the waves being rent by the stem. And most of all, I hear the wind as it swells the sails, making the rigging creak. I know this noise very well; it is the same as the wind in the branches of the big trees at Boucan, the same as the sound of the rising sea that reached as far as the cane fields. But it is the first time I have heard it like this, unfettered from one end of the earth to the other.

The wind-filled sails are beautiful. The *Zeta* is sailing close to the wind and the white canvas undulates from top to bottom. Up forward, the three jibs, tapering like sea birds' wings, seem to guide the ship toward the horizon. Sometimes, after a sudden gust of wind from the east, the sails tighten violently into a flat sheet with a sound like a gunshot. The sound of the sea makes my head swim and I'm blinded by the light. Above all there is the blue of the water, this deep, dark, powerful, sparkling blue. The swirling wind makes me drunk and I have a salty taste in my mouth from the spray of a wave breaking over the bow.

All the men are on deck. They are Indian and Comorian sailors, and there are no other passengers on board. We all feel the same inebriation of the first day at sea. Even Bradmer must feel it. He is standing on the bridge, near the helmsman, with his legs wide apart to resist the rolling of the ship. For hours now he has neither moved nor taken his eyes off the sea. I don't dare ask him any questions, as much as I'd like to. I force myself to wait. I can't do anything but watch the sea and listen to the wind, and there is nothing in the world I would rather do less than go below. The sun beats down on the deck and on the dark sea.

I move away to sit farther away on the bridge, near the end of the vibrating boom. The stern lifts in the waves and then comes down heavily. It creates an endless path broadening as it runs to the horizon behind us. There is no land anywhere. There is only the deep, light-filled water and the sky with its motionless clouds, smoky puffs born on the horizon.

Where are we going? That is what I would like to ask Bradmer. Last night he didn't say anything, as if he was thinking, or didn't want to say. To Mahé perhaps, or to Agalega; the helmsman, an old man the color of baked earth whose pale eyes look directly into yours, told me it depends on the winds. The wind is coming out of the south-southeast, blowing steadily; there are no squalls and we are heading north. The sun is above the *Zeta*'s poop and its radiance seems to fill the sails.

The morning's inebriation continues. The black and Indian sailors remain standing on deck near the foremast, holding on to the shrouds. Now Bradmer is sitting behind the helmsman in his armchair, still looking straight ahead toward the horizon, as if waiting for something to appear. There are only the waves rushing toward us; like beasts they lift their heads with their sparkling crests, butt into the hull, and then disappear beneath it. If I turn around I can see them fleeing, hardly marked by the keel, to the other end of the world.

My thoughts follow the rhythm of the waves as they slap into each other. I feel that I am no longer the same person, that I will never be the same again. The sea is already separating me from Mam and Laure, from Forest Side, from everything that I was.

❊

What day is it? It is as if I have always lived here on the *Zeta*'s stern, looking through the rigging at the sea stretching out before me, listening to its breathing. It seems to me that all I have lived through since our expulsion from Boucan—Forest Side, the Royal College, the W. W. West offices—was nothing more than a dream, and all I had to do to wake up from it was to open my eyes on the sea.

Mingling with the noise from the waves and the wind is a voice deep inside me that endlessly repeats: *The sea! The sea!* And this voice buries all other words and thoughts. The wind pushing us toward the horizon sometimes becomes fiercer, jolting the ship. Then I can hear it cracking the sails and whistling in the rigging. These, too, are the words that carry me farther away. The land I lived on for so long—where is it now? It has become tiny, bobbing on the sea like a lost life raft, while the *Zeta* advances in the sunlight, driven by the wind. It drifts somewhere on the other side of the horizon, a small piece of mud lost in the immense blue sea.

I am so busy looking at the sea and the sky, noting each dark trough between the waves and the spreading lips of the wake and listening with such concentration to the sound of the wind and the water on the bow, that I haven't even noticed that the crew has started eating. Bradmer comes over to me, with the same mocking glint in his little black eyes.

"Well, sir? Has seasickness taken away your appetite?" he asks me in English.

I immediately get up to show him I'm not sick.

"No, sir."

"Well, then, come and eat." It's almost an order.

We climb down the ladder into the hold. Below, the heat is stifling, the air heavy with the smell of cooking and food.

Even though the hatches are open there is very little light. The interior of the boat is just one big cabin, the central part occupied by packing cases and bundles of merchandise, and aft, by the sailors' mattresses on the bare floor. Under the foreward hatch the Chinese cook is busy pouring tea from a big tin kettle and distributing rations of curried rice, which he has cooked on an old spirit lamp.

Bradmer squats in the Indian way, his back leaning against a bulkhead, and I do the same. Here, in the hold, the boat rolls terribly. The cook hands us enamel plates piled with rice and half a liter of boiling tea.

We eat without speaking. In the half-light I make out the crouched Indian sailors drinking their tea. Bradmer eats quickly, using the dented spoon like a chopstick to push the rice into his mouth. The rice is oily and full of fish sauce, but the curry is so strong one can hardly taste it. The tea scalds my lips and my throat, but after the fiery rice it quenches my thirst.

When Bradmer has finished he gets up and puts his plate and liter mug on the ground near the Chinese cook. Just as he is about to climb the ladder to the bridge he digs in his jacket pocket and takes out two strange-looking cigarettes made from a still-green tobacco leaf rolled around itself. I accept one of the cigarettes and light it with his lighter. We follow each other up the ladder and are once again on the deck in the strong wind.

After even a short time in the hold, the light is so dazzling that my eyes fill with tears. Almost groping my way along, bending to get under the boom, I regain my place in the stern and sit down next to my trunk. Bradmer has also gone back to sit in his chair, which is screwed to the bridge; he doesn't talk to the helmsman as he smokes his cigarette and stares into the distance.

The odor of the tobacco is sweet and pungent and it turns my stomach. It doesn't go with the pure blue of the sea and sky, or with the sound of the wind. I put out my cigarette on the deck, but I don't dare throw it in the sea. I refuse to let this foreign body float on its beautiful, smooth surface, so full of life.

The *Zeta* is not a blemish on the seas. It has crossed this and other waters so many times and has gone beyond Madagascar to the Seychelles, as well as south to Saint Paul. The ocean has purified it and made it like the big sea birds gliding in the wind.

The sun sets slowly in the sky, now lighting up the other side of the sails. I can see the shadow of the sails on the sea getting longer by the hour. By the end of the afternoon the wind has lost its strength. A light breeze hardly stirs the sails, smooths and rounds the waves, and makes the water's surface shiver like skin. Most of the sailors have gone below to drink tea and talk. Some of them go to sleep on their mats because they will be standing watch during the night.

Captain Bradmer stays in his armchair behind the helmsman. He seldom speaks, and when he does it is only to mutter a few indistinct words. He constantly smokes his greentobacco cigarettes, whose odor momentarily reaches me when there is a puff of wind. My eyes are burning—do I have a fever? The skin on my face, neck, arms, and back is burning, too. My body is scorched from being in the hot sun all these hours. All day the sun beat down on the sails, on the bridge, and on the sea, without my feeling it. All I saw was that it struck sparks on the crests of the waves and drew rainbows in the spray.

Now the light is coming from the sea, from the depths of its color. The sky is clear, almost colorless. I watch the blue expanse of the sea and the emptiness of the sky until I feel dizzy.

I have always dreamed of doing this. It seems that my life stopped long ago, when I was sitting in the front of the canoe drifting on the Morne lagoon while Denis scrutinized the water, looking for a fish to harpoon. Everything I had thought lost and forgotten—the sound and the extraordinary sight of the sea in motion—comes back as the *Zeta* advances.

The sun sinks slowly toward the horizon, lighting the crests of the waves and opening dark valleys. As the light fades, tinting everything with gold, the sea becomes calm. The wind has died down and the deflated sails hang slack between the masts. Suddenly the heat is heavy and humid. All the men are on deck, either up forward or sitting around the hatches. They smoke, some stretched out on deck, naked from the waist up, their eyes half-closed, perhaps dreaming *ganja* dreams. The wind is calm now and the sea is hardly ruffled by the tiny waves lapping against the boat's hull. It has become a violet color from which light cannot escape. I distinctly hear the voices and laughter of the sailors who are throwing dice on the forward part of the ship; and the monotonous stream of conversation from the black helmsman, who is talking to Captain Bradmer without looking at him, reaches my ears, too.

All this is strange, like a dream that was interrupted long ago. I think of where I'm going and my heart beats more quickly. The sea is a smooth road leading to mystery and the unknown. Gold is in the light around me, and mirrored in the hidden depths of the sea. I think of what awaits me at the other end of this voyage as a land I have already been to many times, but now have lost. The ship glides over the looking glass of my memory. Will I be able to understand it when I get there? Here, in the *Zeta*'s bows, as it slowly advances in the languid twilight waters, the thought of my future gives me vertigo. I close my eyes in order not to see the dazzling sky and the un-broken expanse of sea.

The next day, on board

Despite my distaste, I had to spend the night in the hold. Captain Bradmer does not want anyone on deck during the night. I lay on the bare floor (I didn't have enough confidence in the sailors' mats), head resting on my blanket rolled into a bolster, and I held on to the handle of my trunk because of the incessant rolling. Captain Bradmer slept in a kind of alcove that has been built between the two enormous, barely squared teak beams that support the deck. He has even installed a sketchy curtain that affords him some privacy, but it must be suffocating in the little cubicle, for sometime after midnight I saw that he had drawn the curtain aside.

It was an exhausting night, mostly because of the rolling of the ship, but also because of the closeness of the others. They snored, coughed, and spoke to each other, constantly coming and going from the hold to the hatchways to either breathe some fresh air or to piss overboard in the wind. Most of them are foreigners, Comorians and Somalis whose language has a harsh sound, or Indians from Malabar with dark skin and sad eyes. I was uncomfortable in the hold, but I also didn't sleep at all that night because of the men. In the stifling, shadowy hold, where the flickering night light barely eats into the darkness and the hull whines as it rides the waves, I couldn't keep myself from slowly, and absurdly, being overcome by fear. Among these men, weren't there mutineers, those famous East African pirates whom Laure and I used to read about in the magazines? Were they planning to kill us—me, Captain Bradmer, and those of the crew who weren't in with them—in order to take over the ship? Did they think the old seachest in which I'd put my father's papers actually contained money and precious objects? What I should have done was to open it in front of them, so they could see that it only contained old papers, maps, underwear, and my theodolite. But then, would they think it had a false bottom filled with gold coins? While the ship slowly rode the waves, I felt the warm metal of the trunk against my naked shoulder and stared straight ahead of me, keeping watch in the dark hold. How different this was from the first night spent on the *Zeta*'s deck, as the ship got under way while I slept; how different from when I suddenly woke in the morning and was so dazzled by the huge sea.

Where are we going? Having held a northerly course since our departure, there can now be no doubt that we're heading for Agalega. Most of Captain Bradmer's heterogeneous cargo is for the people of this faraway island: bundles of cloth, rolls of wire, barrels of oil, crates of soap, sacks of rice and flour, beans, lentils, and all sorts of pots and enamel plates held in string bags. All of it will be sold to the Chinese who keep shops frequented by the fishermen and farmers.

The presence of these utensils and the smell of the foodstuffs reassures me. Is this a cargo that pirates would want? The *Zeta* is a floating grocery store, and the idea of a mutiny suddenly seems ridiculous.

But even so I still can't sleep. The men are quiet now, but the insects have begun. Enormous cockroaches run about and sometimes fly with a whirring sound across the hold, and between their gallops and their flight I can hear the high pitched *zzz* of the mosquitoes near my ear. I have to guard against them, too, and cover my face and arms with my shirt.

Not managing to sleep, I go in turn to the gangway and put my head out the open hatch. The night is beautiful. The wind has sprung up again and we're running downwind, the sails

wrung out, the ship driven by a chill wind from the south. After the stifling heat of the hold the wind makes me shiver, but
it is very pleasant. I am going to disobey Captain Bradmer's
orders. Carrying my horse blanket, a souvenir from the days
in Boucan, I go up on deck and walk toward the prow. The
black helmsman is aft, as are two sailors smoking *ganja* and
keeping him company. I settle way up in the bow, under the
wings of the jibs, and watch the sky and sea. There isn't any
moon and the water is the color of night, but my dilated pupils
can see the marks from the spray and the outline of every
wave. The stars are lighting the sea for us. I've never seen them
like this before. Even those other times, in the garden at Boucan, when we walked with our father down the "path of stars,"
they weren't quite so beautiful. On land, the sky is eaten into
by the trees and mountains, faded by the intangible mist, like
breath that pours out of the streams, fields of grass, and the
mouths of wells. The sky is far away and we see it as if through
a window. But here, in the middle of the sea, the night has
no limits.

There is nothing between me and the sky. I lie on the deck
with my head against the closed hatchcover and concentrate
on the stars, as if seeing them for the first time. The sky
rocks between two masts and the constellations turn, stop for
an instant, then fall. I don't yet recognize them. The stars are
so bright here, even the faintest, that they seem new to me.
Orion is to port, and toward the east, perhaps that's Scorpio
where Antares is shining. The ones I can see clearly when I
turn to the stern, so close to the horizon that I only have to
lower my eyes to follow their gentle rocking, are the stars that
form the Southern Cross. I remember my father's voice as he
led us across the dark garden and asked us if we could make
them out where they shone, dim and elusive, above the row
of hills.

As I gaze at this cross of stars I drift even farther away, for they are truly a part of the Boucan sky. I can't take my eyes off them, afraid of losing them forever.

I keep my eyes on the Southern Cross until a bit before dawn, when I fall asleep, rolled in my blanket, my face and hair ruffled by the puffs of wind, listening to the creaking of the sails and the grinding sound of the sea against the bow.

Another day, at sea

I've been watching the sea since dawn, standing still at my place on the stern near the black helmsman. He is a Comorian with the very black face of an Abyssinian, but with luminous green eyes. He is the only one who really speaks to Captain Bradmer, and my status as a paying passenger allows me to sit near him and listen to him talk. He speaks slowly, choosing his words carefully, in very pure French with hardly a trace of creole accent. He says he was a pupil at the seminary in Moroni and was supposed to become a priest. One day he left for no real reason to become a sailor. He has been sailing now for thirty years and he knows every port from Madagascar to the African coast, and from Zanzibar to Chagos. He speaks of the islands, of the Seychelles, of Rodrigues, and also of the most distant ones, Juan de Nova, Farquhar, and Aldabra. The one he likes most is Saint Brandon, which belongs only to the birds and the sea turtles. Yesterday I left the spectacle of the waves and went to sit on deck next to the helmsman, to listen to him talk with Captain Bradmer. Or rather, talk *to* Captain Bradmer; for the captain, like a good Englishman, can stay silent for hours, sitting in his armchair and smoking his little green cigarettes while the helmsman speaks, replying only with a grunt of vague acquiescence, a sort of "hahum" that occasionally reminds one that he's still there. The helmsman tells amusing stories of the sea in his slow, singsong voice as he scrutinizes the horizon with his green eyes: stories of ports, storms, fishing, and girls, stories with no purpose and no end, like his life.

I like it when he talks about Saint Brandon, because he makes it sound like paradise. He is constantly thinking and dreaming about it. He has known many islands and many ports, but for him that is the place all sea routes lead to. "One day I will go there to die," he says. "The water there is as blue and clear as the purest fountain. The lagoon is so transparent that as you glide over it in your canoe you can't even see it; it's as if you're flying just above the ocean bed. There are many islands around the lagoon, ten I think, but I don't know their names. I had just escaped from the seminary the first time I went to Saint Brandon. I was seventeen years old, still a child. I thought I'd landed in heaven, and now I still think it was heaven on earth, in the time before men knew about fishing. I gave the islands my own names: there was Horseshoe Island, and Claw Island, and another was King Island, but I can't remember why I called it that. I came on a fishing boat from Moroni. The men on the boat went there to kill, to fish like beasts of prey. All the fishes ever created were in that lagoon, swimming slowly and fearlessly around our canoe. And the sea turtles came to look at us as if there was no death in the world. Thousands of sea birds flew around us. They perched on the yards and the deck to look at us because I don't think they had ever seen humans before . . . Then we started to kill them."

As the helmsman speaks his green eyes are full of light, and he looks out over the sea as if he is seeing it all again. I can't help following his gaze, beyond the horizon to the atoll, where everything is as new as in the first days of the world. Captain Bradmer puffs on his cigarette and says, "Hahum-hum," like someone who hasn't been fooled. Behind us, two black sailors, one of whom is Rodriguan, listen without really understanding. The helmsman goes on talking about the lagoon he'll never see again except on the day he dies. He speaks of the islands where the fishermen build huts of coral to keep their stores of turtles and fish. He speaks of the storms that come each summer and are so terrible that they cover the islands completely, sweeping away all traces of earthly life. The sea washes over everything when there is a storm, and that is why the islands are always new. But the water in the lagoon, where the masses of turtles and the most beautiful fish in the world live, is always beautifully clear. The helmsman's voice when he speaks about Saint Brandon is soft. It feels as if my sole reason for being on this ship in the middle of the ocean is to hear him talk.

The sea is showing me its secrets, its treasures. I drink in its sparkling light and want to know the color of its deepest parts. I want to understand the sky, the limitless horizon, the endless days and nights. I must learn and receive so much more. The helmsman is still speaking: about the tablelike mountain at the Cape, Antongil Bay, the Arabs who sail in *feluccas* along the African coast, the pirates of Socotra and Aden. I like the sound of his musical voice, his black face with its shining eyes, and his tall silhouette at the wheel as he pilots our ship toward the unknown. The sound and sight of him mingle with the noise of the wind in the sails and the sparkling rainbows in the spray every time the prow cuts through a wave.

Each afternoon, as the day draws to a close, I stand at the stern and watch the glittering wake. It is my favorite time; everything is peaceful, and the deck is deserted except for the helmsman and a sailor standing watch. Then I think of land and the lonely life Mam and Laure lead so far away. I can see Laure's somber face when I spoke to her about the treasure, the jewels and the precious stones hidden by the Unknown Corsair. Was she really listening to me? Her face was smooth and closed, and a strange light I couldn't understand shone deep in her eyes. It is this light I now seek in the infinite sea. I need Laure; I must think of her every day, for I know that without her I'll never find what I'm looking for. She didn't say anything when we left each other, she seemed neither happy nor sad. But when she looked at me on the platform of the train station at Curepipe I again saw that light in her eyes. Then she turned away and left before the train pulled out. I saw her walking in the middle of the crowd on the road to Forest Side, where Mam, who didn't know anything about this, was waiting.

It is for Laure that I want to remember every moment of my life. It is for her that I am on this boat heading farther and farther away. I must conquer the fate that turned us out of our house, that ruined us and killed our father. When I left on the *Zeta,* it felt as if I had broken something, interrupted a chain of events. When I get back everything will be different, renewed.

I think of that and drink in the light until I am drunk. The sun grazes the horizon, but night does not bring anxiety to the sea. On the contrary, a softness covers this world in which we are the only living beings on the surface of the water. The sky becomes gold and purple. The sea, so dark when the sun is at its zenith, is now smooth and calm like a puff of violet smoke blending with the clouds on the horizon and veiling the sun.

I listen to the the helmsman speaking, perhaps to himself, as he stands at the wheel. Beside him Captain Bradmer's armchair is empty, as this is the time he goes into his alcove to sleep or write. In the horizontal twilight the helmsman's tall figure stands out against the glittering sails and seems unreal, like the singsong sound of his words that I can hear without being able to make them out. Night is coming and I think of how the outline of Palinurus must have appeared to Aeneas on the *Argo,* or to Typhis whose words I have never forgotten when he tried to reassure his traveling companions at nightfall:

"Titan set sail on the still sea in order to confirm the good omen. And during the night the wind blew more strongly over the sea and in the sails, and during those silent hours the ship went more quickly. I did not follow the course of the stars that fell from the sky into the sea any longer, like Orion, who had already fallen, or Perseus, who made the waves retain their anger. My guide is the snake with seven stars intertwined in its rings, which is always looking down and is never hidden."

I recite aloud the verses of Valerius Flaccus, which I used to read in my father's study, and for a moment more I believe I am on board the *Argo.*

Later, in the twilight calm, the men come up on deck. Their torsos are naked to the warm breeze, and they smoke and talk or look at the sea like me.

Since the first day I have been impatient to get to Rodrigues and the end of my voyage; but at this moment, I wish this journey would never end and that the *Zeta,* like the *Argo,* would continue to glide eternally on the calm sea, so near the sky with its bright sail like a flame against the already dark horizon.

Night at sea, again

Having fallen asleep against my trunk at my spot in the hold, I am awakened by the stifling heat and the frantic activity of the cockroaches and rats. Insects buzz in the thick air and the darkness only makes their flight more disturbing. To keep one of these monsters from flying right into our faces, when we sleep we cover our faces with a handkerchief or a bit of shirt.

The rats are more circumspect, but more dangerous, too. The other evening a man was bitten on the hand by one of these rodents that he had disturbed in its search for food. The wound became infected despite the arak-soaked rags that Captain Bradmer used to try to heal it, and now I can hear the man raving with fever on his mattress. The fleas and lice also give us hardly any rest, and every morning we scratch at the innumerable bites from the previous night. The first night I spent in the hold, I also had to endure assaults by battalions of bedbugs—the reason that I finally gave up my mattress. I pushed it to the back of the hold and slept on the floor wrapped in my old horse blanket. This way I suffered less from the heat, and was also spared the odor of sweat and brine that permeated the mattresses.

I'm not the only one to suffer from the heat in the hold. One after another the men wake up and either talk among themselves or go on with their interminable game of dice, picking up from where they left off. What do they play for? When I asked Captain Bradmer, he shrugged his shoulders and said simply, "Their women." Despite the captain's orders, the sailors have lit a lamp in the front of the hold, a dim Clark oil lamp. The orange light wavers as the ship rolls and casts a phantasmagoric glow over the sweat-glossed black faces. The whites of their eyes and their white teeth shine in the distance. What are they doing around the lamp? They aren't playing dice and they aren't singing. They're talking in low voices, one after the other—a long conversation punctuated with laughter. The fear of a conspiracy or a mutiny grips me again. What if they really decided to take over the *Zeta?* If they threw us overboard—Bradmer, the helmsman, and me? Who would ever hear of it? And who would ever go and search for them on the distant islands, in the Mozambique canal or on the Eritrean coast? I lie absolutely still with my head turned toward them, looking through my eyelashes at the vacillating light where the red cockroaches and mosquitoes absentmindedly throw themselves into the flame.

Then, like the other night, without making any noise, I climb the ladder toward the hatch and the sea wind. Wrapped in my blanket I walk barefoot on the deck, breathing in the delights of the night and feeling the freshness of the spray.

As the ship glides almost noiselessly over the crests of the waves, being on the sea is like being at the center of the world. The ship seems to fly rather than sail, as if the strong wind blowing in the sails has transformed it into an immense bird with outspread wings.

Again I lie down on the deck, in the bow, against the closed hatchcover where I am sheltered by the edge of the bulwark. I can feel the jib sheets vibrating against my head and the continuous rustling of the sea as it parts before the ship. Laure would love the music of the sea, this mixture of sharp sound with the deep tone of the waves as they break against the stern. I am listening to this for her, so that I can send it across the seas to her, send it as far as the somber Forest Side house where I knew that she, too, is lying awake.

I think again of the look on her face before she turned away and walked quickly toward the road that follows the tracks. I can't forget the fiery light that shone in her eyes at the moment we parted company, a violent and angry light. I was so surprised by it that I didn't know what to do; then I got into the train and didn't think about it again. But now, on the *Zeta*'s deck, sailing toward a destiny I don't know, I remember that look and once more I feel the wrenching ache of our separation.

And yet, I had to go. I had nothing left to hope for back there. I think back to Boucan and to all that could have been saved: the house with the sky-blue roof, the trees, the ravine, and the sea wind blowing in the night, awakening the groans of the runaway slaves from the dark shadow over Mananava and making the bo'sun birds fly away before dawn. I never want to stop seeing this, not even when I am on the other side of the sea and the Unknown Corsair's treasure lies before me.

The ship glides over the waves, light and airy under the starlight. Where is the snake with the seven lights that Typhis described to the sailors of the *Argo*? Is it Eridanus rising in the east in front of Sirius's sun, or the Dragon lying in the north carrying the Etamin gem on its head? No: it isn't either of them. I suddenly see the Big Dipper clearly under the pole star, light and precise, floating eternally in its place in the sky. Lost in the middle of the vortex of stars, we, too, are following its sign. And an endless supply of wind crosses the sky, swelling our sails.

I know now where I am going, and this excites me so much that I have to get up to calm the pounding of my heart. I am going into the void, toward the darkness, gliding in the middle of the sea to a future that cannot be known.

I think again of the two bo'sun birds wheeling above the somber valley, making their rattling noise as they flee from the storm. When I close my eyes I see them, as if they were wheeling above the masts.

A little before dawn I fall asleep while the *Zeta* continues on its way to Agalega. All the men are asleep now. Only the black helmsman keeps watch, his unblinking eyes staring straight ahead into the night. He never sleeps. Sometimes at the beginning of the afternoon when the sun burns the deck he goes into the hold and lies down, silently smoking, his eyes staring in the dim light at the blackened planks above him.

A day on the way to Agalega

How long have we been sailing? Five days? Six? As I go through the contents of my trunk in the stifling, dimly lit hold, this question haunts me with disturbing insistence. What does it matter? Why do I want to know? I try very hard to remember the date of my departure so that I can count how many days I've been at sea. These numberless days seem to have gone by in a flash, even as they seemed very long. It's as if it has been one uninterrupted day that started when I boarded the *Zeta,* a day that is like the sea, where the sky sometimes changes and becomes dark and overcast, and where starlight replaces the sun's rays; but where the wind never stops blowing, nor the waves advancing, nor the horizon surrounding the ship.

As the voyage progresses, Captain Bradmer becomes friendlier. This morning he taught me how to take a bearing using a sextant, as well as how to determine the meridian and the parallel. Today we are at 12° 38 south and 54° 30 east. Finding our position also answers my question about how long I've been at sea; they show me that we are two days away from the island and several minutes too far east, due to the trade winds that have set us to the east during the night. When he has finished taking our position, Captain Bradmer carefully puts his sextant away in the alcove. I showed him my theodolite and he looked at it curiously. I think he even said, "How in hell is that going to help you?" I answered evasively. I couldn't tell him that my father had bought it back when he was preparing to go find the Unknown Corsair's treasure! Back up on deck, the captain sits down again in his armchair behind the helmsman. As I'm nearby, he offers me, for the second time, one of his terrible cigarettes, which I don't dare refuse and which I let burn out in the wind.

"Do you know the queen of islands?" he asks me. He says it in English and I repeat: "The queen of islands?" "Yes, sir, Agalega. It's called that because it is the healthiest and most fertile island in the Indian Ocean." I think he's going to say more, but he falls silent. He merely sinks deeper into his armchair and repeats dreamily: "The queen of islands. . ." The helmsman shrugs his shoulders. He says in French: "Rats' Island. He should call it that instead." Then he begins to tell how the English had declared war on the rats because of the epidemic they spread from island to island. "Once there weren't any rats on Agalega. It was also a little paradise, like Saint Brandon, because rats are the devil's animal; there aren't any in paradise. One day an old boat that nobody knew—and nobody remembers its name now—arrived on the islands from Grande Terre. It was shipwrecked near the island and the islanders saved the packing crates from the cargo, but there were rats even in the packing crates. When they opened them they scattered all over the island and they had babies and they became so numerous that the island belonged to them. They ate all the food supplies in Agalega, the corn, the eggs, and the rice. There were so many of them that the people couldn't sleep anymore. The rats even ate the coconuts from the trees and the sea birds' eggs. First the islanders tried to get rid of them with cats, but the rats banded together and killed the cats and ate them, of course. Then they tried traps, but rats are cunning and they didn't get caught in them. Then the English had an idea. They had dogs sent across the sea, they called them fox terriers, and they promised a rupee for every rat killed. The children climbed into the coconut trees and shook the palms, the rats fell out, and the dogs killed them. I'm told the people of Agalega kill more than forty thousand rats every year, and there are still rats there! Especially in the north of the island. Rats like the Agalegan coconuts very much and they always live in the trees. That's all I have to say about it, but that's why your *queen of islands* should *really* be called Rats' Island."

Captain Bradmer laughs loudly. Perhaps this is the first time the helmsman has told this story. Then Bradmer, sitting in his office chair, begins to smoke again, his eyes squinting against the noonday sun.

When the black helmsman goes to lie down on his mattress in the hold, Bradmer points to the wheel. "Your turn, sir."

He doesn't need to repeat it. Now it is I who am holding the big wheel, my hands squeezing the worn grips. I can feel the heavy waves under the helm and the wind filling the big sails. It's the first time I've steered a ship.

Then a strong gust of wind puts the *Zeta* over her beam, stretching her sails to the breaking point, and I can hear the hull cracking under the strain as the horizon swings in front of the bowsprit. I hold my breath for a long moment, while the ship balances on the crest of the wave. Then suddenly, I instinctively pull hard to port, yielding to the wind. Slowly, the ship straightens in a cloud of spray. The sailors on the deck shout, "Ayoo!"

But Captain Bradmer, his eyes squinting against the sun and with one of his eternal green cigarettes in the corner of his mouth, remains seated and doesn't say anything. I think this man would go down with his ship without leaving his armchair.

Now I am on my guard. I keep an eye on the wind and the waves, and when it feels as if both are getting too strong I yield to them by turning the wheel. I don't think I have ever felt as strong, or as free. Standing on the burning deck, my toes spread for a better grip, I can feel the powerful surge of water under the helm and hull. I can feel the vibrations of the waves as they hit the prow and the gusts of wind in the sails. I have never experienced anything like it. It obliterates everything else—the world, time—and I am surrounded only by the future. My future is sea, wind, sky, and light.

For a long time, perhaps hours, I stand at the wheel in the center of swirls of wind and water. The sun burns my back and neck, then slides down the left side of my body. It is already almost touching the horizon, throwing sparks of fire across the sea. I am so in harmony with the movement of the ship that I know every time the wind is going to drop, every time we are about to go over a wave.

The helmsman is at my side. He doesn't speak and he, too, watches the sea. I know he wants to take the wheel again. I stretch my pleasure out a bit longer so that I can feel the ship slide once more over the hump of a wave, hesitate, and then go on, driven by the wind in the sails. When we are in the trough of the wave I step to one side without letting go of the wheel, and the helmsman's dark hand closes firmly over the grips. When he is not at the helm this man is even more taciturn than the captain. But as soon as his hands are gripping the wheel a strange change comes over him. It is as if he becomes someone else, someone bigger and stronger. His thin, sunburned face, which looks as if it had been sculpted out of basalt, becomes acutely powerful. His green eyes come alive and his whole face reflects a kind of happiness that I can now understand.

Then he starts to speak in his singsong voice, an interminable monologue that gets eaten up by the wind. What is he talking about? I'm sitting on the deck now, to his left, while Captain Bradmer continues smoking in his armchair. The helmsman is not speaking to him or to me. He is speaking for his own pleasure, the way others sing or whistle.

He talks again about Saint Brandon, where women aren't allowed to go. He says, "One day a young woman wanted to go to Saint Brandon, a young black woman from Mahé, tall and beautiful and I don't think more than sixteen years old. As she knew it was forbidden she asked her fiancé, a young man who worked on a fishing boat. She said to him, 'Please take me there!' At first he didn't want to but she said to him, 'What are you frightened of? Nobody will know. I'll go disguised as a boy. All you have to do is say I'm your little brother.' So he ended up saying yes and she disguised herself as a man by putting on an old pair of pants and a loose shirt and cutting her hair, and as she was tall and thin the other fishermen took her for a boy. So she went with them on the boat to Saint Brandon. During the voyage nothing happened, the wind was as gentle as breath and the sky was bright blue and the boat got to Saint Brandon in a week. Nobody knew there was a woman on board, except for the fiancé. But sometimes at night he spoke to her in a low voice; he said, 'If the captain learns about this he'll be very angry and he'll put me off the ship.' She said, 'How will he find out?'

"Then the boat went into the lagoon where it is like paradise and the men started to fish the big turtles that are so gentle they let themselves be taken without trying to get away. Up until this time nothing had happened, but when the fishermen disembarked on one of the islands to spend the night the wind suddenly came up and the sea became violent. The waves went over the reefs and broke in the lagoon. All night there was a terrible storm and the sea covered the rocks on the islands. The men left their huts and took refuge in the trees. Then everybody prayed to the Virgin and the saints and asked them to protect them and the captain lamented as he saw his boat run aground on the shore and then reduced to splinters by the fierce waves. Then a taller wave than all the others appeared and rolled in toward the islands like a savage beast and when it got there it tore up a rock where some of the men were sheltering. Then suddenly it was calm again and the sun started to shine as if there had never been a storm. Then they heard a voice crying and saying, 'Ayoo, ayoo, little brother!' It was the young fisherman who had seen the wave sweep away his fiancée; but because he knew he had disobeyed by bringing a woman to the islands, and was afraid of being punished by the captain, he was crying, 'Ayoo, little brother!' "

By the time the helmsman has finished speaking the light over the sea has become golden, and the sky near the horizon pale and empty. Night is already falling, yet another night. But twilight lasts a long time at sea, and I watch the day very slowly coming to an end. Is this world the same one I knew before? It seems that by crossing the horizon I have entered another world, a world that resembles the one of my childhood at Boucan, where the noise of the sea reigned. It is as if the *Zeta* is sailing backward in time, erasing all that it passes over.

As day turns to night I allow myself to go back into my dreams again. The heat from the sun is still on my neck and shoulders. I can also feel the gentle evening wind that travels faster than our ship. Everybody is silent. Every evening it is like a mysterious rite that everyone observes. Nobody speaks. We hear the sound of the waves against the stem and the dull vibration of the sails and the rigging. As they do every evening, the Comorian sailors kneel on the deck at the front of the ship, to say their prayers facing north. Their voices come to me in a dull murmur mingled with the wind and sea. Never before have I felt the beauty of this prayer—which is addressed to nothing and gets lost in the immensity—as much as I do this evening, when the ship, rocking slightly, glides rapidly across a sea transparent as the sky. I think how happy I would be if you were here beside me, Laure, you who love the muezzin's call that echoes in the Forest Side hills. How I wish you could hear this prayer here and feel the tremor when the ship, like a big sea bird, beats its dazzling wings. I would have liked to bring you with me, like the fisherman from Saint Brandon. I, too, could have said you were my "little brother"!

I know that Laure would have felt the same as I if she had listened at sunset to the Comorian sailors' prayer. We wouldn't have needed to talk about it either. But just as I think of her and feel my heart contract, I realize, too, that I am seeing her now from a different angle. Laure is once again in Boucan, near the house, in the large garden overrun with creepers and flowers; or walking on the narrow path through the cane. She has never left the place she loved. At the end of my journey I can see the surf at the mouth of the river and the sea unfurling on the black Tamarin beach. I left so that I could return. But I won't be the same when I come back. I'll come back like a stranger, and this old trunk full of my father's papers will be full of the Corsair's gold and jewels, the Golconda treasure, or Aureng Zeb's ransom. I'll come back smelling of the sea, sunburned, strong and hardened like a soldier, to reclaim our lost domain. That is what I dream of in the still twilight.

One after the other the sailors descend into the hold to sleep in the heat, which the hull, baked all day by the sun, radiates. I go down with them and stretch out on the wood with my head against my trunk. I listen to the sounds of the interminable game of dice that picks up where it left off at dawn.

Sunday

We have reached Agalega after a five-day passage. The coasts of the twin islands must have been visible very early this morning, from daybreak. I slept heavily, alone in the back of the hold, my head rocking on the floor, oblivious to the movement on deck. The calm waters wake me up. I have become so used to the endless rocking of the ship that its stillness disturbs my sleep.

I immediately go up on deck, barefoot, without bothering to put on my shirt. A thin, gray-green strip fringed with spray from the reefs lies in front of us. This land, though flat and desolate, is a marvel to us, who for days have seen only a blue expanse of sea joined to the vast blue sky. The crew are all forward, leaning over the bulwarks and looking avidly at the two islands.

Captain Bradmer has given the order to drop the sails and the ship drifts several hundred yards away from the coast, but doesn't get any closer. When I ask the helmsman why, he merely says, "You have to wait for the right moment." It is Captain Bradmer, standing next to this armchair, who explains that we have to wait for the ebb tide so as not to be thrown by the currents against the barrier reef. When we are near enough to the channel, we will drop anchor and put the pirogue into the sea to go ashore. The tide won't come in until the afternoon, when the sun starts to set. We have to wait patiently and content ourselves with looking at a shore that is so close, yet so difficult to reach.

The sailors' excitement has passed. They are sitting on the deck now, playing and smoking in the shade of the sail that flaps in the feeble wind. Despite the proximity of the coast, the water is dark blue. Standing on the stern I hang over the bulwarks and watch the big green shadows of the sharks as they pass by.

The sea birds arrive with the low tide. Seagulls and petrels wheel above us, deafening us with their cries. They are hungry and they take us to be one of the fishing boats from the islands; they scream for their due. When they realize their error they fly off and return to the shelter of the coral reefs. Only two or three seagulls continue to make big circles above us, then dive toward the sea and fly on a level with the waves. After all these days spent scrutinizing the empty sea the spectacle of the seagulls' flight fills me with pleasure.

Toward the end of the afternoon Captain Bradmer gets up from his armchair; he gives the orders to the helmsman who repeats them and the men hoist the big sails. The helmsman is at the rudder, standing on tiptoe so he can see better. We are going to land. Slowly, under the soft push of wind from the rising tide, the *Zeta* approaches the bar. Now we can clearly see the long waves breaking against the reefs and hear their continuous crashing.

When the the bow is directly facing the channel and the ship is only several hundred yards away from the reefs, the captain gives the order to cast anchor. The largest anchor, on the end of its heavy chain, is the first to fall into the sea. Then the sailors lower the three smaller frigate anchors port, starboard, and astern. When I ask him why they take so many precautions, the captain tells me about the 1901 shipwreck of the *Kalinda,* a three-master weighing a hundred and fifty tons: anchor was dropped in this same place, facing the opening. Then everybody went ashore, even the captain, leaving the ship in the charge of two inexperienced Tamil ship's boys. Several hours later the tide rose with unusual force, and the current, rushing in the direction of the only channel, was so violent that the anchor chain broke. The people on the shore had seen the ship approaching, very high above the bar where the rollers were unfurling, as if it were going to take flight. Then it plummeted onto the reefs and a receding wave engulfed it and drew it to the bottom of the sea. The following day they found pieces of the masts, bits of wood, and several packages from the cargo, but they never found the two ship's boys.

After finishing his story, the captain gives the order for all the sails to be lowered and for the canoe to be put to sea. I look at the dark water—it is more than ten fathoms deep—and I shiver, thinking of the green shadows of the sharks slipping by, perhaps waiting for another shipwreck.

As soon as the pirogue is in the water, the captain slides down the length of rope with an agility I would never have credited him with and four sailors go after him. In order to get ashore safely two trips have to be made, and I will be on the second. I lean over the bulwarks with the other sailors and watch the canoe rushing to the entrance of the channel. Perched on the crest of a high wave, it enters the narrow opening between the black reefs, disappears for an instant in the trough of a wave, then reappears on the other side of the barrier, in the calm waters of the lagoon. From there it races toward the embankment where the island people are waiting.

We on deck are impatient. The sun is low when the boat comes back and is greeted by the sailors' happy cries. This time it's my turn. Following the helmsman, I slide down the rope to the pirogue and four other sailors come aboard too. As we row, we can't see the channel. The helmsman steers, standing to get the best view. The roaring of the waves warns us that we are close to the barrier. In fact, I suddenly feel our skiff being lifted by a fast-moving wave and we cross over the narrows between the reefs on its crest. Then we are in the lagoon, on the other side, near the long coral wall. At the spot where the waves come to an end, very near the sandy beach, the helmsman has us bring the canoe alongside and ties it up. The sailors jump shouting onto the embankment, then disappear into the crowd of people.

I go ashore in turn. There are many women and children on the seawall, and black fishermen and Indians, too. They all look curiously at me. Apart from Captain Bradmer, who comes when he is carrying cargo, the people must not see whites very often. Besides, with my long hair and beard, my sunburned face and arms, my dirty clothes and my bare feet, I must be a strange kind of white! The children, especially, examine me carefully, not hiding their laughter. On the beach there are some dogs, some thin, black pigs, and some goats trotting about looking for salt.

It is near sunset. The sky behind the islands is becoming yellow above the coconut trees. Where will I sleep? I am about to look for a place on the beach, between the canoes, when Captain Bradmer invites me to join him at the hotel. My astonishment at the word "hotel" makes him laugh. The hotel is an old wooden house, and the proprietor, an energetic half-black, half-Indian woman, lets out rooms to the rare travelers who come to Agalega. It appears she even lodged the chief justice of Mauritius on his only visit in 1901 or 1902! For dinner the lady serves us a crab curry that is really excellent, especially after the indifferent fare of the *Zeta*'s Chinese cook.

Captain Bradmer is very animated and he questions our landlady about the island's inhabitants. He tells me about Juan de Nova, the first explorer to discover Agalega, and he speaks of a French colonist, a certain Auguste Leduc, who organized the production of copra, today the island's only commercial activity. Some of the other islands also produce rare wood: mahogany, sandalwood, and ebony. He speaks, too, about Giquel, the colonial administrator who founded the hospital and revived the island economy at the beginning of the century. I promise myself to take advantage of this port of call— Bradmer has just told me he has to load a hundred barrels of coconut oil—by visiting the forests, which are apparently the most beautiful in the Indian Ocean.

When the meal is over I go stretch out on my bed in the little room at the end of the house. But despite my fatigue, I find it difficult to fall asleep. After all those nights in the stifling hold the calm of this room disturbs me, and even though I try not to, I still feel that I am being lifted by the waves. I open the shutters to breathe in the night air. Outside there is a heavy odor of land, and the toads set the night's rhythm.

Toward Rodrigues, 1910

How I already long to return to the deserted sea, to the sound of the waves against the stern and the wind vibrating in the sails! I want to feel myself cutting through the air and the waves, to experience the power of the void and hear the music of absence. I sit on the battered old chair in front of the open window and breathe in the smell of the garden. I hear Bradmer's voice, his laugh, and the landlady's laugh. They seem to be enjoying themselves a great deal. . . . What does it matter! I fall asleep like that, with my forehead on the window ledge.

Monday morning

I am walking across the island from the south where the village is. The sister islands that make up Agalega are joined to one another, and together they cannot be bigger than the Rivière Noire district. Still, Agalega seems very large after the days on the *Zeta,* when the only activity consisted of walking from the hold to the deck, and from stern to stem. I walk across fields of coconut and cabbage palm planted in straight lines as far as the eye can see. I walk slowly, barefoot, in the earth mingled with sand from the crabs' trenches. The silence disorients me. The sound of the sea cannot be heard here. There is only the wind murmuring in the palms. Despite the early hour (when I left the hotel everyone was still sleeping), the heat is already oppressive. There isn't anyone in the rectilinear avenues, and if their regularity hadn't borne the stamp of something human I might have thought myself on a desert island.

But I am mistaken in thinking there's no one here. Since I started walking across the plantation I have been followed by anxious eyes. The land crabs watch me as I go along the path and sometimes rise up, waving their pincers threateningly. There was a moment when several of them even stopped me from going on by standing together in my path, forcing me to make a detour.

At last I get to the other side of the plantation on the north side of the island. The calm lagoon water separates me from the poorer sister island. There is a hut on the shore and an old fisherman mending his nets near his canoe, which has been pulled up onto the sand. He lifts his head to look at me, then goes back to his work. His black skin shines in the sun.

I decide to return to the village by walking along the coast, on the sandy beach that surrounds nearly the entire island. I can feel the wind from the sea here, but now I no longer have the shade from the coconut trees. The sun is so fierce I have to take off my shirt and use it to protect my head and shoulders. When I get to the other end of the island I can't wait any longer. I strip off my clothes and dive into the clear lagoon water. It is delicious and I swim to the barrier reef until I find the cold layers of water where the rumbling of the waves is very close. Then I swim very slowly back to the bank, floating almost without moving. I open my eyes underwater and look at the multicolored fish darting away from me, but I also keep watch for sharks. The current of cold water coming from the channel, pulling fish and pieces of seaweed along with it, reaches me too.

Back on the beach, I get dressed without drying myself and walk barefoot on the burning sand. Farther on I meet a group of black children who are fishing for octopus. They are the same age we were, Denis and I, when we wandered near Rivière Noire. They look with surprise at the *"bourzois,"* his clothes stained with seawater and his beard and hair full of salt. Do they take me for a castaway? When I approach them, they run away and hide in the shadowy coconut groves.

Before going into the village I shake the sand and salt out of my clothes and comb my hair so that I won't make too bad an impression. From the other side of the reefs I can see the two masts of Bradmer's schooner. The barrels of oil are lined up on the long coral wall waiting to be put on board. The sailors are going back and forth in the canoe, taking them to the ship. There are still about fifty to go.

Back at the hotel I breakfast with Captain Bradmer. He is in a good mood this morning. He tells me that the loading of the oil will be finished toward noon and that we will leave tomorrow morning at dawn. So as not to have to wait for the tide we will sleep on board the ship. Then, to my great astonishment, he speaks to me about my family, about my father, whom he had known in Port Louis.

"I knew about the bad luck he had, about all his problems and debts. It was a very sad business. You lived in Rivière Noire, didn't you?"

"At Boucan."

"Oh yes, that's behind the Tamarin Estate. I was at your house a long time ago, before you were born. It was in the time of your grandfather. I remember it was a beautiful white house with a magnificent garden. Your father had just gotten married to your mother, a very young woman with beautiful black hair and beautiful eyes. You father was very taken by her, it was a very romantic marriage." After a few moments of silence, he adds, "What a pity that it all ended like that. Happiness doesn't last." He looks at the little garden at the end of the porch where a black pig reigns, surrounded by scratching fowls. "Yes, what a pity. . ."

But he doesn't say any more. Almost as if he regrets his frankness, he gets up, puts on his hat, and leaves the house. I hear him talking outside to the landlady, then he reappears:

"This evening the canoe will make its last trip at five o'clock, before the tide starts to come in. Be so good as to be

on the embankment at that time." It is an order rather than
a suggestion.

❖

Thus, I am on the embankment at the said time, after a day
passed dawdling on the south of the island, going from the village to the eastern point, that is, from the hospital to the cemetery. I am impatient to be aboard the *Zeta* again, sailing to
Rodrigues.

As we get farther away from shore it seems to me that all
the men in the boat share my desire to be back on the high
seas. This time I am in the bow and the captain himself steers.
I see the barrier getting closer and the big waves crashing
down and throwing up a wall of spray. My heart beats wildly
when the pirogue rises up against an unfurling wave. I am
deafened by the noise of the surf and the screaming of the
wheeling birds. "Alley-ho!" shouts the captain as the wave recedes; eight paddles pull and we surge into the narrow channel
between the reefs, leaping across on the next wave. Not a drop
of water falls into the boat! Now we are gliding across the deep
blue sea toward the black outline of the *Zeta*.

Later, when we are aboard and the men have gone down
into the hold to play and sleep, I watch the night. Lights shine
on the island where the village is. Then the land darkens and
disappears. Now there is only the nothingness of the night and
the sound of the waves on the reefs.

As on nearly every other night since this voyage started, I
wrap myself in my old horse blanket and lie down on deck to
look at the stars. The sea wind blowing in the rigging announces the tide. I can feel the first waves sliding under the
hull, making the frame creak. The anchor chains grind and
groan. In the sky the stars shine with a fixed radiance. I study

them carefully, as I do every night, as if the secret of my destiny were hidden in their design. Scorpio, Orion, and the faint outline of the Little Dipper are there. Lanis Minor, the Unicorn, and the Argo with its narrow sail and long stern are near the horizon. And particularly on this evening, I look for the stars that most remind me of Boucan, the seven stars of the Pleiades that our father made us learn by heart and that Laure and I recited like the words of a magic formula: Alcyone, Electra, Maia, Atlas, Taygeta, Merope . . . And the last one, which we named only hesitantly because it was so small we weren't sure of having seen it: Pleione. Alone in the night I softly recite their names. It is as if I know that, as a cloud parts, they can also be seen in the sky over Boucan.

At sea, on the way to Mahé

The wind shifted during the night. It is now blowing north, making any thought of return impossible. The captain chose to try to get away from the wind rather than resigning himself to waiting at Agalega for it to pass. The helmsman tells me this in an emotionless voice. Will we someday go to Rodrigues? That depends on how long the storm lasts. Because of the favorable winds we reached Agalega in five days, but now we have to wait for the wind to let us go back.

I am the only one who is anxious about the itinerary. The sailors continue about their way, playing dice as if nothing else mattered. Is it because they welcome any adventure? No, it's not only that. It is that they don't belong to any one person or to any particular land. Their world is the *Zeta* deck and the stifling hold where they sleep at night. I look at their dark, sun- and wind-burned faces, which look like stones polished by the sea. I feel the same irrational, pressing anxiety that I experienced on the night we left. These men belong to another existence, another time. Captain Bradmer and the helmsman are also part of it. They too are indifferent to place and desire, to everything that troubles me so much. Their faces are as smooth as the others' and their eyes have the metallic hardness of the sea.

Perhaps this way I will learn not to ask any more questions. Can one demand anything of the sea? Can one ask the horizon to account for itself? The only realities are the wind driving us, the rolling waves, and the steadfast stars at night guiding us.

The captain speaks to me today. He tells me that he is counting on selling his cargo of oil in the Seychelles, where he knows Mr. Maury well. It is Mr. Maury who will take care of having it transported to England on cargo ships. Captain Bradmer speaks of this with indifference as he sits on deck smoking his green-tobacco cigarettes. Then, when I least expect it, he speaks to me again about my father. He had heard about his experiment to electrify the island. He also knew about all those who had opposed him and had been responsible for his ruin, his brother included. His voice is neutral as he talks about it, and he doesn't comment either. All he says about Uncle Ludovic is, "A tough man." That's all. These events, recounted in the captain's monotonous voice, seem, here on this very blue sea, to come from somewhere far away and almost unknown to me. Even though it is because of them that I am on board the *Zeta,* suspended between sky and sea: not to forget—how can one ever forget?—but to neutralize memory and render it inoffensive so that it slips by like a reflection.

After these few words about my father and Boucan the captain falls silent. He smokes with closed eyes and crossed arms and I almost believe he is half asleep. But suddenly he turns to me and in his choked voice, which can hardly be heard above the noise of the wind and sea, he says, "Are you the only son?"

"Sir?"

He repeats his question without raising his voice: "I asked if you were the only son. Do you have any brothers?"

"I have a sister, sir."

"What is her name?"

"Laure."

He seems to reflect and then he says, "Is she pretty?" He doesn't wait for me to reply but continues, as if to himself, "She must be like your mother, beautiful, and more than that, courageous. Intelligent, too."

To hear this on the deck of this ship, so far from the people of Port Louis and Curepipe, makes me dizzy. For so long I had believed that Laure and I lived in another world, one that was unknown to the privileged people of the Rue Royale and Champ-de-Mars, as if in the derelict house at Forest Side and in the wild Boucan valley we had been invisible. Suddenly my heart beats more quickly and I feel my face redden with anger or shame.

Where am I, then? On the deck of the *Zeta,* an old schooner carrying barrels of oil and full of rats and vermin, lost at sea between Agalega and Mahé. Who is there to care about me and my blushing? Who is there to see my clothes stained with oil from the hold, my sunburned face and my tangled salty hair? Who cares that I have been going barefoot for days? I look at Captain Bradmer's old pirates' head, his wine-colored cheeks and little eyes shut against his stinking cigarette smoke; at the black helmsman in front of him; and farther back, at the silhouettes of the Indian and Comorian sailors, some of whom are crouched on the deck smoking their *ganja* while others play dice or daydream, and I don't feel so ashamed anymore.

The captain has already forgotten it. He says to me, "Would you like to sail with me? I am getting old, I need a second."

I look at him in surprise: "But what about your helmsman?"

"What about him? He's old, too. Every time we lay over I wonder if he'll return to the ship."

Captain Bradmer's offer echoes for a moment in my head. I imagine what life would be like on the *Zeta* deck beside Bradmer's armchair. Agalega, the Seychelles, Amirantes, or Rodrigues, Diego Garcia, Peros Banhos. Sometimes we would sail right up to Farquhar or to the Comoro Islands, or perhaps south to Tromelin. The endless sea, longer than any road, longer than life. Did I leave Laure and break the last link holding me to Boucan for this? As I think of it, Bradmer's offer seems ridiculous, laughable. So as not to offend him I say, "I can't, sir. I have to go to Rodrigues."

He opens his eyes. "I know I've also heard the talk about this dream."

"What dream, sir?"

"The dream of the treasure, of course. They say your father worked very hard on it."

Does he say "worked" ironically, or am I just reading something into it?

"*Who* says so?"

"Everyone knows it, sir. But let's not talk about it, it's not worth it."

"Are you saying you don't believe the treasure exists?"

He nods his head.

"I don't think that in this part of the world"—he indicates the horizon with a circular gesture—"there is any other fortune than the one men have wrested from the land and the sea at the price of their fellow men."

For an instant I feel like telling him about the Corsair's maps and papers that my father had collected, and that I have copied and brought with me in my trunk—everything that has comforted and consoled me in my loneliness at Forest Side. But what good would it do? He wouldn't understand. He has already forgotten his words to me and closed his eyes, giving himself over to the rocking of the ship.

I look at the sparkling sea so that I don't have to think about it. I can feel the gentle movement of the boat as it rises over the waves like a horse clearing an obstacle.

I say again, "Thank you for the offer, sir. I will think about it."

He half opens his eyes. Perhaps he doesn't know what I'm talking about. He grumbles, "Ahum, of course . . . Naturally."

It is over. We won't speak of it again.

❖

In the following days, it becomes obvious that Captain Bradmer has had a change of heart toward me. Now when the black helmsman goes below the captain doesn't give me the wheel. Instead, he himself stands at the helm, in front of the armchair that looks strangely empty and out of place. When he is tired of holding the wheel he calls any nearby sailor and lets him take over.

It doesn't bother me. The sea is so beautiful that one can't think of other people for long. Perhaps out here one comes to resemble the sea and sky, becomes smooth and unthinking. Reason, time, and place no longer matter. Every day is the same as the last and each night begins anew. The sky is empty, the sun beats down, and the constellations are fixed. The wind doesn't change: it blows from the north, driving the boat onward.

Friendships are made and broken among the crew. Nobody needs anyone. On the deck—for since the barrels of oil came aboard I can't stand being shut in the hold—I have gotten to know a Rodriguan sailor, an athletic and childish black man called Casimir. He only speaks creole and a pidgin English that he learned in Malaysia. Through these two languages he tells me that he has made the crossing to Europe several times, and that he's been to France and England. But he takes no pride in it. I question him about Rodrigues, ask him the names of the passes, islets, and bays. Does he know a mountain called the "Commander"? He tells me the names of the principal mountains—Patate, Limon, Quatre Vents, and the Piton. He also tells me about the Manafs, blacks from the mountains, primitives who never come down to the coast.

It is so hot that despite the captain's prohibition some of the sailors come up on deck at night. They don't sleep. They lie with eyes open, talking in low voices. They smoke and play dice.

One evening, just before we arive at Mahé, there is an argument. A muslim Comorian is taken to task by an Indian full of *ganja* for an incomprehensible reason. They grab each other by their clothes and roll around on the deck. The others move away and form a circle around them as if they were fighting cocks. The Comorian is small and thin and is quickly pinned down by the other, but the Indian is so drunk that he falls off him and can't get back up. The men silently watch. I can hear the fighters' ragged breathing, the sound of their awkward blows and their grunts. Then the captain comes up from the hold, looks at the fight for a moment, and gives an order. It is Casimir, the good-natured giant, who separates them. He grabs them both at the same time by the belt and lifts them as if they were bundles of laundry; then he puts one on each end of the deck. With that, order is restored.

❀

The next evening the islands come into view. The sailors utter shrill cries when they see the hardly visible line of land, which looks like a dark cloud beneath the sky. Shortly afterward high mountains appear. "It's Mahé," Casimir says. He laughs with pleasure. "There's Platte Island, and that one there is Frégate." As the ship approaches other islands appear, sometimes so far away that when there is a big wave they are hidden from view. The main island looms larger in front of us. Soon the first seagulls are wheeling and screaming overhead. There are frigates too, the most beautiful birds I have ever seen, shiny black with a huge wing span and long Y-shaped tails floating behind them. They glide in the wind above us, rippling the red sacs at the base of their beaks; they look like shadows come alive.

It is like this every time we arrive at a new land: the birds come to see the strangers from up close. What are these men bringing? Is it death? Or are they perhaps bringing food, fish, squid, even some whales hooked to the sides of the ship?

Mahé Island is before us, barely two miles away. In the warm twilight I can make out white rocks on the coast, coves, sandy beaches, and trees. We sail up the east coast so that we can stay in the wind till the northernmost point, passing close to two small islands whose names Casimir tells me: Conception and Thérèse; then he laughs because these are women's names. The two bluffs are in front of us, the tops of them still in the sun.

After we have passed the island the wind dies down and becomes a light breeze and the sea turns emerald green. We are very near the coral reef fringed with spray. The village huts seem like toys in the middle of the coconut trees. Casimir names the villages for me: Bel Ombre, Beau Vallon, and Glacis. Night falls and the heat is oppressive after all the wind.

When we are in front of the channel we can already see the lights of Port Victoria shining on the other side of the island. Once we are in the roadstead, protected by the islands, Captain Bradmer gives the order for the sails to be lowered and the anchor dropped. The sailors are already getting ready to lower the pirogue in the sea. They are impatient to be on land. I decide to sleep on deck, rolled in my old blanket, at my favorite spot for watching the stars.

The black helmsman, a Comorian, and I are the only ones left aboard. I like the solitude and the calm. The night is smooth and deep and the presence of land, nearby but invisible, is like a cloud, like a dream. I listen to the waves lapping against the hull and the grating rhythm of the anchor chain around which the ship swings, first in one direction then in the other.

I think of Laure and Mam who are so far away now, on the other side of the sea. Are they covered by the same night, the same silent night? I go down into the hold to try to write a letter that I can send tomorrow from Port Victoria. I attempt to write by the light from a night lamp. But the heat is suffocating, and there is the smell of oil and the buzzing of insects. Sweat runs down my face and body. The words will not come. What can I say? Laure warned me when I left, write only one letter, to say: I am coming home. Otherwise don't bother. That's how she is: all or nothing. Too proud to accept not having everything she has chosen to have nothing.

Since I am not allowed to tell her how beautiful it all is here under the night sky, drifting on the smooth water in the deserted boat, why write? I put the writing case and paper back in the trunk, lock it, and go back up on deck where I can breathe. The black helmsman and the Comorian are sitting near the hatch, smoking and speaking softly. Later the helmsman stretches out on the deck wrapped in a sheet that looks like a shroud, his eyes wide open. How many years has it been since he closed them?

Port Victoria

I am looking for a boat to take me to Frégate. Curiosity, rather than real interest, draws me to this island, which my father had once thought he recognized from one of the maps relating to the Corsair's treasure. In fact, it was from the map of Frégate that he realized that the Corsair's map was incorrectly oriented on an east-west axis, and that it had to be rotated 45° to get its correct position.

A black fisherman agrees to take me there; it will take three to four hours, depending on how much wind there is. We leave as soon as I have bought some biscuits and coconuts for thirst from the Chinaman. The fisherman doesn't ask any questions. The only provision he brings along is an old bottle of water. He hoists the slanting sail on the yard and sets it on the long tiller, the way Indian fishermen do.

As soon as we have crossed the channel we are again in the wind and the canoe races forward, leaning over the dark sea. We will be at Frégate in three hours. The sun is high in the sky; it is noon. I sit forward on a stool, watching the sea and the dark receding mass of the bluffs.

We are heading east. On the horizon, which looks like a taut thread, I can see other islands and mountains standing out blue and unreal. Not one bird accompanies us. The fisherman is standing aft leaning on the long tiller.

At about three 'o clock we are just off Frégate's coral reefs. The island is small and flat and is surrounded by sand on which there are coconut trees and some fishermen's huts. We cross the opening in the reef and land on a coral wall where three or four fishermen are sitting. Children are swimming and running naked on the beach. Some way back, buried in the vegetation, a dilapidated wooden house with a veranda sits in the middle of a vanilla grove. The fisherman tells me it belongs to a Mr. Savy. That is, in fact, the name of the family that owns some of the maps my father copied. The island belongs to them but they live in Mahé.

I walk along the beach surrounded by black children who giggle and ask me questions, surprised to see a stranger. I take the road that goes along the Savy property and cross the breadth of the island. There isn't any beach or anchorage on the other side, just rocky coves. The island is so narrow that during heavy storms the spindrift must cover it.

By the time I get back to the embankment, hardly an hour has passed. There is nowhere to sleep and I don't want to waste any more time here. When the fisherman sees me coming he ties the line and hoists the slanting yard along the mast. The canoe glides toward the open sea. The tide is high and waves cover the seawall, passing through the legs of the children who scream with delight. They wave their arms about, then dive into the transparent water.

In his notes my father says that he gave up on the possibility of the Corsair's treasure being on Frégate because of the island's small size and the lack of water, wood, and other resources. From what I have seen he was right. There are no durable landmarks here, nothing that could be used in making a map. The adventurers who roamed the Indian Ocean in 1730 would not have come here. They wouldn't have found what they were looking for, the sort of natural mystery that would defy time and that was so necessary for their purposes.

However, as the canoe gets farther away from Frégate and races west, I feel regret. The clear water in the lagoon, the naked children running on the beach, and the old abandoned wooden house in the middle of the vanilla plants reminds me of Boucan. There *is* no mystery in this world—that is the source of my regret.

What will I find at Rodrigues? And what if it is like Frégate, if there is nothing there either but sand and trees? The sea sparkles now with the slanting rays of the setting sun. In the stern the fisherman still leans on the tiller. His dark face is expressionless, revealing neither boredom nor impatience. He keeps his eyes on the outline of the two bluffs, which are getting bigger; Port Victoria's guardians have already started to disappear into the night.

❖

We are still in Port Victoria. From the *Zeta*'s deck I watch the coming and going of the canoes offloading the oil. The air is warm and heavy, and there isn't a breath of wind. The reflections of light on the shiny sea fascinate me and draw me into a dreamlike state. The noises of the port are far away. Sometimes a bird flies over the ship and its cry makes me jump. I have begun to write a letter to Laure, but will I ever send it to her? I wish that she were here now instead, to read it over my shoulder. Sitting cross-legged on the deck with my shirt open, my hair tangled, my beard long and white with salt like an outlaw's: this is what I tell her. I also tell her about Bradmer, the helmsman who never sleeps, and Casimir.

The hours slip by without leaving a trace. I am stretched out on the deck in the shade of the foremast. After writing only a few lines, I have put the writing case and the paper back in the trunk. Later, the burning sun on my eyelids wakes me. The sky is still as blue and the same bird is wheeling above, screeching. I take up the piece of paper again and mechanically write the lines that came into my mind as I was sleeping:

"Jamque dies auraeque vocant, rursuque capessunt.
Aequaora, qua rigidios eructat Bosporos amnes. . ."

I go back to where I had stopped in the letter. But am I really writing to Laure? In the warm silence of the harbor, in the middle of the sparkling, reflecting light, with the gray coast and the high blue shapes of the bluffs before me, other words come to mind: Why did I abandon everything, for what figment of my imagination? Does this treasure, which I have been chasing for so many years in my dreams, really exist? Are there really gems and precious stones in a vault waiting to sparkle in the sunlight? Is there really a power buried in the earth that can put back the clock and erase unhappiness and ruin and the death of my father in the broken Forest Side house? But I am the only one to hold the key to this secret, and now I'm getting near, closer to it. At the end of my path is Rodrigues, where everything will at last be put in order. I am finally going to fulfill the dream my father had for so long, the one that kept him searching and that haunted my childhood. I am the only one who can do it. My father's will, not my own, must be carried out, since he will never again leave Forest Side. That is what I want to write, but not so that I can send it to Laure. I left to put an end to the dream, so that my life might begin. I am going to take this journey to its conclusion. I know I will find something.

That is what I wanted to say to Laure the day we parted company. But she could see it in my eyes, and she turned away and left me free to go.

I have waited so long to make this journey! It seems to me that I was always dreaming of it. It was in the sound the wind made when the sea rose in the Tamarin estuary, in the waves that ran over the green stretches of cane and in the wind blowing though the filao needles. I remember the unbroken sky above the Tourelle and the dizzying way it bent toward the horizon at dusk. As night fell, the sky would turn violet shot through with darker rays. Now darkness has come to the Port Victoria anchorage and it feels as if we are very close to the place where sky meets sea. Isn't that the sign the *Argo* followed on its course to eternity?

As the light fades, the sailor on watch comes up from the hold where he has slept naked all afternoon in the stifling heat. He is wearing only a loincloth and his body is shining with sweat. He crouches on the bow, facing a porthole in the bulwark, and urinates lengthily into the sea. Then he comes to sit next to me with his back against the mast and starts smoking. In the half-light his sunburned face is bizarrely illuminated by the whites of his eyes. We stay like that for a long time, side by side, without talking.

Friday, I think

Captain Bradmer was right not to try to fight the south wind. As soon as the cargo was unloaded, the *Zeta* passed through the cut the following dawn and found the west wind off the small islands, which would allow us to go back. Lighter, and with full sails, the *Zeta* surges ahead, heeled over like a real clipper. Big waves from the east, perhaps coming from a storm far away on the Malabar coast, churn up the dark sea. They break on the port beam and wash over the deck. The captain has had the forward hatches bolted and the men who are not sailing the ship have gone below. I have been allowed to stay on deck, in the stern, perhaps simply because I have paid for my passage. Captain Bradmer does not seem to be bothered by the waves that sweep the deck and reach as far as his armchair. The helmsman stands with spread legs holding the wheel, and the sound of his words is lost in the wind and turbulent sea.

For half the day the ship advances like this, bent under the wind and drenched in spray. My ears are full of the noise of the elements; they fill my body and vibrate deep inside me. I cannot think of anything else. I watch the captain, his face red from the sun and wind, sitting with his arms hooked through the chair arms, and it seems to me that there is something dark and stubborn and violent in his expression that makes me terribly fearful. Hasn't the *Zeta* reached its limits? The huge waves that hit it portside make it tilt dangerously, and in spite of the din of the sea I can hear its frame cracking. The men have taken refuge aft to avoid the sheets of water. We all stare fixedly in front of us in the direction of the prow. We are waiting for something without knowing what, and it feels as if turning our eyes away for a second could prove fatal.

We stay like this for a long time, clinging to the stays, watching the bow plunge into the dark water and listening to the crashing of the wind and waves. The sea breaks over the helm with such force that the helmsman has difficulty holding the wheel. The veins on his arms are swollen and his face is stretched so tight he looks as if he is in pain. Clouds of smoking spray lit by rainbows rise above the sails. Several times I think of getting up and asking the captain why we are flying all our canvas. But I am stopped by the hard expression on his face, as well as by my fear of falling.

Suddenly, for no reason, Bradmer gives the order to lower the jibs and the staysails and to reef in the mainsails. The helmsman puts the rudder hard left and the ship straightens up. The sails hang loosely, flapping like banners. Everything is normal again. When the *Zeta* is back on course it goes slowly and doesn't heel anymore. The fearsome noise of the wind in the sails has given way to the sound of a gentle whistling through the rigging.

But Bradmer still hasn't moved. His face is as red and closed as ever, and he is still staring straight ahead. The helmsman has gone below to lie down and rest. Casimir the Rodriguan is at the wheel and I can hear his sing-song voice when he speaks to the captain. On the wet deck the sailors have again started up their game of dice and their interminable discussions as if nothing had happened. But did something really happen? Maybe it was just a hallucination from the endless blue sky, the dizzying sea, our wind-drowned ears, the intensity, and the solitude.

The *Zeta* advances easily now and is hardly impeded by the waves. Under the burning midday sun the deck is already dry and glistens with salt. The horizon is still and sharp, the sea fierce. I am flooded with thoughts and memories, and I realize I am talking to myself. But who would notice? Haven't we all been driven mad by the sea—Bradmer, the black helmsman, Casimir, and the others? Who would bother to listen to us talk?

Memories of the secret treasure at the end of this road well up in me. But the sea vanquishes time. From what time do these waves come? Aren't they the same waves as two hundred years ago, when Avery fled from the Indian coast with his fabulous booty, and when Misson's white flag flew over these waters with the words PRO DEO ET LIBERTATE written on it in gold letters. The wind doesn't grow older and the sea is ageless. Sun and sky are eternal.

In the distance I can see each spray-topped wave. I think I know now what I came to look for. It feels as if I can see inside myself, like someone who has been given his dream.

Saint Brandon

After all these days and weeks of not seeing anything but blue sky and sea and the shadow of the clouds, the sailor keeping watch in the bow sees, or rather senses, the gray line of land,

and a name is bandied back and forth on the deck: "Saint Brandon! Saint Brandon!" It is as if it were the most important thing we have ever heard. Everyone leans out over the bulwarks trying to see. Behind the wheel the helmsman screws up his eyes and his face is taut and anxious. "We'll be there before nightfall," Bradmer says. His voice is full of childlike impatience.

"Is it really Saint Brandon?"

My question surprises him. He replies harshly. "What else do you think it could be? There isn't any other land within four hundred miles of here, except for Tromelin behind us and Nazareth, a heap of rocks, to the northeast." Then he says, "Yes, of course it's Saint Brandon."

The helmsman is looking more carefully than anyone at the islands, and I remember his talking about the sky-colored water where the world's most beautiful fishes and turtles and flocks of sea birds live. The islands where women are not allowed to go and the legend of the one the storm swept away. But the helmsman is silent. He pilots the ship toward the still-dark line appearing in the southwest. He wants to enter the channel and get there before nightfall. We are all looking impatiently in the same direction.

The sun is touching the horizon when we come into the archipelago. Suddenly the seabed is visible. The wind dies down. The sunlight is softer, more diffuse. The islands part in front of the ship's prow; there are so many of them they look like a herd of whales. But in fact, it is only one big circular island, a ring from which some coral islets branch off. Is this the paradise the Comorian was speaking about? But as we glide into the lagoon we all feel there is something different here. A kind of peace and slowness come from the clear water, the pure sky, and the silence, that I have felt nowhere else.

Toward Rodrigues, 1910

The helmsman steers the *Zeta* straight toward the first row of reefs. Then we are in very shallow water, and despite the fading light we can clearly see the coral and turquoise seaweed on the seabed. We glide between the black reefs, where every now and then jets of spume from the high seas reach us. The few islands are still far away, looking like sleeping sea animals, but suddenly I see that we are in the middle of the archipelago. Without being aware of it we have come to the center of the atoll.

Captain Bradmer is also leaning over the rail. He is watching the ocean bed, which is so close now that each shell and branch of coral can be clearly seen. Even though the sun is setting behind the islands the clearness of the water cannot be dimmed. We all stay silent so as not to break the spell. I hear Bradmer mutter to himself in English, "Land of the sea."

Night falls over the atoll. It is the gentlest night I have ever known. After the burning sun and wind, the starry, mauve-colored night is a reward. The sailors take off their clothes and dive one after another into the calm waters, swimming soundlessly.

I do the same and swim for a long time in water that is so soft that I can hardly feel it; it surrounds me like a caress. The lagoon water washes me clean and purifies me of all desire and fear. I float for a long time on the mirrorlike surface until the muffled voices of the sailors reach me, mixed with the cries of the birds. Near me I see the dark shape of the island the helmsman says is called La Perle, and a little farther away, surrounded by birds like a whale, Frégate. Tomorrow I will go to their beaches and the water will be even more beautiful. The lights shining through the hatchways of the *Zeta* guide me while I swim. When I climb up the knotted rope attached to the bowsprit the breeze makes me shiver.

Nobody really sleeps that night. The men talk and smoke on deck and the helmsman remains sitting in the stern, watching the reflection of the stars on the atoll waters. Even the captain stays to keep watch, sitting in his armchair. From my place near the mizzenmast I can see the occasional glow of his cigarette. The sea wind catches the men's words and mingles them with the sound of the waves on the reefs. The sky here is vast and pure, as if there were no other land in the world and creation would begin here.

I fall asleep for a while with my head resting on my arms, and when I awake it is dawn. The light is opaque like the lagoon water, azure- and pearl-colored; I haven't seen such a beautiful morning since Boucan. The sound of the sea has risen and become part of the day. Looking around me, I see that most of the sailors are still in the spot where sleep overcame them, lying on the deck or leaning against the bulwark. Bradmer's chair is empty; perhaps he is busy writing in his alcove. Only the black helmsman still stands at his place in the stern. He is watching the sunrise. I go up to speak to him, but it is he who speaks first: "Could there be a more beautiful place in the world?" His voice is husky and full of emotion. "When I came here for the first time I was still a child. Now I am an old man, but still nothing has changed here. It's as if I was here yesterday."

"Why did the captain come here?"

He looks at me as if my question doesn't make sense.

"He came for you! He wanted you to see Saint Brandon. It's a favor he's doing for you."

He shrugs his shoulders and doesn't say any more. Surely he knows that I didn't accept the captain's offer to remain on the *Zeta*; consequently I no longer interest him. He immerses himself in contemplating the sun rising over the huge atoll and the light that seems to leap from the water into the cloudless sky. Birds streak through the sky, cormorants skim the water where their shadows glide, and petrels, high in the wind, are minuscule, whirling specks of silver. They wheel, crossing each other and screeching so loud they wake the men on the deck, who begin talking in turn.

❖

Later I understood why Bradmer had stopped at Saint Brandon. The canoe was put to sea with six crewmen aboard. The captain was at the tiller and the helmsman in the bow with a harpoon in his hand. The canoe glides silently over the lagoon toward La Perle. Leaning over the bow next to the helmsman, I soon see, near the beach, the dark spots that are the turtles. We are silent as we approach them. When the canoe is over them they see us, but it is too late. The helmsman throws the harpoon forcefully; it makes a grating sound as it goes through the shell and blood spurts out. Immediately, with savage cries, the men pull hard on the oars and the canoe races toward the shore, towing the turtle with it. When the canoe is near the beach two sailors jump into the water, pull out the harpoon, and turn the turtle onto its back on the beach.

We are already on our way back to the lagoon where other turtles are waiting without fear. Several times the helmsman's harpoon pierces a turtle's shell. On the white sand streams of blood flow into the sea, staining its clarity. The killing must be done quickly before the sharks smell the blood and chase the turtles to the shallows. The turtles are dying on the white sand. There are ten of them. The sailors dismember them with their swords and line the pieces of meat up on the beach. Then the pieces are put in the pirogue to be smoked on board the ship because there isn't any wood on these islands. The land is barren here; it is a place where sea creatures meet their deaths.

When the butchery is over everyone gets back into the canoe, their hands streaming with blood. I can hear the shrill cries of the birds as they fight over the shells. The light is blinding and I feel dizzy. I want to get away from this island, from this bloody lagoon. During the rest of the day the men busy themselves around the brazier on the *Zeta* deck, where the pieces of meat are grilling. I can't forget what happened that day; I cannot eat the meat. Tomorrow morning at dawn the *Zeta* will leave the atoll and nothing will remain from our stay here except the shattered carapaces already picked clean by the sea birds.

Sunday, at sea

I have been gone for such a long time! A month, or perhaps even longer. I have never gone so long without seeing Laure or Mam. When I said goodbye to Laure she gave me the money she had saved to help me pay for my passage. But I saw that dark flash in her eyes, the spark of anger that said: we might never see each other again. She said "farewell," not simply "goodbye," and she didn't want to accompany me to the port. I needed all these days at sea, the light, the dark, and the burning heat of the sun and wind to understand. I know now that the *Zeta* is taking me to an adventure from which I cannot turn away. Who can know their fate? It is written here, the secret that awaits me and that no one but I can unearth. It is written in the sea, on the spray from the waves, on the sky that covers us during the day, and in the unchanging constellations. How am I to understand what it says? Once again I think of the *Argo* as it sailed over an unknown sea and was guided by the snake of stars. It was fulfilling its own destiny, and not that of the men on board. Of what importance are treasures, lands? Didn't the argonauts have their own destinies to fulfill, some in battle, some in glorious love, and others in death? I think of the *Argo* and the *Zeta*'s deck is transformed. And the dark-skinned Comorian and Indian sailors; the helmsman still standing at his wheel, his face the color of lava and his eyes un-blinking; even Bradmer with his squinting eyes and his drunk-ard's face—haven't they always been wandering from island to island, searching for their destiny?

Has the sun's reflection on the moving waves disturbed my reason? I feel as if I am outside time, in another world, one so different and so far from all I've known that never again will I be able to find what I left. That is why I feel this vertigo, this nausea: I am afraid of giving up what I was, irrevocably, with no hope of reclaiming it. Every hour, every day that passes is like the waves running by the hull, briefly lifting it and then disappearing into the wake. Each one takes me far-ther away from the time I loved, from Mam's voice and Laure's presence.

Captain Bradmer came to me this morning as I stood on the ship's stern. "Tomorrow or the day after we will be at Rodrigues."

I repeat after him: "Tomorrow or the day after?"

"Tomorrow if the wind holds steady."

And so the voyage comes to an end. It is probably because of this that everything seems so different.

The men have finished the store of meat. I am content with spicy rice, but disgusted by the flesh. Every evening for several days now I've felt a fever coming on. Down in the hold, wrapped in my blanket, I shiver despite the heat. What will I do if my body gives out on me? In the trunk I find the bottle of quinine I bought before my departure and swallow a mouthful with my saliva.

Night has fallen without my realizing it.

Late that night I wake drenched in sweat. Beside me, sitting cross-legged with his back leaning against the bulkhead, is a man with a black face on which the night light casts eerie shadows. I push myself up onto my elbow and recognize the helmsman with his staring eyes. He speaks to me in his sing-song voice, but I don't understand very much of what he says. I can hear him asking me questions about the treasure I am going to look for at Rodrigues. How does he know about it? Captain Bradmer must have told him. He questions me and I don't answer, but that doesn't stop him. He waits, then he asks another question, then another. Eventually he loses interest and starts speaking about Saint Brandon, where, he says, he will go to die. I imagine his body lying in the middle of the turtles' shells. The sound of his voice rocks me back to sleep.

In sight of Rodrigues

The island appears on the horizon. In the yellow evening sky it rises from the sea, its high blue mountains thrusting out of the dark water. I think it was the sea birds screeching above us that first alerted me to it.

I go up to the bow to see it better. The sails, swollen by the east wind, make the stem chase the waves. The *Zeda* drives into a trough, then lifts again. The horizon is clear and taut. The island rises and falls behind the waves and the mountain peaks seem to emerge from the depths of the sea.

No land has ever created this impression: the mountaintops resemble the peaks of the Trois Mamelles, but are even higher; they form an impassable wall. Casimir is next to me in the bow. He is pleased to show me the mountains and tell me their names.

The sun is hidden behind the island now. The mountain peaks stand out vividly against the pale sky.

The captain shortens the sails. The men go aloft to reef in. We travel toward the dark island at the speed of the waves, the jibs shining in the twilight like sea birds' wings. As the ship approaches the coast I am filled with emotion. The freedom and happiness of being at sea is drawing to a close. From now on I'll have to look for shelter, speak, ask questions, and be in contact with the land.

Night falls very slowly. We are in the shadow of the high mountains. We enter the channel at about seven o'clock and go toward the red signal light at the end of the jetty. The ship skirts the reefs. I hear a sailor's voice echoing on the starboard side as he shouts out the soundings: "Seventeen, seventeen, sixteen, fifteen, fifteen. . ."

The stone jetty is at the end of the channel.

I hear the anchor fall into the water and the chain unwind. The *Zeta* is motionless alongside the dock, and without waiting for the gangway to be lowered the men jump off the ship, shouting loudly to the waiting crowd. I am standing on deck and for the first time in days, months perhaps, I am fully dressed and have put on my shoes. My trunk is at my feet, ready to go. The *Zeta* will leave by tomorrow, in the afternoon, as soon as the exchange of merchandise is concluded.

I say goodbye to Captain Bradmer. He shakes my hand and obviously doesn't know what to say. It is I who wish him good luck. The black helmsman is already in the hold; he must be lying down, staring at the smoky ceiling.

On the dock the gusts of wind and the trunk on my shoulder make me stagger. I turn back to look once more at the *Zeta*'s silhouette against the pale sky, its raked masts and lacy rigging. Perhaps I should turn back and get on board. In four days I would be in Port Louis; I could take the train, walk in the fine rain to the Forest Side house, hear Mam's voice and see Laure.

A man is waiting for me on the dock. I recognize Casimir's athletic shape by the signal light. He takes the trunk and walks alongside me. He is going to show me the only hotel on the island, which is near Government House; it is owned by a Chinaman and it seems one can eat there, too. I walk behind him in the darkness through the alleys of Port Mathurin. I have arrived.

RODRIGUES, ENGLISH COVE, 1911

ONE WINTER MORNING in 1911 (in August or the beginning of September, I think), I reach the hills that tower over English Cove, where my search will begin.

For weeks and months I have traveled over Rodrigues, from the south where the other channel opens off Gombrani Island, all the way to the chaotic black lava in Malgache Bay; and from the north going over the high mountains in the center of the island, to Mangues, Patate, and Bon Dié Mountain. I have been using the notes I copied from the Pingré book to guide me. "To the east of Grand Port," he wrote in 1761, "there was either not enough water for our canoe, or the water would be too turbulent to carry such a fragile craft as ours. Mr. de Pingré then sent the canoes back by the same road by which they had come with orders to meet us the following day at the *Grandes Pierres Basin at Chaux*." And from another part: "The Quatre Passes mountains are sheer, and as there are hardly any reefs the coast is directly exposed to the wind and the sea breaks so violently on it that it would be highly imprudent to try and get across from this side." Read by the trembling light of my candle in the hotel room at Port Mathurin, Pingré's note reminds me of the famous letter written by an old sailor imprisoned in the Bastille that had started my father hunting for the treasure: "On the west coast of the island at a spot where the sea pounds the coast there is a stream. Follow the stream to its source, where you will find a tamarind tree. Eighteen feet from the tamarind tree the stonework that hides an immense treasure begins."

Very early this morning I walked with feverish haste along the coast. I crossed the Jenner bridge, which marks where Port Mathurin ends, and farther on I waded through the Bambous River in front of the little cemetery. From that point on there are no more houses and the road along the coast gets narrower. I took the road on the right, which goes up to the Cable and Wireless buildings, the English telegraph company at Point Venus. I skirted the telegraph buildings, perhaps from fear of bumping into one on the Englishmen of whom the people of Rodrigues are quite wary.

With a beating heart I climb to the top of the hill. I'm sure now that Pingré came here in 1761—before the astronomers who accompanied Lieutenant Neate in 1874—to observe the transit of Venus, which gave the hill its name.

The fierce east wind makes me stagger. At the foot of the cliff I can see the small waves from the sea, which has come through the channel. Just below me are the Cable & Wireless buildings, long wooden sheds painted gray and screened with bolted-down metal plates like steamships. A little higher, among the vacoas, I can see the veranda of the director's white house with its shutters lowered. At this hour the telegraph offices are still closed. The only person to be seen is a black man sitting on the steps of a shed, smoking and not looking at me.

I continue across the brush. Soon I get to the edge of the cliff and then I see the big valley. In a flash I realize that I have at last found the place I have been looking for.

English Cove opens wide to the sea from each side of the Roseaux River estuary. From where I am I can see the whole valley stretching right up to the mountains. I can make out every bush, tree, and stone. There is no one in the valley; no house nor any sign of humans. There are only stones, sand, the thin strand of the river, and tufts of desertlike vegetation. I follow the line of the river to the head of the valley, where high mountains rise still covered in darkness. I think for a moment of that time at the Mananava ravine where Denis and I stopped, as if on the threshold of a forbidden territory, listening for the high-pitched cries of the bo'sun birds.

There aren't any birds in the sky here, only clouds that rise from the sea in the north and rush toward the mountains, making their shadows run over the bottom of the valley.

I stand for a long time in the fierce wind on top of the cliff, looking for a way down. From where I am it is impossible; the rock face above the estuary is sheer. I clear a path for myself through the brush and go up to the top of the hill. The wind blowing through the vacoa leaves makes a wailing sound that heightens the isolated feeling of this place. Just before reaching the summit of the hill I find a way down: a landslide that has cleared a path to the valley.

Now I am walking in the Roseaux River valley without knowing where to go. Seen from here, the valley seems broad, bordered in the distance by black hills and high mountains. The north wind that enters by way of the river mouth brings the noise of the sea with it and raises little whirlwinds of sand like cinders on a horse track, which makes me think for an instant that people on horseback are coming. The silence is strange because of all the light.

On the other side of the Point Venus hills is the noisy life of Port Mathurin, the market, and the coming and going of canoes in Lascars Bay. Here, everything is silent, like a desert island. What am I going to find here? What awaits me?

I wander in the valley until dusk. I need to orient myself. I want to understand why I came here, what it was that troubled and alerted me. Using a twig, I draw a map of the valley on the dry, sandy riverbank. I draw the entrance to the cove, the course of the Roseaux River that goes up in an almost straight line to the south, then bends before becoming part of the gorge rushing down between the mountains. I don't need to compare it with the Corsair's map in my father's documents: I know I am at the site of the treasure.

Once again I feel drunken and dizzy. There is so much silence here, so much solitude! The only sound comes from the wind blowing in the rocks and brush, bringing with it the faraway sound of the sea on the reefs; this is a world uninhabited by men. The smoking clouds race across the dazzling sky and then disappear behind the hills. I can no longer keep the secret to myself! I want to shout at the top of my lungs so that I can be heard beyond the hills, farther even than this island, to the other side of the sea, as far as Forest Side, where I want my scream to go over the walls and into Laure's heart.

Did I really shout? I don't know. My life is already like one of those dreams in which desire and its fulfillment are one and the same. I run through the valley, leaping over the black rocks and streams, running quicker than I am able through the brush and among the tamarind trees. I don't know where I'm going. I run as if I'm falling through the air with the sound of the wind in my ears. Then I throw myself onto the gray ground. I fall onto the sharp stones without feeling any pain. I am breathless, my body bathed in sweat. I remain on the ground for a long time, my head turned toward the clouds that are still fleeing southward.

❀

Now I know where I am. I've found the place I have been looking for. After these months of wandering I feel at peace again, and my enthusiasm is renewed. In the days following my discovery of English Cove I prepared for my search. At Jeremie Biram in Douglas Street I bought the things I couldn't do without: a pickax and spade, rope, a storm lamp, sailcloth, soap, and food. I completed my explorer's kit with one of the big hats made from vacoa fibers that the Manafs, the blacks from the mountains, wear here. For the rest, I have decided that the few articles of clothing I have and my old horse blanket must suffice. I deposited the little bit of money I have left at Barclay's Bank, where the manager, an obliging Englishman with a wrinkled face, noted that I had come to Rodrigues on business and offered, as he was a representative of the Elisa Mallac postal company, to keep my mail for me.

When I had completed all my preparations I went, as I did each day at noon, to the Chinaman's to eat fish and rice. He knew I was leaving and he came to sit at my table after I'd finished eating. He didn't ask me any questions about my departure. Like most of the people I've met on Rodrigues he believes I am going to pan for gold in the mountain streams. I have taken care not to contradict these rumors. Some days ago as I was finishing my dinner in this very room, two Rodriguan men asked to speak to me. Straight off they opened a little skin pouch and poured onto the table a bit of black earth with shining particles in it. "Is this gold, sir?" From the lessons my father had given me, I immediately recognized the particles as copper pyrites, which have deceived so many prospectors and for that reason are called "fool's gold." The two men were looking at me so anxiously in the light of the oil lamp that I didn't want to disappoint them too cruelly: "No, it's not gold, but it does mean perhaps you are going to find some." I also advised them to get a bottle of aqua regia so that they wouldn't make any more mistakes. Half satisfied they left with their leather pouch. I think it's because of that incident that I acquired the reputation as a prospector.

After lunch I got onto the horse-drawn cart I had hired for the journey. The coachman, an jovial old black, loaded my trunk and the equipment I had bought. I sat down beside him and we departed through the empty Port Mathurin streets for English Cove. We went along Hitchens Street, passed by the Begue house, then up Barclay's Street to the governor's house. Now we're going west, passing the temple and the Depot and traveling across the Raffaut estate. Some black children run for a while after the cart, then give up and go back to swimming in the harbor. We cross the wooden bridge over the Lascars stream. Because of the sun I've pulled my big Manaf hat down over my head, and I can't help thinking how Laure would burst out laughing if she could see me in it, bumping along in this cart with the old black coachman shouting at the mule to make it move forward.

When we get to the top of Point Venus and are in front of the telegraph buildings, the coachman unloads my trunk and tools and the jute sacks containing my provisions. Then after having pocketed what I owed him, he goes off wishing me good luck as he drives away (the prospector legend persists), and I am alone with all my belongings at the edge of the cliff, in the silence of the howling wind, with the strange feeling of having landed on a desert island.

The sun is sinking toward the hills in the east and already its shadow stretches over the bottom of the Roseaux River valley, enlarging the trees and sharpening the points of the vacoa leaves. Once again I feel troubled and confused. I fear going down into the valley as if it were forbidden territory. I stand still on the edge of the cliff, looking out over the countryside I discovered the first time I was here.

The fierce wind makes up my mind for me. Halfway down the landslide there is a platform of stones on which I could take shelter from the night cold and the rain. I decide to make my first camp there and go down with the heavy trunk on my shoulder. Despite the late hour, the sun is still shining on the slope and I arrive on the platform bathed in sweat. I have to rest for quite a while before going back for the spade and pickax, the sacks of food, and the canvas that will be my tent.

The platform is like a balcony; it rests on big blocks of lava that have collected there and juts out over the void. It is certainly very old, for there are large vacoa trees growing on the platform whose roots push through the lava walls. In the distance, above the valley, I can see other identical platforms on the hillside. Who built these balconies? I think of sailors from long ago, American whale hunters coming here to cure their fish. And I think, too, of the Corsair's stay here, which I have come to discover. Perhaps it is he who built these posts, the better to observe the "masonry" in which he had decided to hide his treasure!

Again I feel dizzy and feverish. As I go up and down the slope getting my things, suddenly, on the valley floor, among the withered trees and the vacoa silhouettes, it seems to me that I see, coming from the sea, shadows walking in a line, carrying heavy sacks and pickaxes and going toward the dark hills in the east!

My heart races and sweat streams down my face. I have to lie down on the ground on top of the cliff and look at the yellow twilight sky in order to calm myself.

Night is falling quickly. I quickly finish setting up my bivouac before it is completely dark. On the dry riverbed I find some tree branches left behind from when the river flooded and some smaller pieces of wood for making a fire. I use the big branches to make a rough frame, over which I put the sail-cloth, which I then keep in place with a few heavy stones. When it is all done I am too tired to think of making a fire, and sit down on the platform to eat some ship's biscuits. Night has fallen suddenly, drowning the valley below me and obliterating the sea and the mountains. It is a cold night with a mineral smell and only the sounds of the wind blowing through the brush, the crackling of stones losing their heat, and, in the distance, the rumbling of the waves on the reefs.

Despite my fatigue and the cold, I am happy to be here, in the place I have dreamed about for so long without knowing whether it really existed. I tremble deep inside as I sit with wide-open eyes looking out into the night. Slowly the stars glide to the east and descend toward the invisible horizon. The violent winds shake the canvas behind me as if I were still on the ship. Tomorrow I will go to the valley floor and I will see the place where the shadows passed. Something or someone awaits me. This is why I have come here, have left Mam and Laure. I must be ready for what is going to appear in this valley at the end of the world. I fall asleep sitting in the entrance to my tent, with my back against a stone and my eyes open to the black sky.

I HAVE BEEN IN the valley for a long time. How many days, or months? I should have kept a calendar by cutting notches in a piece of wood, like Robinson Crusoe. I am as adrift in this lonely valley as I was on the vast ocean. Days follow nights, and every new day erases the one before it. So that something will remain to tell of the passing time, I make notes in the exercise books I bought from the Chinaman at Port Mathurin.

What else is there? The repetitive actions I make every day as I travel across the valley searching for landmarks. I get up before daybreak to benefit from the cool hours. At dawn the valley is extraordinarily beautiful: the blocks of lava and shale are rose-tinted, the shrubs and tamarinds and vacoas still black, numbed by the night cold. The wind hardly blows, and beyond the straight line of the coconut trees I can see the still sea, dark blue without any reflections, holding back its crashing waves. This is my favorite time, when everything is suspended as if waiting to begin. The sky with the first sea birds in it—gannets, cormorants, and frigates flying across English Cove to the islands in the north—is still pure and unsullied.

The birds are the only living creatures I have seen here since I arrived, apart from some land crabs who make their holes in the dunes at the estuary and the populations of minuscule sea crabs that run across the mud. When the birds fly over the valley again I know it's the end of the day. I feel as if I recognize each one of them and as if they know me, too: a ridiculous black ant crawling on the bottom of the valley.

Every morning I carry on with my search, using the plans I have made the day before. I measure the valley with the help of my theodolite, going from one landmark to the other, then coming back in a widening arc, so that no piece of earth escapes my perusal. Soon the sun is shining, sparkling on the pointed rocks and forming shadows. Under the midday sun the valley changes to a hard and hostile place, bristling with spikes and thorns. The sun is directly overhead and the heat increases despite the gusts of wind. My face feels like an open furnace and I stagger with eyes full of tears.

I have to stop and wait. I go to the river to drink a little water in my cupped hands, then sit in the shade of a tamarind tree with my back against the roots laid bare by the floods. Unmoving I wait, not thinking of anything while the sun turns around the tree and begins its descent to the black hills.

Sometimes I still think I can see those shadows, those fugitive silhouettes on top of the hills. I walk over the riverbed with burning eyes. But the shadows dissolve into their hiding places and I confuse them with the black trunks of the tamarind trees. This is the hour I fear most, when the silence and heat press down on my head and the wind is like a hot blade.

I rest in the shade of the old tamarind tree near the river. It was the first thing I saw when I woke high up on the platform. It seemed to me the true master of this valley, and as I went to it I thought of the letter about the treasure that spoke of a tamarind tree near the river's source. It is not very big, yet when I sit beneath it, sheltered by its branches, I feel profoundly at peace. I know it well now, its knotty trunk blackened by time,

sun, and drought and its twisted branches with their fine ser-
rated leaves so young and tender. On the ground around it are
long golden pods swollen with seeds. I come here every day
with my exercise book and pencils and, far from the torrid heat
that reigns in my tent, suck the bitter seeds while I think about
my new plans.

I am trying to situate the parallel lines and the five points
that served as landmarks on the Corsair's map. The points are
certainly the tops of the mountains that are at the entry to the
cove. In the evening, before night has fallen, I go to the river's
mouth, and when I see the mountain peaks still lit by the sun
I always have the feeling that something is going to appear.

I constantly draw the same lines on the paper: the bend in
the river that I know and then the rectilinear valley buried between the mountains. On each side above, the hills are basalt
fortresses.

❧

Today, as the sun was setting, I decided to go up to the east
side of the hill again to look for the "mooring ring" marks left
by the Corsair. If he was really here, and it seems more and
more obvious that he was, he must have left these marks on
the rocks on the cliff or on some other unchanging place. The
slope is more accessible on this side, but the higher I get the
farther away the summit is. What had seemed from afar to be
an unbroken line is in fact a series of steps, and this disorients
me. Soon I am so far from the other hillside that I can hardly
make out the white spot of my canvas shelter. The bottom of
the valley is a gray and green desert studded with black lumps
into which the riverbed disappears. At the entrance to the valley I can see the high cliff with Point Venus on it. How alone
I am here, even though people are nearby! Perhaps this is what

heightens my anxiety: I could die here and no one would ever know. An octopus fisherman might one day see the remains of my bivouac and come to investigate, or maybe it would just be swept away by water and wind and become part of the stones and burned trees.

I look carefully at the western hill facing me. Is it an illusion? I can see a capital M carved into the rock, a little above Point Venus. In the oblique dusk light it appears clearly, as if it has been pressed into the rock by a giant hand. Farther up, on a peak, there is a half-ruined stone tower that I had not seen when I set up my camp just below it.

I am tremendously excited by the discovery of these two landmarks, and I immediately rush down the hill and across the valley so that I can get there before nightfall. I splash through the cool water of the Roseaux River, then go up to the eastern hill by way of the landslide I used the first time.

When I get to the top of the slope I search in vain for the M: it has disappeared. The pieces of rock that form the legs of the M are no longer in place, and in the center there is a kind of plateau with tangled bushes that have been flattened by the wind. As I move forward, leaning into the wind gusts, I can hear the dislodged stones tumbling down. Between the euphorbia and the vacoas I see some brown forms slipping away. They are wild goats, perhaps escaped from a herd belonging to Manafs.

At last I am in front of the tower on top of the cliff, which hangs over the valley, already in shadow. How can I have missed it in all the time I've been here? It is made of large blocks of basalt that have been put together without mortar, and one side has crumbled. I can see the remains of a door or opening. I go into the ruin and squat down to protect myself from the wind. Through the opening I can see the sea. It stretches endlessly blue with a darker, more violent thread running through it to the horizon, where, shrouded in gray haze, it becomes one with the sky.

From the top of the cliff I can see over the sea as far as the Port Mathurin roadstead and up to the eastern point of the island. I realize then that this hastily built tower is only here to serve as a lookout for the arrival of enemies. Who built it? It can't have been the British Admiralty, who had nothing to fear from the sea as long as they controlled the India route. Besides, neither the English nor the French navy would have built something so precarious or so isolated. Pingré doesn't speak about this construction in the description of his 1761 voyage. Then I remember the first English camp at Point Venus, in 1810, on the site of the future observation post—that is, at the precise spot that I am on now. The Mauritius Almanac that I read in the Carnegie Library spoke of a little "battery" built inside the gorge to survey the sea. As night falls my mind works with a sort of nervous haste, as in those reveries leading up to sleep. I recite aloud for myself the sentences I read so often in the Unknown Corsair's letter, written in a long and sloping hand on a torn sheet of paper:

> *"For the first sign, find a pgt stone*
> *Take the 2nd V, go from South to North,*
> *it will look like the stern of a ship.*
> *And from the Eastern spring make an angle like an anchor ring*
> *The mark on the sand near the spring.*
> *For* |ᶜ| *pass to the left*
> *For there each of the mark BnShe*
> *There, rub against the pass, where you'll find what you think.*

Seek::**S**
Make x — 1 do m toward diagonal
the Commander's Summit."

At this moment, I am sitting in the ruins of the Commander's Summit as night fills the valley. I no longer feel fatigue, the blasts of cold wind, the solitude. I have just discovered the Unknown Corsair's first clue.

I N   T H E   D A Y S following my discovery of the Commander's
Summit, even though I had a fever that sometimes made
me delirious, I ran from one end of the valley to the other. I
remember now (although the memory comes and goes like a
dream) those boiling days under the April sun during the
windy season; it was like falling down a vertical tunnel. I can
still feel how each breath burned my painfully heavy chest.
From dawn to dusk I followed the sun's path through the
sky, from the solitary hills in the east to the mountains that
dominated the center of the island. I followed the sun, going
in a circular arc with the pickax over my shoulder and using
the theodolite to measure the irregularities of the ground, my
only landmarks. I saw the trees' shadows slowly lengthen over
the ground. The sun burned through my clothes and kept
burning me through the night, keeping me awake as it joined
with the cold coming from the earth. Some nights I was so
tired from walking that I slept where I was when night fell,
between two blocks of lava, awakened in the morning by thirst
and hunger.

One night I awake in the center of the valley and feel the sea
breeze. I can still feel the sting of the sun in my eyes and on my
skin. There is a black moon tonight, as my father used to say.

The sky is filled with stars, and as I ponder them I am full of fever and my obsession. I speak aloud, saying, "I can see the map, it is there, I can see it." The Unknown Corsair's map is nothing more than a drawing of the Southern Cross and its "followers," the "beauties of the night." I can see the lava stones shining over the vast surface of the valley. They are lit like stars in the dusty dark. I walk toward them with wide-open eyes; I can feel their scorching light on my face. Thirst, hunger, and loneliness whirl around inside me, gathering momentum. I hear a voice speaking with my father's inflections. It reassures me at first, then makes me shiver, for I realize it is I who am speaking. Near the large tamarind tree I sit on the ground to keep from falling. I am shivering uncontrollably; I am consumed by the cold coming from the earth and air.

How long did I stay like that? When I open my eyes again I first see the foliage of the tamarind tree above me and the glint of the sun through the leaves. I am lying between the roots. Beside me are a dark-faced child and a girl dressed in tatters like Manafs. The girl has a wet rag in her hands, which she is wringing above my lips.

The water runs into my mouth and onto my swollen tongue. Every time I swallow it hurts.

The child goes away and comes back again carrying a rag that has been dipped in the river. I drink again. Every drop revives my body and makes something else hurt, but it is good.

The girl speaks to the boy in a creole I can hardly understand. I am alone with the young Manaf. When I attempt to get up she helps me to a sitting position. I want to say something to her, but my tongue refuses to move. The sun is already high in the sky and I can feel the heat mounting in the valley. Beyond the shade of the old tamarind tree the landscape is dazzling, cruel. The idea of crossing this zone of light makes me feel nauseated.

The child comes back. He has a red-pepper cake in his hand, which he offers to me with such a ceremonial gesture that I want to laugh. I slowly chew the cake and red pepper soothes my inflamed mouth. I divide up what remains of the cake and offer it to them. They refuse it.

"Where do you live?" I ask.

I have not spoken in creole, but the young Manaf seems to have understood. She points up to the high mountains at the bottom of the valley. I think she says: "Up there."

She is a true Manaf, silent and wary. Since I sat up and started talking she has been moving back; she is ready to leave. The child has also moved back and is stealing looks at me.

Suddenly they go. I would like to call them, keep them with me for a while. They are the first humans I have seen in months. But what good would it do to call them? They walk away without haste, without turning back, jumping from stone to stone then disappearing into the thicket. I see them shortly afterward on the hill on the western side, like the baby goats. They disappear into the bottom of the valley. They have saved my life.

I stay under the tamarind tree until evening, hardly moving. Big black ants run tirelessly but in vain along the roots. Toward the end of the day I hear the cries of the sea birds flying over English Cove. The mosquitoes are dancing. Carefully, like an old man, I start across the valley and eventually get to my campsite. Tomorrow I will go to Port Mathurin and take the first boat out. It might even be the *Zeta.*

THEN COME THE days in Port Mathurin, far from English Cove, days spent in the hospital. The head doctor, Camal Boudou, says only, "You could have died of exposure." "Exposure" is a word I keep inside me. No other word could better describe what I felt that night, before the Manafs gave me something to drink. Still, I can't make up my mind to leave. It would mean I had failed so badly: the Boucan house, Laure, and our chance to live whole lives would all be lost.

So this morning, before dawn, I leave my Port Mathurin hotel and return to English Cove. I don't need a carriage this time: all my belongings stayed at my bivouac, folded in the canvas and held down by stones.

I have also decided to hire a man to help me with my search. At Port Mathurin someone has spoken to me about the Castel farm behind the Cable & Wireless buildings, where I would probably be able to find someone.

I arrive at English Cove just as the sun is rising. I can smell the sea, and in the morning coolness everything has been transformed and seems new to me. The sky above the hills in the east is a very soft pink and the sea shines like an emerald. In the dawn light the trees and the vacoas are unrecognizable shapes.

How can I have forgotten this beauty so quickly? The exultation I feel today is nothing like the fever that maddened me and made me run back and forth across the valley. Now I know what I have come for: I have to do this. The force that draws me is stronger than my will, a memory that began before I was born. For the first time in months, it feels as if Laure is near me, that the distance separating us doesn't matter.

I think of her imprisoned in the Forest Side house and I look at the dawn landscape in order to send this beauty and peace to her. I remember the game we sometimes played in the attic at Boucan, each of us at one end of the dark attic, an old issue of the *Illustrated London News* open in front of us, trying to send the other pictures or words by telepathy. Will Laure still be able to win this game as she always did? I send it all to her: the pure line of the hills standing out against the pink sky, the emerald sea, the wind, and the slow flight of the sea birds coming from Lascars Bay and flying toward the rising sun.

Toward noon, having climbed to Commander's Summit, in the ruined tower of Corsair's Lookout I spot the ravine. I couldn't have seen it from the valley because a mass of fallen earth blocks the entrance. From the lookout, in the bright light, I can clearly see the dark gash it makes on the side of the eastern hill.

I carefully fix it in my mind in relation to the trees in the valley. Then I go see the farmer near the telegraph buildings. His farm, or rather what I had seen of it as I passed it on the road from Port Mathurin, half buried in a hollow, is more a precarious shelter than an actual farm. As I get closer, a black, grunting mass gets up—a semiwild pig. Then it becomes a dog showing its teeth. I remember the lessons Denis gave me in the fields: one stick or stone is of no use; you have to have *two* stones, one for throwing and one for threatening. The dog moves back but guards the door of the house.

"Mr. Castel?"

A black man appears, bare-chested and wearing fisherman's trousers. He is big and strong, with a lined face. He pushes the dog aside and invites me in.

Inside it is dark and smoky. A table and two chairs are the only furniture. At the back of the room a woman in a faded dress is cooking. A fair-skinned little girl stands at her side.

Mr. Castel asks me to sit. He remains standing and listens to me politely while I explain what I want. He nods his head. He will come and help me occasionally, and his adoptive son, Fritz, will bring me something to eat every day. He doesn't ask any questions.

This afternoon I decide to continue my search more to the south, toward the top of the valley. I leave the shelter of the tamarind tree, where I have now set up camp, and walk up alongside the Roseaux River. The river winds along its sandy bed, forming loops and little islands; the thin ribbon of water is nothing more than the external part of an underground channel. As one gets higher up, the river becomes a stream running over a bed of black pebbles in the middle of the gorge. I am already very near the mountain's spur. The vegetation is even sparser here: thornbushes, acacias, and, as always, the vacoas with leaves like cutlass blades.

It is very quiet and I walk as softly as possible. At the bottom of the mountains the stream divides into several springs in the shale and lava ravines. Suddenly the sky blackens and it starts to rain. The drops are big and cold. In the distance, right at the bottom of the valley, I get a glimpse of the sea shrouded by the storm. From the shelter of a tamarind tree I watch the rain advance over the narrow valley.

Then I see her; it is the young girl who saved my life the other day when I was delirious with thirst and fatigue. She has a child's face but she is tall and slim; she is wearing a short skirt, as the Manaf women usually do, and a tattered shirt. Her hair is long and curly like an Indian's. She walks along the valley with a bent head because of the rain. She is coming toward my tree. I know that she has not yet seen me and I dread the moment when she does. Will she cry out in fear and run away? She walks soundlessly, with the supple movements of an animal. She stops to look toward the tamarind tree and then she sees me. Immediately her beautiful smooth face becomes anxious. She stands where she is, balancing on one leg and leaning on her long harpoon. Her wet clothes are sticking to her body and her long black hair makes the copper color of her skin more luminescent.

"Hello!"

I say this in order to break the tense silence. I take a step toward her. She doesn't move, just looks at me. The rain runs over her forehead, down her cheeks and through her hair. In her left hand she is holds a necklace of creepers with fish hanging from it.

"Have you been fishing?"

My voice echoes strangely. Does she understand what I'm saying? She walks up to the tamarind tree and sits on one of the roots, where she is sheltered from the rain. She keeps her face turned toward the mountain.

"Do you live on the mountain ?"

She nods her head. Then she says in her singsong voice: "Is it true you're looking for gold?"

I'm surprised, less by the question than by the way she speaks in almost unaccented French.

"Did someone tell you that? Yes, I'm looking for gold, it's true."

"Have you found any?"

I laugh. "No, I haven't found any yet."

"And do you really believe there is gold around here?"

Her question amuses me. "Why, don't you?"

She looks at me. Her face is smooth and fearless, like a child's. "Everyone is so poor here."

She turns her head again toward Mount Limon, which is hidden by the rain cloud. For a moment we watch the falling rain in silence. I look at her wet clothes, her slim legs, and her bare feet resting squarely on the ground.

"What is your name?"

I ask it almost in spite of myself, perhaps so that I can keep a bit of this strange young woman who is soon going to disappear into the mountain. She looks at me with her dark, deep eyes as if she is thinking of something else. At last she says, "My name is Ouma."

She gets up, takes the necklace of fish and her harpoon, and leaves, walking rapidly along the stream in the lessening rain. I see her supple figure leaping from stone to stone like a young goat; then she disappears into the thicket. It has all happened so quickly that I can hardly believe I didn't imagine this apparition, this young, wild, and beautiful girl who saved my life. I am intoxicated by the silence. The rain is more or less over and the sun is shining brightly in the blue sky. In the light the mountains appear higher, more inaccessible. I vainly scrutinize the slopes over by Mount Limon. The young girl has disappeared, merged into the walls of black stone. Where does she live, in which Manaf village? I think of her strange name and the way she made the two syllables echo; it is an Indian name, a name that disturbs me. Eventually I run down to the bottom of the valley, to my camp under the tamarind tree.

I end the day in the shade of the tree, studying my maps of the valley, and I mark with a red pencil the places where I'll have to make borings. When I go to mark them on the ground, I clearly see a sign not far from the second point that has been indelibly fixed on a stone: four regular holes bored in a square. I suddenly remember the formula in the Corsair's letter: "Seek ∷ S." My heart beats faster as I turn toward the east and see the shape of the Commander's Summit in the diagonal of the north-south axis.

Later that day I discover the first mooring-ring mark on the eastern slope, while trying to establish the east-west line across the Roseaux River at the end of the old marsh. Walking with the compass in my hand and my back to the sun, I cross an uneven gradient that I think is the bed of an old tributary. I reach the eastern cliff, which is very steep here, an almost vertical wall of basalt that has crumbled particularly badly. On a portion of it near the summit I see the mark.

"The anchor ring! The anchor ring!"

I repeat it under my breath. I look for a path to get to the top of the cliff. The stones slip away under my feet, but I pull myself up by grasping the bushes. When I am near the top I have difficulty finding the rock with the sign. Seen from below, the inverted equilateral triangle of the anchor rings used in the corsairs' era had been very clear. As I search for it, I can feel my pulse beating in my temples. Have I been the victim of an illusion? On all the rocks I can see marks forming an angle, which are simply the result of old breaks. I walk back and forth along the cliff edge several times, sliding on the loose earth.

In the valley below, young Fritz Castel, who has come to bring me my meal, has stopped at the bottom of the cliff and is looking at something. The direction he is looking in shows me my error. The sections of basalt all look the same and now I'm sure that the ones I used as reference points are higher up. I climb higher and get to a second plateau, which coincides with the end of the vegetation. There, in front of me, on a big black rock, shines the triangle of the anchor ring. It is magnificent, inscribed on the hard rock with a regularity that only someone with a chisel could achieve. Trembling, I approach the stone and touch it gently with my fingertips. The basalt is hot from the sun, soft and smooth like skin, and I can feel the cutting edge of the inverted triangle, like this:

Following an east-west line, I will certainly find the same mark on the other side of the valley. The other hillside is some distance away; even with a telescope I wouldn't be able to see the mark. The western hills are already in shadow, so I put the search for the other anchor ring off till tomorrow.

After young Fritz has left I go up the hill again. I stay there for a long time, sitting on the crumbly rock, watching night fall over English Cove. It feels as if for the first time I'm not seeing it with my own eyes, but through the eyes of the Unknown Corsair who came here a hundred and fifty years ago and drew the map of his secret on the gray river sand, then let it be washed away, leaving only the signs chiseled into the hard stone. I imagine how he held the chisel and mallet to etch the sign, and how the blows must have rung through the deserted valley. In the peaceful cove, with the roar of the sea and the rustle of the wind, I can hear the sound of the chisel on the stone and the answering echoes in the hills. That evening, lying on the ground between the roots of the old tamarind tree, wrapped in my blanket as I had been on the *Zeta* deck not so long ago, I dream of a new beginning.

❖

Today, as soon as dawn comes I make for the foot of the western slope. The pale light hardly shows up the black rocks, and in English Cove the sea is a translucent blue, lighter than the sky. The same as every morning, I can hear the cries of the sea birds crossing the bay, flocks of cormorants, gulls, and gannets screaming shrilly as they fly toward Lascars Bay. I have never been as happy to hear them as I am today. They seem to be greeting me as they fly over the cove, and I shout back a greeting too. Terns with enormous wings and swift petrels fly above me. They wheel near the cliff, then join the others over the sea. I envy their lightness and the rapidity with which they glide through the air, the fact that they are not earthbound. I see myself attached to the bottom of this sterile valley, taking days and months to see what the birds take in with one sweeping glance. I like to see them; in some small way it makes me feel part of the beauty of their flight and their freedom.

What need do they have of gold or riches? The wind is enough for them, the morning sky, the sea full of fish, and the rocks jutting from it their only shelter during storms.

I have let myself be guided by my intuition to the black cliff, whose jagged outline I had seen from the other cliff. The wind buffets me and makes me tipsy as I climb, clutching the brush. Suddenly the sun rises above the hills in the east and dazzling sparks scatter over the sea. It is magnificent.

I examine the cliff piece by piece. I can feel the warmth of the slowly rising sun. Toward noon I hear a shout: young Fritz is waiting for me at the bottom near my camp. I come down for a rest. My enthusiasm of the morning has evaporated. I feel tired and discouraged. In the shade of the tamarind tree I eat the white rice with Fritz. When he has finished he waits silently, staring into the distance, sitting impassively as the blacks from here typically do.

I think of Ouma, so wild and mobile. Will she ever come back? Every evening before sundown I walk along the Roseaux River to the dunes, looking for traces of her. Why? What would I say to her? Yet it seems to me that she is the only person who would understand what I seek here.

That night, when the stars appear one by one in the north of the sky, the Little Dipper, then Orion and Sirius, I suddenly realize my error: when I located the east-west line, starting from the anchor ring, I followed my compass in a northerly direction. But the Corsair, when he was drawing his map and marking his landmarks on the rocks, didn't use a compass. He must surely have used the North Star to guide him; this was his reference when he established the east-west perpendicular. Since the magnetized north and the stellar north are off by 7°36, it makes a difference of more than a hundred feet at the bottom of the cliff—that is, on the other section of rock that forms the first spur of the Commander's Summit.

I am so excited by this discovery that I can't bear to wait until the next day. Barefoot and carrying my storm lamp I walk to the cliff. The wind is blowing violently, bringing clouds of spindrift with it. In my shelter among the roots of the old tamarind tree I had not heard the storm, but here, out in the open, it blows me about, whistling in my ears and making the flame in the lamp waver.

I get to the bottom of the black cliff and start looking for a way up. The rocky face is so steep I have to hold the lamp between my teeth as I climb. I reach a crumbly ledge about halfway up and start looking for the sign on the side of the cliff. Lit by the lamp, the basalt wall looks strange and ghostly. Every indentation and crack makes me start. I go over the whole ledge until I get to the ravine that separates this section of the cliff from the peak overlooking the sea. The fierce cold wind and the roar of the nearby sea stun me and water streams over my face. I am exhausted, but just as I'm about to descend I see a large rock above me, and I know the sign has to be there. It is the only rock that can be seen from everywhere in the valley. To get to it I have to make a detour and follow a path of crumbling rock. When I am at last in front of the rock, with the lamp swinging between my teeth, I see the anchor ring. It is so clearly etched I would have been able to see it without the lamp. Its edges are as sharp under my fingers as if they had been chiseled yesterday. The black stone is cold and slippery. The triangle is drawn with its point going up, the inverse of the anchor ring in the west. It looks like a mysterious eye on the rock, looking out from the other side of time, eternally contemplating the other side of the valley without ever relaxing its gaze, day or night. A shiver goes through me from head to foot. I have found the way into a secret whose power is stronger and more lasting than my own. How far will it take me?

❧

After this I exist in a kind of waking dream in which the voices of Laure and Mam on the veranda at Boucan, the Unknown Corsair's message, and the shadowy picture of Ouma gliding between the bushes, heading to the top of the valley, are intermingled. Loneliness squeezes me tight. Apart from young Fritz Castel, I don't see anyone, and even he doesn't come as regularly as before. Yesterday (or the day before, I'm not sure which) he put the pot of rice on a stone in front of the camp, then left, scaling the western hill and not replying to my calls as if he were afraid of me.

At dawn, the same as every morning, I went to the estuary. I took my toiletry kit containing my razor, soap, and brush, as well as my laundry. Propping the mirror against a stone, I began to shave my beard, then cut my hair, which came down to my shoulders. The mirror reflected a thin sunburned face and eyes shining with fever. My nose, which is thin and aquiline, like those of all the L'Étang males, further accentuated my lost expression. I looked half-starved. Because I was following in his footsteps, I think I had begun to resemble the Unknown Corsair who had inhabited these parts.

I like being here at the estuary of the Roseaux River; the dunes start here and I can hear the slow breaths of the nearby sea as the wind swirls through the spurge and reeds, making the palms squeak. The dawn light is soft and calm and the water is smooth as a mirror. I have finished shaving, bathing, and washing, and am getting ready to go back to my camp, when I see Ouma. She is standing beside the river with her harpoon in her hand, watching me. There is no fear on her face; in fact, she has a mocking look in her eyes. I have often hoped to meet her here on the beach at low tide, when she comes back from fishing, yet her presence surprises me and I stand stock-still with my wet laundry dripping at my feet.

In the dawn light, standing close to the water, she is even more beautiful than before, with her calico dress and shirt soaked with sea water and her copper-colored, lava-colored face shining with salt. She stands with one leg forward and her weight on her left hip; in her right hand she holds the reed harpoon with its ebony point, while her left hand rests on her right shoulder. Her damp clothes fall in drapes around her and she looks like an antique statue. I stare at her without daring to speak, and I can't help thinking of the beautiful and mysterious Nada from the old magazines in the dimly lit attic of our childhood. I step forward and it immediately feels as if the spell has been broken. Ouma turns away and strides off along the river bank.

"Wait!" I shout without thinking as I run after her.

Ouma stops and looks at me. I can see the fear and suspicion in her eyes. I want to say something to keep her here, but I haven't spoken to anyone for so long that I can't find the words. I want to tell her how I've looked for her footprints on the beach in the evening before the tide comes in. But it is she who speaks first, saying to me in her mocking singsong voice, "Have you found any gold yet?"

I shake my head and she laughs. She squats down, a little way back from me, on top of a dune. In order to sit she brings her skirt between her legs with a movement that I have never seen any other woman make. She leans on the harpoon.

"And you, have you caught any fish?"

It is her turn to shake her head.

"Are you going back to your place in the mountains?"

She looks at the sky. "It's still too early. I'm going to try again, near the point."

"Can I come with you?"

She gets up without replying. Then she turns to me: "Come."

She walks off without waiting. She walks quickly in the sand with her animal gait, the long harpoon slung over her shoulder.

I throw the bundle of wet clothes onto the sand without worrying about the wind that could carry it off. I run behind Ouma. I catch up to her near the sea. She is walking along the unfurling waves with her eyes fixed on the ocean. The wind flattens the wet dress on her slim body. My bird companions are flying overhead in the still pearly morning sky, screeching and making their rattling sound.

"Do you like the sea birds?"

She stops and lifts her arms toward them. Her face shines in the sunlight. She says, "They are beautiful!"

The young girl leaps lithely and effortlessly over the sharp rocks at the end of the beach. She continues on to the point and stands in front of the deep, steely-blue water. When I reach her she makes a sign for me to stop. Her long silhouette leans over the sea; she has the harpoon raised and is searching the depths near the coral banks. She stays like that for a long moment, perfectly still, then suddenly she throws herself forward and disappears into the water. I watch the surface, looking for a bubble, ripple, or shadow. Then, when I don't know where else to look, she resurfaces several arm's lengths away from me, out of breath. She swims slowly up to me and throws a speared fish onto the rocks. She gets out of the water with the harpoon, her face pale with cold. She says, "There is another one over there."

It is my turn. I take the harpoon and dive with my clothes on into the sea. Under the water I can see the disturbed bottom and the sparkling, spangled seaweed. The waves breaking on the coral reef make a sharp, crunching sound. I swim under-water toward the coral with the harpoon tight against my body. I go round the coral twice without seeing anything. When I surface Ouma is bending toward me. She shouts: "There, over there!"

She dives. I see her black shape gliding near the bottom. The seawife comes out of her hiding place in a cloud of sand and swims slowly past me. Almost by itself the harpoon springs from my hand and nails the fish. Blood clouds the wa-ter around me. I surface immediately. Ouma is swimming be-side me and climbs onto the rocks. She seizes the harpoon, then kills the fish by clubbing it on the black rock. I am breath-less and stay seated, shivering with cold. Ouma pulls my arm.

"Come, you have to walk!"

Holding the two fish by the gills she is already jumping from rock to rock down to the beach. In the dunes she looks for a reed to tie the fishes onto. Then we walk together to the Roseaux River. At the spot where the river forms a deep pool the color of the sky she puts the fish on the bank and dives into the soft water, then sprays herself with water like an animal taking a bath. Standing at the edge of the river she says I look like a big wet bird and that makes her laugh. I also throw myself into the water, making a big splash, and then for a long while we laugh and throw water at each other. When we come out of the water I am surprised that I don't feel cold anymore. The sun is already high and the dunes near the estuary are burning hot. Our wet clothes stick to our skin. Ouma kneels on the sand and wrings out her skirt and shirt from top to bottom, lifting one sleeve first and then the other. Her copper-colored skin shines in the sun and water streams off her heavy hair and runs down her cheeks and neck. Gusts of wind ripple the river water. We don't speak anymore. Standing beside the river in the bright sunlight, listening to the sad sound of the wind in the reeds and the noise of the sea, it feels as if we are the only people left on earth, the last inhabitants perhaps, come from nowhere, brought together by a chance shipwreck.

I never imagined this could happen to me, that I would feel something like this. A force has been born in me that spreads through my body, filling me with desire. We sit for a long time on the sand waiting for our clothes to dry. Ouma doesn't move either, squatting on her heels the way Manafs do so well, with her long arms folded around her legs and her face turned to the sea. The sun shines on her tangled hair: I can see her pure profile, her straight forehead, and the ridge of her nose and lips. Her clothes billow in the wind. It seems to me that nothing else has any importance.

Ouma decides to leave first. She suddenly gets up in one movement and gathers her fish together. Then, squatting on the riverbank, she prepares them in a way I have never seen before. With the tip of the harpoon she cleaves their stomachs and guts them. She washes their insides with sand, then rinses them in the river water. She throws the offal some distance away to the waiting army of crabs.

She has done all this quickly and silently. Then she cleans away whatever traces remain on the riverbank with water. When I ask her why she does this she replies, "We Manafs, we're maroons."

Further on I retrieve my almost dry laundry, which is covered with white sand. I walk behind her to my camp. When she gets there she puts the fish I harpooned on a flat stone and says, "It's yours."

I protest and try to give it back to her, but she says, "You are hungry. I'll make you something to eat."

She quickly gathers some dry branches. With some green reeds she makes a kind of grid that she lays on top of them. I offer her my tinderbox but she shakes her head. She prepares some dry lichen and, squatting with her back to the wind, repeatedly strikes two flintstones together very quickly until the heated stones rain sparks. The lichen starts to smoke. Ouma takes it carefully in her hands and gently blows on it. When the flame springs up she puts the lichen under the dry branches and soon the fire is crackling. Ouma stands up. Her face is lit with childlike joy. The fish is cooking on the green reed grid and there is an appetizing smell already. Ouma is right, I'm dying of hunger.

When the fish is cooked Ouma puts the grid on the ground. By turns, burning our fingers, we pull off mouthfuls of the flesh. I am sure I will never eat anything better than this fish grilled without salt on a grid of green reeds.

When we have finished eating Ouma gets up. She carefully puts out the fire by covering it with black sand. Then she takes the other fish, which she had covered with earth to keep it from the sun. Without saying a word or looking at me she leaves. The wind shows the shape of her body in her clothes faded by sea and sun. The sun is shining on her face, but her eyes are two black spots. I understand why she has not spoken. I understand, too, that I must stay where I am, that this is part of her game, the game that she is playing with me.

Supple and fleet like an animal she slips between the bushes and jumps from rock to rock at the bottom of the valley. Standing beside the old tamarind tree I see her for one instant more, climbing the side of hill like a wild goat. She neither stops nor looks back. She walks toward the mountain, toward Mount Lubin, and disappears into the shadow covering the western slopes. I listen to the beating of my heart and my mind moves very slowly. The loneliness returns to English Cove, but it is more frightening now. Seated near my camp I face the setting sun and watch the advancing shadows.

❁

The days that follow pull me still further into my dreamlike existence. I find more of what I am looking for every day, and its force fills me with happiness. From sunrise till nightfall I walk across the valley, looking for the landmarks, the signs. I am intoxicated by the dazzling light that precedes the winter rains, the cries of the sea birds, and the gusts of wind coming from the northwest.

Sometimes I see a stealthy shadow flitting between the basalt blocks midway up the slope; it is only a quick glimpse and I am never quite sure of having really seen anything. Ouma, come down from her mountain, watches me from behind a

rock or from the vacoa thickets. She is occasionally accompanied by a mute young boy of extraordinary beauty who she
says is her half-brother. He stays beside her without daring to
come closer, looking wild and curious at the same time. His
name is Sri; Ouma says it is a nickname given him by his
mother because he has been specially sent by God.

Ouma brings me strange food to eat wrapped in margosa
leaves: rice cakes and dried octopus, and manioc and pepper
cakes. She puts the food on a flat stone in front of my camp
like an offering. When I tell her about my discoveries she
laughs. I have marked the signs I have found during the course
of the days in an exercise book. She likes me to read it aloud to
her: stones marked with a heart, two points, and a crescent-
shaped moon. Stone marked with the letter M; stone marked
with a cross. A snake's head, a woman's head, and three chiseled points forming a triangle. Rock marked with a chair or a
Z reminiscent of the Corsair's message. Truncated rock. Rock
sculpted into a roof. Stone decorated with a big circle. Stone
whose shadow forms a dog. Stone marked with an S and two
points. Stone marked with a 'Turkish dog" (a creeping dog
with no paws). Rocks with a line of chiseled points going
south-southwest. Broken and burned rock.

Ouma also wants to see the signs that I've brought back
with me: strangely formed lava, obsidian, and fossils. She takes
them in her hands and looks carefully at them as if they were
magic. Sometimes she brings me strange objects she has
found. One day she hands me an iron-colored stone that is
smooth and heavy. It's a meteorite, and the feel of this body,
fallen from the sky perhaps thousands of years ago, makes me
shiver as if I had touched something supernatural.

Ouma comes almost every evening now to English Cove.
She waits beneath a tree at the top of the valley while I measure
distances and bore holes, because she is afraid the noise might

bring down the people who live in the vicinity. Several times young Fritz and farmer Begue have come to see me and have helped me dig the holes near the estuary. Ouma does not appear on these days but I know she is somewhere nearby, hidden behind some trees or in a hollow where she blends with her surroundings.

With Fritz's help I set out marker rods. They are reeds I have specially prepared for this and they have to be placed every hundred feet so that they will make straight lines. I am working toward the top of the valley, using the signs I have identified: chiseled stones, marked angles, a heap of pebbles making a triangle, etc. I use the theodolite to make sure the lines are straight, so that they will conform with the original design (the Corsair's grid). The sun beats down, making the black stones sparkle. From time to time I shout to young Fritz to come and give me a new rod. If I squint I can see all the lines coming together on the riverbed, as well as junctions where I will be able to bore my holes.

Later with Fritz I dig some holes near the western hill at the foot of Commander's Summit. The ground is hard and dry and our picks hit basalt rock at once. Every time I begin a new hole I am very impatient. Are we at last going to find a sign or trace of the Corsair's passage, perhaps the beginning of the "masonry"?

One morning while Fritz and I are digging at the foot of the hill in the sandy ground, I suddenly feel something soft under my pick that, in my maddened state, I at first take to be the skull of some sailor buried there. The object rolls over the sand and suddenly shows it legs and claws! It is a big land crab that I have abruptly awakened. Young Fritz, quicker than I, kills it with a blow from the spade. Full of joy, he interrupts his work to go and put water in the pot, and having lit the fire he prepares a court-bouillon.

❧

In the evening when the light is fading and the valley is still and calm, I know that Ouma is not far. I can feel her looking at me from the top of the hills. Sometimes I call to her, and then listen to the echo repeating her name right to the bottom of the valley: "Ou-ma-a!"

She is far away and close by at the same time, like a bird in flight that one is unaware of until it briefly blocks the sun. Even when I don't see her for a long time, because of Fritz Castel or Begue (for no Manaf woman ever shows herself to the inhabitants of the coast), I have a pleasant feeling that she is looking at the valley and that her eyes are on me.

Perhaps all this belongs to her and her people and she is the true mistress of the valley. Is she the only one who believes in the treasure that I am looking for? Sometimes, when the day has not yet really begun, I think I see her walking through the lava blocks accompanied by Sri, bending to examine the stones as if she were following an invisible track. Or she is walking on the beach where the sea is breaking, going along the river to the estuary. She is standing by the clear water, looking toward the horizon beyond the coral reef. I come up to her and also look at the sea. Her face is strained, almost sad.

"What are you thinking of, Ouma?"

She starts, then turns to face me, her eyes full of sadness. She says, "I'm not thinking of anything. I only think of impossible things."

"What is impossible?"

But she doesn't reply.

The day breaks then, putting everything into relief. Ouma stands unmoving in the cold wind that blows away the tips of the waves running over her feet. She shakes her head as if she wants to chase away a disturbing thought, then she takes me by the hand and draws me toward the sea. "Come, we are going to fish for octopus."

She takes the long harpoon that she has stuck into the dune in the middle of the other reeds. We go east where the coast is still in shadow. The Roseaux River curves behind the dunes and reappears very near the black cliff. Tufts of reeds grow right up to the edge of the sea. As we approach them, clouds of minuscule silver birds fly up cheeping, *wiiit! wiiit!*

"We'll find octopus here, the water is warmer."

She walks toward the reeds, then suddenly she takes off her skirt and shirt. Her body shines in the sunlight, long and slim. She leaps over the rocks to the sea and disappears under the water. Her arms and the harpoon surface for a moment, then there is only the sea and tiny waves. Soon the water parts, and Ouma slides out as quickly as she went in. She comes to where I am, unhooks the octopus dripping ink and turns it inside out. She looks at me. There is no shame in her, she looks wild and beautiful.

"Come!"

I don't hesitate. I undress too and dive into the cold water. Suddenly I have the same feeling I had long ago at Tamarin when Denis and I used to swim naked through the waves: a feeling of happiness and tremendous freedom. I swim underwater near the bottom with my eyes open. I can see Ouma close to the rocks, burrowing in the craggy parts with the harpoon as a cloud of ink comes out. We swim together to the surface. Ouma throws the second octopus onto the beach after turning it inside out. She holds the harpoon out to me. The smile on her face is brilliant, her breathing slightly raspy. I also dive near the rocks. I miss the first octopus but get the second on the sandy bed the moment it jumps backward, spewing ink.

We swim together in the clear lagoon water. When we are very near the reef Ouma dives in front of me and disappears so quickly that I can't follow her. She appears a moment later with a seawife at the end of her harpoon. Then she detaches the still-living fish and throws it toward the bank. She gestures to me not to say anything. She takes my hand and together we let ourselves sink into the water. Then I see the threatening shadow coming and going in front of us: a shark. It turns two or three times, then swims off. With no more breath left in our lungs we surface. I swim to the bank while Ouma dives again. When I get to the beach I see she has retrieved the fish. She runs beside me in the white sand. Her body sparkles in the sun like basalt. With precise, rapid movements, she picks up the octopuses and the seawife and buries them in the sand near the dunes.

"Come. We are going to dry ourselves."

I am lying on the sand. On her knees beside me she takes dry sand in her hands and powders my body from top to bottom.

"Now you put sand over me too."

I take the fine sand in my hands and let it trickle over her shoulders, back, and chest. Now we look like two clowns full of flour, which makes us laugh.

"When the sand falls off we will be dry," Ouma says. Dressed in white sand we sit on the dune near the reeds. The only sounds are the wind in the reeds and the crashing of the rising sea. We are alone except for the crabs who come out of their holes one after the other, waving their claws. In the sky the sun is at its zenith, burning in the center of our solitude.

I look at the sand drying on Ouma's shoulders and back and falling off in little streams, uncovering her glistening skin. I am filled with such fierce desire that it burns me like the sun. When I put my lips on Ouma's skin she trembles but does not move away. Her long arms are folded around her legs and she rests her head on her knees, looking somewhere else. My lips trail along her neck and over her soft shiny skin, from which the sand is falling like silver rain. I start to shiver and Ouma lifts her head and looks anxiously at me. "Are you cold?"

"Yes. . . No." I'm not quite sure what is happening to me. I am shaking badly and finding it hard to breathe.

"What's the matter?"

Suddenly Ouma gets up. She quickly gets dressed. She helps me put on my clothes as if I were sick.

"Come and rest in the shade, come!"

Is it fever or fatigue? My head is spinning. With difficulty I follow Ouma through the reeds. Her body is very erect as she walks, holding the fish by its gills while the octopuses hang from the end of her harpoon like flags.

When we get to my camp I lie down under the tent and close my eyes. Ouma stays outside. She prepares the fire to cook the fish. She also cooks the flat bread that she brought with her this morning. When the meal is ready she brings it into the tent and watches me eat without having any herself. The meat of the grilled fish is exquisite. I eat greedily with my fingers and drink the fresh water that Ouma has gotten from far upstream. After that I feel better. Wrapped in my blanket in spite of the heat I watch Ouma's profile looking into the distance, as if she is keeping watch. Later it starts to rain, finely at first, then harder with big drops. The wind shakes the canvas above us and makes the branches of the tamarind tree squeak.

When daylight starts to fade the girl speaks to me about herself, her childhood. She speaks hesitantly in her singsong voice, and there are long pauses during which her words mingle with the noise of the wind and rain on the tent.

"My father was Manaf, a Rodriguan from the high mountains. But he left here to be a sailor on a British India boat, a big boat going to Calcutta. He met my mother in India, married her, and brought her back here because her family was against the marriage. He was older than she was, and he died from fever on a voyage. When I was eight years old my mother took me to Mauritius, to the nuns at Ferney. She didn't have enough money to raise me herself. I also think she wanted to remarry and thought I would be an embarrassment. . . At the convent I liked the mother superior very much, and she liked me, too. When she had to return to France, as my mother had abandoned me she took me with her. But when I was thirteen I got sick with tuberculosis and everybody thought I was going to die . . . Then my mother wrote from Mauritius to say she wanted me to come back and live with her. In the beginning I didn't want to, I cried and I thought I was crying because I didn't want to leave the mother superior, but I was really crying because I was fearful of going back to my mother and the poverty on the island and in the mountains. The mother superior cried, too, because she liked me very much and had hoped I would also become a nun, and as my mother was not Christian and had kept her Indian religion, the mother superior knew I was going to be turned away from the religious life. All the same I had to go. I traveled alone on the long voyage through the Suez Canal and across the Red Sea. When I got to Mauritius my mother was waiting, wrapped in her veils, but I didn't remember her and I was surprised to see that she was so small. A little boy was at her side and she told me he was Sri, the one specially sent by God. . ."

She stops talking. It is nearly night. Outside the valley is already in shadow. The rain has stopped but we can still hear water dropping on the tent when the wind blows through the branches of the old tamarind tree.

"It was difficult in the beginning for me to live here because I didn't know anything about the Manaf way of life. I didn't know how to do anything, I couldn't run or fish or make a fire, I didn't even know how to swim. And I couldn't speak because no one spoke French, even my mother only spoke Bhojpuri and creole. It was terrible, I was fourteen years old yet I was like a little child. In the beginning the people made fun of me, they said my mother should have left me with the bourgeoisie. I would have liked to run away but I didn't know where to go. I couldn't go back to France because I was a Manaf and nobody would have wanted me. Also, I liked my little brother Sri very much, he was so sweet, so innocent, I think my mother was right to say he was a messenger from God. Then I began to learn all that I didn't know. I learned to run barefoot on the rocks, to catch a kid while it was running, to make a fire, and to swim and dive for fish. I learned how to be a Manaf, to live like the maroons by hiding in the mountains. But I also liked being here with them because they never lie and they never hurt anyone. The people who live on the coast at Port Mathurin are the same as those in Mauritius, they lie and deceive and that is why we stay hidden in the mountains. . ."

Now it is night. The cold has come into the valley. We are lying against each other with our legs intertwined. I can feel the warmth of Ouma's body on my body. Again it is if we are the only living beings on earth. English Cove is lost, it drifts into the background on the cold sea wind.

I'm not trembling anymore and I don't feel any fear or haste. Ouma, too, has forgotten that she has to flee and hide all the time. As earlier in the reeds, she takes off her clothes, then helps me undress. Her smooth warm body is still covered with sand in places. She laughs as she brushes the remaining sand from my back and chest. Then, without my knowing how, we are inside each other. Her head is thrown back and I can hear her breath and feel her heartbeat; her heat is inside me, infinite and hotter than all those scorching days on the sea and in the valley. How we glide, how we fly through the night sky in the middle of the stars, silently, without thought, listening to our breathing, which has become one, like the unified breath of sleepers. Afterward we remain pressed against each other so as not to feel the cold from the stones.

❀

I have at last found the ravine where there was once a spring. It's the one I saw when I first arrived at English Cove, but I thought it was too far from the riverbed to figure on the Corsair's map.

The more rods I put in, forming straight lines between the first landmarks, the farther east I am led. One morning, walking at the bottom of English Cove near the drawing of the east anchor ring, I decide to search along the line that goes from the anchor ring to the stone with four points that I found on the first spur of the east cliff, which was designated "Seek :: S."

Having the ends of reeds placed at irregular intervals to follow, it takes me a long time to climb from the bottom of the valley. I reach the summit of the east cliff a little before noon, having gone over and staked out more than a thousand feet. As I get to the top of the cliff I see, simultaneously, the break in the ravine and the stone that points to it. The stone is a block of basalt about six feet high, and it has been planted in the crumbly ground in such a way that it must be visible from the bottom of the valley where the old estuary is. It is the only one of its kind, fallen from the basalt overhang at the top of the cliff. I am certain that it has been carried here by men, perhaps rolled over logs and then straightened like the druid rocks. The notches for the ropes can still be clearly seen on its sides. However, my eyes are immediately drawn to an indentation on top of the rock, at its center: a straight groove, about a finger thick and about six thumbs long, has been hollowed into the stone with a chisel. This groove is in the exact place for the continuation of the line that I have followed from the anchor ring in the west, and points toward the ravine opening.

I go closer with a pounding heart and see the ravine for the first time. It is an eroded corridor that crosses the breadth of the cliff, getting narrower toward English Cove. Its entrance is obstructed by a mass of fallen stones, and because of them I have never thought to explore it before. Seen from the valley the entrance to the ravine looks like all the other rockfalls from the cliff. And from the top of the east hill it resembles a mass of collapsed earth without any depth.

There is only one path that can take me to it, and that is the line I have constructed, which starts at the anchor ring in the east, crosses the Roseaux riverbed at an angle of 95 degrees (the exact intersection of the north-south line), passes through the center of the stone marked with four points (the point S in the Corsair's document), and then goes to the basalt block, where it joins with the groove cut by the Corsair's chisel.

I am so excited by this discovery that I have to sit down in order to calm myself. The cold wind quickly brings me back to my senses and I hastily climb down to the bottom of the ravine. I find myself in a kind of open pit shaped like a horseshoe, about twenty-five feet wide and a hundred feet long, with one end leading down to the earth mass that blocks the entrance.

I am absolutely sure that I will find the key to the mystery here. The vault, the sailor's chest that was usually fixed to the ship's prow, in which the Unknown Corsair locked his fabulous riches to keep them safe from the English and the cupidity of his own men, must be buried somewhere here. What better hiding place could he have found than this natural break in the cliff wall, invisible from the sea and the valley, and locked with a natural bolt fashioned from both landslide and alluvium from the mountain stream? I am too impatient to wait for help. I return to my camp and come back with everything I'll need: pick, spade, the long iron sounding rod, a rope, and some drinking water. I continue until evening without stopping, breaking and boring at the bottom of the ravine at the spot that I believe corresponds with the groove in the basalt block.

Toward the end of the day when the bottom of the ravine is darkening, the drill enters the dirt at an angle that lays bare a hiding place half filled with earth. Moreover, this earth is of a lighter color—proof, according to me, that it has been put there to seal the underground cave.

Using my hands to pull away the pieces of basalt I enlarge the opening. My heart pounds in my head and my clothes are soaked with sweat. Once the hole is bigger it reveals an old cavity fortified by means of dry stones placed in a circular arc. Soon it is big enough for me to stand up in. There is not enough room for me to maneuver the pick and I have to dig with my hands, moving the blocks of stone by leaning on the drillbit and using it as a lever. Then metal echoes on stone. I can't go any farther. I've reached the bottom. The hiding place is empty.

❧

Night has almost fallen. The empty sky above the ravine is slowly darkening. But the air is so warm it seems as if the sun is still burning down on the stone walls, on my face, on my hands and inside me. Sitting at the bottom of the ravine in front of the empty hiding place I drink all the water I have left in my water bottle, but it is warm and tasteless and doesn't quench my thirst.

It feels as if I am coming out a dream, and for the first time in a long while I think of Laure. What would she think of me if she could see me like this, covered with dust, sitting at the bottom of this trench with hands bloody from digging? She would look at me with her dark piercing eyes and I would feel ashamed. I am too tired now to move, think, or even feel. I am hungry for the night, filled with desire for it, and I lie down where I am, my head leaning against the black stones that I have pulled from the ground at the bottom of the ravine. Above me, the sky between the high stone walls is black. I look at the stars: fragments of broken constellations whose names I no longer know.

❊

When I emerge from the ravine in the morning I see Ouma. She is sitting under a tree near the camp waiting for me. Sri sits motionlessly beside her, watching me approach.

I come up to the girl and sit down next to her. In the shadow her face is dark but her eyes are shining with great force. She says, "There isn't any more water in the ravine. The fountain has dried up." In the creole way, she says "fountain" for "spring." She says it kindly, as if it were water I was looking for in the ravine.

The morning light is shining on the stones and the leaves of the trees. Ouma fills the pot with water from the river and prepares the flour porridge that Indian women make, *kir.* When it is ready she gives it to me on an enamel plate. She herself eats with her fingers from the pot.

In her calm singsong voice she speaks again of her childhood in France, in the convent, and of her life here when she came back with her mother to live with the Manafs. I like the way she tells me this. I try to imagine her the day she came ashore from the big steamship, wearing her black uniform, dazzled by the bright sunlight.

I also tell her about my childhood at Boucan, about Laure and the lessons with Mam on the veranda in the evening and my adventures with Denis. When I tell her about our trip to Morne in the pirogue her eyes shine.

"I, too, would like to go to sea." She gets up and looks toward the lagoon. "There are many islands on the other side, where the sea birds live. Take me there to fish."

I like it when her eyes shine like that. We have decided we'll go to the islands, to Gannet Island, to Baladirou, and perhaps even as far south as Gombrani. I'll rent a pirogue in Port Mathurin.

❊

For two days and nights the wind blows fiercely. I stay curled up under my tent, eating salted biscuits and going out only when necessary. On the morning of the third day the wind dies down. The sky is radiant blue and there aren't any clouds. I find Ouma standing on the beach as if she hasn't moved since I last saw her. When she sees me she says, "I hope the fisherman will bring the pirogue today."

An hour later it's there. Taking some water and a box of biscuits with us we board. Ouma stands in the prow with her harpoon in her hand, looking at the surface of the lagoon.

We let the fisherman off at Lascars Bay and I promise to give him back the pirogue the following day. The sail is taut in the east wind as we glide away. Rodrigues's high mountains rise up behind us, still pale in the early morning light. Ouma's face shines with happiness. She shows me Limon, Piton, and

Bilactère. When we pass through the channel the swell makes the pirogue pitch and we are enveloped in spray. But farther on we are once again in the lagoon, sheltered by the reefs. Yet the water here is dark, pierced through with mysterious reflections.

An island appears in front of us: Gannet Island. Before even being able to see them, we can hear the din of the sea birds. The sound is a continuous screech that fills sky and sea. The birds have seen us and are flying above the pirogue. Terns, albatrosses, black frigates, and giant gannets scream as they wheel around us.

The island is no more than fifty yards away to starboard. There is a ribbon of sand near the lagoon, and toward the open sea big rocks on which the waves break. Ouma comes to stand near me at the rudder, saying in a low voice next to my ear, "It's beautiful. . ."

I have never ever seen so many birds at one time. There are thousands of them on the rocks, which are white with guano; they dance around, take flight, then land again, and the sound of their wings is like the droning of the sea. Waves break on the reef and cover the rocks with dazzling waterfalls, but the gannets are not afraid. They spread their mighty wings and lift into the wind above the water until it recedes, then alight again on the rocks.

A screeching flock flies above us in tight formation. The birds wheel around the pirogue, darkening the sky, flying against the wind with their huge wings outstretched and their cruel eyes turned toward the strangers they hate. They become more and more numerous and their strident screams deafen us. Then some of them attack us, pecking at us from behind, and we have to get away from them. Ouma is frightened. She presses herself against me and blocks her ears with her hands. "Let's get away from here! Let's get away from here!"

I put the tiller to starboard and the sail creaks as it takes the wind. The gannets have understood. They move away, but continue to watch us as they wheel. On the island rocks the bird population continues to leap above the cascades of spray.

Ouma and I have not yet recovered from our scare. We race away in the wind, but for a long time after leaving the island we still hear the shrill cries of the birds and the beating of their wings. About a mile from Gannet Island we find another island on the barrier reef. On the northern side the waves crash onto the rocks with a noise like thunder. There are almost no birds here except for some terns gliding above the beach.

As soon as we land Ouma takes off her clothes and dives into the water. I see her dark body shining under the surface, then she disappears. She comes up several times to breathe, holding her harpoon straight up toward the sky.

Then I, too, undress and dive in. I swim with eyes open near the bottom. There are thousands of fish in the coral whose names I don't even know: silver ones, and yellow-and-red zebra-striped ones. The water is very soft and I glide effortlessly near the coral. I look for Ouma but can't see her.

When I get back to the shore I stretch out on the sand and listen to the sound of the waves behind me. The terns float in the wind. There are even some gannets come from their island to look at me and screech.

A long time afterward, when the white sand on my body has already dried, Ouma emerges from the water in front of me. Her body gleams in the sunlight like black metal. She wears a seaweed belt around her waist to which she has attached her prey: a *dameberi*, a *capitaine*, and two catfish. She sticks the harpoon into the sand with the tip pointing up, then takes off her belt and puts the fish in a hole in the sand that she covers with wet seaweed. Then she sits down and powders her body with sand.

I can hear her rasping, tired breathing. The sand shines on her dark skin like gold dust. We don't speak. We look at the water in the lagoon and listen to the mighty sound of the sea behind us. It's as if we've been here for days and have forgotten everything we ever knew. In the distance Rodrigues's high mountains slowly change color; the coves are already in shadow. It's high tide now. The lagoon is full and smooth, deep blue. The pirogue's stern barely touches the beach. With its curved prow it looks like a huge sea bird.

❀

Later, when the sun is no longer so high, we eat. Ouma gets up and a fine rain of sand spills off her body. She gathers together some dry seaweed and bits and pieces of wood left by the tide. I use my tinderbox to light the twigs. As the flame springs up it illuminates the wild joy on her face and I draw closer to her. She makes a grid with some damp twigs, then prepares the fish. When she is ready she douses the flame with a handful of sand and puts the grid on the glowing wood. The smell of the grilling fish fills us with delight and soon we are burning our fingers in our haste to get at the meat.

Some sea birds have been attracted by the waste. They fly in big circles against the sun and then land on the beach. Before eating they look at us with their heads cocked to one side.

"They won't harm us, they know us now."

The gannets do not land on the beach. They dive for the scraps and fly up with them in a cloud of sand. Even some crabs come out of their holes, looking fierce and timid at the same time.

"There's quite a crowd here!" Ouma laughs.

When we have finished eating Ouma hangs our clothes on the harpoon and we go to sleep on the hot sand, in the shadow of her improvised umbrella. We bury ourselves in the sand next to each other. Ouma falls asleep like that as I look at her face with its closed eyes and beautiful smooth forehead, on which wisps of hair move in the wind. When she breathes the sand slides off her chest, making her shoulder shine in the light like a stone. I stroke her skin with my fingertips. She doesn't stir. She breathes slowly with her head resting on her folded arms while the wind blows the sand on her long body into tiny streams. The sky in front of me is empty and Rodrigues is hazily mirrored in the lagoon. Sea birds fly above us and some walk on the beach a few steps away from us. They aren't afraid of us any more, they have made friends with us.

I think that this day, like the sea, will never end.

❊

Yet evening comes and I am walking on the beach surrounded by anxiously screeching birds. It is too late to think of going back to Rodrigues. The tide has gone out, the coral platforms are exposed, and we risk running aground or damaging the pirogue. Ouma joins me at the island's point. We have gotten dressed again because of the cool sea wind. The sea birds fly with us, landing on rocks in front of us and uttering strange cries. The sea is open here, unfettered. We watch the waves unfurling at the end of their journey.

When I sit down beside Ouma she puts her arms around me and rests her head on my shoulder. Her scent and her warmth are all around me. The twilight wind comes, already bringing darkness with it. Ouma shivers. She is disturbed by the wind.

It alarms the birds, too, making them leave their resting places and fly high into the sky, screeching at the last rays of sun above the sea.

Night comes quickly. Already the horizon is fading and the spray has no more shine to it. We walk against the wind to the other side of the island. Ouma makes us a bed for the night by laying out dried seaweed on the dune far up the beach. We wrap our clothes around us to protect us from the damp. The birds have stopped their panicked flight. They have settled on the beach not far from us and in the darkness we can hear the clicking of their beaks and their noisy chattering. Pressed close to Ouma I breathe in the smell of her body and her hair and taste the salt on her skin and lips.

Her breathing slows and I lie motionless with my eyes open onto the night, listening to the sound of the waves rising behind us, coming closer and closer. There are hundreds of stars in the sky and they are as beautiful as when I slept on the *Zeta's* deck. In front of me, near the dark patches of the mountains of Rodrigues, are Orion and the "beauties of the night," and right at the top, near the Milky Way, I search, as once I used to, for the twinkling spots of the Pleiades. I try to find Pleione, the seventh star, and Alcor at the end of Big Dipper. Lower down in the sky, to the left, I recognize the Southern Cross, and then the great ship Argo slowly appears as if it is really gliding over a black sea. I would like to be reassured by Ouma's voice, but I don't dare wake her up. Her chest moves gently against me and her breath becomes one with the rhythmic sound of the sea. After the long, light-filled day, the deep slow night penetrates and transforms us. We have come here to this entrance to the high seas to experience, far from other people, this day and night among the birds.

Did we really sleep? I don't know. I lay still for such a long time, feeling the wind above me and hearing the terrific clamor of the waves breaking on the coral shelf. It seemed as if I watched the stars slowly gyrating until dawn.

In the morning Ouma is pressed into the hollow of my body; she sleeps on in spite of the sun shining on her eyelids. Sand, damp with dew, sticks to her dark skin, trickles in little streams along her neck, and is all over her clothes. The lagoon water in front of me is green and the birds have left the beach; they have started their day, and with wings spread in the wind they look down with piercing eyes, searching the sea. The Rodrigues mountains, Piton, Bilactère, and Diamant, isolated on the shore, are clearly outlined against the sky. Pirogues glide over the water with swollen sails. In a few moments we must put on our sandy clothes, get into the boat, and let the sail fill with wind. Ouma will be half-asleep, lying forward at the bottom of the pirogue. We will leave our island and go to Rodrigues, and the birds will not come with us.

Monday, August 10 *(1914)*

Alone at the bottom of English Cove this morning I tally up the days. Several months ago, like Robinson Crusoe, I started doing this, but having no wood to put notches in I make my marks on the covers of my exercise books. That is how I arrived at this date. Extraordinarily, it tells me that I came to Rodrigues exactly four years ago. This discovery troubles me so much that I have to do something. I quickly slip my dusty shoes on my bare feet and take the gray jacket, a souvenir of my days in the W. W. West offices at Port Louis, from the trunk. I button my shirt all the way up but can't find a tie, having used mine during a storm to attach the flaps of the canvas I have made into a tent. Hatless and very sunburned, my hair and beard so long that I look like a castaway, and wearing this bourgeois jacket and old boots, I would have been the laughingstock of the people on Rempart Street at Port Louis. But here on Rodrigues they are less demanding, and hardly anyone takes any notice of me.

The Cable & Wireless offices are still empty at this hour. There is only an Indian employee who looks at me indifferently, even when I ask my absurd question with exquisite politeness.

"Excuse me, sir, what day is it today?"

He appears to think. Without moving from his place on the stairs he says, "Monday."

I insist, "But, what's the date?"

After another silence he announces; "Monday, August tenth, nineteen-fourteen."

❊

As I go down the long road between the vacoas toward the sea, I feel kind of dizzy. I have been living for such a long time in the isolated valley, with only the ghost of the Unknown Corsair as company! Alone, except for the shadowy Ouma who sometimes disappears for such long periods that I'm not sure she really exists. I have been away from home and those I love for an eternity. Memories of Laure and Mam tug at my heart like a premonition. The blue of the sky dazzles me and the sea looks as if it is on fire. I feel as if I am coming from another world, another time.

When I get to Port Mathurin I am suddenly part of a crowd. It is either the fishermen returning home to Lascars Bay or the mountain farmers who have come to market. Laughing black children run beside me, but when I look at them they hide their faces. I think that from living in the Corsair's territory I have come to look like him. An odd kind of corsair, emerging all dusty and tattered from his hiding place and without a boat.

After I pass the Portalis house I am in Barclay Street, in the center of town. While I draw the last of my savings from the bank (to buy sailor's biscuits, cigarettes, oil, coffee and a harpoon tip for fishing octopus), I hear the first rumors of the war into which the world appears to be throwing itself. A recent copy of the *Mauricien* on the wall of the bank gives the telegraphed news from Europe: Austria's declaration of war against Serbia following the assassination at Sarajevo, the mobilization of troops in France and Russia, and preparations for war in England. This information is already ten days old!

I wander for a long while through the streets of this town where nobody seems aware of the destruction threatening the world. There are crowds in front of the shops on Duncan Street, at the Chinaman's on Douglas Street, and on the road to the wharf. For a moment I think of going to the dispensary to speak to Doctor Camal Boudou, but I am ashamed of my tattered clothes and my long hair.

There is a letter for me at the Elias Mallac Company. I recognize her beautiful sloping handwriting on the envelope but I can't bear to open it immediately. There are too many people here. I hold it in my hand while I walk down the Port Mathurin streets, doing my shopping. Only when I am back in English Cove, sitting at my campsite under the old tamarind tree, do I dare open the letter. On the envelope I read the date it was sent: July 6, 1914. It was posted only a month ago.

It is written on a sheet of Indian paper that is light, fine, and opaque. I recognize it from the crackling sound it makes between my fingers: it is the same paper our father used to write and draw his plans. I thought these sheets had all disappeared after we left Boucan. Where had Laure found them? I think she must have kept them all this time, as if saving them to write to me. When I see her elegant slanting script, I am so moved that I cannot see for a moment. Then I read the words softly to myself:

My dear Ali,

> *You see, I haven't kept my promise. I swore I wouldn't write except to say two words to you: come back! And here I am writing to you without even knowing what I am going to say.*
>
> *First I am going to give you some news, which, as you might imagine, is not very good. Since your departure every-thing here has become even sadder. Mam has stopped doing anything, she won't even go to town to try and keep our af-fairs in order. It is I who have had to go several times to plead with our creditors. There is an Englishman, a certain Mr. Notte (no one could have invented such a name), who threatens to seize the few remaining pieces of furniture we still have at Forest Side. I have managed to stop him by making promises, but for how long? Enough of this. Mam is very weak. She still speaks of going to find refuge in France, but all the news we get is about the war. Yes, everything looks very bad at the moment and we don't have much hope for the future.*

My heart contracts as I read these lines. Where is the Laure who never complains, and who refuses to indulge in what she calls "jeremiads." The anxiety I feel is not about the war threatening the world. It comes from the distance between me and my loved ones, which separates me irrevocably from them. But in the final lines I catch a trace of the old Laure's teasing voice:

*I can't stop thinking about the time at Boucan when we were
so happy and the days never ended. I hope that where you
are you are enjoying days just as beautiful and happiness
instead of treasure.*

There is no formal ending; she signs it only with the letter
L. She never approved of handshakes or kissing. What is left of
her on this old sheet of Indian paper?

I carefully fold the letter and put it in the trunk with my
papers, next to the writing case. Outside the midday light
sparkles, making the stones at the bottom of the valley shine
brightly and putting an edge on the vacoa leaves. The wind
brings the sound of the rising tide. Gnats dance at the tent entrance—do they sense the storm? It seems to me that I can still
hear Laure's voice calling to me for help from across the ocean.
Despite the noise of the sea and wind there is nothing but silence and my loneliness shimmers in the light.

I walk haphazardly across the valley, still wearing the gray
jacket that is too large for me, and boots whose leather has
dried out and hardened, scraping at my feet. I follow the route
along the initial sections and lines of the Corsair's map, which
form a large hexagon ending in six points that has the shape of
the star of Solomon's seal and corresponds to the two inverted
triangles of the anchor rings.

I cross English Cove several times, keeping my eyes on the
ground and listening to my footsteps echoing in the valley. I
scrutinize all the stones and bushes that I know so well; on the
dunes near the Roseaux River's estuary there are still traces of
my footsteps in the sand that the rain has not washed away. I
raise my head and stare at the inaccessible blue mountains at
the bottom of the valley. It is as if I want to recall something
that is far away, something forgotten, perhaps the great dark
Mananava ravine where night begins.

I can't wait anymore. That evening, as the sun is descending over the hills going down to Point Venus, I go to the entrance to the ravine. I feverishly scale the stones blocking it and swing the pickax furiously at the ravine wall, risking being buried under a landslide. I don't want to think about my marker posts and my calculations. I can hear my heart thudding and the harsh sound of my labored breathing, as well as the din from the earth and shale as it shatters under the pickax. This work calms me down and my anxiety disappears.

In a fury I hurl hundred-pound blocks of rock against the basalt walls at the bottom of the ravine; an odor of overheated salt peter hangs in the air. I am drunk, drunk from solitude and silence, and because of it I am shattering these stones and talking to myself, saying, "It's here! It's here . . . Over there! Over there. . ."

I swing the pick at a group of basalt stones at the bottom of the ravine; they are so big and ancient that there is no doubt in my mind that they've been rolled down from the top of the black hills. Several men are needed to get them out of the way, but I can't bear to wait for the blacks from the farms—Raboud, Adrien Mercure, and Fritz Castel. With an enormous effort, having dug a hole under the first basalt stone, I manage to slide the tip of my pickax under it and try to use the handle as a lever. The block of stone moves slightly and I can hear earth falling into a deep cavity. But then the pick handle breaks in half and I fall heavily against the rocky cliff.

I stay there for a while, stunned. When I come to, I can feel something warm running over my hair and cheeks: blood. I am too weak to get up and I have to remain at the bottom of the ravine, leaning on one elbow and holding my handkerchief to the back of my head to stanch the blood.

A little before nightfall I am drawn out of my torpor by a sound at the entrance to the ravine. In my delirious state I take up the pickax handle to defend myself against what might be a wild dog or a hungry rat. Then I recognize Sri's slim form, which appears darker in the twilight. He is walking at the top of the ravine and when I call he comes down by way of the landslide.

He looks scared but he helps me get up and walk to the entrance to the ravine. I am hurt and weak but I say to him like a frightened animal, "Come, let's go, come!" We walk together to the camp at the bottom of the valley. Ouma is waiting for me. She brings water in the pot and putting some in the hollow of her hand she washes my head where the blood has congealed in my hair. She says, "Do you really love gold so much?"

I tell her about the hiding place I found under the basalt stones and the signs indicating these stones, this ravine, but I am confused and too vehement and she must think I am mad. The treasure means nothing to her; like all Manafs she holds gold in contempt.

Once my head has been bound with my blood-stained handkerchief I eat the meal that she has brought me, dried fish and *kir.* After I have finished she sits beside me and we stay silent for a long time under the pale sky that precedes night. Groups of sea birds are flying across English Cove to their resting places. My impatience and anger have dissipated. Ouma leans her head against my shoulder, as when we first came to know each other. I breathe in the scent of her skin and hair.

I speak to her about what I love, the fields in Boucan, the Trois Mamelles, and the dark and dangerous Mananava where there are always two bo'sun birds flying. She listens without moving, thinking of something else. I can feel that her body isn't relaxed. When I want to reassure her with a caress, she moves away and puts her arms around her long legs, like when she is alone.

"What is it? Are you angry?"

She doesn't reply. Night has just begun as we walk to the dunes. The air is so soft and light now at the beginning of summer and the empty sky is just beginning to fill with stars. Sri stays seated near the camp, still and erect like a guard dog.

"Tell me again about when you were a child."

I speak slowly as I smoke a cigarette, inhaling the honey odor of the English tobacco. I tell her about all of it, our house, Mam teaching us on the veranda, Laure going to hide in her tree of good and evil, and our ravine. Ouma interrupts to ask me questions about Mam, and especially about Laure. She questions me so much about her, wanting to know what kind of clothes she wore and about her likes and dislikes, that I think she is jealous. That this wild girl should want to know so much about a bourgeois young woman amuses me. I don't think, not for one moment, that I haven't understood what she is feeling, what is tormenting her and making her so vulnerable. It is so dark now that I can hardly make out her form seated beside me in the dunes. When I want to get up and go back to the camp she pulls me down again.

"Stay a bit longer. Tell me more about Boucan."

She wants me to tell her again about Mananava, about the cane fields that Denis and I used to run through, the ravine that started in the mysterious forest and the slow flight of the sparkling white birds.

Then she tells me again about her stay in France; the sky that is so dark and low that one feels that daylight is going to be extinguished forever, the prayers in the chapel and the hymns that she loved. She speaks to me about Hari and Govinda, who grew up among the herds in her mother's country. One day when Sri was alone in the mountains he made a flute from a reed and started to play it, and this is how her mother knew that he was God's envoy. When she came back to live with the Manafs it was he who taught her how to catch a running kid and he who took her for the first time to the sea to fish for octopus and crab. She also talks about Soukha and Sari, the pair of pale birds who know how to talk and who sing for God in the Vrindavan country. She says it was they I saw at the entrance to Mananava.

Much later we go back to the camp. We have never spoken before like this, so softly, without being able to see each other as we sit in the shelter of the big tree. It is as if time doesn't exist anymore, and as if there is nothing else in the world except for this tree, these stones. Very late that night I lie down to sleep on the ground in front of the tent with my head resting on my arms. I wait for Ouma to come and join me. But she stays where she is, watching Sri, who is sitting on a stone a little farther away. Silhouetted against the sky, they look like guardians of the night.

❖

As the sun comes up behind the mountains, I sit cross-legged in front of the trunk that serves as my desk, drawing a new map of English Cove, on which I join together all the lines between the markers, bringing into view, little by little, a kind of spiders' web whose six points form a big Star of David.

I am not thinking of the war today. Everything feels new and pure. Suddenly I lift my head and see Sri looking at me. I don't recognize him at first, but think he is one of the children from Raboud's farm who has come down with his father to go

fishing. Then I recognize him by his eyes, which are wild and
anxious, but also soft and bright. He is looking straight at me.
I leave my papers and walk slowly toward him so as not to
frighten him. When I am ten paces away from him he turns
and walks off. He doesn't hurry as he bounds over the rocks
and often stops to wait for me.

"Sri! Come back!" I have shouted even though I know he
can't hear me. But he continues walking to the bottom of the
valley. I follow him then without trying to catch up to him.
He springs lightly over the black rocks and his slim form
dances in front of me for a moment before disappearing into
the brush. I think I have lost him but he is always there, under
a tree or in between some rocks. He only comes into view
when he starts walking again.

I follow Sri for hours across the mountains. We are very
high, way above the hills on the bare mountainside. Below me
I can see the rocky slopes and the dark patches of vacoas and
thornbushes. There is no vegetation here, only minerals. The
sky is a magnificent blue, with clouds racing across it from the
east, throwing enormous shadows over the valley as they
quickly pass by. We continue to ascend. Sometimes I can't see
my guide, and when I catch sight of him, far in front of me,
dancing lightly on his toes, I am not sure whether it is he or a
goat or wild dog.

I stop for a moment to look at the distant sea. I have never
seen it from this high up before; it is immense, hard, and shiny
as steel, crossed by a long silent fringe of breaking waves.

The gusts of cold wind bring tears to my eyes. I sit down on
a stone to catch my breath. When I start walking again I think
I have lost Sri. I squint and look up the mountain and over the
dark glens. Then, just when I am about to give up on him, I
see him on another part of the mountain, surrounded by children and a herd of goats. I call, but the echo of my voice makes

the children flee and they disappear with their goats into the brush and rocks.

I can see traces of people here. There are circles of dry stones similar to the ones I found when I first arrived at English Cove. I can also see paths through the mountains; they are hardly visible but I can see them because the wild life I have led during four years in English Cove has taught me to be able to spot any signs of humanity. As I get ready to go down to the other slope to find the children I suddenly see Ouma. She comes up to me and without saying anything takes me by the hand and leads me up toward the top of the cliff to a place where the ground forms a kind of overhanging bank.

On the other side of the glen, on an arid slope along a dry mountain stream, I can see huts made from stone and branches as well as some tiny fields protected from the wind by dry stonewalls. The dogs have caught our scent and are barking. It is the Manaf village.

"You mustn't go any farther," Ouma says. "If a stranger went there the Manafs would have to retreat farther up the mountain."

We are walking along the cliff to the north side of the mountain. The wind is blowing in our faces. Below the sea is dark, infinite, dotted with white horses. In the east the lagoon looks like a turquoise mirror.

"At night we can see the town lights," Ouma says. She points at the sea. "And over there we can see the boats coming."

"It's beautiful!" I say this almost in a whisper. Ouma is sitting as she usually does, on her heels with her arms folded round her legs. Her dark face is turned to the sea and the wind ruffles her hair. She turns to the east, to the hills.

"You must go down, it will be night soon."

But we don't move and stay seated as the wind blows around us, like birds soaring very high in the sky; we are unable to leave the sea. Ouma doesn't speak to me but I feel as though I know everything that is inside her, desire as well as despair. She never talks about this, but it is what makes her like to go to the beach so much, to dive into the sea and swim out to the waves with her long harpoon in her hand and then, from behind the rocks, to watch the coastal people.

"Do you want to leave with me?"

The sound of my voice, or rather my question, makes her jump. She looks angrily at me with flashing eyes. "Leave to go where? Who would want me?"

I try to find the right words to pacify her, but she says furiously, "My grandfather was a maroon, one of the black runaway slaves from Morne. He died when his legs were crushed in a cane mill because he had joined Sacalavou's people in the forest. Then my father came to live here on Rodrigues and became a sailor. My mother was born in Bengal and her mother was a singer, she sang in honor of Govinda. Where do you think I could go? To France, to a convent? Or maybe to Port Louis to serve those who killed my grandfather, those who bought and sold us as slaves?"

Her hand is icy as if she had a fever. Suddenly she gets up and walks to the west slope where the paths separate, to the place she was waiting for me earlier. Her face is calm again but her eyes are still sparkling with anger.

"You must go now. You mustn't stay here."

I want to ask her to show me her house but she has already gone; without turning back she goes down to the little glen where the Manafs' huts are. I can hear children's voices and barking dogs. It will soon be night.

I rush down the mountainside, running through the thornbushes and the vacoas. I can no longer see the sea, nor the horizon; there is nothing but the shadow of the mountains growing larger in the sky. When I get to the valley in English Cove it is dark and rain is falling softly. Under my tree in the shelter of my tent I curl up and stay there, unmoving. I am cold and lonely. I think then of the noise of destruction, rumbling like a storm, getting louder every day, rolling over the earth and making a clamor that no one can ignore. That night I decide to leave for the war.

T HEY ARE ALL there this morning at the ravine entrance: Adrien Mercure, a huge black with Herculean strength who once was a foreman in the copra plantations at Juan de Nova, Ernest Raboud, Celestin Prosper, and young Fritz Castel. When I told them I had found the hiding place they left what they were doing and came immediately, each one carrying a spade and a length of rope. If anyone could have seen us crossing English Cove, the men with their spades and big vacoa hats and me at their head, bearded with long hair and tattered clothes and a handkerchief still bound around my head, they would have thought we were staging a masquerade, imitating the return of the Corsair's men to dig up their treasure!

Our enthusiasm is high in the cool morning air and we begin to dig around the basalt blocks at the bottom of the ravine. The ground is soft at the surface but becomes as hard as rock as we go farther down. We take it in turns to wield the pickax while the others clear away the debris at the broadest part of the ravine entrance. While we are doing this I suddenly realize that these stones and earth at the ravine entrance, which I had taken for a natural lock caused by runoff from the old stream bed, are actually debris from when the Corsair's men dug these hiding places at the bottom of the ravine. I have the strange feeling once again that the whole ravine is man-made. Starting with a simple break in the basalt cliff, they dug and burrowed until they managed to create the impression of a gorge, a gorge that has been remodeled for more than two hundred years by the rains. It truly is an odd feeling, almost scary, as diggers must have when they uncover ancient Egyptian tombs in the silent, cruelly bright desert.

At around noon the base of the largest basalt block has been dug out to such an extent that a simple push will tip it onto the ravine floor. We all push on the same side and the rock rolls several yards in an avalanche of dust and small stones. In front of us, exactly at the point indicated by the groove chiseled into the rock on top of the cliff, is a gaping hole that the dust still obscures. I can't wait any longer, and I get down on my stomach and wriggle through the opening. It takes several moments for my eyes to get used to the dark. "What's in there? What's in there?" I hear the blacks behind me saying impatiently. After a long while I wriggle out again. The blood pounds in my head and throat, making me dizzy. From what I have seen this second hiding place is empty, too.

Using the pickax I enlarge the opening. Soon a kind of pit is revealed, which comes to a deadend at the base of the cliff. The bottom of the pit consists of the same rust-colored rock that alternates at the bottom of the ravine with basaltic rock. Young Fritz goes into the shaft and disappears from sight. When he comes up again he shakes his head. "It's empty."

Mercure shrugs his shoulders scornfully. "It's a goat's spring."

Is it really only one of those old watering places for the herds? But why would someone have gone to all that trouble when the Roseaux River is only two feet away? The men leave with their spades and rope. The sound of their laughter disappears when they get beyond the ravine entrance. Only young

Fritz Castel stays with me, standing in front of the gaping hiding place as if he is waiting for my instructions. He is ready to begin work again, to put in new rods and bore new holes. Perhaps he has succumbed to the same fever as I, a madness that has made me abandon everything and everyone for a mirage, a golden bolt of light.

"There's nothing more to do here." I speak to him in a low voice as if speaking to myself. He looks at me with shining eyes, not understanding.

"All the hiding places are empty."

Then we, too, leave the fiery bowels of the ravine. From the top of the slope I look over the valley, at the dark green tufts of the tamarind trees and the vacoas, the fantastic shapes of the basalt rocks, and especially the thin, sky-blue ribbon of water snaking toward the marsh and dunes. The palm and coconut trees form a moving screen in front of the sea, and when the wind blows I can hear the noise of the waves, the regular breathing of a sleeper.

Where should I look now? Near the dunes in the marsh where the sea used to lap? In the caves on the other bank at the foot of the ruined tower, the Commander's Lookout? Or up there, very high up in the wild mountains of the Manafs, at the source of the Roseaux River where the goats live in the crags hidden by the thornbushes? It seems to me now that all the lines on my maps are dissolving, and that the signs on the stones have been left there by storms, etched by lightning and constant wind. I am filled with despair and my strength is gone. I want to say to Fritz, "It's over. There's nothing more to find here. Let's leave."

The young man is looking at me so insistently, with such eager eyes, that I can't bear to make him miserable too. As firmly as I can I start walking to my camp. I say, "We are going to search on the west side. We'll have to bore and plant rods. You'll see, in the end we'll find it. We're going to look everywhere, on the other side and then at the top of the valley, too. There won't be an inch of ground left that we haven't gone over. We'll find it!"

Does he believe me? My words seem to have reassured him. He says, "Yes, sir, we'll find it, if the Manafs don't find it before us!" The idea of the Manafs finding the Corsair's treasure makes him laugh. Then suddenly he becomes serious and says, "If the Manafs find the gold they'll throw it in the sea!"

And what if he's right?

❖

The anxiety I have been feeling for weeks, this noise that rumbles from across the sea like a tempest and that I can't forget, is with me day and night, and today I feel its full impact.

I leave early in the morning for Port Mathurin in hopes of finding another letter from Laure, but as I walk through the brush and vacoas in front of the Cable & Wireless buildings at Point Venus I see a crowd of men near the telegraph offices. The Rodriguans are waiting on the veranda, some standing and talking while others sit in the shade on the steps, absentmindedly smoking cigarettes.

Over the last two days of madness at the bottom of the ravine, while looking for the Corsair's second hiding place, I had forgotten about the gravity of the situation in Europe. Yet the other day, as I was passing by the Mallac & Company building, I stopped with everyone else and read the official notice from Port Louis posted at one side of the door. It spoke of the general mobilization that had already begun in Europe. England had declared war on Germany on the side of France. Lord Kitchener was appealing for volunteers from the colonies and dominions in Canada and Australia, and also in Asia, India, and Africa. I read the notice, then returned to English Cove, perhaps hoping to find Ouma and talk to her about it. But she didn't come, and after that the din we made at the bottom of the ravine must have scared her and kept her away.

As I come nearer the telegraph building no one pays any attention to my ragged clothing and over-long hair. I see Mercure and Raboud, and a little apart from them the giant Casimir, a sailor from the *Zeta*. He recognizes me too and his face lights up. With shining eyes he explains that the men here are waiting for their enlistment orders. That is why there are only men here! Women do not like war.

Casimir talks to me about the army and the battleship on which he hopes to sail. The poor, good giant! He is already talking about the battles he is going to wage in countries he doesn't know, against an enemy whose name he doesn't know either. Then an Indian man, an employee of the telegraph company, appears on the porch. He starts to read the list of names that is to be forwarded to the recruiting office in Port Louis. A heavy silence hangs in the air as he very slowly reads them in a singsong nasal voice, with an English accent that deforms the syllables.

"Hermitte, Corentin, Latour, Sifflette, Lamy, Raffaut. . ."

As he reads the names, the wind takes them and scatters them over the brush among the vacoa blades and black rocks; the names already echo strangely, like names of the dead, and suddenly I feel like running away, going back to my valley where no one will be able to find me, disappearing without a trace into Ouma's world among the reeds and dunes. The voice goes on slowly calling out the names and I shiver. I've never had this feeling before; it's as if I'm waiting for him to call my name with the others, as if my name has to be there with the others who are going to leave their country to go and fight our enemies.

"Portalis, Haouet, Céline, Bégué, Hitchen, Castor, Pichette, Simon. . ."

I can still leave. I think of the ravine and the crisscrossing lines over the bottom of the valley that make the landmarks stand out like beacons, of all I've seen and heard during these months and years, the sound of the sea and the birds, the radiant beauty of it all. I think of Ouma, of her skin, her smooth hands, her black metallic body gliding underwater in the lagoon. There is still time for me to leave, to get far away from this madness where men laugh and exult when the Indian calls their name. I can leave, find a place where I'll forget all this, where I won't be able to hear the noise of the war above the sound of the sea and wind. But the singsong voice continues calling out names, names that already sound unreal, the names of men from here who are going to die somewhere else for a world they know nothing about.

"Ferney, Labutte, Jérémiah, Rosine, Médicis, Jolicoeur, Victorine, Imboulla, Ramilla, Illke, Ardor, Gramcourt, Salomon, Ravine, Roussety, Perrine, Perrine junior, Azie, Cendrillon, Casimir. . ."

When the Indian calls his name, the giant stands and leaps with a whoop into the air, both feet together. There is an expression of naive happiness on his face, as if he had just won a bet or heard some good news. Yet it is his death that has just been called. Perhaps because of him I didn't flee to English Cove. I think it is because of him, because of his happiness when he heard his name called.

When the Indian has finished reading the names on his list he stands still for a moment, his paper fluttering in the wind, and asks in English, "Are there any other volunteers?"

And almost against my will I walk up the metal stairs to the porch and give him my name to add to the list. Earlier Casimir

had shown his joy, and now most of the Rodriguans are dancing on the spot and singing. When I come down the stairs
some of them surround me and shake my hand. The party atmosphere carries over onto the coast road that leads to Port
Mathurin, and in town the streets are full of noisy crowds ac-
companying us to the hospital for the medical examination. It
is only a formality and doesn't last more than one or two minutes. We go in turn with bare chests into the hot cubicle where
Camal Boudou, flanked by two nurses, summarily examines
the volunteers and gives them back a stamped travel warrant.
I expect him to ask me some questions but he only looks at my
teeth and eyes. He hands me the travel warrant, and as I leave
he says in his soft, serious voice, with an expressionless face,
"So, you're going to the front, too?" Then he calls the next
man without waiting for my reply. I read the date of departure
stamped on the travel warrant: December 10, 1914. The name
of the ship has been left blank but its destination has been written in: Portsmouth. It is done, I am going to war. I will not
even be able to see Laure and Mam before going to Europe because the ship will go via the Seychelles.

❁

Nonetheless, I return to the ravine every day, as if I were at last
about to find what I've been searching for. I cannot wrench
myself from this crack in the valley that has neither grass nor
trees; nothing lives in this crevice where the light reflects off
the basalt rocks and the rusty mountain slopes. In the morning
before the sun is too hot, and then again at dusk, I walk to the
deadend and look at the holes I discovered at the bottom of the
cliff. I lie down on the ground, and as my mind drifts I let my
fingers run round the pit opening, which water once honed as

smooth as glass. My furious blows with the pickax have left gouges on all sides of the bottom of the ravine, and the ground is full of craters that the dust is already beginning to fill. When the howling wind forces its way inside the ravine, coming in violent gusts from the top of the cliff, small avalanches of black earth run into these holes, making the stones at the bottom of the hiding places reverberate. How much time will it take for nature to reseal the Corsair's shafts that I opened? I think of all those who are going to come after me, ten years from now, or maybe even a hundred, and I decide to close the hiding places up again for them. I find big flat stones in the valley and carry them with difficulty to the mouth of the pits. Smaller stones that I pick up from the ground around me do to fill in the chinks, and then I heap big spadefuls of the red earth on top of the hiding places. Young Fritz helps me with this, not understanding why we are doing it but without asking questions. Since the beginning it has been a series of incomprehensible and rather frightening rituals to him.

When everything is finished I have a sense of satisfaction as I look at the mounds that cover the Corsair's two hiding places at the bottom of the ravine. It feels as if in accomplishing this work I have taken a new step in my quest, and have now become in a way the accomplice of this mysterious man whose tracks I have been following for so long.

I particularly like to be in the ravine in the evening. As the sun approaches the jagged line of the western hills near Commander's Summit, the light comes almost to the bottom of the long stone corridor, strangely illuminating the rock walls and the mica in the shale. I sit at the entrance to the ravine, watching the shadow advance across the silent valley. I study it in detail, noting each change in this landscape of stones and thorns. I wait for the arrival of my friends the sea birds who leave the Pierrot and Gombrani islands on the south coast each evening to fly to their refuge in the north, where the sea breaks on the coral reef. Why do they do it? What secret order leads them along the same path above the lagoon? As I wait for the sea birds, I also wait for Ouma, hoping to see her walking along the river bed, slim and dark, carrying octopuses on the end of her harpoon or a necklace of fish.

Sometimes she comes. She plants her harpoon in the sand near the dunes, as if signaling for me to come see her. When I tell her that I have found the Corsair's second hiding place and that it, too, was empty, she bursts out laughing. "So, there isn't any more gold, there is nothing here!" I feel irritated at first, but her laughter is infectious and soon I am laughing with her. She's right.

When we discovered the pit was empty the looks on our faces must have been something to see! Ouma and I run to the dunes and as we pass through the reeds clouds of cheeping silver birds take flight in front of us. We quickly take off our clothes and dive together into the clear lagoon water, which is so soft that we can hardly feel our bodies entering this different element. We swim for a long time underwater without coming up for breath. Ouma doesn't even look for fish to catch. She just amuses herself by chasing them and driving the old red mullets from their dark recesses. We have never been as happy as we have been since we discovered that there is no treasure in the hiding places! One evening, while we are watching the stars appear over the mountains, she says:

"Why are you looking for gold here?"

I want to tell her about the house at Boucan and the endless garden, about everything we lost, which is really what I am trying to find. But I don't know how to put it and she adds in an undertone, almost as if speaking to herself,

"Gold is worthless. You mustn't be scared of it. It's like scorpions who only sting those who are afraid of them." She's not trying to show off. She says this simply but firmly, like someone who is sure of her words. "All of you out there, you desire gold above everything because you think there is nothing more powerful. You make war for it. People everywhere will die because of this obsession."

My heart races when I hear her say this, and I immediately think of my enlistment. For a moment I want to tell Ouma everything, but my throat tightens. I have only a few more days left in the valley near her, and so far from the rest of the world. How can I talk about the war to Ouma? For her it is something evil. She wouldn't forgive me for enlisting and would flee from me.

I can't speak to her about it. I hold her hand in mine and squeeze it tight so that I can feel her warmth. I put my lips on hers and breathe in her breath. It is a gentle summer night, the wind having died down, the sky full of beautiful stars. There is only peace and joy. I think it is the first time that I feel time passing without impatience or desire, but with sadness because I know that there will be no coming back to what I have here, that it is going to be destroyed. I am on the point of telling Ouma several times that we are soon not going to see each other again, but her laughter, her breath, the smell of her body and the taste of the salt on her skin stop me. How can I spoil this peace? I can't prevent what is going to be shattered, but I can still believe in miracles.

❦

Every morning, like most of the Rodriguans, I stand in front of the telegraph building waiting for news. The communiqués from Europe are posted on the porch to one side of the building's entrance. Those who can read translate what is written into creole for the others. There is a great crush of people around the notice, but I manage to read a few lines: they deal with French's and Haig's armies, with Langle and Larrezac's French troops, with battles in Belgium, with threats on the Rhine, with the front on the Oise near Dinant, and in the Ardennes near the Meuse. I know these names because I learned them at the College, but what do they mean to most of the Rodriguans? Do they imagine them belonging to islands where coconut and Bourbon palms sway in the breeze, and where the sound of the sea breaking on the reefs can always be heard? I feel angry and impatient, for I know that in very little time, maybe only a few weeks, I'll be there, on the banks of unknown rivers, in the midst of a war that has swept all names into one hat.

❈

When young Fritz Castel came this morning I made a kind of will. Using my theodolite, I calculated one last time the east-west line that passes directly through the two anchor ring signs on the sides of the valley, and determined the spot where this line meets the north-south axis calculated by the North Star. At the point where these two lines meet on the Roseaux River in the center of the valley, at the end of the marshland that forms a tongue of land between the two arms of the river, I have put a heavy basalt stone as a marker. To get the stone to this spot I had to slide it with young Castel's help, along a path of reeds and rounded branches that we had laid in the riverbed. I tied a rope around the stone and, pushing and pulling by turns, we carried it more than a mile to the other end of the valley, to the point that I'd marked with a B on my map. We elevated it slightly on a mound of earth that goes into the estuary and is surrounded by water at high tide. This took us nearly all day. Fritz Castel helped me without asking any questions. Then he went back home.

The sun is low in the sky when I start, using a cold chisel and a big stone as a mallet, to inscribe my message for the future. On top of the stone I etch a groove three inches long that corresponds to the line linking the east-west anchor rings. Then on the south face of the stone I chisel the principal landmarks corresponding to the Corsair's markers. The capital M represents the points of Commander's Summit, the ∷ chiseled into the rock, the groove for the ravine, and the point indicating the northernmost stone at the beginning of the estuary. On the north face of the stone I mark the Corsair's five principal markers with five points: Charlot, Bilactère, and Mount Quatre Vents, which form the first south-southeast alignment; and Commander and Piton, which form the slightly divergent second alignment.

I would also have liked to etch the triangles of the Corsair's grid inscribed in the circle that passes through the anchor rings and the northernmost stone, of which this stone is the center. But the surface of the stone is too uneven for me to draw something so precise with such a blunt chisel. I have to be content with putting my initials, AL, in capitals at the bottom of the stone, and below them the date in Roman numerals:

X   XII   MCMXIV

This afternoon, certainly the last that I will spend here in English Cove, I want to take advantage of the full summer heat by having a long swim in the lagoon. On the deserted beach where I used to come with Ouma I undress in the reeds. Today the valley seems to me even more silent, faraway, and abandoned. There are no clouds of twittering silver birds rising from the reeds, no sea birds in the sky, only soldier crabs fleeing for the muddy marsh with their claws raised. I swim for a long time in the very soft water, lightly brushing the coral that the sea washes over. With my eyes open underwater I watch the fish coming out of the shallows: *kofs*, pearly needle fish, and even a splendid and poisonous *lafa* fish with its dorsal fins standing straight up like ship's rigging. Very near the coral reef I chase a seawife from its hiding place and it stops to look at me before fleeing. I don't have a harpoon, but even if I did I don't think I would have had the heart to use it against one of these mute creatures and see their blood stain the water red.

Back on shore in the dunes I cover myself with sand and wait until the setting sun makes it run down in little streams over my body, as when I was with Ouma.

I watch the sea for a long time as I wait. I am waiting in the twilight for Ouma to appear on the beach with her ebony-tipped harpoon in one hand and some octopus like a trophy in the other. The valley is filled with shadow when I walk back to the camp. I stare with anxiety as well as desire at the tops of the blue mountains, as if eventually I would see a human shape emerging from the stones.

Did I call, "Ouma-ah"? Perhaps, but if I did it was in such a weak, strangled voice that it didn't even rouse an echo. Why isn't she here when I need her more than on any other night? Sitting on my flat stone under the old tamarind tree, I smoke a cigarette and watch night come into English Cove. I think of Ouma and how she listened when I spoke to her of Boucan; I think of her face hidden by her hair and the taste of salt on her shoulder. Then I realize she has to know, she must know my secret, and when she came to be with me that last night it was to say goodbye. That was why she hid her face and why her voice was hard and bitter when she spoke to me about gold, when she said "all of you out there." Because I didn't understand I feel angry now, angry with her and angry with myself. I walk feverishly in the valley, then come back to sit under the big tree where it is already becoming dark and crumple the papers and maps in my hands. They are no longer important! I now know that Ouma will not come. To her, I have become like the others, like the coastal people that the Manafs watch from afar, waiting for them to go.

I run across the valley in the hazy twilight and climb to the top of the hills in order to escape the eyes that look at me from all sides. I stumble over pebbles and clutch at the basalt blocks, and I can feel the earth crumbling under my feet and hear it falling to the bottom of the valley. In the distance, under the yellow sky, the mountains are black and compact without light or fire. Where do the Manafs live? On Piton, on Limon, in the east, or on Bilactère above Port Mathurin? But then, they never stay two nights in the same place. They sleep in the warm cinders of their fires that they put out at dusk, just as the black maroons in the mountains of Mauritius used to. I want to go higher, to the foothills of the mountains, but night has come and I bump into rocks and tear my clothes and hands. I call Ouma again, with all my strength now, "Ou-maaa," and in the darkness my shout echoes off the gullies and makes a strange rumbling sound, an animal cry that frightens me, too. Then I stay half lying against the slope, waiting for the valley to be silent again. When it is, everything becomes smooth and pure, invisible in the night, and I don't want to think about what is going to happen tomorrow. I want to be as if nothing has happened, the way it was before.

YPRES, WINTER 1915
THE SOMME, AUTUMN 1916

T HERE ARE NO LONGER any novices among us. We've all had our share of misery and danger. All of us, the French Canadians of the 13th infantry Brigade and the colonial Indians of the 27th and 28th divisions, have lived through the Flanders winter: the beer freezing in its barrels, battles in the snow, the fog and poison gas, the incessant bombardments, the outbreaks of fire in the shelters. So many men are dead. We hardly ever feel fear now. We've become indifferent, as if in a dream. We are the survivors.

We've been digging into the mud on the riverbanks for months, day after day, without knowing why we are doing it and without even having to be asked. We have been here for so long, listening to the cannons thunder and the crows sing their songs of death, that we don't notice the passage of time. Has it been days, weeks, or months? Or rather one day that is always the same and that every new dawn drags from our sleep on the frozen ground weakened by hunger and fatigue—the same day rotating slowly with the pale sun behind thick clouds.

It is the same day as when we rallied to Lord Kitchener's appeal, so long ago now that we don't remember when this day began, or even if it had a beginning. There was the embarkation in the Portsmouth mist on the *Dreadnought,* a steel fortress. Then the train across the north and the convoys of horses and men walking under the rain along the railway to Ypres. Did I really live through all that? When was it? Was it months or years ago? What happened to my companions as winter approached on the road to Flanders: Rémy from Quebec, Le Halloco from Newfoundland, and Perrin, Renouart, and Simon, whose origins I don't know—all those who were there in the spring of 1915 to relieve the Expeditionary Force, which had been decimated in the battles at La Bassée? Now we don't know anyone. We dig trenches in the clay earth and advance, creeping, toward the Ancre River, day after day, yard by yard, like hideous moles moving toward the dark hills that overlook this valley. Sometimes, in the heavy silence of the empty fields, we start as we hear the *tac-tac* of machine guns and the reports of the exploding shells in the distance behind the line of trees.

When we speak to each other, we do so in low voices; the words come and go as they pass along the lines—repeated orders, contradictions, distortions, stories of interrogations, and news of people we don't even know. One night when the cold keeps us all awake in our freezing holes someone starts to sing; then suddenly the song stops, and no one asks him to continue or tells him it is more painful when there is silence.

In spite of the rain there is a shortage of water and we are devoured by lice and fleas. We are all covered in a crust of mud mixed with our own filth and blood. Very different from the first sunny days in London, when we proudly showed off the light-beige uniforms and feathered hats of the volunteers from overseas, marching through the streets in the freezing December air with the infantrymen dressed in red, the squadrons of grenadiers, and the lancers of the Indian army's 27th and 28th divisions in their tunics and high white turbans. I remember the New Year celebrations in the Saint Paul district that we wished would never end, the procession in the frost-covered gardens, the drunkenness of the last nights, the joyous embarkation on the platform at Waterloo, and the misty dawn on the deck of the immense *Dreadnought*. I remember the spray-drenched men in their khaki greatcoats, volunteers full of hope from the four corners of the world, standing there looking out to the horizon, waiting for the dark line of the French coast to appear.

All of that is so far away now—did it really happen? Fatigue, hunger, and fever have played havoc with our minds and darkened our memories. Why are we here today? What are we doing buried in these trenches, our faces black with smoke, our clothes in rags, stiff with dry mud, wallowing for months in this odor of latrines and death?

❧

We have become familiar with death and are indifferent to it now. Little by little it has decimated the ranks of those I knew during the first days, when we rolled along in the armored trains to Boves station. I caught glimpses of a huge crowd every now and then from between the slats that boarded the windows, walking in the rain toward the valley of the Yser, scattered along the roads, divided, reunited, and then separated again. Morland's 5th division, Snow's 27th, Bulfin's 28th, and Alderson's 1st Canadian: the October veterans who we, along with the Territorial Army and the Expeditionary Force, were going to join. We thought of death in those days, but it was a glorious death that we envisioned when we spoke of it among among ourselves in the evenings: like that of the Scots officer who, with only a sabre in his hand, had mounted an

attack against the German machine guns. The men waited impatiently on the Comines canal for the order to attack, intoxicated by the sound of the cannons rumbling day and night
like subterranean thunder. When the order came and we were
told that General Douglas Haig's troops had started their
march toward Bruges, there was an explosion of childlike
joy. The soldiers shouted, "Hurrah!" as they threw their helmets into the air, and I thought of the men at Rodrigues waiting in front of the telegraph building. The cavalrymen of the
French squadrons joined us on the banks of the Lys. In the
dusky winter light their blue uniforms seemed unreal, like a
bird's plumage.

Then we started our long walk to the northwest, going up
the Ypres canal toward Hooge wood, where we could hear the
rumble of the cannon thunder. We met up with other troops
every day, Frenchmen and Belgians who had managed to live
through the Dixmude massacre and were coming back from
Ramscappelle, where the Belgians had caused an immense
flood by opening the sluice gates of the canal. Bloody and
in rags they told terrifying stories of the Germans, who kept
on coming in endless, frenzied, screaming hordes; of battles in
the mud with cold steel, bayonets, and daggers; of bodies
pulled along in the current, caught on barbed wire, trapped in
the reeds.

I keep hearing their awful stories. A circle of fire has closed
around us, in the north at Dixmude and Saint-Julien, in the
Houthulst forest, and in the south on the banks of the Lys and
near Menin and Wevicq. We advance over a deserted, destroyed landscape where the only things left are the charred
trunks of branchless trees. We advance very slowly. It is more
like crawling. Sometimes in the morning we see the gully at
the end of a field and the ruined farm that we know we will
not reach before evening. The earth is so heavy here, it weighs

our legs down and clings to our soles and makes us fall flat on our faces. Some of us don't get up again.

We crawl along the trenches we dug before dawn, listening to the cannon thunder and the rat-tat-tat of the machine guns that are very near now. Far away, behind the hills on the Ypres side, the French are also fighting. But we don't see any men, only their black smoke soiling the sky.

In the evening, Barneoud, who comes from Trois Rivières, talks about women. He describes their bodies, their faces, and their hair. His voice as he tells us this is husky and sad, as if all the women he's describing are dead. When he first started we laughed because it seemed so incongruous to have all these naked women with us in the war. War has nothing to do with women—on the contrary, it is the most sterile possible meeting of men. His talking about these women's bodies while we lay in the mud, inhaling the stench of urine and rotting flesh and with the circle of fire burning day and night around us, made us shudder and filled us with revulsion. We would shout at him in English and French: *Assez,* shut up, *tais-toi!* Stop talking about women, shut up! One evening as he went on with his delirious descriptions, a huge devil of an Englishman started savagely beating him with his fists, and might have killed him if an officer, the second lieutenant, had not arrived carrying a service revolver. The next morning Barneoud had disappeared. It was said he was sent to the 13th infantry Brigade and died in one of the Saint-Julien battles.

I think we had already become indifferent to death then. Its sounds reached us every hour of every day: the dull reports of the shells when they hit the ground, the staccatos of the machine guns, and a bizarre noise that came directly after, the voices and footsteps of men running through the mud along with the shouted orders of the officers, the commotion before the counterattack.

April 23: Following the first release of gas above the French lines, we counterattack with the 13th Brigade and the batallions of the Canadian 3rd Brigade under Colonel Geddes. All day long we advance in a northeasterly direction toward Houthulst forest. In the middle of the plain, the bombs, which are hollowing out huge craters nearer and nearer to us, force us to make shelters for the night. We hastily dig ten-foot ditches, which six or seven of us squeeze into like crabs. Curled up with our steel helmets pulled down on our heads we stay there until the following day, hardly daring to move. Behind us we hear the English cannons responding to the German ones. In the morning, as we sleep leaning one against the other, we are startled awake by the whistling of a shell. The combustion is so strong that, despite the narrowness of the trench, we are lifted and hurled against each other. Crushed underneath my comrades I feel a warm liquid running down my face: blood. Am I wounded, perhaps dying? I push off the bodies that have fallen on me and see that it is my comrades who have been killed. It is their blood running over me.

I crawl to the other holes full of men and call for the survivors. Together we drag the wounded to the rear, looking for somewhere to take shelter. But where? Half our company has been killed. The second lieutenant who stopped Barneoud has been decapitated by a shell. We reach the rear lines. At five o'clock in the evening, joined by the English under General Snow, we attack again, taking ten-yard leaps across the crater-filled field. At half past five, as the twilight is deepening into dark, a huge yellow-green cloud suddenly appears in the sky fifty yards ahead of us. The light breeze spreads it slowly southward. Other closer explosions give rise to new wreaths of deadly smoke.

My heart stops and I am paralyzed by horror! Someone shouts, "Gas! Go back!" We run for the trenches, hurriedly making masks out of handkerchiefs and strips torn from our coats and anything else within reach, which we moisten with our meagre water supply. The menacing cloud slowly advances toward us, copper-colored in the twilight. The acrid smell is already in our lungs, making us gag. The men turn away from it and their faces reflect their hatred and fear. When the order to fall back to Saint-Julien comes, many of the men have already begun to run, bending close to the ground. I think of the wounded who had to stay in their holes, over whom death is now passing. Then I also run across the field pitted with shell craters, through the charred thicket with the muddy, water-soaked handkerchief pressed against my face.

❧

How many are dead? How many can still fight? After experiencing the horror of that lethal, dusky-yellow cloud, so much like one in a twilight sky, we stayed huddled in our trenches, keeping our eyes heavenward day and night. We mechanically called the roll, perhaps in the hope of making those men whose names no longer belonged to anyone appear again: Simon, Lenfant, Garadec, Schaffer . . . Adrien, the little redhead, Gordon, that was his surname, Gordon . . . Pommier . . . Antoine, whose surname I had forgotten, who came from Joliette, and Leon Berre and Raymond, Dubois, Santeuil, Reinert. . . . But were those really their names? Did they really exist? We'd viewed death differently when we first arrived from our distant countries: glorious, in broad daylight, with a little star of blood on the chest to mark the fatal wound. But death isn't like that. It's deceitful and insidious, keeping its whereabouts secret until it wants to pounce, then doing so without telling anyone. It seizes sleeping men during the night, drowns others in the bog and in pools of mud at the bottom of ravines, suffocates some by dragging their faces in the dust, and freezes the bodies of those sleeping under torn hospital tents, men with livid faces and emaciated thoraxes riddled with dysentery, pneumonia, and typhoid. When someone dies it takes us a while to realize they are no longer there. Where are they? Perhaps they have had the good fortune to be sent to the rear, or perhaps they lost an eye or a leg and will never go to war again. But somehow we know, there is something about their absence and the silence that surrounds their names when they are called that tells us they're dead.

※

It is as if some monstrous animal comes during the night to disturb our uneasy sleep, to snatch some men and carry them off to be devoured in its lair. These absences hurt and the wounds go so deep we can never forget them, whatever we do. Since the gas attack on April 24 we have not moved. We stay in the trenches, the same ones we started digging six months ago when we arrived. Then the countryside in front of us was still intact, waving glens of trees still rust-colored from the winter, farms in their fields, pastures dotted with water, paddocks, rows of apple trees, and in the distance the faint outline of Ypres, with its stone steeple emerging from the midst. Now all I can see over the machine gun's sights is ravaged ground and charred trees. The exploding shells have dug out hundreds of craters, destroying forests and hamlets, while the Ypres belfry leans to one side like a broken branch. Silence and emptiness have replaced the hellish din of the first weeks' bombing. The circle of fire is dying down, like a flame that has consumed everything and is going out because there is nothing left to burn. We barely hear the occasional rumbling batteries, or see the plumes of smoke where the allied shells have hit.

Is everyone dead? One night as I sit on a box doing guard duty, protected by the trench from machine gun fire, this idea crosses my mind. In order to curb my desire to smoke I chew a stick of licorice that a Canadian soldier whose name I don't even know gave me. It is a cold, cloudless night, another winter's night. I can see the stars, but some of them belong to the northern skies and I don't recognize them. In the light of the rising moon the torn, crater-filled ground appears even more alien and void.

It is so quiet that it feels as if the world has been emptied of men and beasts, like a high plateau stranded in a region from which all life has fled forever. I feel death so strongly that I can't bear it. I go to a comrade who is sleeping sitting with his back against the trench wall. I shake him. He looks dazedly at me as if he doesn't remember where he is. "Come and see! Come!" I drag him to the observation post and make him look over the deadly machine gun at the frozen moonlit countryside. "Look: there isn't anyone left. It's over! The war is over!" I speak in a low voice but my tone and the look in my eyes must be worrisome because the soldier recoils.

He says, "You're mad!" I repeat in the same strangled voice, "But look! Look! I tell you there isn't anyone left, they're all dead! The war is over!" Other soldiers who have been woken up are approaching us. The officer is there and he says in a loud voice, "What's going on?" They reply, "He's nuts! He says the war is over." Others chime in, "He says everyone's dead." The officer stares at me as if trying to understand. Perhaps they'll see that it's true, that it's all over now because everyone is dead.

The officer seems to be listening to the silent night around us. Then he says, "Go back to sleep! The war isn't over and we have a lot to do tomorrow!" To me he says, "You go sleep, too. You're tired." Another man takes over guard duty and I burrow into the bottom of the trench. I listen to the breathing of the men who have gone back to sleep, the only living beings left in the world, buried in this hacked earth.

The Somme, Summer 1916

We walk across this plain like a column of ants on the banks of a huge, muddy river. Always along the same roads, following the same grooves and digging innumerable holes in the same fields without knowing where we're going. We hollow out underground runs, corridors, and tunnels in the heavy, black, humid earth, which turns to mud as we dig at it. We have stopped asking questions. We don't want to know where we are or why we are here. For months, day after day, we dig trenches along the river opposite the hills. When we first ar-rived on the banks of the Ancre, shells started to fall to the right and left of us and we threw ourselves onto our stomachs in the mud with the sinister whistling of the missiles in our ears. The shells exploded on the ground, blasting away the trees and houses and starting fires that burned red in the night, but there was no counterattack. We waited and then began to dig trenches again and the convoys of mules continued bring-ing wooden posts and cement and sheet metal for the roofs. In spring a fine light rain fell, creating a mist that hid the sun's rays. Then the first airplanes came, flying beneath the clouds. Odilon and I squinted to see whose they were. They turned and went off toward the south. "They must be French," Odilon said. The Fritzes only have airships. We sometimes see them going up into the sky at dawn like fat slugs. "You'll see, just you wait. The French planes will put out their eyes!"

Odilon is my friend. He comes from Jersey and has a funny accent that I don't always understand. He's eighteen and has an angelic face. His beard hasn't grown in yet and the cold makes his skin red. For months we've been working side by side, and we share the same space to eat and sleep as well. We don't really ever speak to each other except for a few words—the essentials, just questions and answers. He joined the army after me and as I had been made a corporal after the battle of Ypres I chose him as my orderly. When they wanted to send him to the front at Verdun I requested that he be allowed to stay with me. I felt as soon as I met him that it was my duty to protect him in this war, almost as if I were his older brother.

Summer has come and the days are beautiful, but the star-filled nights are even more beautiful. At night when everybody is asleep we listen to the toads croaking in the marsh and on the riverbanks. There the men from our contingent make barbed-wire fences and observation posts and cement the platforms for the cannons. But at night, when we can't see the barbed wire or the trench ditches that look so like open graves, thanks to the innocence of the toads' song we are able to forget for a while that there is a war going on.

The dead horses arrived by train at Albert station. Then they were transported in tip-carts along the muddy roads to the banks of the Ancre. Every day the tip-carts brought mountains of dead horses' carcasses and spilled them out in the grass fields near the river. Before they arrived we could hear the cawing of the ravens and crows following the carts. One day we were walking along the Ancre to go and work on the trenches and we crossed a large field of oats and stubble that was full of the cadavers of horses killed in the war. The bodies were already black and rotting and flocks of screeching carrion-seeking crows were flying above them. None of us were neophytes, we'd all seen death, friends hurled back by machine gun bullets, doubled up as if they had been punched by an invisible fist; others torn apart or decapitated by a shell.

But when we crossed this field of hundreds of carcasses of dead horses our legs shook and the bile mounted in our throats.

What we didn't know was that it was only the beginning of the war. We thought then that the fighting was nearly over, that all the country around us had been deserted like the field that had served as an open grave for the horses' bodies. It was like the sea in front of us: a vast stretch of almost unreal hills and forests, very dark despite the summer sunlight, over which only the crows had the right to fly.

What was to the other side of them? Our silent, invisible enemies. They lived there, spoke, ate, and slept like us, but we never saw them. Sometimes the noise of machine-gun fire in the distance, in the northwest or the south, reminded us that they were still there. Or the piercing drone of an airplane passing between two clouds and then out of sight.

We were working on making roads. Every day the trucks brought their cargo of pebbles and tipped them in heaps in intervals along the banks of the Ancre. Soldiers from the Territorial Army and the New Army came with us to build these roads and the railroad that was to cross the river to Hardecourt. After a few months, no one would recognize this country. Where, at the beginning of the winter, were only pastureland, fields, woods, and some old farms, there now stretched a network of stone roads, railroad tracks, metal shelters, and hangars for the trucks, planes, tanks, cannons, and munitions. Over all this the camouflage teams had put huge brown canvas sheets that resembled the scurfy grasslands. When the wind blew the canvas crackled like a ship's sails and we could hear the strident sounds through the barbed wire. The powerful cannons had been buried in the center of huge craters and looked like giant ants or evil land crabs. The trucks came and went, constantly bringing in loads of shells: the 37's and 47's as well as 58's and 75's. Beyond the railroad men hollowed out trenches on the banks of the Ancre, building concrete platforms for the cannons and constructing fortified shelters. In the plains, to the south of Hardecourt, near Albert, Aveluy, and Mesnil, where the valley narrows, we built a stage set: false ruins and false wells that hid the machine guns. We made puppets out of old uniforms stuffed with hay to look like soldiers' corpses lying on the ground and we built hollow trees to hide the lookouts, Bren guns, and howitzers, out of bits of sheet metal and branches. The roads, railroads, and bridges were covered with huge grass-colored raffia curtains and bundles of hay. From an old barge brought from Flanders the Expeditionary Force fashioned a floating cannon that could down the Ancre as far as the Somme.

Now that summer has come, bringing the long days, we have been reinvigorated. It is as if everything we see taking place here is only a game, and we don't think of death. Odilon, after despair of the winter months spent in the Ancre's mud, has become confident and lighthearted. At night after the day's work on the roads and railroads he drinks coffee with the Canadians and chats with them until curfew. The sky is full of stars, and I remember the starry skies at Boucan and English Cove. For the first time in months we confide in each other. The men speak of their parents and fiancées, wives and children. Photographs are passed round, old bits of dirty moldy cardboard on which, in the trembling lamplight, smiling faces appear, distant shapes, as unreal as ghosts. Odilon and I do not have any photos, but I have Laure's last letter in my jacket pocket, which I received in London before boarding the *Dreadnought*. I have read and reread it so many times that I have committed its half-teasing and rather sad words to memory.

She speaks about Mananava and how one day when all this is over we will go back there. Does she really believe it? One night I talk to Odilon about Mananava and the two bo'sun birds wheeling above the ravine at twilight. Does he hear what I'm saying? We're sitting in the subterranean shelter that serves as our barracks, and I think he's put his head on his knapsack and fallen asleep. I don't mind. I want to go on talking, not for him but for myself, so that my voice will reach beyond this hell to the island where Laure lies awake in the silent night, listening to the pattering rain as she used to in the house at Boucan.

We have been working at setting up this imitation landscape for so long that we no longer believe the war is real. Ypres and the forced marches of Flanders seem very far away. Most of my present comrades were not with me back there. In the beginning they treated our work on the false landscape as a joke, they wanted to smell gunpowder and hear the cannons thunder. Now they don't understand what the purpose of all this is and have become impatient. "Is this what war is?" Odilon asks after an aggravating day spent digging trenches and runs for the mines. The sky above is leaden. The storm breaks with a heavy downpour, and when we are relieved from duty we are as soaked as we would be if we had fallen in the river.

In the evening in our underground shelter the men play cards and dream out loud as we wait for curfew. News of the battles at Verdun circulates and for the first time we hear these strange-sounding names that we will hear so often again. Couaumont, the Dame ravine, the Vaux fortress, and the name that makes me shiver in spite of myself, Mort-Homme: "Man-Death." A soldier, an English Canadian, speaks to us about the Tavannes tunnel crammed with the wounded and dying while above the shells went on exploding. He tells of the flashes of light from the explosions, the smoke and the ripping noise of the 370 mortars, and all the men they mutilated and burned. Can it already be summer? Some evenings the sun setting above the trenches is extraordinarily beautiful. Huge scarlet and violet clouds lie suspended in a gilded gray sky. Can all those who are dying at Douaumont see it too? I imagine what life must be like high in the sky, if one had wings like the bo-'sun birds. One would not be able to see the trenches, nor the holes from the shells; one would be far from it all.

We all know that the battle is near now. We've been pre-paring since early winter and now everything is ready. Teams of workers no longer go to the canal every day, and the trains hardly run. The cannons are in their hiding places under the canvas and the machine guns are in the rotundas at the ends of the trenches.

Toward the middle of June, Rawlinson's soldiers begin to arrive. English and Scottish, Indian and South African batal-lions, and Australian divisions, all coming back from Flanders and Artois. We've never seen so many men before. They come along the roads and railroads from all quarters and install themselves in the miles of trenches we have dug. The word is that the attack will take place on June 29. The cannons start firing on the 24th. All along the banks of the Ancre and in the south, on the banks of the Somme where the French forces are firing, cannons make a thunderous, deafening noise. After the days of silence and the long, uncomfortably squashed wait we are intoxicated and feverish, trembling with impatience. Day and night the cannons thunder and the sky above the hills turns red.

But over on the other side there is silence. Why don't they respond? Have they left? How can they withstand this hail of fire? For six days and nights we scan the countryside in front of us. On the sixth day it begins to rain, a torrential rain that soon turns the trenches into muddy streams. The cannons are quiet for several hours; it is as if the sky itself has entered the war.

Crouched in the shelters we watch the falling rain all day, and by evening we have become anxious. It seems as if it will never stop again. The English talk about the floods in Flanders when hordes of green uniforms were swimming in the swampy Lys. For the most part we are disappointed to have the attack set back again. We keep looking at the sky, and when, toward evening, Odilon announces that the clouds are not as thick and that a patch of blue can even be seen, everybody shouts, "Hurrah!" Perhaps it isn't too late? Perhaps the attack can take place during the night? We watch night slowly falling over the Ancre valley and swallowing the forests and hills in front of us. It is a strange night and no one really sleeps. Toward dawn I doze off with my head on my knees and the hullabaloo of the attack wakes me with a start. It is already very light, very bright, and the air blowing through the valley is the dryest and warmest I have felt since leaving Rodrigues and English Cove. A light, sparkling mist is rising from the still-wet banks, and what immediately comes to mind is the smell of the ground and the grass in summer. I also see gnats dancing in the light and swinging in the wind between the shelter posts. For an instant I experience such a feeling of peace that everything appears to be suspended, hanging motionless in the air.

We are all standing in the muddy trench, helmets pushed down on our heads and bayonets fixed. We are looking over the slope at the pale blue sky, where white clouds float as light as down. We relax as we listen to the sweet summer sounds, the water running in the river, the strident insects, and the singing lark. We wait in this peaceful silence with painful impatience, and when the first cannon fire thunders from north, south, and east, we shudder. Soon the large-bore English guns begin roaring behind us, and in response to their powerful blows the earth rumbles and trembles, echoing the impact of the shells form the other side of the river. The bombardment is extremely fierce and echoes incomprehensibly in the clear sky with its beautiful sparkling summer light, coming as it does after the previous day of rain.

After a seemingly infinite period of time, the uproar stops. The silence that follows is dizzying and full of pain. At exactly seven-thirty the sergeants and corporals pass the order to attack from trench to trench. As I shout in turn, I look at Odilon's face for the last time. Then I am running, bending forward with my two hands clutching my gun, to the banks of the Ancre where the pontoons are full of soldiers. I can hear the *tac-tac* of the machine guns in front of and behind me. Where are the enemies' bullets? Without slowing we run across the moored pontoons in an clatter of boots against wooden slats. The river water is thick, the color of blood. Men slip in the mud on the opposite bank and fall, not getting up again.

The dark hills are above me; they threaten us as if they have eyes everywhere. Black smoke is rising on all sides, smoke without fire, smoke that has killed. Isolated rounds of gunshot ring out. We can hear the staccato of machine guns coming from the ground somewhere in the distance, but we don't know from where. Without trying to hide I run behind a group of men toward the designated objective, which has been drilled into us for months: the burned hills that separate us from Thiepval. To our right other running men join us on the crater-filled field; they are from the 10th Corps, the 3rd Corps, and Rawlinson's divisions. In the middle of the huge empty field the bushes burned by the gas and the shells look like scarecrows. As I near the end of the field, machine-gun fire suddenly clatters out, right in front of me. Little clouds of bluish smoke float here and there within the confines of the dark hills; the Germans are entrenched in the shell holes and they sweep the field with their automated rifles. Already shattered men are falling, puppets without strings, collapsing in groups of ten and twenty.

Did someone give the orders? I didn't hear anything but I am lying on the ground looking for cover, a shell hole, a trench, a lump of earth attached to a stump. I crawl on my stomach in the field. Around me other shapes are crawling, too, looking, their faces hidden by their guns, like big slugs. Others are motionless, face-down in the mud. The crackling of the guns continues to echo in the empty sky and the *rat-a-tat* from the automatics is all around me, leaving little transparent blue clouds floating in the warm wind. Crawling on the soft ground I find what I am looking for: a chunk of rock hardly as big as a ballard. I press against it with my face so close to the stone that I can see every crack and bit of moss. I stay there, motionless. My body hurts and my ears are still full of the din from the bombs that have now stopped falling. I think I say aloud: Now it's our turn to give it to them! Where are the other men? Are there still men on this earth, or only these sad and pitiful larvae crawling along, only to stop and disappear in the mud? I stay for such a long time with my head pressed against the rock, listening to the automatics and the guns, that my face turns as cold as the stone. Then I hear the cannons behind me. The shells explode in the hills and black clouds of smoke rise into the warm sky.

Again I hear the orders to attack being given by the officers. I run straight ahead toward the shell holes where the automatics are positioned. And they are there, looking like big burned insects, and the bodies of the dead Germans seem like their victims. The men run in tight formations for the hills. The guns hidden in other holes sweep the field, killing men by tens and twenties. With two Canadians I roll into a shell hole full of German bodies. Together we throw the bodies up over the sides. My comrades are pale, their faces mud- and smoke-stained. We look soundlessly at each other; in any case, the noise of the guns would drown out our words. It drowns out even our thoughts. Protected by the armor plate of the automatic, I look at the goal that I have yet to reach. The hills of Thiepval are still as dark, still as far away. We'll never get to them.

Around two o'clock in the afternoon I hear the retreat being sounded. Immediately the two Canadians jump out of the shelter. They run to the river so quickly that I can't keep up with them. I can smell the smoke from the cannons in front of me and hear the shriek of the heavy shells passing above us. We have only a few minutes to get back to the base and the safety of the trenches. The sky is full of smoke, and the sunlight that was so beautiful this morning is now soiled and tarnished. When I finally get back to the trench, out of breath, I look at those who are already there and can hardly recognize their tired faces, or the empty, absent eyes of men who have escaped death looking back at me. I look for Odilon and my heart begins to pound because I can't find him. I run through the trench as far as the night shelter. "Odilon, where are you? Odilon, where are you?" The men look dazedly at me. Do they know who Odilon is? There are so many missing. For the rest of the day, as the bombardment continues, I hope against all reason that I'll finally see him appear at the edge of the trench, with his calm child's face and smile. That night the officer calls the roll and puts a cross by the names of the absent. How many have we lost? Twenty, thirty, perhaps more. Slumped against the trench wall I smoke as I drink bitter coffee and look at the beautiful night sky.

The next day and those that follow, the rumor goes round that we were defeated at Thiepval, as at Ovillers and at Beaumont-Hamel. They say that Joffre, the Commander of the French forces, told Haig to take Thiepval at any price, and that Haig refused to send his troops into another massacre. Have we lost the war?

Nobody speaks. Everyone eats quickly and silently, drinks lukewarm coffee, and smokes without catching his neighbor's eye. It's the ones who didn't come back who shame and disturb us. Sometimes, when I am still half-asleep, I think of Odilon as if he is still alive and when I wake up I look around for him. Perhaps he was wounded and is in the hospital at Albert, or was sent back to England? But deep down, I know very well that he fell on his face in the dark mud, despite the sunlight on the dark row of hills that we couldn't reach.

❖

Now everything has changed. Our division, decimated since the attack on Thiepval, has been divided among the 12th and 15th corps to the south and north of Albert. We are fighting under Rawlinson, acting as a "hurricane." Every night the infantry columns slowly advance from one trench to the next, crawling silently across the wet fields. We are penetrating far into enemy territory, and without the magnificent star-filled sky I wouldn't know that we are heading farther south each night. My experiences on board the *Zeta* and during the nights in English Cove have let me know this.

The cannons begin their bombardment before daybreak, burning the forests, hamlets, and hills in front of us. Then as soon as it is light the men start attacking, taking up their positions in the shell holes and firing on the enemy lines. A moment later the retreat is sounded and we all crawl backward, safe and sound. On July 14, after the attack, for the first time the English cavalry openly charges across the bomb craters. We enter Pozières together with the Australian Corps. It is nothing but a heap of rubble.

It is a very hot summer, and day after day the sun beats down. The heat is intense. We sleep where the last attack has led us, anywhere, even on the ground, protected from the evening dew by a piece of canvas. We can't think of death anymore. Every night we advance through the hills in Indian file, under the stars. Sometimes there is a flash of light from a rocket and the clatter of guns being fired haphazardly. These are warm, empty nights, devoid of insects or animals.

At the beginning of September we rejoin General Gough's 5th Army, and with the men who remain under Rawlinson's command we march even farther south toward Guillemont. At night we walk northeast, along the railroad track, going toward the woods. They surround us, dark and menacing: the Trones woods behind us, the Leuze woods to the south, and in front of us the Bouleaux woods. The men wait sleeplessly in the quiet night. I don't think any of us could keep from imagining what had been here before the war; the beauty of these quiet birch forests, where we could hear the hoot of the screech owl, the murmuring streams, and the bounding of the wild rabbit. These are woods where lovers used to go after the ball and where entwined bodies would laughingly roll on grass still warm from the sunlight. Woods along whose paths the silhouettes of shrunken old ladies tying up bundles of firewood would be seen in the evening, when blue smoke started rising from the calm villages. None of us sleep. We keep our eyes wide open on the night—perhaps our last? We listen carefully and our bodies pick up the slightest vibration, the slightest suggestion of life, which seems missing from here. We wait with painful dread for the moment when the first cannon shells will tear through the night behind us, raining down a hurricane of fire on the big trees, eviscerating the earth and opening the awful way for the attack.

Before dawn it starts to rain, a fine, cool drizzle that penetrates our clothes, wets our faces, and makes us shiver. Then, almost without the support of the bombardment, the men throw themselves in successive waves into the attack of the three woods. Behind us the night is fantastically lit on the Ancre side where the 15th Army launches a diversionary attack. But for us it is a silent and cruel battle, mostly fought with cold steel. One after the other waves of infantrymen pass over the trenches, taking possession of the automatics and chasing the enemy into the woods. I can hear the crackle of gunfire very near us in the Bouleaux woods. Lying in the wet ground we shoot haphazardly into the undergrowth. Rockets burst noiselessly into light above the trees, then fall in a shower of sparks. As I run to the woods I trip over an obstacle: it is the body of a German stretched out on his back in the grass. He is still holding his Mauser in his hand, but his helmet has rolled a few steps away. The officers are shouting, "Cease fire!" We have taken the woods. In the gray dawn light, the ground is littered with the bodies of Germans lying in the grass under the fine rain. Dead horses cover the field, and already the sad cawing of crows can be heard. Despite their fatigue, the men are laughing and singing. Our officer, an Englishman with a red and jovial face, tries to explain to me: "The bastards didn't expect us!" But I turn away and as I do I hear him repeating the same phrase to someone else. I feel nauseated and so deeply weary that I stagger. The men bivouac in the undergrowth in the German encampment. Everything was ready for reveille to be sounded; it seems the coffee is still warm. The Canadians happily drink it. I stretch out under the big trees with my head against the tender bark and fall asleep in the beautiful morning light.

❀

The heavy winter rains arrive, and the Somme and Ancre rivers overrun their banks. We are prisoners in the captured trenches, stuck in the mud, huddled in the makeshift shelters. We have already forgotten the intoxication of the battles that brought us here. We have captured Guillemont, Falfemont farm, Ginchy, and on September 15, Morval, Gueudecourt, and Lesboeufs, pushing the Germans back to their last trenches on top of the hilly slopes at Bapaume and Transloy. Now we are imprisoned in the trenches on the other side of the river, prisoners of the rain and mud. The days are gray and cold and nothing happens. Sometimes in the distance we can hear the sound of the cannons on the Somme and in the woods around Bapaume. Sometimes, too, we are awakened in the middle of the night by flashes of light. "On your feet!" shout the officers. We pack our knapsacks in the dark and leave with bent backs, running through the frozen mud that sticks to everything. We go south along the furrowed roads near the Somme, but we can't see where we're going. What do these rivers we are always talking about look like—the Yser, the Marne, the Meuse, the Aisne, the Ailette, the Scarpe? They are rivers of mud flowing under low skies, thick, heavy water carrying debris from the woods, burned beams, and dead horses.

Near Combles we meet up with the French divisions. They are paler and look more battered than we do. Their eyes are sunken and their uniforms are torn and splattered with mud. Some of them don't even have shoes anymore, and their feet are bound with bloody scraps of cloth. There is a German officer in their convoy. The soldiers give him a rough time, insulting him because of the gas that killed so many of us. Despite his tattered uniform he carries himself proudly, and suddenly he pushes them back. He shouts in perfect French: "But you were the first to use gas! It's *you* who forced us to fight in this way! It's *you!*" The silence that follows this outburst is impressive. Everyone lowers their eyes and the officer takes his place again among the prisoners.

Later we get to a village. I never knew the name of this village that we entered in the gray dawn with its deserted streets and its houses in ruins. Our boots echo strangely in the rain. It feels as if we have arrived at the end of the world, maybe even at the edge of the void. We camp in the destroyed village, and throughout the day convoys and Red Cross vans pass by. When the rain stops a cloud of dust veils the sky. Farther on, in the trenches that start where the village streets end, we hear the rumbling of the cannons again and farther still the hiccups of the falling shells.

Sitting at fires built in the corners of ruined houses, Canadian, Territorial, and French soldiers fraternize and exchange names. Others have nothing to say and we don't ask them anything. They continue to wander the streets, unable to stop. They are exhausted. In the distance we can hear gunfire, but it is as slight as school children's firecrackers. We are adrift in a strange country, in an incomprehensible time, being endlessly tormented by the same day and night. It has been such a long time since we had a real conversation. Such a long time since we talked to a woman. We hate the war with all our being.

We are surrounded by destroyed roads and crumbling houses. On the miraculously intact railway the cars have been disemboweled and turned upside down. Bodies dangle from them like cloth puppets. In the fields surrounding the village are horse cadavers as far as the eye can see, bloated and black like dead elephants. The crows somersault above the carrion, their grating cries making the living jump. Columns of sick and wounded prisoners move pathetically through the village. With them come mules, limping horses, and thin donkeys. The air is poisoned with smoke and the stench of corpses. The noxious smell like that of a dank cellar is everywhere; a German shell has sealed a tunnel in which the French had taken shelter to sleep. A lost man searches for his company. He attaches himself to me and repeats: "I'm from the 110th infantry. From the 110th. Do you know where they are?" In a shell hole at the bottom of the ruined church the Red Cross has erected a table where the dead and dying are heaped on top of each other. One night we sleep in a trench at Frégicourt, the next night in one at Portes-de-Fer. We continue marching across the plain. At night the minuscule lights of the artillery posts are our only landmarks. Sailly-Saillisel is in front of us, enveloped in a huge black cloud that looks as though it had come from a volcano. Cannons thunder very nearby, to the north on the Batack hills and to the south in the Saint-Pierre-Vasat woods. There are grenade and pistol battles in the village streets at night. From the windows of ruined cellars the automatics sweep the crossroads, mowing down men. I can hear them hammering as I breathe in the smell of sulphur and phosphorous from clouds of dancing shadows. "Wait! Hold your fire!" I am huddled in a ditch with men I don't know (French? Haig's English?). It is full of mud. There has been no water for days. My body is burning with fever and I am wracked with constant vomiting. The acrid odor fills my throat and I can't keep from shouting, "Gas! The gas is coming!" It is dawn and blood is running everywhere; it keeps rising and floods the trenches and ditches, coursing through the ruined houses and streaming over the ploughed-up fields.

Two men are carrying me. They are holding me under my armpits and dragging me to the Red Cross station. I lie on the open ground for such a long time that I become like a burning coal. Then I am in a truck that jolts and zigzags to avoid the bomb holes. The doctor in the hospital at Albert looks like Camal Boudou. He takes my temperature and squeezes my stomach. He says: "Typhoid." He adds (but maybe I only imagined it), "In the end it's the lice who win wars."

TOWARD RODRIGUES, SUMMER, 1918–1919

FREEDOM AT LAST: the sea. This is what I was waiting for during all those terrible, death-filled years: the moment when I would stand amid a crowd of discharged soldiers on the deck of a ship returning to India and Africa. We keep our eyes fixed on the sea from morning 'til night, and keep staring at it when the moon rises and illuminates the wake. Once we have passed through the Suez Canal the nights become so soft and inviting that we creep up from the hold to sleep on deck. I roll myself up in my army blanket—the only souvenir, along with my khaki jacket and the canvas pouch with my army papers, that I have kept from the war. We have slept in the mud for so long that the wooden deck with the star-filled sky above us feels like paradise. We converse in creole and pidgin, sing songs and tell endless stories. The war has already become legend, constantly transformed by each different storyteller. There are men from the Seychelles, Mauritius, and South Africa on deck; but none of the Rodriguans who had volunteered in front of the telegraph office is here. I remember Casimir's joy when his name was called. Can it be that, thanks to the lice, I am the only survivor, the only one who has escaped the slaughter?

❊

I think of Laure often these days. When it is allowed I go up to the prow, near the capstan, and watch the horizon. As I watch the dark-blue sea and the clouds I think of Laure's face. We are in the open sea now, near Aden; then we pass Cape Gardafui and are making for the big ports of Mombasa and Zanzibar, which Laure and I dreamed about at Boucan. We are sailing toward the Equator and the days are already burning hot, the nights dry with glittering, starry skies. I watch the flying fish, albatross, and dolphins. And every day the picture I have of Laure becomes stronger; I can hear her voice more clearly, catch her ironic smile and glimpse the light in her eyes.

Near Oman we are caught in a magnificent storm. When it starts there is not a cloud in the sky, only a fierce wind that makes the waves crash into the ship. The ship is like a moving wall against which sea rams are butting their heads. Buffeted on both sides, the ship rolls considerably and waves sweep over the lower deck where we are. Like it or not, we have to leave paradise and go down into the disgusting, furnace-hot hold. The sailors tell us we are experiencing the tail of a storm passing over Socotora, and in fact that same evening torrential rains deluge the ship and flood the holds. We take turns pumping while streams of water sweep through the bilge, running between our legs and carrying off the trash and debris. But when sea and sky are calm again the light is dazzling! We are surrounded by the vast, blue ocean where long waves fringed with spray advance slowly alongside the ship.

The stops in Mombasa and Zanzibar and the journey to Tamatave pass very quickly. I hardly ever leave my place on deck, except when the afternoon sun is at its fiercest and when there are sudden downpours. I don't take my eyes from the sea, but watch it constantly as it changes color and mood:

sometimes smooth and waveless, rippling in the wind; at other times hard, horizonless, gray with rain, roaring, giving us a piece of its mind. I think again of the *Zeta* and the voyage to English Cove. It seems like such a long time ago that I saw Ouma gliding along the riverbed, harpoon in hand, or felt her sleeping body pressed against mine as we lay under the star-filled sky. Here at last, thanks to the sea, I find my rhythm and dare to dream again. I know that I have to go back to Rodrigues. Its pull is stronger than I; I have to go back. Will Laure be able to understand that?

❀

When the long pirogue that ferries between the ship and Port Louis finally reaches the dock, I am assailed by the crowd, the din, and the smells. My head swims as it did in Mombasa, and for a moment I want to get back on the steamship and continue my journey. But suddenly, under the trees at the Commissariat, I see Laure. The next moment she is hugging me, then pulling me through the streets to the station. In spite of our emotion we speak quietly and slowly, as if we had only parted yesterday. She asks me about the journey and the military hospital, tells me about the letters she wrote. Then she says, "Why have they cut your hair like a convict?" I reply, "Because of the lice!" There is a moment of silence. Then she begins to ask me again about England and France, as we walk to the station through streets I don't recognize anymore.

The years have changed Laure and I don't think I would have recognized her if she hadn't been wearing the same white dress she wore when I left for Rodrigues, or standing slightly apart from everyone else. In the second-class compartment going to Rose Hill and Quatre Bornes I notice the pallor of her skin, the dark circles around her eyes, and the bitter lines on either side of her mouth. She is still beautiful, the same light flares up in her eyes, and the nervous energy I like so much is still there, but it is all weaker, as if she has been tired out.

My heart contracts as we approach the Forest Side house. Under rain that looks as if it hasn't stopped for years, it seems even sadder and more somber. With a first glance I take in the crumbling porch, the little garden with its overgrown grass, and the broken tiles that have been repaired with gummed paper. Laure follows my eyes and says in a low voice, "We're poor now." My mother appears, starts down the porch steps, and then stops. Her face is tense and anxious; she doesn't smile and she puts her hand up to her eyes as if to see where we are, even though we are only a few feet away. I realize that she is almost blind. When I am in front of her I take her hands. She holds me to her for a long time without saying anything.

In spite of our impoverished circumstances and the neglected house, for that evening and the days that follow I am happier than I have been for a long time. It feels as if I have come home, as if I have found myself.

❈

December: Despite the rain that falls every afternoon on Forest Side, that summer is the most beautiful and carefree that I have known in years. Thanks to the pile of money I received the day I was discharged—along with the Médaille Militaire and the Medal for Distinguished Conduct, as well as a promotion to Warrant Officer, first class—we are safe from want for some time and I am able to explore the region as much as I wish. Laure often comes with me, and on the bicycles I bought in Port Louis we cross the cane plantations and cycle to Henrietta and Quinze Cantons. Or we take the cart-filled road toward Mahébourg and go as far as Nouvelle France, then take the muddy paths to Cluny or cycle across the Bois Chéri tea plantations. In the morning, when we emerge from the mist that covers Forest Side, the sun shines on the dark foliage and the wind makes the cane wave in the fields. Nothing troubles us as we zigzag between the puddles, me in my uniform jacket and Laure in her white dress with a big straw hat on her head. In the fields the women in gunnies stop working to watch us pass. On the road to Quinze Cantons, at about one o'clock, we meet up with the women coming from the fields. They walk slowly in their long swinging skirts, balancing their hoes perfectly on their heads. They call out to us in creole and make fun of Laure, who pedals with her dress bunched between her legs.

One afternoon Laure and I are cycling beyond Quinze Cantons, and we cross the Rempart River. The path is so difficult that we have to abandon the bikes and hastily stash them in the cane. In spite of the burning sun the path is muddy in places and we have to take off our shoes. We walk barefoot in the warm mud as we used to, and Laure knots her white dress between her legs, Indian style.

My heart starts to pound as I walk in front of her toward the Trois Mamelles peaks, which dominate the cane fields like strange termite heaps. The sky, which earlier was so clear, has filled with big clouds. But we don't pay any attention to them. Propelled by the same desire we walk as fast as we can through the sharp cane leaves. The plantation ends at the Papayes River. After that there are big fields of grass with heaps of black stones rising out of them; Laure calls them martyr's tombs because of all the people who died working in the cane fields. At the end of this steppe, between the Trois Mamelles peaks, you get to the stretch of country that borders the sea, from Wolmar down to Rivière Noire. When we get to the pass we are blown about by the wind from the sea. Big clouds race across the sky. After the heat of the cane fields the wind makes us dizzy. We stop for a moment to look at the countryside stretching out in front of us, and it is as if time has stood still, as if it were only yesterday that we left Boucan. I look at Laure. Her face is hard and closed but her breath is coming short, and when she turns to me I see that her eyes are shining with tears. It is the first time she has revisited the scene of our childhood. She sits down on the grass and I sit beside her. We don't speak as we gaze at the hills, the dark shadows of the streams, the uneven ground. I search in vain along the Boucan River for our house behind the Tourelle. All signs of habitation have disappeared and in place of the woods there are large burned wastelands. It is Laure who speaks first, as if answering my questions.

"Our house isn't there anymore. Uncle Ludovic had the whole property razed to the ground, while you were on Rodrigues, I think. He didn't even wait for the final judgment to be handed down.

My voice is thick with anger.

"But why? How could he have dared?"

"He said he wanted to use the land for cane. He didn't need the house."

"How despicable! If I'd known, if I'd been there. . ."

"What could you have done? We couldn't do anything. I hid it from Mam so as not to upset her more. She wouldn't have been able to stand his ruthlessness, wanting to hurt us so much that he even destroyed the house."

My eyes cloud over as I look at the sea sparkling in the light of the setting sun and the lengthening shadow of the Tourelle, this magnificent countryside spread out before our eyes. I am studying the banks of the Boucan so hard, and it seems to me that I can see something like a scar in the brush where the house and garden were, near the dark spot of the ravine where we used to perch on the old tree. Laure goes on speaking, trying to console me. Her anger has subsided now and her voice is calm.

"You know, it isn't important anymore that the house is gone. The life we had there happened such a long time ago, it's over now. What's important now is that you've come back. Mam is old and she needs us both. It was only a house after all. An old decaying dump with a leaking roof. It's no good wanting what no longer exists."

But I say in a strangled voice full of rage, "No, I can't forget it. I will never forget it!"

I stare for a long time at the still countryside under the moving sky. I look at it in detail, scrutinizing each river and thicket from the Rivière Noire gorge as far as Tamarin. On the banks of the river I can see smoke coming from Gaulette, near Grande Rivière Noire. Perhaps Denis is there in old Cook's hut. I am staring so hard at this golden light on the sea and shore that at any moment I expect to see shadows of the children we once were running barefoot through the high grass, faces scratched and clothes torn, racing at twilight across a world that stretched forever to watch the flight of the two bo'sun birds above the mysterious Mananava.

THE HEADINESS OF homecoming passed quickly. First there was my job in the W. W. West offices, the same job I'd held for so long and that everybody pretended I'd left to go to war. The same smell of dust, the same humid heat filtering in through the shutters, the same din from Rempart Street. The same bored employees, clients, merchants, accountants . . . For all these people nothing has changed. The world has stayed the same. Yet Laure tells me that one day in 1913, when I was in Rodrigues, the starving people, reduced to penury by the cyclones, all gathered in front of the station. The crowd of Indians and blacks from the plantations, the women in gunnies with their babies in their arms, stood there without shouting or making a sound, waiting for the train from the mountains, the one that came every day from Vacoas and Curepipe, bringing the whites who owned the banks, shops, and plantations to town. They waited for a long time, patiently at first, then gradually showing their anger and despair as time passed. What would have happened if the whites had come to town that day? But having been warned of the danger in advance they didn't take the train to Port Louis. They stayed at home waiting for the police to settle the affair. The crowd was dispersed. Some of the Chinese shops were robbed, some stones were thrown through the windows of the Foncier Bank and even through those of the W. W. West offices. That was how the affair was settled.

At the W. W. West offices my cousin Ferdinand, Uncle Ludovic's son, is now the boss. He pretends not to know me and treats me like a servant. I get angry, but because Laure wants me to keep the job so much I don't argue with him. The same as before, every free moment I have I spend walking along the quays on the port, among the sailors and dockers, near the fish market. What I would like more than anything is to see the *Zeta* again, and Captain Bradmer, and the Comorian helmsman. I often stand under the trees at the Commissariat, hoping to see the schooner with its armchair come into port. I already know that I'll have to leave again.

At night, in my room at Forest Side, I open the old trunk, which has rusted from its stay on English Cove, and look through the accumulated papers, maps, sketches, and notes concerning the treasure, which I had sent from Rodrigues before leaving for Europe. When I look at them I see Ouma, diving cleanly into the water, swimming easily, her ebony-tipped harpoon in her hand.

Each day my desire to return to Rodrigues grows stronger, my desire to be once more in the silent, peaceful valley where the sky, clouds, and sea don't belong to anyone. I want to flee from "high society," from their meanness and hypocrisy. Ever since the *Cernéen* printed an article, "Our World War Heroes," in which my name was cited and various, purely imaginary acts of bravery attributed to me, suddenly Laure and I are on all the guest lists for parties at Port Louis, Curepipe, and Floréal. Laure accompanies me dressed in her same old white dress, and we chat and dance. We go to the Champ-de-Mars or have tea at the Flore. All the time I think of Ouma and the cries of the birds that fly over the cove every morning. It is the people here who seem imaginary and unreal to me. I'm tired of the false honors they insist on giving me. One day, without telling Laure, I leave my gray office worker's suit at Forest Side and put on the old khaki jacket and pants I brought back from the war, both of them dirty and torn from the days in the trenches, but adorned with my officer's insignia and my decorations. That afternoon when the W. W. West offices close, I go and sit in the Flore tea room after having drunk several glasses of arak, still wearing this costume. From that day on, like magic, the society invitations stop coming.

But my boredom and desire to flee are so great that Laure can't help noticing. One evening she is waiting for me at Curepipe Station the way she used to. The constant Forest Side drizzle has wet her white dress and hair, and she is holding a big leaf over her head to try to keep dry. I tell her she looks like Virginie, which makes her smile. We walk along the muddy road, alongside Indians going back to their houses before nightfall. Suddenly Laure says, "You're going away again, aren't you?"

I search for a reply that will reassure her, but she repeats, "You're going to leave soon, aren't you? Tell me the truth." Without waiting for my reply, or maybe because she knows it, she becomes angry. "Why don't you say anything? Why must I always hear about you from other people?" She hesitates, then says, "That woman there, the one you lived with like a savage! And that stupid treasure you still think exists!"

How does she know? Who can have told her about Ouma?

"We'll never be the way we were before. There will never be a place for us here."

Her words hurt because I know they're true. I say, "But that's why I have to leave. That's why I have to find the treasure."

What would have been a good way to tell her? She has already pulled herself together. She wipes away the tears running down her face and cleans her nose with the back of her hand like a child. The gloomy Forest Side house stands before us like a boat stranded atop a hill after a flood.

That evening, after dinner with Mam, Laure is happier. We sit on the porch talking about my voyage and the treasure, and Laure says animatedly, "When you find the treasure we'll come and join you. We'll have a farm that we'll work ourselves like the pioneers in the Transvaal."

Then, little by little, we let our dreams become more grandiose, as they used to in the attic at Boucan. We speak about the farm and the animals we'll have when our new lives begin, far away from the bankers and lawyers. I find François Leguat's narrative among my father's books and read aloud the passages dealing with the flora, climate, and beauty of Rodrigues.

Drawn by the sound of our voices, Mam comes down from her room. She comes out to where we are, and her face in the light of the storm lamp looks as young and beautiful as it was at Boucan. She listens for a while to our extravagant ideas, then she kisses us and holds us close. "You're dreaming again."

That night the old crumbling Forest Side house really is a ship crossing the sea, making its way as it pitches and creaks under the soft patter of the rain to a new life.

BEING ON THE *Zeta* again makes me feel as if I've re-discovered life and freedom after years of exile. I am in my same place on the stern, next to Captain Bradmer sitting in his armchair screwed to the deck. We have already been sailing for two days with a tail wind along the 20th parallel in a north-easterly direction. When the sun is high Bradmer rises from his chair and, as he used to, turns to me. "Would you like to try your hand, sir?" Just as if we had been sailing together all these years.

Standing barefoot on the deck with my hands gripping the wheel, I am happy. The deck is deserted except for two Co-morian sailors with white turbans on their heads. It is good to hear the wind in the rigging again and see the prow rise up against the waves. The *Zeta* looks as if it could go up as far as the horizon where the sky begins.

It seems only yesterday that I was on my way to Rodrigues for the first time, standing on deck with the taste of salt on my lips, feeling the ship move beneath me like an animal as the bow mounted the big waves. Surrounded by silence and the vast sea it is as if I have always been here at the *Zeta* helm, fol-lowing a course that never ends, as if everything else that hap-pened was nothing but a dream. A dream of the Unknown

Corsair's gold in the ravine at English Cove, of my love for Ouma with her lava-colored skin, of the lagoons and sea birds. The war was a dream, too: the freezing nights in Flanders, the rain at Ancre and Somme, the clouds of gas, and the flashes from the exploding shells.

When the sun begins to set behind us and I can see the sails' shadows on the sea, Captain Bradmer takes back the helm. Standing in front of the wheel with his red face and his eyes squinting against the sun on the waves, he looks just the same. Without being asked he tells me about the helmsman's death.

"It was in nineteen-sixteen, or maybe at the beginning of nineteen-seventeen . . . We got to Agalega and he became sick. He had diarrhea and fever and was delirious. He couldn't eat or drink. The doctor came and said it was typhoid and ordered the whole boat to be put into quarantine. He was afraid of an epidemic. He never came back and the next day the helmsman was dead. Then, sir, I got angry. Since they didn't want anything to do with us, I had all the merchandise we were carrying thrown overboard in front of Agalega, then we left and went south to Saint Brandon. That's where he wanted to end his days . . . We tied a weight to his feet and threw him into the sea in front of the reefs, where the water is so deep and blue. When he had sunk we said prayers, then I said: Helmsman, my friend, now you are home forever. Rest in peace. And the others said: Amen. We stayed for two days in front of the atoll. It was so beautiful, there wasn't a cloud in the sky and the sea was so calm. We watched the birds and turtles swimming near the ship. We caught several turtles to smoke and then we left."

His voice wavers and is drowned by the wind. The old man stares straight ahead past the bulging sails. In the twilight his face suddenly looks tired, indifferent to what the future might bring. Now I understand how deluded I was: history happened here just as it did everywhere else; the world is not the same anywhere. There have been crimes, transgressions, a war, and because of it our lives have come apart.

"It's funny, but I haven't been able to find another helmsman. He knew the sea so well, even as far as Oman . . . It's as if the boat doesn't really know where it's going anymore . . . It's funny, isn't it? He was the true captain of this ship. It belonged to him."

As I look at the sparkling wake drawing a path on the impenetrable waters, I become anxious again. I'm afraid of arriving at Rodrigues, afraid of what I'll find. Where is Ouma? The two letters I sent her, first from London, before leaving for Flanders, then from the military hospital in Sussex, were not answered. Were they even delivered? Does one write to Manafs?

At night I don't go down into the hold. Protected by the cargo stowed on deck, I sleep rolled in my blanket with my head on my knapsack, listening to the sea and the wind in the sails. When I wake I go urinate over the side, then come back and sit and watch the star-filled sky. What an eternity time at sea is! With each hour that passes more of my troublesome memories are washed away, and I come closer to the immortal helmsman. Is it *he* whom I must find at the end of my journey?

Today, the wind having turned, we are on a beam reach, the masts at a sixty-degree angle, and the recalcitrant sea slaps at the stem, bringing up clouds of spray. The new helmsman is a black with an impassive face. Despite the tilt of the deck, Captain Bradmer is sitting beside him in his old armchair, watching the sea as he smokes. Every attempt I make to engage him in conversation is stopped by two words, which he grunts without looking at me: "What, sir?" and "No, sir." We are being buffeted by fierce gusts of wind, and most of the men, except for the Rodriguan merchants who do not want to leave their parcels unattended on deck, have taken refuge in the hold. The sailors quickly close the hatches and pull an oilskin over the merchandise. I slide my knapsack under the oilskin and, in spite of the sun, wrap my blanket around me.

The *Zeta* is making a huge effort to dominate the sea, I can feel every creak of the hull, every groan of the masts. Because she is heeling so far over, huge steaming waves break on the deck and wash over us. At three o'clock the wind is so fierce that it makes me think it might be a hurricane, but there are very few clouds, only pale mare's tails that cross the sky in huge arcs—not a sky that heralds a storm.

The *Zeta* is having trouble staying on course. Bradmer himself is at the helm, bracing himself on his short legs and grimacing because of the spray. Even with few sails set, the force of the wind still makes the ship whine. How long will he be able to control it? Then suddenly the squalls become less violent and the masts straighten up. It is nearly five in the evening, and the light is warm and beautiful as the mountains of Rodrigues slowly rise above the sharp horizon.

Suddenly everyone is on deck. The Rodriguans sing and shout and even the usually taciturn Comorians speak. I stand in the bow with everyone else, and with a pounding heart stare at the deceptively blue line as if it is a mirage.

This is how I imagined arriving all the time I was in the hellish war, stuck in the trenches, ankle deep in mud and waste. My dream comes true as the *Zeta* races like a skiff over the dark sphere of water, amid bursts of spray, toward the transparent mountains on the island.

That evening, accompanied by the frigates and terns, we go past Gombrani, then Plateau Point, where the sea becomes oily. We can already see the beacon lights shining in the distance. Night has fallen over the northern slopes of the mountains. My fear has passed, and now I'm impatient to go ashore.

The ship glides along with all sails set and I watch the dike getting closer. I lean over the side with the Rodriguans, bag in hand, ready to jump ashore.

The children are already coming aboard when, as I am about to disembark, I turn round to look at Captain Bradmer. But he has finished giving his orders, and in the dim light of the beacons I can only see the outline of his face and body marked by tiredness and loneliness. Without looking at me, he goes down into the hold to smoke and sleep, and perhaps to think of the helmsman who never left the ship. As I walk toward the lights of Port Mathurin I carry this disturbing picture with me. I don't realize that this is the last time I will ever see Captain Bradmer.

❊

At dawn I arrive in my domain, at Commander's Summit, where a long time ago I saw English Cove for the first time. Here it seems as if nothing has changed. The big valley still stretches to the sea, black and isolated. While I descend the slope between the vacoa blades, making the ground under my feet crumble, I try to recognize all the places I have been, the ones I know well: the dark stain of the ravine, the big tamarind tree, the basalt blocks with their etched signs, the thin line of the Roseaux River that snakes between the bushes to the marsh; and farther away, the mountain peaks that were my landmarks. There are trees whose names I don't know, and Indian almonds, coconuts, and spurge.

When I get to the middle of the valley, I look in vain for the old tamarind tree where my camp was, under which Ouma and I had slept when the nights were warm. There is a mound of earth where the tree used to be, criss-crossed with thornbushes. I realize that the tree is still there, sleeping under the earth—it must have been hit by a storm—and that this mound covers its roots and trunk almost like a tomb. Despite the sun beating down on my back and neck, I sit on the mound in the middle of the brush for a long time, trying to retrace my steps. I decide to build my shelter where the old tree used to be.

I no longer know anyone on Rodrigues. Most of the men who responded to Lord Kitchener's appeal and left with me haven't come back. During the war years there was a famine because of the blockade, when the boats didn't bring any food— rice, oil, tinned goods. The population was decimated by sickness; typhoid especially killed the mountain people because they didn't have any medicine. Rats are everywhere now; they run through the Port Mathurin streets in broad daylight. What happened to Ouma and her brother in the desertlike mountains, without any resources? What has become of the Manafs?

The only person I know is Fritz Castel, who didn't go to war and stayed in the isolated farm near the telegraph offices. He is a young man of seventeen or eighteen now, with an intelligent face and a deep voice, and I have difficulty seeing in him the child who helped me set the posts. The other men, Raboud, Prosper, Adrien Mercure, have disappeared like Casimir, like all those who responded to the call-up. *"Fin-'mort,"* repeats Fritz Castel when I say their names: dead.

With Fritz Castel's help I build a hut of branches and palms before the tomb of the old tamarind tree. How long will I stay? I know my days are limited. I don't need money (my discharge pay is almost intact, it's time that I don't have. I've been weakened by what I have gone through. I realize this as soon as I return to the silent cove, surrounded by the power of the basalt walls, listening to the continuous swell of the sea. Can I really still hope for something from this place, after how the world has been destroyed? Why have I come back?

❄

For days I sit without moving, like the blocks of basalt at the bottom of the valley that look like ruins from a city long disappeared. I don't want to move. I need to be enveloped in this silence, this stupor. At dawn I go to the reeds on the beach. I sit on the spot where Ouma covered me with sand to let me dry in the wind. I listen to the roar of the waves breaking in arcs, waiting for the moment when the sea will climb the neck of the channel in a cloud of spray. Then I listen to it coming closer, gliding over the oily river bed and emptying into the secretive pools. In the morning and at night the flight of the sea birds across the bay marks the day's beginning and end. I think of the beauty of those simple fearless nights in the valley, the nights when I waited for Ouma, or when I wasn't waiting for anyone, and the nights when I kept watch on the stars, each one in its place in the cosmos. But now as night falls I become disturbed and anxious. I listen to the sound of the stones contracting and notice how cold it is. Most nights I curl up at the back of my hut with my eyes wide open, shivering and unable to sleep. My anxiety is sometimes so great that I have to go back to town to sleep in the Chinaman's narrow hotel room, after barricading the door with the table and chair.

What has happened to me? The days pass slowly in English Cove. Young Fritz Castel often comes to sit on the mound of the old tree in front of my hut. We smoke and speak, or rather, *I* speak, about the war, the attacks with naked bayonets in the trenches, and the bright glare of the bombs. He listens to me patiently, saying, "Yes, sir" or "No, sir." So as not to disappoint him I send him to dig some holes. But the old maps I drew don't mean anything to me now. The lines become a jumble as I look at them; the angles distort and the landmarks sink into each other.

After Fritz Castel has left I go sit under the big tamarind tree at the entrance to the ravine, and as I smoke I watch the changing light in the valley. Several times I go into the ravine to feel the burning heat on my face and chest. The ravine is just as I left it: the rocks that concealed the first hiding place, the marks from the pickaxes, and big groove-shaped notch on the overhanging basalt are still there. What did I come to look for here? It all feels so empty and abandoned, like a body wracked by fever where everything that once was hot and palpitating has been reduced to a feeble tremor. But I still enjoy the light in the ravine, and the solitude. I also like the sky, which is so blue, and the shape of the mountains above the valley. Perhaps it is for all this that I have come back.

In the evenings, while the twilight deepens, I sit in the sand on the dunes and dream of Ouma and her metal-colored body. I make a drawing of her with a sharp piece of flint on a basalt block near where the reeds start. But when I want to write the date I realize that I don't know what day or month it is. For a moment I think of running to the telegraph office as I did before, to ask: What day is it? But then I realize that it wouldn't mean anything to me, that the date is of no importance.

❀

This morning, as soon as the sun has risen, I make for the mountains. At first it seems to me that the path I'm following between the bushes and vacoa trees is one I know, but soon the sun becomes so hot my vision blurs. Below me the hard blue stretch of sea encircles the island. If Ouma is here I will find her. I need her; it is she who holds the key to the prospector's secret. My heart beats fast as I climb Mount Limon by way of the landslide. Was this the way I came when I was trying to follow Sri as he ran up the mountain? The sun is at its zenith and no shadows are left. I don't recognize anything and there is nowhere to shelter from the blistering rays.

I am lost in the middle of the mountains, surrounded by stones and bushes that all look alike. Burned peaks point from all sides into the sparkling sky. For the first time in years I shout her name: "Ou-ma-ah!" I stand facing the fawn-colored mountain and scream: "Ou-ma-ah!" The burning, blinding wind is screaming, too. It reeks of lava and vacoa and numbs my brain. "Ou-ma-ah!" I turn northward again, this time to where I can see the churning sea. Then I climb to the top of Limon where I can see all the other mountains around me. The bottom part of the valley is already in shadow. In the east the sky is clouding over. "Ou-ma-ah!" It feels as if I'm shouting my own name into this desertlike landscape, trying to call up the echo of my life lost during all those years of destruction. "Ouma! Ou-ma-ah!" My voice becomes hoarse as I wander over the high plateau, searching in vain for some traces of habitation, a goat's corral, a fire. But the mountain is empty. There are no signs of human beings, no broken branches, no disturbance of the dry ground. Only the occasional tracks of a centipede between two stones.

❧

Where am I? I must have wandered for hours without realizing it. When night comes it is too late for me to think of going back down again. I look around for a place to take shelter, a craggy spot in the rocks that will protect me from the night chill and the rain that has started to fall. On the side of the mountain, which is already in shadow, I find a kind of bank covered in short grass and settle there for the night. The wind whistles above my head. Exhausted, I fall asleep immediately. I am awakened by the cold. The night is pitch black and in front of me the waxing moon shines with a brilliant, surreal light. Time is suspended in the beauty of the moon.

As day breaks I slowly start to make out the shapes surrounding me. I am moved when I realize I've spent the night in the ruins of an old Manaf camp. I dig at the dry ground with my hands and discover traces of what I am looking for between the stones: bits of glass, rusty cans, shells. Now I can clearly see the circles of the pens and the bases of the huts. Is this all that remains of the village Ouma lived in? What happened to all of them? Abandoned by everyone else, did they all die of fever and starvation? If they left, they didn't have time to cover their traces. They must have fled. I stand in the middle of the ruins, feeling completely disheartened.

After the sun has risen I go back down the slopes of Mount Limon through the thornbushes. Soon I can see the vacoas and the dark foliage of the tamarinds. At the end of the long Roseaux River valley, the sea that keeps us prisoner glitters harshly in the sun.

S UMMER, WINTER, ONCE again the rainy season. I have spent all this time in English Cove, dreaming, with nothing to guide me, not knowing what was happening to me. Gradually I've started searching again, measuring the distance between the rocks and drawing new lines in the invisible network that covers the valley. All my movements take place on this spider web.

I have never felt as close to uncovering the secret as I do now. The feverish impatience of seven or eight years ago, when every day I discovered a sign or symbol, no longer plagues me. Then I came and went between the slopes of the valley, jumping from rock to rock and boring holes everywhere. I was so impatient and violent. I couldn't hear Ouma, or see her. I was totally blinded by this stony landscape while I watched for shadows that would uncover a new secret.

Today, all that is over with. Now I have what I lacked before: faith. I have faith in the basalt blocks, in the ravines, in the narrow river, in the sand dunes. Where did it come from? Perhaps from the sea that encircles the island, from its deep and vibrant roar. Everything here is a part of me; I finally understood this by coming back to English Cove. It is a power that I'd believed lost. So now there isn't any need to hurry. Sometimes I sit motionless for hours in the dunes near the estuary, watching the waves, the petrels and seagulls flying by. Or, in the shelter of my hut, when the sun is at its zenith, after having dined on several boiled crabs and some coconut milk, I write in the exercise books that I bought from the Chinese traders at Port Mathurin. I write letters to Ouma and Laure that they will never receive, in which I describe unimportant things, what the sky looks like, the shape of the clouds, the color of the sea, and the thoughts I have sitting here at the head of English Cove. At night when the sky is cold and the full moon stops me from sleeping, I light the storm lamp and sit cross-legged at the entrance to the hut, smoking and drawing maps on other exercise books, keeping a record of the progress I am making in unraveling the secret.

I bring back odd things from my walks on the beach, things that have been thrown up by the sea; shells, sea urchin fossils, and *tek-tek* shells. I carefully put these objects in the empty biscuit box. I remember the things that Denis used to bring back to Laure from his wanderings, so I am keeping them for her. Young Fritz Castel and I bore into the sand on the cove floor and I pick up strangely shaped pebbles and half-broken bits of shale and flint. One morning we are following the Roseaux River's old course, taking turns digging with the pickax near the spot where it forms an elbow, when we un-cover a big, smoky, black basalt stone that has a series of nicks made on its tip with a chisel. Kneeling in front of the stone I try to decipher it. My companion watches me curiously and fearfully: Who can this god be that we have brought forth from the river sand?

"Look! Look here!"

The young man hesitates, then kneels beside me. I show him how the nicks on the black stone correspond to the moun-tains in front of us at the back of the valley: "Look, here is

Limon. There are Lubin and Patate. Over there is big Malartic. Over here, Bilactère and the two Charlots and there, Commander's Summit and the Lookout. Everything is marked on this stone. This is where he disembarked, and I'm certain he moored his canoe on this stone. These are all the landmarks he used to draw his secret map." Fritz Castel gets up. The same look I saw before is in his eyes, curiosity mixed with fear. What or who is he afraid of? Me, or the man who marked this stone so long ago?

❀

Fritz Castel has not come back since that day. It's probably better this way. Alone, I can more easily understand the reasons for my being in this sterile valley. Now nothing separates me from the stranger who came here nearly two hundred years ago to leave his secret before dying.

How could I exist in such ignorance of what was around me, looking only for gold, ready to flee from here as soon as I had found it? Boring all those holes and laboring so hard to move the rocks was a violation. Alone and at peace with myself, I finally understand: this whole valley is like a tomb. Mysterious and savage, it is a place of exile. I remember Ouma's words when she spoke to me the first time, and her hurt tone when she asked: "Do you really love gold so much?" I didn't understand then; I was amused by what I thought was her naïveté. What else could there be to take from this harsh valley? Not for one moment did I think that this wild, strange girl could possibly know the secret. Now, it is probably too late.

There is only me in the middle of this pile of stones, with these bundles of papers, maps, and exercise books in which I have written the story of my life as my only support!

Toward Rodrigues, Summer, 1918–1919

I think back to the time when I started discovering the world in the Boucan valley. I remember the times I ran through the grass to catch sight of the birds eternally wheeling above Mananava. I've started to talk to myself as I used to. I sing the words from the chorus of the song that we used to sing with old Cook when he rocked us gently on his knees:

> *Waï, waï, mo zenfant,*
> *faut travaï pou gagne so pain . . .*

I hear that voice again. I watch the Roseaux River running toward the estuary in the soft dusk. I forget the heat, the frustrating search at the bottom of the cliff, and all the holes I bored for nothing. Night falls, and with it the hardly perceptible ripple of wind through the reeds and the soft noise of the sea. This is how it used to be when I sat near the Tourelle de Tamarin watching darkness cover the glens, peering into the dim light to catch the curls of smoke rising over Boucan.

❁

At last I have rediscovered the freedom of the nights when I lay on the ground with open eyes, communing with the center of the sky. Alone in the valley I watch the galaxy unfold, the still cloud of the Milky Way. One by one, the stars of my childhood appear: Hydra, Leo, Orion's Dog, proud Orion carrying his jewels on his shoulders, the Southern Cross, and as always, the Argo, sailing eastward through space, its stern lifted by the invisible waves of the night. I lie in the black sand near the Roseaux River, neither sleeping nor dreaming. I feel the soft light of the stars on my face, and the movement of the earth. In the peaceful summer silence, with the sea rumbling in the distance, I realize that the constellations are a key. I can see all the different roads across the sky, the spots that shine more brightly like beacons. I can see secret paths, dark pits, and traps. I think of the Unknown Corsair who might have slept on this same beach so long ago. Did he also know the old tamarind tree, which now lies underground? Did he also watch the stars that had guided him here? Lying on the soft ground after the violent battles and killings, protected from the sea winds by the coconut trees and euphorbias, he must finally have found peace here. I cross time in a rush of vertigo as I watch the star-filled sky. The Unknown Corsair is here, too; he breathes my breath and I look at the sky through his eyes.

Why didn't I think of it earlier? The configuration of English Cove is the same as that of the universe. I had constantly enlarged the simple map of the valley and filled it with signs and sticks, and the truth of this place was soon hidden behind all the intertwined lines. With a pounding heart I leap up and run to my hut, where the night light is still burning. In the wavering light from the lamp I search in my bag for the maps, documents, and grids. I take the papers and the lamp outside and facing south, compare my maps with the designs in the vault above. In the center of the map, where I had previously put my boundary marker, the intersection of the north-south line with the axis of the mooring rings corresponds to the Cross shining in front of me. In the east, above the ravine of the same shape, Scorpius bends back its body, in whose center is red Antares, pulsating at the place where I discovered the Unknown Corsair's two hiding places. I look to the east and see, above the three points forming the M of Commander's Summit, the three Marys of Orion's belt, which have just appeared above the mountains. In the north, toward the sea, is the Big Dipper, light and fleeting, designating the entrance to the pass; and further on, the curve of the ship *Argo,* which traces the shape of the bay, and whose stern goes up the estuary as far as the end of the ancient riverbank. It is so dizzying that I have to close my eyes. Am I in the grip of a new hallucination? But the stars have always been there, and the ground below them follows their outline. The secret I have been looking for has always been hidden in the firmament, where there is no room for error. Without realizing it, I have been seeing it since I first started looking at the night sky in the "path of stars."

Where is the treasure to be found? Is it buried in Scorpio or Hydra? Is it in the Southern Triangle, which joins at the center of the valley points H, D, and B that I first found? Is it in the *Argo's* stem or in the stern, marked by Canopus and Miaplacidus, shining so brightly every day in the two basalt rocks on either side of the bay? Is it in Formalhaut, that jewel of a star that stands by itself, shining with the clarity of a piercing glance above the high sea, rising high in the sky like a night sun?

That night I keep watch, unable to sleep, tingling from the sky's revelation, looking at every constellation, every sign. I remember the star-filled nights at Boucan when I crept silently out of the hot room into the cool of the garden. Then, like now, I believed I could feel the position of the stars on my skin, and as dawn started breaking I would use sharp little pebbles to draw these positions in the ground or in the sand of the ravine.

Morning comes and I fall asleep at last in the light as I used to, not far from the mound that contains the old tamarind tree.

❖

Now that I know the secret of the Unknown Corsair's map I no longer feel any need to hurry. For the first time since I came back from the war it feels as if my quest has changed meaning. Before I didn't know what I was looking for, *whom* I was seeking. I was trapped by an illusion. It feels as if a weight has lifted from me, enabling me to live and breathe again. I can take walks again, and swim and dive into the lagoon water to fish for sea urchins, as when I was with Ouma. I've made a harpoon from a long reed and put an ironwood tip on it. Imitating Ouma, I dive into the cold dawn water when the current from the rising tide passes through the opening in the reefs. I look for fish where the coral is: catfish, seawives, and *damberis*. Occasionally I spot a shark's blue shadow and turn to face it, staying absolutely still and not letting out any air bubbles. I can swim now for as long as Ouma did, and as quickly. I know how to grill fish on the beach, too. I've planted corn, beans, sweet potatoes, and cauliflower near my hut, and I've put the young papaya tree that Fritz Castel gave me in an iron pot.

In Port Mathurin people start to ask questions. One day when I come to withdraw some money, the manager of Barclay's says, "What's this? How come we see you in town so often these days? Does this mean you've given up finding your treasure?

I smile at him and answer with confidence, "On the contrary, sir. It means I've found it." Then I leave before he can ask any more questions.

❧

In fact, I go to the seawall every day in hopes of seeing the *Zeta*. It hasn't docked at Rodrigues for months. Cargo and passenger transport is now handled regularly by the *Frigate,* a steamship from the all-powerful British India Steamship Company, which is represented in Port Louis by Uncle Ludovic. This boat brings the letters Laure has been sending me for several weeks now about Mam's illness. Laure's last letter, dated April 22, 1921, is even more urgent. I keep the envelope in my hands without daring to open it. Surrounded by the bustle of sailors and dockers, I stand under the canopy on the wharf, looking at the clouds gathering in the sky. There has been talk of an approaching storm and the barometer has been steadily falling. At around one o'clock in the afternoon, when there are few people left, I finally open Laure's letter and read the first words:

"My dear Ali, when you get this letter, if you ever do, I don't know if Mam will still be with us. . . ."

My eyes mist over. I know this is the end. There is nothing to keep me here, now that Mam is so ill. The *Frigate* will return in a few days and I'll leave with it. I send a telegram to Laure telling her of my plans, but a feeling of numbness has come over me and it accompanies me wherever I go.

❧

That night as I lay awake worrying, the storm begins as a continuous, slow wind blowing through the thick black night. In the morning I watch the clouds race across the sky above the valley, in ragged pouches through which the sun glints. Sheltering in my hut I can hear the crashing waves. The noise is terrifying; it sounds like the roaring of a huge animal, and I realize that the island is going to be hit by a hurricane. There's not a moment to lose. I grab my knapsack and, leaving everything else behind, quickly start to climb the hill toward Point Venus. Only the telegraph buildings will be able to withstand the force of the hurricane.

When I get to the big gray sheds everyone in the vicinity is there—men, women, children, even the dogs and pigs they've brought with them. An Indian employee of the telegraph company announces that the barometer has already fallen below 30. At around noon the wind comes screaming over Point Venus. The buildings start shaking and the electric light goes out. Torrents of rain beat down on the metal walls and roof; it sounds as if the sky has burst apart. Someone lights a storm lamp that distorts people's faces fantastically. The hurricane blows all day. That night, exhausted, we sleep on the shed floor, listening to the wind shrieking as it tears through the tin houses.

At dawn I am awakened by the silence. The wind has grown weaker but I can still hear the sea thundering on the reefs. Everyone is massed on the promontory in front of the main telegraph building. As I get closer I see what they are looking at: a ship has been wrecked on the coral reef in front of Point Venus. From our position, we can clearly see the broken masts and split hull. Huge waves break over the shipwreck, throwing up clouds of spray; only the stern of the ship is still there, pointing up to the sky. The name of the boat is being passed through the crowd, but by the time it gets to me I have already recognized the ship; it is the *Zeta*. The old armchair screwed to the deck is visible on the stern. But where is the crew? Nobody knows. The shipwreck happened during the night.

I run down to the shore and walk along the devastated beach. I look for a pirogue and someone to help me, but I search in vain. There is no one on the beach. Perhaps the lifeboat at Port Mathurin? But I am too anxious, I can't wait. I take off my clothes and get into the sea by sliding over the rocks on which the waves are pounding. The sea is very rough; it has come over the coral reef and is churning like a river in spate. I try to swim against the waves but they are too strong and I can't make any headway. The waves are breaking just in front of me. I can see the jets of spray being thrown up to the black sky. The wrecked ship is no more than a hundred yards away; the sharp reef has cut it in two between the masts. Sea covers the deck and washes over the empty chair. I can't go any closer without being pounded against the reef myself. I shout out, "Bradmer!" But my voice is drowned by the crashing waves, I can barely hear it myself. I swim a while longer against the sea, which has flooded over the reef. There's no sign of life on the shipwreck; it looks as if it could have been there for centuries. The cold water is weighing down my body and tightening my chest. I have to give up and go back. I let the swell slowly carry me back along with the debris from the storm. When I get back to the beach I am so tired that I don't even feel where I slashed my knee against a rock.

At noon the wind dies down completely and the sun shines over the devastated land and sea. It is over. On shaky legs, close to losing consciousness, I start to walk to English Cove. A crowd of people stands near the telegraph buildings, laughing and talking loudly now that they have been released from their fear.

When I get to the top of English Cove I see a ravaged land. The Roseaux River has been turned into dark mud, running noisily through the valley. My hut has disappeared; the trees and the vacoas have been torn up by their roots and my vegetable garden is no more. Blocks of basalt have been pushed through the ground and the valley floor is a crisscross of earth and streams. Everything I left in my hut has gone—not only the clothes and pots, but my theodolite and most of the papers concerning the treasure, too.

Daylight is fast fading in this place that looks like the end of the world. I walk along the valley floor searching for something, anything that might have escaped the hurricane. I look in all the familiar places, but it has all changed and is already unrecognizable. Where is the pile of stones that formed the

Southern Triangle? And these basalt rocks near the bank—are
they the ones that guided me when I first found the mooring
rings? The twilight is copper-colored, like molten metal. For
the first time since I have been here the sea birds are not flying
across the cove. Where have they gone? How many of them
survived the hurricane? For the first time, too, rats have come
to the bottom of the valley, chased from their nests by the torrents of mud. They scurry around me in the half-light, emit-
ting sharp, frightening little cries.

In the center of the valley, near the overflowing river, I see
the big basalt slab on which I had etched the east-west line and
the two inverted triangles of the mooring rings before leaving
for war. The slab has withstood the rain and wind and has
merely sunk a bit farther into the ground; standing in the middle of this ruined land it looks like a monument to the dawn of
civilization. Will someone find it one day and understand what
it means? The valley in English Cove has taken back its secret,
closed the doors that had momentarily opened for me. The
eastern cliff is bathed in the last rays of the setting sun as I go
to the ravine entrance one final time. But as I get closer I can
see that the weight of the gushing water has caused part of the
cliff to crumble, stopping up the access passage. The torrent of
mud gushing from the ravine has devastated everything in its
path, even the remains of the old tamarind tree.

I stay for a long time, until night has fallen, listening to the
noises in the valley: the river coursing so strongly, carrying
trees and earth away with it; the water streaming from the
shale cliffs; and in the distance, the thundering sea. I spend all
of the two days left to me looking at the valley. Every morning I leave my narrow room in the Chinaman's hotel and go to
the top of Commander's Summit. But I don't go down into
the valley. I stay seated in the brush near the ruined tower,
watching the long black-and-red valley where all trace of me

has already disappeared. In the sea, suspended on the coral reef, looking quite surreal, the *Zeta's* stern doesn't move as the waves rush past it. I think of Captain Bradmer, whose body hasn't been found. Apparently he was alone on the ship and didn't try to save himself.

As I stand on the deck of the new *Frigate,* heading toward the open sea, its metal hull vibrating from the machinery that powers it, I look at Rodrigues for the last time. In front of the high, bare mountains shining in the morning sun, the ship-wrecked *Zeta,* sea birds wheeling above it, balances eternally at the edge of deep waters, looking like the carcass of a sperm whale cast up by the tempest.

MANANAVA, 1922

SINCE MY RETURN, Forest Side feels too strange and quiet. The old house—the dump, as Laure calls it—is like a leaking ship carelessly patched with pieces of sheet metal and tarpaper, through which water seeps all the same. The dam and rot will soon claim the house as their own. Mam doesn't speak or move and she hardly eats; Laure stays with her day and night. I don't have the same stamina. I walk through the cane near Quinze Cantons, where I can see the peaks of Trois Mamelles and the sky sloping down to the other side of the island.

I have to work, and following Laure's advice I present myself once again at W. W. West, whose director is now my cousin Ferdinand. Uncle Ludovic is old and has retired from the business; he lives in the house he built near Yemen, where our land formerly began. Ferdinand receives me rudely, which at one time would have made me furious. Now I don't care. When he says, "So, you've come back to the place you used to—" I suggest, "haunt?" Even when he speaks of "war heroes being a dime a dozen," I don't react. In the end he offers me the job of foreman on their Médine plantations, and I have to accept. So now I'm a sirdar!

I live in a cabin near Bambous and every morning I ride across the plantations, overseeing the work. I spend the afternoons in the noisy refinery where I check the arrival of the cane, the size of the bundles, and the quality of the syrup. It's exhausting work, but I prefer it to the stifling atmosphere of the W. W. West offices. The refinery manager is an Englishman by the name of Pilling who has been sent from the Seychelles by the Agricultural Company. Ferdinand had spoken ill of me, but he is a fair man and our relations are good. He often speaks about Chamarel, where he hopes to go. He promises that if he is sent there he will try to have me come, too.

Yemen is lonely. In the morning, the men and women in gunnies advance like a ragged army over the vast fields. The noise of the billhooks has a slow, regular rhythm. At the end of the fields, around Walhalla, the men break the "stumps"—heavy stones—which they pile into pyramids. I ride across the plantation to the south, listening to the noise of the billhooks and the barked orders of the sirdars. Sweat streams down my body. On Rodrigues I was intoxicated by the sun's rays as I watched it sparkle on the stones and vacoas. But here, the heat lying thickly on the dark green expanse of the cane fields makes me feel even more alone.

I now think often about Mananava, my last refuge. I have carried it with me for such a long time, since the days when Denis and I would walk to the beginning of the gorge. As I ride through through the cane I often look to the south and imagine the hiding places at the river's source. The time has come for me to go there.

❖

I saw Ouma today.

They've started cutting the virgin cane at the top of the

plantation. Men and women have come from all sides of the coast with anxious faces because they know that only a third of them will be hired. The others will have to take their hunger back home again.

On the road to the refinery, a woman in gunny is walking apart from the others. She half turns and looks at me. Though her face is hidden by a large white veil, I still recognize her. She disappears into the crowd dividing up along the many paths through the fields. I try running after her, but I bump into the workers and the women politely refuse to give way and we are all enveloped in a cloud of dust. When I get to the fields all I can see is the thick green wall waving in the breeze. The sun is beating down on the dry earth, burning my face. I choose a path at random and run down it calling, "Ouma! Ouma! . . ."

Women in gunnies stop cutting the grass between the cane and raise their heads. A sirdar calls after me in a hard voice. I question him, distraught. Are there any Manafs here? He doesn't understand. People from Rodrigues? He shakes his head. There are, but they're in the refugee camps at Morne and Ruisseau des Créoles.

❀

Every day I look for Ouma on the road that the gunnies take to come to the fields, and in the evening I wait by the accountant's office where everyone gets paid. The women realize what I'm doing and they make fun of me, shouting insults and jeering at me. After a while I feel too shy to walk with them through the cane, and I wait for night to fall before I cross the fields. I pass children gleaning, but they know I wouldn't tell anyone and they show no fear. How old must Sri be now?

I spend my days galloping through the plantations in the dust and burning sun that makes my head spin. Can she really be here? Every fragile, gunny-clad woman bent over her own shadow, working with a billhook or hoe, looks like her. Ouma only appears that one time, as she did once before near the Roseaux River. I remember our first meeting, when she fled through the valley between the bushes and climbed up the mountain, agile as a young goat. Was it only a dream?

That's when I decide to give it all up, throw it all away. Ouma has shown me what I have to do, told me in her wordless way, simply by appearing before me like a mirage amid all the people who come to work on land that will never be theirs: blacks, Indians, and half-castes, hundreds of men and women coming every day to Yemen, Walhalla, Médine, Phoenix, Mon Désert, Solitude, and Forbach. Hundreds of men and women piling stones to make walls and pyramids, pulling out the cane stumps, tilling the land, planting the young cane, then thinning out the leaves throughout the growing season and keeping the ground free of weeds and grass, and then in the summer moving square by square over the plantation, cutting from morning to night, only stopping to sharpen their sickles, working until their hands and legs are covered in bloody cuts from the sharp leaves, working until the sun makes their heads swim and fills them with nausea.

Almost without realizing it I have gone to the south of the plantation, where the chimney of an old ruined refinery still juts out of the ground. The sea is not far away but can't be seen or heard, yet sea birds occasionally fly across the blue sky. They are free. The men here are clearing new land for planting. Under the scorching sun they break the ground with their hoes and load their tip-carts with black stones. When they see me they stop working as if they're frightened of something. I start pulling stones from the ground and throw them on the tip-cart with the others. We work steadily, the setting sun burning our faces. As soon as a tip-cart is full of stones and stumps it is replaced by another. The old walls stretch into the distance perhaps reaching as far as the shore. I think of the slaves who built them, the ones Laure calls "martyrs," who died in these fields, or who escaped to the mountains in the south. The sun is very near the horizon now. Today I feel it has purified and freed me the way it used to on Rodrigues.

A woman in gunny has arrived. She is an old Indian with a wrinkled face. She is bringing the workers something to drink, sour milk that she draws from a pot with a wooden ladle. When she gets to me she hesitates, then hands me the ladle. The sour milk soothes my dust-filled throat.

The last full cart rolls off. In the distance the sharp whistle of the generator signals the end of the working day. The men take their hoes and leave, in no hurry.

When I get to the refinery Mr. Pilling is waiting for me in front of his office. He looks at my sunburned face and dust-covered clothes. When I tell him that in the future I want to work in the fields, cutting and clearing, he dryly interrupts me: "You wouldn't be able to do that work, and anyway it's impossible. No white has ever worked in the fields." He adds more calmly, "I shall take it that you need a rest and have come to hand in your resignation." That is the end of the conversation. I walk slowly along the now-deserted dirt road. In the light of the setting sun the fields are as big as the sea, and chimneys of the other refineries, which I glimpse every now and then, look as though they belong to steamships.

❀

Rumors of rioting are what bring me once again to the hot Yemen lands. It appears that the Médine and Walhalla plantations are burning and unemployed men are threatening the refineries. Laure tells me the news in a low voice so as not to disturb Mam. I quickly get dressed. In spite of the fine morning rain I go out wearing only my army shirt, without a jacket or hat, and my bare feet pushed into my shoes. When I get to the top of the plateau near Trois Mamelles, the sun is shining over the fields. Columns of smoke are rising from the plantations over in Yemen. I count four fires, perhaps five.

I start down the cliff, cutting through the brush. I think of Ouma who must be below. I remember the day I was with Ferdinand and saw the Indians throw the white foreman into the furnace, and the silence that fell after he had disappeared into the gaping fiery mouth.

I get to Yemen at about noon. My face is scratched and I am soaked in sweat and covered with dust. People are crowded near the refinery. What is happening? The sirdars keep on contradicting themselves. It appears that some men set fire to the sheds and then fled to Tamarin. They are being chased by mounted police.

Where is Ouma? The refinery buildings are surrounded by police who bar my way. In the courtyard, guarded by militiamen with guns, men and women crouch in the shade with their hands on their necks, waiting for their fate to be decided.

I go back across the plantations toward the sea. If Ouma is here I am sure she'll look for refuge near the sea. In the middle of the fields, not far from me, I can hear the shouts of the men fighting the fire. Somewhere deep in the fields I hear guns firing. But the cane is so high I can't see above the stalks. Not knowing which direction to go, I run wildly from one side of the cane to the other with the sound of gunshots ringing in my ears. Suddenly I stagger; I'm out of breath and have to stop. My legs are trembling and I can hear my heart thudding. I've come to the end of the plantation. It is quiet here.

When I climb to the top of a stone pyramid I see that the fires have already been put out. There is only one column of clear smoke in the sky: the cane-trash furnace is working again.

It's all over now. When I get to the black-sand beach I stand still in the midst of the debris brought up by the storm. I do this so Ouma can see me. The coast is deserted; it is as wild as English Cove. I walk along the bay in the light from the setting sun. I'm sure Ouma has seen me. She follows me silently, without leaving any tracks. I mustn't try to see her. This is her game. When I once spoke to Laure about her she said in her mocking voice, "Sorceress! She's cast a spell on you!" I think Laure is right.

It's been so long since I was here last. It feels as if I am walking in my own tracks, the ones I left when I went with Denis to see the sun glittering on the sea. When night falls I am on the other side of the Tamarin River. Lights from the fishing village twinkle before me. Bats fly through the clear sky. It is a warm, calm night. For the first time in a long while I get ready to sleep under the stars. I lie down in the black dune sand at the foot of some tamarind trees, my arms behind my neck. I watch the sky filling. I listen to the soft murmur of the Tamarin River as it merges with the sea.

The moon comes out. It rises to the middle of the sky, making the sea beneath it sparkle. Then I see Ouma sitting not far from me in the shining sand. Her face is in profile and she's sitting as she always does, with her arms folded around her legs. My heart starts to pound and I tremble. I'm afraid she'll turn out to be nothing but an illusion and disappear. The wind blows over us, bringing with it the sound of the sea. Ouma comes up to me and takes my hand. Then she removes her dress the way she used to in English Cove and walks to the sea without waiting for me. We dive together into the cool water and swim against the waves. Long waves from the other side of the world wash over us. We swim for a long time in the moonlit black sea before going back to the shore. Ouma pulls me to the river and we lie on the pebbles on the riverbed and wash the salt from our bodies and hair. When we get out the cool air makes us shiver and we speak in low voices so as not to wake the dogs in the vicinity. We powder our bodies with the black sand as we used to and wait for the wind to make it slide in little streams from our shoulders and stomachs.

There are so many things I want to say to her that I don't know where to start. Ouma has things to say, too. She tells me about how the typhoid brought death to Rodrigues and how her mother died on the boat bringing the refugees to Port Louis. She tells me about the camp at Ruisseau des Créoles and the salt works at Rivière Noire, where she and Sri worked. By what miracle did she know I was at Yemen? "It's no miracle," Ouma says. Her voice is almost angry. "I waited for you every moment of every day at Forest Side, or I would go to Port Louis to Rempart Street. When you came back from the war I had waited so long I could afford to wait some more. I followed you everywhere. When you went to Yemen I was there, too. I even worked in the fields so that you'd see me." I feel dizzy and my throat tightens. How could it have taken me so long to understand?

Now we have stopped talking. We lie, holding each other very close against the cold night air. We listen to the sea and the wind blowing through the filao needles and nothing else in the world exists.

THE SUN IS RISING above Trois Mamelles. Outlined against the bright sky, the blue-black volcanoes are just the same as when I spent my days wandering around with Denis. I remember that I always liked the southernmost peak, the one that looks like a hook, around which the sun and moon turn.

I sit for a while in front of the Barachois sandbar, watching the calm river flow by. Terns, cormorants, and quarrelsome seagulls skim the water, waiting for the fishing boats. Then I walk up along the Boucan River to Panon, moving slowly and carefully as if I have to avoid landmines. The mild, sweet smell of the sugar cane is in my nostrils, and through the leaves I can see the road to Yemen in the distance, where steam is already rising. Higher up, on the other side of the river, I can also see Uncle Ludovic's new, gleaming-white house.

I feel sick inside, for I know where I am now. This is where our garden began, and a little farther up, at the end of the path, I would have been able to see our house with its blue roof glittering in the sun. I walk through the high grass without feeling the thornbushes scratch me. There is nothing there. The burning, destruction, and plunder took place so many years ago. Was it here that the veranda began? I think I recognize some of the tamarinds, mangoes, and filao, but the next moment I see ten exactly like them. I stub my toes against stones I never knew and stumble over new holes. Was it really here we lived, and not in a totally different place?

As I walk on the blood pounds in my head and I feel feverish. I want to find something of ours. Later, when I speak to Mam about Boucan, I'm sure her eyes light up. I squeeze her hand tightly, trying to pass some of my strength to her. I speak as if our house still existed, as if nothing had ever ended, as if the lost years were going to be resurrected in the same suffocating heat as when Laure and I sat on the veranda listening to her read the Bible to us.

I wish I could hear her voice now as I stand in the wild brush among the piles of black stones that once formed the foundations of our house. As I walk toward the hills I suddenly see the ravine where we spent so many hours perched on the tree's highest branch, watching the nameless stream rush by. I hardly recognize the spot. Everywhere else the ground has been overtaken by high grass and scrub, but here it is empty and dry, as if it had been burned. My heart beats very fast because this was where Laure's and my domain really was; this was our secret place. Now it is nothing more than a ravine, a dark, ugly, lifeless fissure. Where is the tree, our tree? I think I recognize it in an old black trunk with broken branches and hardly any leaves. It is so ugly and small that I can't understand how we were able to climb it. When I lean over the ravine I can see the famous branch we used to lie on, an emaciated arm stretched out into the void. The moving water at the bottom of the ravine is filled with broken branches, pieces of tin, and bits of plank. After our house was demolished the ravine was used as a dumping place.

I don't tell Mam any of this. It is of no importance. I speak to her about how it used to be, which is more real than the ruined land I saw. I speak to her of what she loved most, the garden full of hibiscus, poinsettias, arum lilies, and her special white orchids. I talk about the oval basin in front of the veranda where we used to hear the toads croaking. I also tell her about what I loved so much and would never forget, the sound of her voice when she read us a poem or recited the night prayers, and the path down which we walked so soberly, watching the sky as our father explained the stars to us.

I stayed there until nightfall, wandering through the brush, searching for signs, smells and souvenirs, any traces of us. But the land has been wrecked and is dry, too; the irrigation canals became clogged over the years. There are no more mango and loquat trees. The only remaining trees are thin, tall tamarinds like those on Rodrigues, and the banyans, which never die. They have been withered by the sun. I was looking for the chalta tree, the tree of good and evil. I felt that if I could find it I would know that something from our past had managed to survive. I remembered it as being at the bottom of the garden, at the end of the fallow land, where the road to the mountains and the Rivière Noire gorge begins. I crossed the scrub and quickly went to the upper part of the ground from where Mount Terre Rouge and Brise-Fer could be seen. Suddenly, I saw it in the middle of the brush in front of me, bigger than it used to be, with a lake of shade under its dark leaves. As I got closer I recognized its smell, a sweet disturbing smell that made us turn our heads away when we climbed its branches. The tree did not yield and it was not destroyed. All the time I'd been away, far from the protection of its leaves and branches, had been no more than a moment for it. There had been hurricanes, droughts, and fires; men had demolished our house, trampled the flowers, and let the water in the canals dry up; but the tree had remained, the tree of good and evil that sees and knows everything. I looked for the marks Laure and I made when we inscribed our names and heights with a knife and the place where the hurricane had torn away one of its branches. Its shade was dark and sweet; the smell of it made me dizzy. Time stood still. The air was vibrating with insects and birds and the ground beneath the tree was moist and alive.

Here, hunger and unhappiness were unknown. War didn't exist. The world was held at bay by the chalta tree's strong branches. Our house was destroyed and our father was dead, but now that I had found the chalta tree there was no need for despair. Under it I could sleep. Night was falling and the mountains disappeared. Everything I had done, everything I'd searched for, was all so that I could be there at the entrance to Mananava.

❀

How much time has passed since Mam died? Was it yesterday or the day before? I don't remember. During the last days and nights we took turns watching over her, me during the day and Laure at night, so that she always had a hand to hold in her thin fingers. Every day I told her the same story, the one about Boucan where she was always young and beautiful and where the blue roof always sparkled in the sunlight. This place doesn't exist except for us three. In talking about it, a little of its immortality became part of us, bound us and gave us the strength to bear the approaching death.

Laure doesn't speak. In fact she refuses to; it is her way of fighting Mam's death. I brought her a small branch from the chalta tree, and when I gave it to her I saw she hadn't forgotten it. Her eyes shone with pleasure as she took the branch from the bedside table where she had put it, or rather carelessly thrown it, in the way she has with objects she loves.

There was that terrible morning when I woke to see Laure standing beside my cot in the empty dining room. I remember how tangled her hair was, and the hard, angry light in her eyes.

"Mam is dead."

That was all she said, and still puffy with sleep I followed her into the dark room where the night light was still lit. I looked at Mam, her thin face with its regular features and her beautiful hair spread out over the pure white pillow case. Laure went to take her turn on the cot and fell asleep immediately, her arms shielding her face. I stayed alone in the dark room with Mam, dazed and bewildered, sitting on the creaking chair in front of the trembling night light, ready to start telling my story again, ready to talk softly about the big garden where we used to walk together in the evenings along paths strewn with tamarind pods and hibiscus petals, looking at the stars and listening to the sharp buzz of the mosquitoes dancing around our heads; and when we returned, the joy of seeing my father smoking and looking at his maps of the sea, his big illuminated study window standing out against the velvet-blue night.

This morning, standing in the rain in the cemetery near Bigara, I listen to the earth falling on the coffin and I keep my eyes on Laure's very pale face. Her hair is covered with Mam's black shawl and raindrops roll down her cheeks like tears.

❈

How long, since Mam was still alive? I can't believe it. It is finished, I will again never hear her voice coming out of the dim light on the veranda, never smell her perfume or feel her eyes on me. When my father died it felt as if I had started going backward, traveling toward a forgetfulness that would distance me forever from my youth, my strength, and this I couldn't accept. There is no way of getting to buried treasure; it is impossible to find. It's "fool's gold," like the stuff the black prospectors brought me when I first got to Port Mathurin.

Laure and I are alone now in this old, cold, empty wreck with its closed shutters. When the night light goes out in Mam's room, I light another and put it among the useless phials on the bedside table.

"Nothing would have happened to her if I'd stayed . . . It's all my fault, I should never have left her."

"But you had to go, didn't you?" Laure asks herself this question.

I look at her with concern. "What will you do now?"

"I don't know. Stay here, I suppose."

"Come with me!"

"Come with you where?"

"To Mananava. We'll be able to live on the *geometric pitch*." Her look is full of sarcasm.

"Just us and the Sorceress?" That is what she calls Ouma. Her eyes become cold and her face shows how weary she's grown, how distant from me. "You know it's impossible."

"But why?"

She doesn't answer. She looks through me. I suddenly realize that in the course of my years of exile I lost her. She has followed another path and become someone else; our lives no longer coincide. Her life is with the nuns of the order of St. Elizabeth, where women go when they have no money and no home. She belongs beside the cancerous Indians who beg for a few rupees, a smile, some words of sympathy. She will cook pots of rice for the feverish children with distended stomachs and squeeze some money for them out of the "bourzois" of her caste.

For a moment her voice is as full of concern as when I used to cross the room in bare feet to go out into the night. "What will you do?"

I say in a boastful voice: "I'm going to pan the brooks, like in the Klondike. I'm sure there's gold in Mananava."

There it is: for a second more her eyes shine with amusement, and we are as close as we once were when people used to call us "the lovers."

Later I watch as she packs her small suitcase to go live with the nuns in Lorette. Her face has become calm and impassive again, and only her eyes glitter with a kind of anger. She covers her beautiful black hair with Mam's shawl and then goes, without turning back, carrying her little cardboard case and her big umbrella. She is tall and erect and from now on nothing will hold her back or change the course of her life.

❀

I spend the whole day at the estuary by the Barachois sandbar, watching the tide go out and rediscovering the black beach. At low tide, looking like waders in the coppery water, some tall black adolescents come to fish for octopus. The most daring of them come closer to get a better look at me. One of them is deceived by my army shirt and, believing me to be an English soldier, addresses me in that language. So as to not disappoint him I reply in English and we chat for a moment, he standing and leaning on his long harpoon, I sitting in the sand smoking a cigarette in the shade of the veloutier trees. Then he rejoins the other young men and their voices and laughter gradually recede as they cross to the other side of the Tamarin river. The only people left now are the fishermen standing in their pirogues, gliding slowly over water that sends their reflections back up at them.

I hear the first wave unfurling on the beach as the tide starts to come in. The wind from the sea is blowing over me and the sound of the sea makes me shiver as it always did. I put my army bag over my shoulder and go upriver toward Boucan. Before I get to Yemen, I swerve off toward the thicket where our road used to start, the big red-earth path cut between the trees that went all the way up to our white house. I remember us walking down this path after the bailiffs and Uncle Ferdinand's lawyers came to drive us away. The road is no longer there: it, and the world it led to, have been eaten up by grass.

How beautiful and soft the light is here, like the light that used to bathe me when I stood on the veranda watching dusk envelop the garden. It is the only thing I recognize. I walk through the brush and don't even try to find the chalta tree or the ravine again. I am impatient and slightly anxious, like the sea birds at the end of the day. I walk quickly south, using Mount Terre Rouge as my guide. Suddenly I come upon a pool shimmering in the light: it's the lake at Aigrettes, where my father installed the generator. No one has been here in years, and it is surrounded by high grass and reeds. Nothing remains of my father's great project. The dynamo was sold to help with the debts, and the iron structures that supported the dynamo were carried off long ago. Water and sludge have obliterated my father's dream. Screeching birds fly out of the reeds as I skirt the basin to get to the path leading to the gorge.

When I get past Brise-Fer, the Rivière Noire valley stretches below me, and farther on, between the trees, I can see the sea sparkling in the sun. Bathed in sweat, breathless and anxious, I have reached the beginning of Mananava. As I walk into the gorge I feel a moment's apprehension. Is this where I have to live, now that I am truly a castaway? In the violent light of the setting sun the shadows cast by Machabé and Pied de Marmite

make the gorge seem even blacker. The red cliffs above Mananava are an insurmountable wall. Mananava is the end of the
world, the place from where one can see without being seen.

I am in the heart of the valley now, walking through the
shadows cast by the big trees. Darkness is falling. The wind is
blowing over the sea and I can hear the sounds of the leaves'
invisible movements as they flutter and dance in the breeze. I
have never been this far into Mananava before. As I move
through the shadows, under a sky that is still very light, the
endless forest opens in front of me. I am surrounded by ebony
trees with their smooth trunks: terebinths, pines, wild figs,
and sycamores. My feet sink into a carpet of leaves, and I can
smell the musky odor of the earth and the dampness in the atmosphere. I follow the bed of an old mountain stream, picking
red guavas, and maroon-colored pistachios as I pass. The freedom of this place intoxicates me all over again. Isn't this where
I was always meant to come? Isn't this the forgotten valley indicated on the Unknown Corsair's maps, situated along the
course of the ship *Argo?* Walking between the trees, my heart
beats loudly as it did once before, not so long ago, in English
Cove. I've had this feeling before: I am not alone here. Not far
from me, someone else is walking through the forest, following a path that will soon meet up with mine. Someone is gliding soundlessly through the leaves; I can feel someone looking
at me with a look that pierces everything and bathes me in its
light. I am above the forest now, near the river's source where
the foliage undulates down to the sea. The sky is dazzling as
the sun slips under the horizon. I am going to sleep here, facing
east, among the lava blocks still warm from the sun. My house
will be here where I can always see the sea.

Then I see Ouma coming toward me out of the forest, with
a light step. Two white birds appear at the same moment.

Soaring in the wind, high up in the colorless sky they wheel around Mananava. Have they seen me? Like two white comets, one beside the other, hardly moving their wings, they silently watch the halo of sun on the horizon. They are here; the world stops and the stars are suspended in their course. Only their bodies move in the wind . . .

Ouma is beside me. I sense her body's scent, its heat. I say softly, "Look! Those are the birds I used to see! They're the ones . . ." As the sky darkens they fly off toward Mount Machabé. Then they disappear behind the mountains, diving down toward Rivière Noire. Night has fallen.

❀

Our life on Mananava, far from other people, is like an exquisite dream. We live like primitives, concerned only with the trees, coves, grass, and water flowing from the springs in the red cliffs. We hunt for crayfish in a tributary of the Rivière Noire and find shrimp and crabs under the flat stones near the estuary. I remember the stories old Cap'n Cook told us about Zako the monkey who used to catch shrimp with his tail.

Nothing is complicated here. At dawn we glide into the forest, which is heavy with dew, to pick red guavas, wild cherries, and cabbages, Madagascan plums, bullock's hearts, and *bredes-songe* and margosa leaves. We live in the same place as the maroons in Senghor and Sacalavou's time. "Look there! Those were their fields. They kept their pigs, goats, and fowl there. And over there they grew beans, lentils, yams, and corn." Ouma shows me the crumbled dry stonewalls and the piles of pebbles hidden by the brush. Farther on we find a thornbush growing against the lava cliff, hiding the entrance to a cave. Ouma brings me heavily scented flowers. She puts them in her thick hair, behind her ears. "Cassia flowers."

She has never been more beautiful, her black hair framing her smooth face, and her body in her faded and patched gunny slim and supple. She is more beautiful than I have ever known her.

I hardly ever think of the gold; I don't desire it anymore. My pan stays on the edge of the stream near the spring as I run through the forest behind Ouma. My clothes have been ripped by the branches and my hair and beard have grown as long as Robinson Crusoe's. Ouma has plaited me a hat from vacoa blades and when I wear it I feel unrecognizable.

We have been down to the mouth of the Rivière Noire several times, but Ouma is afraid of being seen because of the gunnies' revolt. Still, one dawn, we go as far as the Tamarin estuary where we walk on the black sand. It is still covered by the dawn mist and the wind is cold. Half-hidden in the middle of the vacoas, we watch the rough sea tossing up clouds of spray. There is nothing in the world more beautiful.

Sometimes Ouma goes fishing alone, either in the lagoon near the Tourelle or in the one near the saltmarsh so that she can see her brother. She comes back in the evening with fish and we grill it in our hiding place near the river's mouth.

Every evening as the sun sinks toward the sea, we sit very still in the rocks, waiting for the arrival of the bo'sun birds. When they come they are high up in the orange- and pink-tinged sky, slowly gliding like stars. They have made their nest at the top of a cliff near Mount Machabé. They are so white and beautiful, they fly above Mananava on the sea wind for so long that our hunger, tiredness, and fears about the future eventually dissipate. Haven't they always been here? Ouma says they are the two birds who sing the praises of God. We wait for them every day at twilight because they make us happy.

And yet, when night falls, something makes me feel anxious. There is an empty expression on Ouma's dark, copper-colored face, as if what she sees around her doesn't really exist. She says several times in a low voice: "One day I'll leave here . . ."

"Where will you go?" I ask. But she says no more.

The seasons pass; a winter and summer have gone by already. It's been so long since I've seen another person! I can't remember anymore what it used to be like at Forest Side and Port Louis. Mananava is vast; it is all I need. The only person with whom I still have any connection in the outside world is Laure. When I speak of her, Ouma says, "I'd like to meet her." But then she adds, "It's impossible, though." I remember how Laure went to beg from the rich people of Curepipe and Floréal for the poor women and all those who had been damned by the cane. I tell Ouma about the rags she got from the wealthy to make shrouds for the old Indian women who were going to die. Ouma says in a clear voice, "You should be with her." I'm hurt and troubled by her words.

❦

Tonight it's crystal cold, a winter night like those on Rodrigues when we lay on the sand in English Cove and watched the sky fill with stars.

It is absolutely quiet. Time stands still, not only here but in the whole universe. Lying on a carpet of vacoa leaves, wrapped in the army blanket with Ouma, I watch the stars: in the west, Orion, and squeezed against *Argo's* sail, Orion's Dog, in which Sirius, the "sun of the night," shines so brightly. I love talking about the stars. I say their names aloud, as I used to when I recited them to my father while we walked along the "path of stars:" "Arcturus, Denebola, Belletrix, Betelgeuse, Acomar, Antares, Shaula, Altair, Andromeda, Fomalhaut . . ."

Suddenly the sky above me starts to rain stars. Trails of light illumine the sky on all sides and then die out; some darken very quickly while others sparkle for so long that when we close our eyes they are engraved on our retinas. We get up so we can see better and stand with our heads thrown back, dazzled by this spectacle. I feel Ouma's body tremble against my own. I want to warm her but she pushes me away. I touch her face and feel her tears. She runs to the forest and hides under the trees so she doesn't have to see the sparkling plumes covering the sky. When I join her she speaks in a hoarse voice full of fatigue and anger. She talks about the war's horrors, which she says will return; about the death of her mother and the plight of the Manafs, who have always been chased from their homes, and who are now being forced to leave Mauritius. I try to calm her down. I want to tell her that they were only meteorites falling from the sky! But I don't dare say it, and besides, were they really only meteorites?

Through the foliage I can see the shooting stars gliding silently through the icy sky, pulling other suns and stars along with them. The war will return, she said; perhaps what we saw was telling us that the heavens will soon be lit again by bombs and fires.

We hold each other for a long time, standing under the trees that shield us from the signs of our fate. Then the sky grows calm and the stars begin to shine again. Ouma does not want to go back among the rocks. I cover her with the blanket and fall asleep sitting by her, like a useless watchman.

❀

Ouma has gone. Under the canopy of branches streaming with the morning dew there is only the vacoa mat from which the imprint of her body has almost disappeared. I tell myself she is going to come back, and to keep from thinking about it I go to the stream to wash sand in my pan. The mosquitoes dance around me, and mynah birds call to each other with their sarcastic cries. Every now and then I think I see her shadow flitting between the trees in the thick forest, but it's never more than monkeys who flee at my approach.

I wait for her every day near the river's mouth, where we used to swim and hunt for red guavas. While I wait I play on the grass harp, for *we* had used it to send messages, too. I remember the afternoons when I was waiting for Denis and heard the squeaky signal from the middle of the high grass, sounding like a strange insect repeating *vini, vini, vini . . .*

But this time no one answers. Night falls over the valley. Only the mountains float above it: Brise-Fer, Mount Machabé, and in the distance, rising up before the metallic sea, Morne. The wind comes in with the tide. I remember what Cook used to say when the wind echoed in the gorge: "Listen! Sacalavou is wailing because the whites have pushed him off the mountain! It is the voice of the great Sacalavou!" I listen to the sound as I watch the fading light. The red rocks of the cliff behind me are still hot, but down below in the valley wisps of smoke have already started to rise from the chimneys. Every moment I think I am going to hear the sound of Ouma's footsteps coming from the forest, smell the warmth of her body.

❖

The British soldiers have surrounded the refugee camp at Rivière Noire. The camp has been cordoned off for several days by barbed wire to stop anyone getting out or in. Those who are in the camp—Rodriguans, Comorians, people from Diego Suarez and Agalega, and Indians from India and Pakistan—all have to have their papers inspected. Those whose papers are not in order have to go back to where they came from. An English soldier tells me this when I try to get into the camp to look for Ouma. Behind him, in the dust between the huts, I can see children playing in the sun. Poverty is the reason the cane fields are set afire; it is what fans the people's anger and drives them wild.

I wait for a long time in front of the camp in hopes of seeing Ouma. That night I don't want to go back to Mananava. I sleep in the ruins of our old property at Boucan, in the shelter of the chalta tree. Before falling asleep, I listen to the toads croaking in the ravine and feel the breeze rise with the moon; I hear the waves lapping at the fields of grass.

At dawn, some men arrive with a sirdar and I hide in the tree in case they're coming for me. But they aren't looking for me: they're carrying *macchabées*—heavy, cast-iron pincers that are used to pull out stumps and big stones. They also have picks, pickaxes, and axes. A group of women in gunnies accompany them, balancing their hoes on their heads. There are also two horsemen, whites—I can tell from the way they give orders. One of them is my cousin Ferdinand and the other is an Englishman I don't know, probably a field manager. I can't hear what they're saying from my hiding place, but I have no trouble understanding. They're surveying the land for the last time, before it is cleared to plant cane. I watch them indifferently. I remember the despair we all felt when we were forced from our land, and how slowly we drove down the straight, dusty main road in the truck full of furniture and trunks. I remember how Laure's voice shook with anger as she repeated, "I wish he were dead!" and how Mam gave up trying to make her be quiet. Now it is as if it all belonged to another lifetime. The two horsemen have left and from my hiding place I can hear the sounds, muted by the foliage, of the pick hitting the ground, the *macchabées* squeaking as they grip the rocks, and the slow, sad song the blacks always sing as they work.

When the sun is at its height I feel hungry and go to the forest to look for guavas and pistachios. My heart aches as I think about Ouma, put in the prison camp because she chose to join her brother. From the top of the hill I can see the smoke from the camp at Rivière Noire.

Toward evening I see the dust rising on the road from the long convoy of trucks going to Port Louis. I get to the edge of the road as the last ones are passing by. Under the half-open awnings, I can see the dark, weary, dust-stained faces. I realize they are being taken away to be put in the hold of a ship and sent back to their own country, so that they won't ask us for water, rice, or work, and won't set fire to the white man's fields. Ouma is being taken away, to be sent somewhere, so long as it's somewhere else. I run after them for a while in the dust, but then I lose my breath and, feeling as if I've been stabbed in the ribs, I have to stop. The people there look at me without understanding.

I wander for a long time along the shore. Above me the Tourelle with its jagged rocks looms like a lookout over the sea. I climb through the brush as far as the Étoile and find myself on the same spot where, thirty years ago, I watched the coming of the big hurricane that destroyed our house. Behind me is the horizon, the source of the black clouds that bring rain and lightning. It seems that only now, thirty years later, can I really hear the screaming wind and all the other terrifying sounds of approaching disaster.

❧

How did I get to Port Louis? I walked in the sun behind the military trucks until I was exhausted. I ate pieces of sugar cane

that had fallen from the carts onto the road and an Indian gave
me some rice and a bowl of *kir* in his hut. I avoided the villages
because I didn't want to be mocked by the children, nor found
by the police, who were still looking for arsonists. I drank water from stagnant pools and slept either in the brush at the side
of the road, or hidden in the dunes at Point Sable. At night I
swam in the sea the way I used to with Ouma, cooling my feverish body. I floated motionlessly over the waves as if I were
asleep. Then I powdered my body with sand and waited until
the wind made it stream down my skin.

As soon as I reach the port I see the boat on which all the
people from Rodrigues, the Comoros, and Agalega had already been loaded. The *Union La Digue* is a large, new ship
belonging to Abdool Rassool. It is far out in the roadstead and
nobody can get near it. The customs buildings and warehouses
are being guarded by British soldiers. I spend the night under
the trees at the Commissariat with the bums and drunk sailors.
I am awakened by the gray morning light. There is no one left
on the docks. The soldiers have returned in their trucks to Fort
George. The sun slowly rises, but the docks remain deserted as
if it were a holiday. Then the *Union La Digue* pulls up its anchors and steams away across the calm sea with birds flying
round its masts. First it heads west until it is nothing more
than a dot on the horizon, then it turns north, to the other side
of the horizon.

❧

I go back to Mananava, the most mysterious place in the
world. I remember when I believed the night started its journey here before flowing downriver to the sea. I walk slowly
through the damp forest, following the stream. I can feel
Ouma everywhere; her footsteps rustle in the wind and the

scent of her body mingles with the perfume from the leaves of the ebony trees.

I stay near the springs, listening to the water running over the pebbles. The treetops sparkle in the wind. Through gaps in the foliage I can see the dazzling sky, the pure crystal light. What can I expect from this place? Death hangs over Mananava, which is why no one ever comes here. It belongs to the ghosts of Sacalavou and the runaway slaves.

I hastily gather the few objects I have left in the world: my khaki blanket, army bag, and gold panning tools—pan, sieve, and bottle of aqua regia. I carefully erase my tracks the way Ouma taught me, brush away the signs of my fires, and bury my waste.

The sun is still shining on the eastern part of the countryside. In the distance, on the other side of Mont Terre Rouge, I can see the dark stain of Boucan where the ground has been cleared and burned. I think of the road that goes through the hunting grounds where the dispossessed live to the top of Trois Mamelles, and of the dirt road that cuts through the cane field to Quinze Cantons. Laure might be waiting for me, but she might also not be. When I arrive she will finish an ironic and funny sentence, as if it were only yesterday that we left each other, as if time did not exist for her.

I get to the Rivière Noire estuary at dusk. The water is black and smooth, and there is no wind. Some pirogues glide along the horizon with their triangular sails attached to the rudder, looking for some wind. The sea birds are beginning to arrive from the south and north, crossing paths with each other as they skim over the water, screeching anxiously. I get what papers I still have relating to the treasure out of my bag—the maps, sketches, and books of notes that I made here and on Rodrigues—and I burn them on the beach. A wave rolls onto the sand and washes the cinders away. I now know that this is what the Corsair did after taking his treasure out of the hiding places in the ravine on English Cove. He destroyed everything and threw it into the sea. Then one day, after having lived through so much slaughter and so much glory, he retraced his footsteps and undid everything he had created so that he could at last be free.

I walk across the black sand toward the Tourelle. I have nothing left.

❀

I stop for the night on the slope of the Étoile with the Tourelle in front of me. On my right, already in darkness, is the Boucan valley, and a bit farther to the right, the smoking Yemen chimney. Have the laborers finished clearing the land that used to be our estate? Perhaps they have chopped down the big chalta tree, our tree of good and evil. If so, not a single trace of our occupancy remains on that land.

I think of Mam. I think she must still be sleeping somewhere, alone in her big brass bed under a cloud of mosquito netting. I wish I could whisper to her about things that have no end, about memories, fragile and transparent like a mirage: of our house and its blue roof, the garden full of birds where night is falling, the ravine, and the tree of good and evil that stands at the entrance to Mananava.

Here I am again in the same spot where I saw the big hurricane arrive, in my eighth year, before we were driven from our house and thrown into the world like a second birth. On the Étoile I feel the noise of the sea swelling inside me. I'd like to talk to Laure about Nada the Lily, whom I found instead of treasure, and who has now returned to her island. I'd like to speak to her too about journeys round the world, and see her eyes shine as they used to when, from the top of a pyramid, we would see the huge expanse of the sea.

I'll go to the port to choose my ship. There's mine; it is fine and light, like a frigate with huge wings. It is called the *Argo*. Surrounded by birds, it glides slowly over the black water toward the open sea in the dusky light of day's end. Soon it will be sailing under the stars, following its destiny written in the sky. I am on the deck, on the stern, enveloped in wind, listening to the waves slapping against the hull and the wind crackling in the sails. The helmsman is singing his monotonous song without end, and I can hear the voices of the sailors playing dice in the hold. We are the only ones on the sea, the only living beings. Ouma is with me again. I can feel her breath, the warmth of her body, her heartbeats. Where will we go together? Agalega, Aldabra, Juan de Nova? There are countless islands. Perhaps we'll brave the interdiction and go as far as Saint Brandon, where Captain Bradmer and his helmsman found their refuge. We'll go to the other side of the earth, to a place where we need fear neither signs in the sky nor the wars of men.

Now night has fallen. To the depths of my being I hear the living sound of the rising sea.

ABOUT THE AUTHOR

Jean-Marie Gustave Le Clézio was born in Nice in 1940, of French and British parents. His first novel, *The Interrogation*, won the Prix Renaudot in 1963 and established his reputation as one of France's preeminent contemporary writers. He has since published over twenty works of fiction and anthropology (many of them translated into English), including *The Flood, The Giants, War, Terra Amata,* and *The Mexican Dream.* Another novel, *Desert,* is forthcoming in Verba Mundi. Mr. Le Clézio has lived in France, Mauritius, Thailand, Mexico, and Panama. He currently divides his time between Nice and New Mexico.

ABOUT THE TRANSLATOR

Carol Marks is a writer and translator, most recently of a monograph on Paul Klee by Philippe Comte. She lives in Boston.

THE PROSPECTOR

was set in Linotron Bembo, a typeface based on the types used by Venetian scholar-publisher Aldus Manutius in the printing of *De Aetna*, written by Pietro Bembo and published in 1495. The original characters were cut in 1490 by Francesco Griffo who, at Aldus's request, later cut the first italic types. Originally adapted by the English Monotype Company, Bembo is one of the most elegant, readable, and widely used of all book faces.

Typeset by BookMasters,
Ashland, Ohio.
Printed and bound by Haddon Craftsmen,
Scranton, Pennsylvania.